The fiery brilliance of the Ze[...] on the cover is created by "laser holography." This is the revolutionary process in which a powerful laser beam records light waves in diamond-like facets so tiny that 9,000,000 fit in a square inch. No print or photograph can match the vibrant colors and radiant glow of a hologram.

So look for the Zebra Hologram Heart whenever you buy a historical romance. It is a shimmering reflection of our guarantee that you'll find consistent quality between the covers!

INNOCENT TEMPTRESS

"What are you doing here?"

Starlin thought quickly. "I came to . . . to meet someone. A man. A very big man," she added. "He'll be here any moment."

"I don't think so . . ." he drawled, his eyes raking over her.

Starlin was surprised to feel nettled. "And why not?" she demanded peevishly.

His lips twitched. "By the looks of you, I'd say slaying fairy-tale dragons is more your style."

"And I'd say ravishing helpless women, yours!" She gasped as his hand went to his knife and he took a step toward her. "Are you going to kill me?"

She saw a flash of white teeth. "I don't kill infants."

"And the devil take me if I am to believe that," she shot back.

"Careful, little wildcat, for he may be closer than you think" was the laconic reply.

Yes, she thought, meeting his gaze, he might at that. "I . . . never thought him to have green eyes," she said before she could stop herself.

He grabbed her wrists, imprisoning them easily with one hand.

"What are you going to do?" she asked in a choked voice.

With infuriating dominance, he forced her to drop to her knees, then knelt before her. Before she could protest, he had crushed her lips with his.

She could feel every inch of him pressed against her, and knew then what he really intended . . .

PIRATE'S CONQUEST

MARY MARTIN

ZEBRA BOOKS
KENSINGTON PUBLISHING CORP.

ZEBRA BOOKS

are published by

Kensington Publishing Corp.
475 Park Avenue South
New York, NY 10016

First printing: April 1987

Printed in the United States of America

For the Molick duo—my devilishly handsome brother, John, and his vivacious temptress, Theresa—my soul-partners and memory-makers. Thanks, you two, for always being there.

Prologue

A kiss—soft and tantalizing—roused him from the misty depths of sleep. The woman came into his arms with a breathless sigh and a promise of exquisite ecstasy. Without even opening his eyes, he envisioned her perfectly, welcomed her. It was the same as so many other nights. Dream lover . . . temptress of seduction, she was no stranger to him. She was a part of him in every way; his destiny, it seemed. Her cloud of ebony hair, the texture of the finest silk, swirled like a cloak around him, floating down over his powerful naked body. His hand involuntarily reached to grasp it . . . stroke it with a lover's sure touch, then lace his fingers through it and with a possessive jerk of his wrist, draw her over him.

Scorpio, fierce ruler of the vast, wild sea and a man of many legends, willingly surrendered all to this woman whom he knew only beyond his conscious thought. They were of one mind, one desire, and nothing could keep them apart.

The temptress pressed her lithe form against his

long, hard length, and all reason left him. Tresses scented softly by roses floated down about her delicate, porcelain perfection. But it was her eyes that would bind a man to her for all eternity should he gaze into them. They were wide and beautiful, their alluring violet depths tinged with mystery and shimmering with promise. Her body, supple and sleek, as her legs lay entwined about his. He moved his hand to cup her breasts, caress their lush firmness and a slow, smoldering fire ignited within him. His long fingers moved over her, aroused her, and urged a quivering pink crest to his seeking lips. The sweetness of the taut, round bud began a trembling in his limbs. Desire, white hot and overwhelming, swept him into a spiraling vortex of passion. He lingered there in a haze of ecstasy, savoring the sweetness of her lips and the promise they conveyed. Persuasive and hungry they moved over his, their dew softness urging him toward shivering depths of pleasure. Elusive . . . wrapped within the mists of dreams . . . she invaded, taunted, and remained just beyond total surrender. Deep within the spiritual passages of their souls they had met many times. They were bound by their hearts, not by time. Love . . . that had yet to exist.

Later, he would awaken and find her gone, and he would be left with only a dream-haunted memory.

Dawn came. The tall sea captain awoke to emptiness. He pondered the wisdom of her presence in his dreams. Who was she? A part of his past that he had chosen to forget? Or a link to his future that had yet come to pass? He tossed restlessly on the tangled sheets knowing that somehow she was a connection to everything that he sought.

He knew he would never find peace until he revealed her significance in his life. And he knew also that she would somehow help him put to rest the demons within that made him hell-bent on vengeance, and were very close to destroying completely the man he had once been. He tried to remember his other life, so different from this one of pirating, the raiding and bloody battles upon the seas. He was barely able. He had walked on the other side for too long now—the dark side that was a part of every man should he choose to unleash it. An intense feeling of need suddenly threatened to overwhelm him. Scorpio cast the baffling emotion aside, knowing that for him such deep caring for anyone was impossible. He had only one single emotion inside him that he must concentrate on—hate. With single-minded determination he turned his thoughts—and his thirst for revenge was restored.

Chapter One

Borne on the hushed breath of darkness, fragrant wood smoke from the Gypsies' fires drifted upward into the night. Wild music filled the sultry air, the Gypsies' beribboned tambourines and soulful violins blending in a pulsing rhythm of celebration throughout their encampment that graced the curving bay.

Overhead the moon was rising higher in the forbidding black sky, full and blood-red, its fiery light shining down on the colorfully dressed Gypsies who leaped and pirouetted about the flaming bonfires to the throbbing beat of the music. Heavy racing clouds pushed onward by ocean trade winds cast ominous shadows upon the whirling figures.

High atop a cliff overlooking the Sargasso Sea, a man stood on the veranda of a gracious old cottage observing the stormy emotion of the scene. He had deliberately sought solitude tonight for he was feeling

11

overwhelmed by distant memories. Up here, alone, he was able to sort out his thoughts and contemplate the journey ahead of him. He was almost certain of his destination. His dreams had somehow charted his course.

An image suddenly appeared from the deepest core of his memory, blurring his vision and stirring the anguish ever present within him. It was a woman, a madonnalike creature, lithe and lovely, with hair as dark as a raven's wing and eyes like glittering smoke-violet crystal.

"I await you, my dark lord. Come, seek your destiny in my arms and passion like you've never known. I am yours, you've only to reach out to me."

Within his head, he heard her siren's vow, and fought to remain strong. It was merely an illusion, nothing more, he told himself. Yet, he knew he could not dispel the image for long. For at night, when he slept, she would come. Somehow, she was inevitably linked to his future. As quickly as it had appeared, the vision narrowed and vanished. Sheer animal power emanated from him as his eyes, as green and restless as the sea, stared down upon the wildly dancing Gypsies. Lean fingers curled around a slim black cigar and brought it to his lips. He dragged deeply, then slowly released the pungent smoke through flaring nostrils.

"An outcast in paradise lost," he murmured huskily, "that is what I have become of late, and tonight must seek to change."

Tawny hair, thick and unruly, caught in the breeze and tumbled across slashing brows. Appearing like some dark angel fallen from heaven's grace he stood sentinel on that seaside bluff, certain that the night would yet yield what he was seeking. His hawklike gaze drifted to the willowy form of the Gypsy Queen.

Bettina, passionate and knowing, circling, spinning about the orange tongues of fire, red skirts swirling high about her golden legs, was the one woman who truly understood his purpose and his moods.

She moved like a lithe, young tigress, a fine sheen of moisture on her soft skin, her every gesture an expression of seduction. Long black hair tumbled down her back and about her half-naked shoulders. Full, high breasts threatened to spill from her low-cut blouse as she writhed and twisted to the sensuous music.

The tip of her tongue slipped between her sulky lips, ran suggestively across their fullness.

He could feel her eyes upon him now, hot and promising, roaming over him. She was dancing for him, he knew that, yet the realization gave him no pleasure.

Once, and not very long ago, they'd been very close. She'd been good for him then. But no more. His dream temptress was the only woman who moved him. He assessed Bettina's flushed face, the dreamlike expression.

He still thought she was lovely. She was not a classical beauty; her face was too long and her features too prominent, but her earthy sensuality exuded an untamed magnetism that could still fire his blood if he would allow it. And if she'd not married Salvador while he'd been away this last time, he'd be down there with her now, dancing, feeling the heat of her passion reaching out to him.

Instead, her husband was her partner, hopeful dark

eyes trained upon her like an adoring puppy.

"Poor bastard," he exhaled, "soon, but still too late, you will discover that she is not the woman of your dreams. And Bettina . . . you witch . . . you'll break his heart without a single regret."

His mind drifted back to recall his conversation with Bettina after he'd returned from his voyage to find her in her bed, body entwined about Salvador's sleeping form. She'd looked up at him and had smiled in welcome—as if finding his friend in her bed was nothing for him to concern himself over.

And after he'd gotten over the first shock, he'd had to agree. Salvador had always loved her beyond reason. And it was better this way, for everyone. So, with a wry smile and a shrug of his broad shoulders, he'd turned around and left without so much as a whisper exchanged between them.

Bettina had quickly run after him, firing off a rapid stream of explanations. He recalled her words.

"You are still my special man, Scorpio. This silly marriage need not come between us." She'd laughed lightly. "I did it on impulse, you know how I am. A bit too much wine and dancing . . . and you'd been gone so long. I was lonely, that's all."

He'd kept walking, Bettina trotting along beside him, her lush body covered by only a thin white shift. Even now, he remembered how tempting she'd looked standing there in the moonlight. "And so you just decide to marry him to help fill in the long hours until my return. Is that it, Tina?" he'd drawled mockingly, laughing harshly.

"Well . . . and perhaps to make you just a bit jealous, my handsome brigand," she'd purred, arms already

14

slipping through his, seeming to delight now in telling him how Salvador was a disappointment as a lover, and that she hoped they could continue as before . . . without her husband knowing, of course. "Please," she'd purred. "I've missed you so."

He recalled how she'd stomped her foot in aggravation when he'd smiled into her face, then kissed her thoroughly that last time before calmly turning away, and calling over his shoulder.

"Salvador is a good man. You'll have a fine life together. Just give it some time, Tina."

Bettina had screamed in indignant fury, her scorching epithets mingling with that of the gulls soaring overhead.

He had left her shouting after him, and had not looked back, nor touched her again. And she was miffed, of that he was certain. He studied her expression now. It was obvious by her flashing eyes that she was deliberately trying to lure him back to her bed.

His mind turned to more urgent matters, to the sight of the moon rising higher in the sky. He snarled softly. "Hurry, wench. Dawn will soon be upon us. I have no time to waste on these games of yours." He knew she was deliberately making him wait. Bettina could be such a spiteful bitch when it suited her.

As if she'd somehow heard every word, Bettina suddenly glanced upward, her night-black eyes glinting wickedly meeting the smoldering jade of his. Her primitive dance became more frenzied, her movements teasing, promising as if she were searching for some dizzying pinnacle as yet out of reach.

She was a whirlwind of passion with her uninhibited

dance, dark hair tangled wildly about her face, arms like slender reeds in swaying motion. Wispy tendrils of smoke curled about her, caressed her dusky form, then soared upward through night's haze to drape about him like a flirting lover.

Bettina smiled into his narrowed eyes, her coral-tinted lips mouthing his name, appearing to whisper through the wind. "Scorpio, come, it is time."

She spun away, leaping gracefully before the fire, bare feet skimming across the sand as she clapped her hands over her head, the wind whipping her sweeping skirts high about her sleek thighs. The music built to a crescendo. Bettina swayed upon her feet, then suddenly crouched low, her jet hair cascading around her as she bowed her head. A graceful chimera of seduction, he thought, but for him, there was only one thing to lure him this night. The music ended abruptly and the dancing ceased.

Knowing that the time had come, he strengthened his resolve, and with little difficulty, set aside nagging doubt. Everything was going to go just as he'd planned for so long. With careful plotting and cunning, he would seek his revenge on those few that were left. He might not be certain who they were as yet, but he would find out. Retributive justice—and by his hand. Lips full and generous suddenly lifted at the corners in a cynical smile. Revenge, bittersweet, thrummed within his chest and hardened his heart to the task ahead. There was absolutely no doubt in his mind that his plans would succeed. His self-assurance came easily, borne by years sailing the seas facing all that man and nature could hurl at him, continually emerging unscathed and undaunted by it all. So many events . . . so long away from his homeland.

A footstep came, a shadow fell. He was already down the stairs and waiting. Overhead, gray clouds swept onward by the ever-changing zephyr drifted lazily through a twilight haze, the persistent breeze tugging at the hem of his cloak, sending it swirling about his lithe frame.

Suppressing a tremor of excitement, he breathed deeply the salty aroma of the sea. It soothed him. He respected its power. It was the only thing that he could not readily predict, or control. Perfectly calm now, he greeted the young girl who had been sent to escort him.

"Hello, Jamie," he called to her. "Your sister is ready for me?"

The young girl nodded shyly. "Yes, she will be waiting for you."

He took her hand and smiled affectionately at her. Looking charming and fresh in a yellow patterned skirt with a scarlet sash tied about her tiny waist, Jamie returned the gesture. She was a sweet girl, fresh and innocent, nothing like Bettina. Perhaps, he reasoned, because they'd had different mothers. Jamie's mother had been an English captive who had never truly been converted by the Gypsies, and who'd secretly taught her daughter the ways of the "gorgios."

"Lead the way, little princess."

Jamie's blue eyes twinkled and then suddenly lost their sparkle. Her voice trembled when she spoke. "You will be careful, Scorpio, and will take good care of your brother for me? You know I have not looked forward to this time."

"Aye, I will, young friend." He ruffled her shining locks. "I'll never give those that pursue me the pleasure of seeing me swinging from a British yard-arm, have no fear of that."

She paused for a moment to delve into the large pocket of her skirt. "I have something for you." She handed him a black raven's feather.

His fingers unconsciously caressed it. It was soft and silky, and he found himself comparing its texture to the hair of the temptress in his dream.

"Bettina says it is a powerful charm that will enable your ship to skim swiftly over the water like a bird and easily escape your enemies," Jamie added as they continued onward.

"It pleases me very much, thank you."

As they approached the secluded cottage of the Gypsy Queen, Jamie halted and looked up into his intense face. "Scorpio, no one really knows what awaits you when you leave here again. Already, in just a few short years, your name has become legend in every seaport. I know there are those who swear you are responsible for many crimes, yet most of it is untrue, is it not? You are seeking to uphold your family honor in what you do, correct?"

"Yes," he replied quietly.

"I thought as much." She placed a chaste kiss on his lips. "May your path be guided in the right direction, my friend. Godspeed."

Bettina's eyes slitted like a she-wolf's upon stepping forward from her tent and noticing her little sister embracing Scorpio. Honest affection was not something she understood.

"Jamie!" she yelled. "Go help Salvador with the fishing nets that need to be set out . . . now!"

The young girl sensed her sister's hidden fury and

spun quickly to hurry along the path that led to the sea.

Scorpio fixed a narrow-eyed glare on Bettina. "That was uncalled for, Tina. She was only telling me good-bye."

Bettina laughed harshly. "You do not see what is right before your eyes. I hope your vision is decidedly more accurate with your enemies."

They stood staring heatedly at each other. With a stiff nod of her head, Bettina indicated a place before the campfire. "Come, sit down, for I wish to see if the leaves can help chart your path."

The alluring Gypsy sat with Scorpio upon the sand surrounded by the misty darkness of the night. Between them a fire hissed and crackled, silhouetting Bettina's form in harsh shadow as she stared intently at the lacy-patterned leaves forming unusual shapes in the earthen bowl cradled in her hands. Her dark eyes bore a faraway expression.

Scorpio watched her closely, observed the play of emotions on her face. Something about her expression made his heart beat faster. The full moon shone brightly on the white sand around them as she began to speak in a trancelike voice. Lulled by the sound of her voice and the crashing of the surf against the boulder-strewn shore, Scorpio sat motionless, captivated by the spell of the moment. He closed his eyes and Bettina's voice was everywhere.

As before in the dream, a rainbow of colors danced behind his eyelids, swirling like an artist's brush, graceful lines forming, merging, becoming a single image: the woman's face from his dreams, beautiful and spellbinding. Why did her image fill him with such unease? Quickly he opened his eyes to dispel the vision.

19

Displaying no outward sign of emotion, he listened quietly to Bettina's words.

"You are torn between two distinct worlds, two separate identities. Soon, the two must merge if your soul is ever to have peace. I . . . I can see your ship traveling a great distance—to a place you know well. Here, you will meet an ally—and an enemy." She hesitated for a brief moment, her silky brow furrowing. She shook her head. "It is very confusing . . . and I am not certain . . . yet I feel that you must walk carefully in their midst for danger surrounds both."

"What sort of danger?"

Bettina's black eyes bore a veiled expression as they fixed upon his. "I do not know." Slowly she closed her eyes and turned her face upward, her arms reaching toward the starlit sky. Echoing across the waters of the Sargasso Sea, her strong voice splintered through the hovering shadows.

"Upon this island we have all lived free, and have been happy—yet one among us is not. Ever restless, his heart has room only for vengeance, even as his soul longs for peace. His search has been long, but shall soon come to an end."

Suddenly, Bettina trembled and cried out softly. She bowed her head. "I see a ring of brilliant colors . . . and within the circle is a woman. Outside that ring is a man with two faces. Love shines on one face, hate distorts the other. The man must penetrate the brilliant aura and temper the anger within him, for this woman is the answer to many things."

"Who is she?" Scorpio urged. "I must know."

Smoke from the fire spiraled in clinging wisps about them.

"A princess of sorts . . . one with a will of steel and a heart of ice who shall soon make you doubt all that you believe . . . even the proud heritage you seek to uphold."

Scorpio grabbed her by the arm, his cool demeanor shaken. "For love . . . or hate . . . ally or enemy? How will this woman come into my life?"

Bettina's head snapped up and her body quivered. "I honestly do not know, Scorpio," she replied, almost fearful. "I can only tell you what the leaves appear to reveal. And that is all that I see. The rest you must seek out on your own."

He released her arm and sat back to stare into the shadows, remembering, unable this time to stop the haunting memories. Images came out of the darkness in a kaleidoscope of spinning, tumbling scenes. Times long past, once so full of happiness, had ended in sorrow. And so unnecessarily. Hate had quickly become his single emotion, and now consumed his life.

From the first, he'd vowed revenge against the man who was responsible and any of his descendants, swearing to destroy them all with the same ruthlessness and cunning as his family had been destroyed.

Life had been very hard for Scorpio in the beginning. He remembered the humiliation of having people whisper behind his back, knowing they were eagerly discussing sordid details and unfounded rumors. Once, he'd almost killed a man for snide remarks made about his mother. That had been the day he'd decided to leave England. A young man disillusioned with life, he'd signed on a pirate vessel and taken to the seas. He'd never returned to his homeland. The young man learned quickly, and soon he'd become master of his

21

own ship. He assumed a new identity, one that could not be linked to his family.

At sea, he called himself Scorpio, and his ship flew the black flag. Instead of the pirate symbol, however, the sinister curved shape of a scorpion graced the fluttering silk, the symbol "m" representing the eighth sign of the zodiac in script beneath it.

In the years that followed, Scorpio was rumored as deadly as his symbol and became feared by virtually every seagoing man. Yet, if the truth were told, only the ships of one particular salvor from Key West were attacked by his pirate band. His battles with other merchant ships were in self-defense of his own vessel.

Nevertheless, to stay on the safe side, smart merchants charted courses far away from the Florida, Bermuda coasts.

There were those who scoffed at his warnings and deliberately sailed near Antare. Scorpio frowned, recalling those few who'd been foolish—greedy treasure-seekers who'd ventured too far and too near his private island in the lost sea. He was certain they'd heard the reputed stories of the English galleon—rumored to have been sunk years ago during a hurricane, and now lying in a watery grave near his island.

The treasure-hunters allowed their avaricious natures to draw them to the Triangle, where legend claimed the sea, and the ghostly apparition of a lovely woman protected the vast treasure on the ocean's floor. There were reports from some, whether tale or true, of the sea periodically relinquishing bits of gold and jewelry that could be found along the Triangle's beaches—if one dared to try.

Over the years the stories became more absurd, as did the treasure-hunters' greed. Their numbers increased and they ventured more often to the lost sea. The battles to protect his privacy became more frequent and intense. But after a smart exchange of iron, the intruders always scattered like mists before the morning sun, swearing they'd sooner tangle with the devil himself than ever confront the Devil's Triangle, or Scorpio, again.

Antare, a lush tropical island, was Scorpio's oasis from the madness of the world—his self-proclaimed kingdom. He guarded it, and the waters surrounding it, with a fierceness that few dared challenge.

Located in an area of the Western Atlantic between Bermuda, Florida, and the 40th meridian, Scorpio lived within an invisible triangle of danger and speculation. It was virtually uncharted, and respected by wise seamen.

Scorpio did not care that it was the source of many unexplained incidents: the loss of entire ships and crews, the sudden appearance of eerie fogs, violent storms that raged for hours and then abruptly whirled away. It was home to him. He did not fear it, and only felt truly alive when he was at his gracious plantation on the island and far from maddening society.

Shaking off black thoughts, Scorpio looked up and smiled ruefully at Bettina. "When all is said and done, I suppose in the end a man is always alone, isn't he, Tina?"

"Only because he chooses to be, Scorpio," she returned, watching him closely. Her expression abruptly softened as her eyes caressed his rugged face. "I feel there is one last thing I must tell you, for it might prove important."

Scorpio was surprised at the tender look on her face. She could be just as cold and calculating as he, but at this moment her innermost feelings were plainly visible.

"Go on," he murmured thickly.

"Only this. Look to their eyes, and you will know."

They sat silently. Scorpio trembled visibly, seeing violet eyes in the purple shadows. Then in one smooth motion he came to his feet and regained his self-control.

"I appreciate your concerns, and your words, Bettina. However there is no magic involved in what I am seeking to do. I have known for some time now where it is I must go. And prophecy or no, come first light, I set sail."

Bettina stood and watched his tall form move along the beach toward the longboat that waited to take him out to his ship, the *Tempest,* that was anchored in the bay. She'd known he would only shrug off any of her warnings, for he was not one of them, after all.

It was sometime later, just before the break of dawn, when the wind at last ceased howling about the island and crept away to linger in swaying palmettos, that the *Tempest* prepared to set sail.

The crew scrambled to their assigned positions, each of them no stranger to his task. The mainsail was quickly run up the mast where it fluttered to life in the morning breeze. At a command from their captain, thirty-two men bent their backs to the capstan bars on the quarterdeck to haul the anchor cable through the hawsepipes. Scorpio stood watching, his keen eyes observing their practiced motions. As the cable was

24

withdrawn from the sea, several sailors hurried forward with broom and buckets to scrub the line clean of sand and mud. They had heard their captain say many times how even the slightest bit of mud on the deck could send a man sliding into the ocean, and death's jaws. The crew did not doubt his word. Dedicated, they worked swiftly and efficiently.

Moist tropical breezes blew steadily across the *Tempest*'s quarterdeck, drying the sweat from the men's brows and bare backs as they worked feverishly to get the ship under way. Their grunts and soft snarls drifted on predawn winds to where Scorpio stood, long legs braced against the rolling motion, observing their precise movements. Admiration shone in his eyes. They were all good men, loyal and true. But then, that was to be expected; after all, he'd hand-picked each one himself. And he would trust any one of them with his life if need be.

Faint shafts of purple-gold light pierced through lingering shadows, silhouetting their muscular forms through the billowing folds of the ship's wind-whipped sails. The sun peeked over the horizon. Anticipation wavered in the breeze. The huge ship shuddered, then caught the crests of the waves and began gliding toward the open sea.

The men shouted joyfully. Hoots and whistles echoed in the air. Mugs of rum were passed among them and quick toasts proposed.

"'Tis free as a bird, we are!"

"T' England . . . and me darlin's own sweet arms."

"T' me doxy, Lula May," another chimed in, "and heaven here on earth."

Everyone laughed good-naturedly. Scorpio fixed his

point of vision in the direction of the English coast. He knew now where his destiny lay. In four weeks he would confront it. He stared out at the endless sea for several seconds before glancing down at the broadsword he held in one hand.

They were sailing smoothly over the water now, charted on a definite course, unhindered by anything but God and nature. With a wide smile, he suddenly wielded the gleaming blade upward, swinging it overhead in a fiery arc of brilliant silver and gold. As always, the weapon felt good in his hand, like it had been created just for him. Chased in intricate detail, it was a cherished weapon that had been passed down through his family from the famous English buccaneer, Henry Morgan.

"To England!" he shouted before his men, "and revenge . . . sweet and long coming!"

Chapter Two

The coastline of Torquay, England

"Race with the wind, Abra." Starlin Cambridge urged her mount through the stable doors and out into the concealing darkness of night. She leaned low over the mare's sleek white neck whispering words to spur the horse onward.

The animal's ears twitched in acknowledgement of the girl's command, and after sailing smoothly over the stone wall which encircled the Cambridge estate, the leggy mare stretched out into a rolling gallop across the isolated shoreline, her dainty hooves sending bits of shale and wisps of seagrass flying from beneath pounding hooves.

Starlin wrapped long slim legs tightly about Abra's middle and entwined her fingers in the flowing mane. Horse and rider became a blur of motion as they tore over the expanse of beach that bordered the wild craggy bluffs and pounding sea near the Cambridge country estate, Laurelwood.

Starlin loved this place, loved its wild natural beauty

and even the fierce storms that blew in off the ocean and raged sometimes throughout the night—keeping her wide-eyed in her bed for hours envisioning how the sea would look as it lashed back in furious protest.

She enjoyed prowling the isolated coastline bordering Laurelwood, particularly late at night when everyone else lay sleeping. At nineteen years of age and having just been released from a stuffy, girls' finishing school, Starlin Louise Cambridge was madly in love with life itself. Possessed of intelligence and spirited daring, she was given to unconventional behavior that tended to explode into unsuppressed rebellion on nights as wild as her mood. If it suited her, she did it, if it hinted of danger, all the better, for she was a born adventurer, and was particularly fond of the sea. It was so mysterious and totally free. Something that the granddaughter of the Earl of Eaton could never totally hope to be. She glanced out at the tumultuous ocean as her mount carried her swiftly along the foam-dashed edge.

There was something about its raging beauty during a storm, such as the one now threatening, that filled her with awe. The sea, all powerful and unhindered, symbolized to Starlin everything that she longed for, and could not have. For she was a Victorian woman, after all, and as such, could not expect to do anything more with her life than marry well and produce fine children.

However, tonight she thought she could take on any role, act just as she pleased, for there was no one here to place any restrictions on her—not one single soul.

Starlin knew she was a young woman given to impulse if it suited her purpose. And that most of the time it did. At the prim finishing school in Liverpool, she'd been reprimanded often and more than any other girl, yet had adamantly refused to bend to dictated rule. It was not that she was a featherbrain, or did not seriously consider a situation before acting, she mused. It was just that she made up her mind quickly and reacted with a bit more vigor than her peers. More than one instructor had told her she simply feared too little and wondered altogether too much.

Feeling the blue velvet ribbon tear free of her unruly riot of black hair—and not caring a fig—she had to agree that it was probably true.

The one thing she had considered most gravely before she'd slipped from her room were the consequences should it be discovered that she'd left the house. She was well aware that the household would be in a dither if Miss Eggie awakened and went to Starlin's bedroom to check on her and discovered her missing. The incident would be reported to her grandfather just as soon as they reached London next week. And for certain, she'd be in for another of his firm lectures on the proper behavior of young women from respectable families. Poor Grandfather, lucky for both of them that he had gone on ahead to oversee matters at the London house, for he just did not understand his impetuous granddaughter. Having some time to himself after their long summer together would do him a world of good.

Pushing aside her thoughts, she leaned into the biting wind, reveling in the salty spray that blew across her face and whipped her midnight tresses out behind her like a glorious sable cloak.

Starlin had promised herself this one last ride to her

special place before leaving to begin her new life in the city under her grandfather's rule. Not that the earl was an ogre, or that she didn't love the old bear. She did, immensely. Without him, she had no one, and it had been her grandfather who had come to Key West after her parents' death and confronted her stepbrother with a revised will naming the earl as her guardian.

Ah well, she thought, one last venture, Starlin, and then you will have to resign yourself to the whirl of the London season that is fast approaching. She knew it was expected of her, and it was final.

"Isn't everything, where we women are concerned?" she yelled bitterly over the roaring of the crashing breakers. "And it's totally unfair!"

To forever live one's life under a husband's rule, without freedom, without excitement, why it is just too horrible to even contemplate, she thought. And soon she'd be spending every day cooped up in Grandfather's rambling old house. She'd be expected to wear long, fancy gowns that forced you to walk just so—or one would find oneself hopelessly entangled in yards of silk—just to sit and exchange subtle banter with foppish dandies and worry over her every word. It was enough to send the headstrong girl into a fit of outright rebellion this night.

She didn't wish to marry! she fumed inwardly. She had dreams! She wanted to savor every drop of life until there was absolutely nothing left to experience. Perhaps when she was thirty, and old, she might wish to settle down. Yes . . . perhaps then.

With a firm hand the girl reined the mare toward a lofty cove high in the cliffs where she might look out upon the wind-tossed sea and wish for that certain someone who might take her away to a special place to share her hopes and dreams. Someone like herself, who understood how very precious freedom of thought and deed was to man, or woman.

The breeze whirled about her with a wistful sigh as Abra topped the first jutting sand bluff and was brought to a skidding halt. The mare stood tossing her regal head, impatient to be off again. Starlin held her close as her gaze roamed over mist-covered cliffs. She knew she'd have to search carefully for the narrow opening, since it had been difficult enough to find even in daylight.

The moon peeked out briefly from behind a murky cloud bank, a shaft of piercing light dancing along the granite walls as if indicating the way. The girl smiled and urged Abra slowly along their base, the delicate scents of flowering vines entwined about the rocky crevices tantalizing her senses. Then, she saw it.

The jagged fissure was before her. She slid from the mare's back, tied off the reins, and walked over to sit cross-legged upon the very edge of the cliff. She smoothed her white muslin skirt over her knees and stared out from her lofty perch, her nerves tingling with awareness. Looking at the bewitching sight before her, Starlin knew she could never have imagined the absolute savage beauty of this place at night. She was glad now that she'd taken the risk to come.

Silvery sea grass far below did a graceful wavering dance above the sand drifts. Rain threatened, and thunder continued to rumble. The wind howled unexpectedly through the honeycombed passages behind her, as though pining for a long-lost lover. Gooseflesh quivered on the girl's bare arms, yet she

31

refused to leave. Lightning, so bright it nearly blinded her, charged through the heavens plunging into the soaring whitecaps, and took Starlin's breath away. Ghostly tendrils of fog weaved steathily in and about huge angry waves like the slithering tail of some fearsome sea serpent bent on ensnaring its awesome power. Undaunted, the breakers hurtled against the shore eliminating anything that dared to stand in their way. It was stunning to behold, and Starlin was to think later that perhaps that was why she had not immediately noticed the ship heading in from the ocean toward the calmer bay. Her attention had been drawn to the fury of the elements and not the distant horizon.

At first, when it finally caught her eye, she was confident that it must be a figment of her vivid imagination, for surely no one, not even the best of seamen, could have guided a ship so well amid the ocean's fury. She rose to her feet, just barely able to make out the great hull of the vessel plunging in and out of the choppy water, riding high each crest with graceful ease. She marveled that it didn't capsize or become dashed upon the reefs so dangerous in the area.

It was like nothing she'd ever witnessed before, this battle between sea and vessel, and it left her trembling with emotion and envious of the confrontation. "Where did it come from so suddenly?" she pondered out loud, thinking in the back of her mind that it appeared Zeus had somehow sent it up from the bottom of the sea to do battle with mighty nature.

The full moon appeared once again, and she saw that the ship was as black as night, for only the billowing white sails unfurled in the wind could be easily discerned. Starlin was breathless and did not move—

for how long she wasn't certain—but it came as a jolting shock to suddenly realize that the ship had been maneuvered into the sheltering bay below her lofty perch and was now weighing anchor.

Her captain must have decided to seek shelter from the approaching storm until morning, Starlin assumed, and agreed with his wise decision—until she noticed the swaying beacon of light from high atop the ship's rigging, and felt the cold hand of fear slowly clutch her in its wake. Back and forth, back and forth, the flashing light came: some sort of signal, she felt certain. She was unable to take her eyes off it. And then she realized why they'd come!

"Smugglers!" she gasped, "coming to this cove to meet someone!"

Heavens, but hadn't she heard countless stories of such goings-on in this isolated area where few dared venture, save fearless pirates and one foolish girl? A thrill of excitement shot through her. Then, glancing down at her white blouse and skirt swirling about her in the breeze like a beckoning banner, she dropped quickly to her stomach. She could only hope that they hadn't been drawn by the sight of her white clothing. Oh, dear! Had she been the one to draw them to this location?

It was the only time in her life that Starlin knew complete terror. She could not move, could not breathe, she could only lie there and watch as a longboat was lowered and directed toward the shore.

Abra's soft whinny brought Starlin to her senses. Rigid with apprehension, she whirled away from the bluff's edge and forced herself to think calmly. She knew if she tried to leave here now that she might be shot, or worse, captured. Dressed in white, upon a white mare, she'd be spotted in a moment. And these men were undisputedly pirates. They would take no chances, but shoot first and worry about asking questions later.

Her mind quickly sought a solution to her predicament. If she sent the mare on alone, and stayed hidden, perhaps they would think that the horse had been the white vision on the cliff that had caught their attention. Maybe they'd even leave without investigating further.

"Yes . . . oh yes . . . please work," she prayed fervently, giving Abra a desperate hug before untying the reins and slapping her soundly on the rump. "Run Abra . . . my very life depends on you!"

As if she understood, the mare hesitated only momentarily, then trotted off down the only trail to the beach. Starlin watched her go, then her gaze darted quickly over the shoreline, saw that the boat was docked and that a group of ferocious-looking men— outlaws!—were now walking her way with lighted torches.

Why didn't they look over and see the mare! she thought in panic. Were they blind! Glancing around for something to use as a weapon, Starlin gave an anguished cry when she saw nothing that looked very intimidating. What could she do? She just couldn't stand here like a ninny and let them do with her whatever they wanted. Think, Starlin! she demanded, or your life may well be over. She released a pent-up sigh when she saw one of the pirates point toward the galloping horse. The group halted, appeared to be conversing in earnest.

One man stood out from the rest. He was a good

head taller than his counterparts and did not appear to share in their discussion. A black cloak swirled about his lithe form, catching in the breeze, revealing clinging breeches tucked into turned-down jackboots. He continued onward, his targeted destination perfectly clear. His determined strides sent Starlin into a flurry of motion, and upon spying a good piece of driftwood lying to one side, she rushed over and snatched it up before plunging into the dark opening of the cave.

"It must have been the horse that I seen, Captain!" a burly pirate called after the intimidating form striding purposefully away from them, leaving the group staring after the fleet-footed horse fast retreating in the distance.

"Perhaps," came back the deep masculine reply.

"If Giles were here he'd have signaled back by now and sent someone out to meet us!" another man shouted.

The knot of ruffians watched their captain walk steadily toward a tower of cliffs that rose high above sea level. Their gazes met: uneasy, for they were always mindful of a trap. Only one shrugged before separating from them and trotting after his captain.

"Scorpio!" he yelled out, "wait before you go charging up there! It could be an ambush! This is not where we usually meet up with Giles!" He managed to catch up to the captain at last and grabbed his elbow, pulling hard.

"Dammit, Ely," Scorpio growled, turning up his heel. "I know what I'm doing. Now go on back with the men and try to keep them calm. If it was the mare that we saw, then we have nothing to fear. We just missed our location because of the weather, that's all." He attempted to smile reassuringly at the younger man. "We can lie low here and ride it out until morning, then be on our way."

"I don't like this place. Come back to the ship with us," Ely urged.

"I'm going to have a look around, Brother, then if I find that I am truly alone, I think I'll pick a spot where I can see everything that moves, and stand guard for the night." Scorpio pounded his brother's back good-naturedly. "Rest easy. I'll send a signal back to you, then you'll know all is well. Take the men and go back to the ship. You can all get a good night's rest knowing I can easily spot anything from up there."

Ely hesitated, his expression one of concern. "I do not know what you're up to . . . or why you suddenly felt such a need to take the ship into the bay, but by the look in your eyes . . . it's far more than even I realize, isn't it?"

"Is it?" Scorpio parroted huskily, before continuing onward.

"Yes!" Ely shouted. "Since leaving Antare over three months ago, you have been like a man possessed. Why?"

There was no answer, just a curt order called back gruffly. "Ely, go back to the ship with the men."

"Aye-aye, sir," Ely retorted tersely, pausing to chew his lower lip for a moment, still uncertain what he should do. He stood watching his brother move away with that light, predatory stride of his that could catch even the most aware of men off guard it was so deadly silent. He knew something was amiss, and whatever it was, it had been gnawing at Scorpio the entire trip. And his brother was not ready to share it with him, that was certain. Ely recognized Scorpio's desire to be alone and sort out his thoughts, and resolved to let him do so. They had been at sea for months. Scorpio's responsibilities had been many. He felt confident that his brother could take very good care of himself. He had managed so far. His apprehension eased somewhat, Ely turned back toward the grumbling men and allowed his brother to walk onward.

Starlin had listened to the echo of voices that had drifted up to her hiding place, and forced herself to stay back in the cave, not to move a muscle, or even to breathe raggedly.

There had been a total of eight men. She gripped the driftwood tighter and pressed her body flat against the cavern wall. How could she manage to hold off so many? Perhaps if luck was with her, they would not see her in the darkness. She whispered a silent prayer.

The pirate captain paused at the cave's entrance to peer into the absolute darkness. He thought he heard a flutter of movement inside, or a slight gasp, or perhaps . . . destiny whispering? He glanced over at the flaming torch in his hand, contemplating his next move. He wasn't exactly certain what he might find within, but he felt almost driven to continue. Who, or what, waited for him here on this desolate strip of land?

His emotions in turmoil, he tried to calm his racing heart before venturing farther. Some inner voice seemed to tell him that it was not Giles in the cave. He would have to wait until daybreak now, and a short while longer before disposing of the goods he'd pirated from Benton Cambridge. When he'd first felt compelled to guide his ship into the cove, after hearing his man in the crow's nest report sighting a white banner, he'd assured himself it was only the smuggler, Giles, whom he was scheduled to meet along this coastline. Then, after quickly taking note of the unfamiliar region, his gut impulse had been to turn away. Yet, he hadn't, even though he'd known staying here overnight meant holding onto the goods, a dangerous risk in these waters. And any other time he would never have weighed anchor carrying such a prized haul. Except that this was not like any other time. Taking a deep breath, he stepped just inside the entrance.

Starlin's heart almost leaped into her throat upon observing the flickering light just ahead. Her mouth grew dry, her head was spinning, and for the only time in her life, she felt certain she might swoon. She pressed back against the cavern wall, her grip tightening on the piece of driftwood. She knew if she fainted, that she'd surely tumble out into their path. And if she did that . . . Oh, she did not want to die! She wished she could call back these past hours! At the moment, even going to London did not seem so terrible. Dying was terrible! Shaking badly, she tried to regain some measure of self-control.

Scorpio could feel the presence of another, and somehow sensed their fear. He felt his own heart pounding frantically in his chest. With fluid strides he moved forward through the tunnel.

Starlin watched the light grow brighter, saw the shadowy form of a man wavering against the shale wall, and raised her weapon with both hands in readiness. A sob bubbled in her throat, and she could not contain her small outcry. Immediately, the torch was abruptly extinguished and she screamed when she felt steellike fingers close about her left wrist. Yet,

38

before she could react, he'd dragged her willy-nilly along behind him to the cave's entrance.

Once in the moon's light, he halted and turned back toward her. He leaned forward slightly and found himself staring into wide, frightened eyes.

"What the hell . . . why, you're just a bit of a girl!" he breathed, clearly astonished.

Recovering her voice, Starlin hissed, "Let go of me this instant, you blackguard." She stared up through the shadows at the fiercest man she'd ever seen. Remembering her weapon, and forgetting her initial fear, she swung the driftwood as hard as she could and caught him a glancing blow on the shoulder.

He didn't even flinch, just knocked the crude weapon easily from her hand and flung her unceremoniously upon the sand. She fell back on her bottom, teeth jarring together, and glared up at him. He stood towering over her as if he were deciding whether he might devour her instantly or save her for a midnight tidbit. Even in deep shadow, their eyes challenged each other, smoky violet smoldering . . . hard jade glittering.

"Just what the deuce are you trying to do?" he growled, scowling down at her. "I mean you no harm."

Starlin was almost too numb with shock to answer. She just sat there watching his every move, waiting, she felt certain, for him to ravish her.

Something about the frantic expression in her eyes tore at his heart. She was like some beautifully savage sea nymph with those alluring, soulful eyes. His pulse jumped. My God, those eyes, those incredible violet eyes. Bettina's words rang in his head. He knelt swiftly beside her. "Who are you? . . ."

Starlin's stomach knotted in panic as he came forward out of the darkness, appearing even more threatening in size as he drew nearer. Lord, but this man was terribly wide of shoulder and fierce of expression, if that was a scowl that she could just barely make out on his face. In the shimmering hues of silvery light that backlit his powerful physique he appeared more dark prince summoned by sorcery to meet the night than mere mortal man.

Irritated with what he assumed was a deliberate refusal to answer him, Scorpio's eyes blazed. "Answer me, chit!" his growl echoed off the walls.

"I . . . I . . ." She found herself stammering, unable to stop.

"Lucifer's twisted tail," he muttered savagely. Grasping hold of her wrist once again, he yanked her up to stand before him. "Answer me, now!"

"I came here to . . . to meet someone. A man . . . a very big man," she blurted in a rush, head craned back to better watch his every gesture. "And he'll be here any moment."

He studied her silently for a moment, those all-knowing jade eyes holding her own unwavering gaze. "I don't think so . . ." he drawled at last.

"Yes, it's true . . . we always meet here after dark," she hurriedly added.

"A lovers' tryst?" He laughed softly. "You?"

Starlin was surprised to feel nettled by his arrogant tone. "And why not?" she retorted peevishly.

"Forgive me, if I wound your pride, girl, but by the looks of you, I imagine you're more some poor chap's rebellious offspring who's managed to escape for a night of unchaperoned adventuring." His mouth

40

twitched. "I'd say slaying fairy-tale dragons is more your style."

"And I'd say ravishing helpless women, yours!" Starlin lashed back, stung. She watched him carefully, eyes widening as he moved his hand toward his sword. Oh dear God, but she never had known when to keep still! He would surely have his way with her, then kill her for such a remark! Without a tremor, she forced herself to stand bravely before him. When, after a few moments she felt nothing more than his amusement, her eyes flew to his and met his twinkling gaze.

"You mean you aren't going to . . . and kill me . . . after?" she croaked.

"After? After what?" he drawled mockingly.

"I just thought . . . I mean . . ." Her lips clamped firmly shut. Damn him, he was purposely baiting her, looking every bit like he found it all so humorous. "Why would I want to kill you?" A flash of white teeth danced in shadow. "Besides . . . I don't kill infants."

"And the devil take me if I am to believe that," she shot back.

"Careful, little wildcat, for he may be closer than you think" was the laconic reply.

Yes, she thought, meeting his gaze head-on, he might at that. "I . . . never thought him to have green eyes," she heard herself saying before she could stop the words.

"I have been told that he can appear in any form that you wish him to." His voice was entrancing.

Starlin looked warily at him, tensing when he drew her a heartbeat closer. His head dipped forward, nearer than she liked, yet she found herself mesmerized by everything about him.

41

His features were difficult to discern clearly in the fused moonlight, but what she could see was enough to give her pause. His hair was worn rakishly long, curling about his collar, and was partially covered by a dark piece of cloth knotted at the back of his neck. A glimmer of a gold earring in one ear caught her eye, but it was upon his chiseled features that her gaze kept returning. She thought that his jawline appeared rigid and unyielding, but otherwise could find little fault with the way he looked.

Scorpio stared down at her feeling as though everything Bettina had told him would come to pass was at this moment being set into motion.

As before in the dreams, he wanted to turn away; run as fast and far from her haunting violet eyes as he possibly could. Yet he knew it was useless. This bewitching girl with her haunting eyes was somehow linked with his future, and whether he liked it or not, he knew he could not turn about and simply walk away from her.

Bloody hell! Had he envisioned one so young? Even in the moon's light he could tell she was of tender years. How he longed to take her outside beneath the moon and look upon her soft features. Her high cheekbones and wide-set brows bespoke of fine ancestry, and he knew that she would be breathtaking to gaze upon, of that he had no doubt. His eyes shifted to her wild, thick mane floating about her and down her trim back, imagined where it might curve out over her shapely backside. He shook himself. Stop it, you fool, he raged inwardly, before she has you dangling from that British yardarm you brag so often of avoiding.

Her head was thrown back, the slim white column of

her neck inviting as he heard her whisper chokingly, tentatively, "Please . . . let there only be you . . ."

It was a plaintive sound, as if she could read the message in his eyes. It tore at his heart, yet he knew he must not weaken. If he sought answers, then he would have to appear unmoved.

"Pirates always share the spoils, don't you know that, beauty?" The words were clipped even to his own ears, and sounded heartless.

Starlin squirmed in his tightening embrace. "Let me go and I promise I'll never breathe a word to anyone of your being here!" She watched with trepidation as he shook his head.

"That, I cannot do."

His reply, ringing with finality, sent her into a flurry of desperate motion. She thrashed about like a wounded animal ensnared in a deadly trap, and now, when moonbeams caught his features, Starlin saw something that made her blood chill. Was it just the eerie cast of its rays that made it suddenly appear that there was another man entirely behind those beautiful, mocking eyes. Fear and desire stirred together.

"Let me go . . ." she demanded in a choked voice.

"I cannot," he whispered.

Frantic now, she instinctively struck out and clawed the side of his face with her nails, yet felt gratification upon hearing his grunt of pain.

Searing emotions blotted out his reason. He felt possessed, driven by something even he could not identify.

She cried out and began twisting in his grasp. "No . . . I don't wish this!"

"It really doesn't matter anymore what you wish,

43

love, for it appears that the die has already been cast." He grabbed her wrists, imprisoning them easily with one great hand until the tendons felt crushed. With infuriating dominance, he forced her to drop to her knees, then knelt before her. "You are mine, goddess of the night, and I, your master."

She could feel every inch of him pressed against her, and knew then what he really intended. In one smooth motion, he pulled her down with him to the sand. Startled into action, Starlin rolled swiftly onto her stomach and tried vainly to scramble away. He grasped her easily about the hips, dragging her flailing limbs back into the circle of his arms . . . then slid that long, steel-honed body over hers.

Frustrated tears escaped from beneath her thick lashes to drop upon the silt floor. She felt their wetness upon her face as he slowly pressed her cheek into the sand. His lips brushed the throbbing pulse behind her ear.

"Hush, don't fight me." He held her gently close now, battling the burst of desire raging through his veins and losing. It came as a shock to him to realize how much he wanted her—like no other female he'd ever known, he wanted her.

With a muffled groan, he slowly lowered his head until his lips found that warm place at the nape of her neck that tasted and smelled sweetly of woman.

Chapter Three

As soon as his mouth pressed against her rose-scented skin he was lost in a fiery haze of passion. His lips parted, tasting of her, savoring her upon his tongue. It was an instinctive action, brought about by his first glimpse into those illusive smoke-violet eyes, so captivating that they seemed to draw him into her very soul. His emotions and reasoning were shattered by her.

There was nothing upon the face of the earth that could have stopped him from taking her, for he realized now, with possessive male acceptance, that she was his, and that very soon she would realize it, too. One could not freely exorcise the other. They were of one mind, one desire, one destiny.

"Don't do this . . ." she whispered, confused by the feelings that were awakening deep within her.

He felt her resistance melting. "Ah, love, even if hell beckons it will not stop us. You were made for this moment, and for me." The soft words were near her ear as his lips brushed her lobe.

Without touching her with his hands he sought to take away the fear that he knew held her in its wake. He had never experienced anything so all-consuming in his life. He longed to tell her so much. "Your innocent provocativeness is enough to set my blood afire as no courtesan has ever done," he murmured against her cloud of thick hair. How his hands ached to roam over her, his body to join with her, yet he knew he must go slowly. She had been created for him, and had surely known no other man's touch.

Starlin was intensely aware of his lips doing strange, erotic things to the back of her neck, behind the shell of one delicate ear. His mouth was hot and moist now nibbling at that sensitive place just beneath the lace edge of her collar. She could feel the firm hardness of his jaw, the roughness of his unshaven chin against her upper back as he deftly unfastened the first few tiny buttons of her blouse and lightly placed a kiss there. The rippling muscles of his arms now held her prisoner, making her very much aware of the unsettling strength of him. He was big, big enough that he could easily encompass her entire body and keep her quieted beneath him.

Something warm and sticky trickled upon her bare skin. His blood . . . from the wound she'd inflicted on his cheek warm upon her back, in marked contrast to the cold steel of his blade that lay pressed against her side. Did he intend to seduce her tenderly, then force her to succumb to him . . . then kill her just as ruthlessly? And if so, how could she find the strength to stop him? At the same time every limb and nerve she possessed felt as if they were drowning in a sea of honey. Was there indeed something evil within her to make her feel so . . . so filled with desire for him? Even as Starlin's mind had fleetingly conjured up the violent image of her own demise, another had quickly replaced it. One that surprisingly reassured her. It seemed impossible, yet she felt she knew at that precise moment what he was feeling. They were as one in every thought and emotion. Shocked at the revelation, and her body's slow awakening to his hungry, persuasive mouth moving over the indentation at the base of her spine, she gasped hoarsely.

"This is absolute madness. The moon and the night have caught us in its spell." Tears of confusion spilled from her eyes.

He brushed a soft kiss across one shoulder. "It is not my touch that frightens you any longer, but you still tremble. Tell me what you fear," he whispered.

Her breathing was hoarse and ragged. "I feel as if our very emotions intermingle . . . as if there is only one of us and not two."

"Because I think . . . we were meant to meet this way," he said quietly. "And soon, you and I shall be one in every way." He nuzzled her ear. "Does that frighten you?"

"This can't be happening. It . . . has to be nothing more than a dream."

"It's much more than that, love, you will know it, too, very soon."

"But . . . but, is this not wrong?" she asked.

"No . . . no," he whispered feverishly, "it is not wrong. Nothing this beautiful could be wrong."

All expectations of a violent demise by this man's hand flew from her mind. In its place, and just as consuming to the emotions, awakened passion so heady it nearly took her breath away. He held her in his willful vise against his hard body and, of a sudden, she found a tingling warmth begin in the pit of her stomach, spreading to the very ends of her toes and fingertips. His caress was as gentle as a kiss.

Passion was fanned with exquisite care until, at last, throaty sounds of breathless wonder escaped her. Nothing and no one, she realized, had ever prepared her for these feelings now coursing through her, or for a man such as him.

Scorpio's own blood thudded in his ears. He was stunned by everything he was experiencing. Every fiber of his being intermixed with hers. Some inner voice kept telling him that she was the one . . . the temptress of his dreams. Never in his life had he felt this way about a woman. Temptress or shy maiden—what was she? And even more important—who was she?

After his first all-consuming rage and mingled passion had come rushing to a head, he'd regained some measure of control, his taut muscles had relaxed, and he'd begun to entice her slowly.

It excited him further to know that she was beginning to respond to him. With slow languid movements he awakened the woman in her. And then so swiftly that she wasn't even aware, he allowed his fingers to skim along the back of her thin blouse, unfastening the last tiny button with ease before sweeping aside the material to fix his smoldering gaze upon the creamy smoothness of her naked back. She was trembling beneath him.

Shaken by an inexplicable sensation of yearning, Starlin's fingers reached forward, wanting so to touch him, only to clench the sand, waiting . . . longing . . .

She wanted him . . . terribly . . . yet was no less unsettled by the thought. She was spinning toward some boundless apogee of pleasure, totally out of control and no longer able to resist the heady fires he stirred inside her.

Gently, his hands kneaded the tense muscles along her slender spine until she was soft as a kitten in his arms.

Starlin writhed against him, feeling like screaming for him to touch her everywhere, not to torture her further.

At last his hands slipped inside her blouse and beneath her, playing skillfully over her pliant form, long fingers sliding sensuously up and down her belly. Finally, when she could stand no more and cried out in passion, he cupped her breasts with rough expertise. The satiny tips of her nipples firmed against his palms, reveled in his touch. He encircled the rigid buds gently with his fingertips, rolled the sensitive flesh slowly . . . so achingly slowly between thumb and forefinger.

Starlin shuddered beneath him, intense feelings of longing searing her every nerve and claiming the last vestige of her reasoning. She wondered what it was like to have a man inside you—to love you in every way. Arms like steel clasped her tightly against him. His hips moved against hers, the hard swell of him letting her know just what it was that she longed to feel within her.

"Now you know," he said in a voice heavy with desire, "what it is that will claim you as truly mine."

She could feel the hard length of him throbbing hotly against her through her skirt and moaned down deep in her throat. Long lashes fluttered shut when she felt him reach down and impatiently tug the material up over her hips, leaving her partially naked and vulnerable and consumed by her own need. However mad it might seem, she was powerless to resist the raging fires he'd awakened.

"Take me now if it is to be," she said urgently, "for you have surely bewitched me . . . I want you so."

He made no verbal acknowledgment, only his hands stroking over her body with a lover's sure touch. The back of a silken shoulder bared to his view sent shock waves of desire through him. He caressed it, placed his lips there, just behind her arm where it joined her body, found the flesh heated and velvety soft to the touch.

Lightning snapped across the sky again and again, the storm hitting at last with gale force. Rain fell in torrents, the flashing streaks of silvery light bursting into the shadowy cavern, playing across their bodies in tempo with their movements.

Instinctively, the roundness of her hips arched involuntarily against him, and he could think of little else at that moment to take his mind away from that one place that he longed to possess.

"Turn over," he commanded raggedly.

Wild pleasure washed over her like nothing she'd ever experienced before, prompting Starlin to unhesitantly comply, her arms coming up to wrap about his neck as his mouth slanted hard across hers. His skin smelled of sea wind and lime, an elusive scent that suited him well. Her fingers touched the shaggy curls near his collar and longed to burrow in the silky mane. Without hesitation, she slipped the knotted cloth from his head, freeing his thick hair to her touch. She pulled him closer, clinging to him. Her mouth moved in erotic surrender to his kiss, and she thrust her tongue deeply into his mouth, offering him all she had to give.

She was his. He knew that he would cherish her forever. Their bodies clung in a heated passion as boldly electrifying as the storm.

Something cold as ice brushed across the back of his neck—a serpent's caress, Scorpio was chilled by thinking.

His fingers caught in her hair, tearing her lips free of his and dragging her head back. His eyes held her pinned. Starlin did not like what she saw in his. They were aglitter with rage.

Unbidden words—his own now recalled—broke through his haze of passion.

"For love . . . or hate . . . for love or hate?"

Bettina's voice echoed back at him. "One will be an ally, the other, an enemy."

Was this lovely beauty . . . the enemy? It is in her eyes, fool, taunting back at you in violet hues! Please, God, why did it have to be so, he thought angrily, then snarled savagely.

"How in the hell did you come by it, girl?"

"By . . . by . . . what?" Starlin rasped, her eyes wide, bottomless pools. She thought he must surely be possessed by some strange madness brought about by the full moon.

"You appear so sweet . . . so pure. But I think that is a clever ruse—I know you cannot be!" he hissed bitterly, lips but inches from hers. "You refuse to tell me how you came into possession of it, don't you? But then, I am not surprised. I am certain you must be one of them—and I know what I must do." The fingers of one hand, relentless and cruel now, where once they'd been so tender, snaked out to encircle her throat,

51

squeeze slowly.

"Please . . . you're choking me," she gasped, her hands clawing at his.

"I'll do more than that if I don't get the right answers . . . I promise you," he threatened. "Tell me . . . my enemy . . . how did you know that I sail these waters? Were you spying for someone?"

"I have no idea what you're talking about," she sobbed, absolutely rigid with fear. She viewed the dark hatred in his eyes and knew he meant every word.

"This," he spat, jerking her hand up between their faces, "is what I'm damned well talking about!"

The ring given to her by her stepfather the day that he'd disappeared in a boating accident along with her mother sparkled before her eyes.

"How is it you came to wear this ring?" he demanded.

Her thoughts swirled. Feeling degraded and used, Starlin experienced an overwhelming need to strike back. Frightened but defiant, she choked. "Go to hell, sea wolf, for I owe you no explanations."

"You speak bravely, but for how much longer." Looking at her now, hatred flared, mingling with lusty desire. He wanted to destroy her and everything painful that she represented with the same driving intensity that he'd yearned so tenderly for her just moments before. Long-smoldering hostility overwhelmed awakened desire, and he unsheathed his sword and held the razor-sharp blade up before her eyes. "I seek answers, now."

Starlin swore to face death bravely. "Slay me if you will, for I would rather be impaled by cold steel than by your mad man's flesh."

With a cool, derisive laugh Scorpio released his grip on her throat and yanked her hand downward, pressed it between their bodies. "Would you now," he sneered, holding her fingers firmly against his pulsing desire. "The devil's own son if I should mistakenly give you what you prefer."

Her chin tilted forward haughtily, and her purple gaze did not waver from his all-consuming eyes, yet he saw the vulnerability in her trembling, kiss-ravaged mouth and a flicker of awakening horror in her look.

"So, that is what you fear now even more than death," he said tersely. "Pure as an angel? Aye, I think so." He smiled cruelly. "But not for very long . . . for nothing can stop me from marking you justly. You will remember, my beloved enemy, having confronted me, and lost."

Starlin felt the pressure of his throbbing flesh against her crushed fingers and lapsed into a breathless plea. "Not this way . . . oh, God, no."

"Yes, exactly this way," he growled at length, his face contorted by something she did not wish to define.

With revenge in his eyes, he tossed aside the sword then lay his hand upon her bare thigh. She heard cloth slowly ripping, felt long fingers seek out her moist warmth. I will not cry out, she told herself firmly, trying not to flinch as his touch seared virgin flesh. One finger delved . . . then withdrew.

"You *are* chaste as a new budding flower," he said throatily, passion and hate all at once firing in his eyes.

Starlin was so overwhelmed with contempt that she didn't think of the possible consequences, but spat directly into his face. He froze in motion, did not move a muscle. She did not dare. Spittle ran down his ravaged cheek, yet he paid it no heed. He shook his head as if to clear the red mist before his eyes, tawny hair spilling in wild confusion over scowling brows.

She was to think then that if ever there were truly demons sent up from hell that this man was surely one of them.

Long suppressed hatred burst from him in sudden blinding fury. No longer was she but an innocent girl he sought to woo, but an enemy of past events that even now tormented his soul. Rising swiftly to his knees, he grabbed her behind the legs and yanked her hips to him. She screamed, trying to entangle her legs within his to keep him from her. She fought like a tigress, with teeth and nails and spirit. He only sneered at her futile efforts, enjoying the battle and the lusty awakening of other senses. Then, tiring of the game, he grasped her beneath the arms and pulled her thrashing body up against him, jade-hard eyes staring straight into hers that were slitted like a cat's and filled with hate.

"Place your legs about my waist," he ordered huskily, and when she did not respond, grabbed her beneath the buttocks and forced the slender limbs there himself.

The relentless pressure from one hand encompassed the back of her skull and pushed her head forward until their lips touched, and caught fire.

Hungrily, his mouth moved over hers seeming to draw every drop of fight from her. Starlin was shocked to feel a perverse pleasure amidst humiliating shame as their lips clung in a fiery kiss. What was wrong with her, she screamed inwardly? Never had a man's kiss excited her before. This was awful, wasn't it? He was an unfeeling monster who was hell-bent on degrading her, not making love to her. His tongue darted in and out of her mouth, plundering the sweetness within and her reason, until she moaned in despair. Her body shuddered against him. It was as if she realized that she could not fight him and hope to win. She lay limply in his arms, tears streaming down her face, the final debasement.

That small indication of defeat should have made him feel triumphant. After all, that was what he sought from her wasn't it? He wanted to ravish her, punish her flesh until she was broken and shamed and lay sobbing in his arms while he took her. Yes, that was exactly how it was to be! His lips and hands continued their arrogant assault, but his mind just could not continue. Buried in the back of his hatred lay a strong conviction that to do this thing was wrong, and that he would, for some reason, regret it terribly after.

"Damn you . . . damn you . . ." he growled suddenly, chokingly. Raising his head, he stared upon her features as though dazed. "Oh, God, what are you to me?"

Eyes blurred by tears, Starlin looked up at him, stunned by the pain she glimpsed in his dark gaze. Neither moved for a moment, but just clung to each other, studying, searching, raw emotions plainly visible to see.

At first when he dipped his head forward and his lips brushed across hers she automatically drew back. But they proved no threat this time, moving languorously over hers, sending sparks of fire to all of her nerve endings. In her innocence, she had no conception of how devious a man like him could be, or how persuasive. His ardent pursuit of her senses thrilled her

55

treacherous body, and he knew now that there was yet another way. She would come to him . . . and it would be enough.

Starlin was lost in his web of passion and helpless to her own emotions. Somehow, without her awareness, he subtly untied her chemise and pushed aside the offending garment. Then his hands and lips were everywhere, touching, kissing, his mouth so warm against her skin. The curious hunger inside her kept building, seeking something more, until it became unbearable, and she cried out to him in a sweeping rush of desire.

He was totally calm now, but ever devious. What she'd almost made him do sickened him, and he vowed that she would pay double. Beneath him she writhed in her passion, and she was magnificent to behold. He kissed her pale throat, her lush breasts, suckled the rosy nipples until they stiffened pertly in response. She was totally his now to take when he was ready, and he surrendered to his own desire as his lips grazed downward across her quivering belly to tantalize intimate hollows, raven black curls, kissing lingeringly her soft, vulnerable flesh until it was trembling and grew moist and warm against his mouth.

Again and again he plundered the delicate folds and pulsing bud with the tip of his tongue until, at last, long wracking shudders encompassed her body and a bubble of a sob tore from her lips.

Unfastening his breeches with deliberate slowness he positioned his hips between her legs, supporting his weight on his hands as he stared down at her. Vulnerable violet eyes held his, seemed to be begging for a reassuring word.

"You are truly the most fiery little thing I've ever come across," he whispered raggedly, and felt a measure of satisfaction when he saw her flinch as if he'd just struck her across the face.

Her lips bared back from her teeth and she screeched in fury. "You despicable bastard! I hate you . . . I hate you! And I swear as God is my witness I will live to see you hang!" She bucked her hips against his, wild now to escape the final loathsome act that would mark her his conquest.

A voice seeming far off in the distance echoed through the cave passages. It was some minutes before Starlin's shocked brain realized that he'd moved away from her to rearrange their clothing, and for some reason known only to him, was shielding her body from the intruder's eyes.

"Scorpio! For the love of heaven will you answer me!"

Starlin looked up to see a glimpse of another man dashing through the entrance, a flaming torch in hand. She quickly pulled her tattered garments closer about her and huddled behind Scorpio.

"It sounded like you were tangling with some wild she-cat as I approached," Ely said to his narrow-eyed brother. "What is going on in here?" He stared at Scorpio, barely able to glimpse the disheveled girl shielded by his body. His eyes registered shock. "And who is she, Scorpio?"

"Go back to the ship, Ely," Scorpio growled.

"The hell I will!" Ely replied heatedly. "Why did you not signal me as you said? This place makes me uneasy." He stuck the end of the torch into the sandy floor, his eyes peering over his brother's shoulder at the cowering girl. "No need to answer that. I think I can see very well what was going on. She was the white vision that we saw, wasn't she?"

"Aye, one of Lucifer's own, she is." Scorpio wiped his sweat-dampened face with the back of his arm. "Leave us, now, we have something to settle between us."

Ely stood his ground, his blue-green eyes filled with disbelief. "You can't really mean to do what it is I think you were about when I came in here?"

"You have no idea what this is all about . . . so don't interfere!"

"Have you taken all leave of your senses? She is only a young thing, man, barely out of school."

"Oh, she is more than that, Brother . . . much more," Scorpio said bitterly. He twisted around toward Starlin, but was drawn up short by Ely grabbing his shoulder. He spun about angrily, coming to his feet and appearing as one possessed to swing on his brother.

"Are you crazy or something?" Ely ducked the blow of his fist, leaving Starlin to stare in mute disbelief at both men.

The two men faced each other. One overwhelmed by emotion, the other, stunned by his.

It gave the girl the briefest opportunity to slide backward across the sand into the dark shadows along the cave wall. Upon feeling her back come up against a solid surface, she stood on wobbly legs and inched the shale until she was able to dart unseen through the entrance and was swallowed up by the night.

Neither man had been paying her notice they were so intent on dodging the other's blows. After a while, Scorpio's pent-up rage finally abated, and he fell down on his knees in the sand, breathing labored, sweat pouring down his body.

Ely did the same, but kept a guarded eye on his brother. He gingerly touched his bruised jaw where one of Scorpio's smashing blows had clipped him. Being the younger and lighter of the two, he'd managed to dodge Scorpio's first blind swings, leading him around in a circle, carefully ducking to avoid those lethal fists, until his brother had at last exhausted his fury.

Sides heaving, they faced each other. Their eyes met. Ely saw that Scorpio's were now clear. What he had glimpsed in them earlier had almost unnerved him. He had never seen his brother behave in this way.

"Are you feeling better?" Ely posed with a careful smile.

Scorpio breathed deeply, nostrils flaring wide. "I can't feel any worse." Remembering the girl, his head jerked around in search of her. He saw that she had fled. An overwhelming mingling of loss and bitter gall assailed him. "For the love of God, why?" he ground out tersely.

Misunderstanding his brother's harsh statement, he sought to ease the moment. "She got away while you were stalking me about," Ely stated, relief flooding through him that she had escaped. "And now that the chippy has flown, can we get on with our mission?"

Scorpio jumped to his feet and swept up his sword in one smooth motion. "I'll go after her."

"No! Enough. We're getting out of this place!" Ely snarled. "That storm is the worst I've seen in a long time. The men are edgy and I need you to come back to the ship and calm them down." He was grateful when he saw his brother hesitate. "You have a responsibility

59

to the men. As their captain, they look to you to guide them in times such as these." Ely was betting on the fact of his brother's loyalty to his crew to keep him from tracking the girl and possibly getting himself captured in the process. "Let her go . . . there will be others."

Scorpio's eyes were dark and brooding. "Not like this one there won't.

Starlin Cambridge awakened with a dreadful sense of unease in her bed, the covers clutched tightly about her neck. She watched a stray beam of sunlight come peeking through the partially separated window coverings. It was morning, the storm had passed—and last night did not happen, she tried to convince herself. A bad dream . . . yes . . . that was all that it was. Wasn't it?

She lay that way for a long while, trying not to think about him by forcing herself to mentally tally the ornately cast plaster garlands in the ceiling.

An image appeared there from the distant corners of Starlin's mind that she could not banish nor turn away from: that of a lean, chiseled face in shadowy relief with eyes that were like that of a storm-lashed night, and hands that were her complete undoing. Something she could not readily identify rushed through her body, and then was recalled. Heat, throbbing and intense, pulsated between her thighs, made her automatically tighten her legs together. She remembered his sure touch . . . her breathing quickening with each writhing movement of her hips . . . her breasts growing full and aching, longing, even as she hated herself, for his total possession. From within, she recalled that deep, husky voice and surrendered to the simplicity of physical satisfaction. Even as she recognized what was happening to her body, she felt the embers of desire flame out of control, and rushed with a breathless sigh to meet it.

Afterward, a peculiar weakness settled within her and she slept peacefully without dreams.

When she woke again it was late morning. She tried to convince herself, in innocent naïvete, that he had simply been some demon of dreams that she would exorcise, but by the time that she had dressed to meet the new day, she realized with sinking despair that she had failed to banish him from her mind.

Chapter Four

London after dark was exciting to behold, for it was then that the city truly came alive. On this evening, Edmond, Earl of Eaton, was hosting a fashionable soirée for his granddaughter, Lady Starlin Cambridge. Invitations bearing the Winfield coat of arms had been received by every prestigious household. The acknowledged king of the capital's hosts, the earl's spectacular parties were eagerly anticipated by every member of the elite *haut ton*. They were well aware of his search for a suitable husband for her ladyship, and of the sizable fortune she would one day inherit. Young lords of the aristocracy were encouraged to pursue the wealthy Lady Cambridge without reserve. They did so in droves. For within this glittering realm, one's life work was the pursuit of pleasure. Therefore, no one who was a member would dream of not responding to, or failing to attend the soirée.

The appointed hour drew near. The light rain which had plagued the day lifted, storm clouds skimming past a slivered moon revealing a faint dusting of stars highlighting the sky. Laughter drifted on the breeze, echoing across the tree-lined streets surrounding Hyde Park, mingling with the sound of iron-shod hooves and the menagerie of rumbling coaches beginning to arrive at Eaton Hall.

The elegant mansion, situated but a stone's throw from Hyde Park, was aglow with dazzling lights. Footmen in top hats and black tails attentively waited to assist the lords and ladies from their conveyances and into the gilded salon where the Earl and Lady Cambridge waited to receive them.

Starlin stood beside her grandfather, smiling warmly and making polite conversation. There wasn't one who would have recognized her as the hoyden who had arrived in London just a short year ago. It had been that long since Starlin's encounter with the pirate, Scorpio, and if anything, the time had only served to enhance her spirited loveliness. She had forced herself to put the explosive encounter in the cave from her conscious mind, but sometimes at night, in dreams, it still returned to haunt her. And if she would chance to think of it in the light of day, she would have to say it was because of Scorpio—and those dreams—that she had not yet chosen a husband. He alone had been the one who'd awakened lusty yearnings, virginal passions, such as no other man had been able to do.

Starlin Cambridge projected the perfect image of the aristocrat's granddaughter, appearing poised, cultured, and very much a lady. The earl had spared no expense to educate her. Adept in several languages, an accomplished artist and musician, she'd been carefully molded to become a dutiful Victorian wife.

Young bachelors hovered a short distance away,

murmuring among themselves.

"Mmmm, Courtland appears to have gained her favor . . . lucky bloke."

"Beauty and wealth, what more could a man wish?"

"But rather a strange bird, though . . . or so I've been told."

"There are ways of silencing that lovely mouth," a brash lad sneered.

The group of young men laughed softly.

Starlin heard their amused chuckling and turned to favor the circle of bachelors with a haughty look of displeasure. Immediately, there were embarrassed coughs and averted eyes. Unobtrusively, they observed her cool beauty, each man secretly longing to hold her just once.

Intoxicating in a pale lavender silk with an overnet woven through with silver threads and a décolletage that revealed a hint of full ripe breasts, Lady Cambridge did indeed make a ravishing picture that tempted many to dream of what it might be like to possess her. Her long dark hair, the color and texture of sable, was fashioned becomingly on top her head in a coronet of lustrous curls. Sculpted, high cheekbones, complemented by skin the color of fine porcelain, only served to enhance the slight poutiness of her moist, pink mouth. A mouth just made for kissing, more than one admirer had been heard to exclaim. And if her lips were temptation, then her eyes were a man's undoing. They were truly her most captivating feature. Set beneath delicately arched jet brows and thick, sooty lashes, they appeared culled from sparkling amethysts which slanted exotically at the corners. Ever changing with her mood, they innocently beckoned and promised, teased and foretold. Yet not one of London's fine young men had ever sampled the secret passion hidden in their depths. It was in her favor that she accepted her classic beauty quite naturally and was not one to dwell on her physical appearance.

Yet, the ton was ever puzzled by her behavior. The usual gossip-mongers were in attendance and sat in a group on one side of the room, quizzing and dissecting each guest as they arrived, heads bobbing in agreement, eyes shining brightly. Occasionally, they'd paused in mid-sentence to draw breath and exchange comments about their hostess. They laughed amusedly, watching from behind secretive smiles as the Earl and Lady Cambridge stood underneath a crimson banner emblazoned with the family crest, and greeted the last of their guests. It was entertaining for them to observe the proceedings. The dowagers were quite familiar with Starlin's reputation of being an Ice Princess. Her league of scorned suitors were many, and the dames were quick to agree that the name suited her perfectly. It would have surprised and undoubtedly pleased the tale-carriers immensely if they would have had any idea that these very same concerns were on the earl's mind at that moment.

The earl watched his granddaughter unobtrusively, seeking some indication that she found at least one of the eligible young lads to her liking. Firmly, he recalled his earlier decision to see her properly wed before the season's end. Regardless of how the stubborn minx balked at the idea, it was time she began to accept the responsibilities of womanhood. And if not soon, then he'd be forced to form an alliance for her. He had tried to avoid doing so, but, she stood to inherit a sizable fortune from him when she came of age.

One year, and she could do as she pleased. And if not under some husband's wing, what then would she think to do? Gad, but the very idea made him extremely nervous. However, there was hope. For already, she'd received countless proposals, and all from titled gentlemen he held in the highest esteem who would make his granddaughter the perfect match. In the past, and much to his chagrin, with each new offer of marriage, she had turned up her classic nose and politely refused. Perhaps now that she was a tad more mature and approaching twenty-one, she might seriously consider a future offer. He recalled his having asked of her why she'd previously declined such wonderful matches, and had been stunned when she'd simply replied, "I know you're trying to look out for my best interest, Grandfather. But I do not love any of the young men in question. I am beginning to wonder if such an emotion even exists for me." She'd sigh wistfully. "Yet, I do not intend to marry without it, so I have decided to remain unattached and continue to live here with you."

"But, it is unheard of, my sweet," the earl stammered. "No one of our class ever waits for love to marry. It is expected that you will marry well, produce fine heirs . . . love? Well, that may come after."

Yet Starlin Louise had remained firm in her convictions. "I will not be some man's brood mare, Grandfather." She had observed his distressed face sympathetically. "I am sorry to have to talk to you in such a fashion, but you must realize how I feel. If I ever marry, and I say 'if,' it will be to a man who views me as his equal. One who believes in love, as I do, and who may very well just sweep me off my feet." She had laughed at the latter, wondering herself if such a man even existed, and never, never allowing her thoughts to dwell on the one man who had, quite naturally, done so.

The earl would reply testily, "These ridiculous views of yours, Granddaughter, are driving all of your suitors away. I am finding it increasingly difficult to seek out new lads to invite to these affairs. Soon you must chose one, or I will do so for you." He had ignored the pugnacious uplifting of her chin. "Milady, your position in life demands it. I will not have the same thing happen to you that befell your mother after your natural father's death."

"Because she married Carl, of whom you did not approve, and allowed him to adopt me and took me to live with them in Key West, you mean, don't you?" It was bluntly stated, but without rancor.

"More so, because the man was an adventurer. A shiftless treasure-hunter who ran some shabby salvage business off the Florida coast," the earl shot back with an air of disdain.

"A very profitable one, I might add," Starlin returned firmly. "And we were all very happy for five years, if I may remind you."

"Ill gotten gains, I have no doubt," the earl grumbled. "I still can't believe your mother gave up everything for that man. Why, I can't tell you the numerous tales that drifted back to me over the years concerning Carl Cambridge."

Starlin sighed. "Your estrangement hurt her deeply, but she did love him, you know. And you've told me countless times, how if they'd lived like normal folk and not have gone looking for the devil's treasure, that my mother and Carl would still be alive." She placed her hand on his arm, sharing his pain. "It's part of the past now, Grandfather. They're gone . . . and no treasure was ever discovered." She smiled gently. "And we are lucky to have each other. I will never forget how happy I was when you sent for me. Benton felt obligated to care for me—we never got on too well as you know. I spent all of my time with Mammy Juno. Benton had the salvaging firm to occupy his time. I am so grateful for your invitation on my behalf."

Fury flashed in the earl's eyes. "That shiftless scoundrel. He's never loved anyone or anything except money. I will never forgive him for keeping you a virtual prisoner of that desolate estate in the Keys." he shook his head sadly. "I regret my obstinancy. It kept me from my daughter in her last days . . . and almost doomed you to a lonely life with Benton Cambridge."

"Hush now," Starlin urged gently. "Mother knew it was your pride that kept you away. We tried to understand, and loved you no less. And all was not lost, for you still have me." She squeezed his arm. "In all fairness, Benton is the way that he is because his father always seemed disappointed in him, yet doted on me. Benton was envious of my relationship with Carl. When the will stipulated that I should receive half of Carl's holdings, Benton was outraged."

"It was only right that you should receive a part of it," the earl huffed. "After all, it was your mother's inheritance that allowed Carl to remain operating the shoddy affair." He snorted. "Not that I shall ever allow you to interact with Benton. You will have my inheritance, and it will be substantial."

"With one stipulation, of course," Starlin said, meeting his eyes.

"My child, I have catered to your every whim, but not this time. You must have a husband soon to oversee my vast holdings." He saw her mouth tighten grimly. "I am growing tired. I wish to see you properly wed and your future secure."

She grew silent and thoughtful, observing the earl. "You do look peaked. Are you up to this evening, sir?"

"Yes, of course," he blustered. "It's just time for you to accept your destiny, darling. I regret now ever having discussed my business with you. Too late, I see my error."

"It was definitely to my benefit." She tossed her jet black locks.

"Poppycock!" the earl replied, frowning. "It has only served to further your ridiculous ideals that all men are silly fops with only one thing on their minds where women are concerned!"

"I do not feel that way about you," Starlin stated with a charming smile.

"Hmph," he grumbled, color fusing his pale cheeks. "That will be enough of that."

"Very well," she agreed. "I understand that Benton's attorney, Malcolm Wells, sent you a wire last month?"

The earl frowned. "You've been talking to my secretary again, have you?"

"Briefly. Is there a problem with the salvaging firm?"

"No."

She sighed. "You aren't going to discuss it with me, are you?"

The earl was careful of his answer. He knew how wily Starlin Louise could be. And he did not wish to discuss

70

Malcolm Wells, of all people. His personal association with the Cambridge attorney was something he did not want known—could not afford to have known. It prompted him to reply, "The Cambridge salvaging business is doing fine. That's all that should be important to you."

"And Benton . . . is he all right?" she queried, careful not to pry too much, for she knew how the earl was irritated by the turn of the conversation.

"Just remember—that part of your life is over, child. However, it can do no harm to tell you that Benton is doing as well as can be expected. You are aware of how unstable he has been since the boating accident. Wells does his best to keep things going—that's the most we can hope for."

Starlin's silky brow furrowed and she purposely avoided making any vows that were impossible to keep. "By your unease each time that Benton's name is mentioned, I tend to think there is something about my parents' death that you have not told me. Is there?"

The earl quickly shook his head. "No—there is nothing."

It was then several guests arrived and their conservation terminated. Starlin forced a smile, yet her mind was racing furiously. She was remembering the look on her grandfather's face as she'd posed that very important question regarding her parents' reported demise. Never before had she seen the earl look so distraught and unsure. She wished there had been time to hear his reply, and decided to delve into the matter further at a more opportune time.

At last, the receiving line dwindled, and with it, Lord Winfield's hope of sparking Starlin's interest in one of the young men. He sighed tiredly. Somewhere, there had to be a man who would measure up to Starlin's high ideals, for the very thought of coercing her into marriage left a bad taste in his mouth. Yet, he felt it was imperative to find a suitable husband for his granddaughter soon. He was aware that when Starlin became of age she would no longer be under his guardianship. She would also acquire half interest in the Cambridge salvaging firm. The earl did not want her to return to Key West. Therefore, he had vowed to see her married before she turned twenty-one.

As he shook the hand of their last guest, he found himself unknowingly regarding the lad's face with intensity. A gesture that prompted Starlin to whisper in a discreet, yet amused, voice, "I say, sir. It would do to soften the look in your eyes. The last young chap to shake my hand was doing well to suppress a tremble."

The earl favored her with a rueful smile. "I did not realize. Perhaps that has been the problem all along, hmmm, Granddaughter?"

She regarded him with dubious eyes. "In what way do you mean that, sir?"

"Simply, with me constantly at your side the lads are kept a distance. I see how they watch your every move. It's time to choose one, my dear."

"I have no interest in any of them." Starlin smiled softly at him. "We have a fine life together, Grandfather. It is enough for me."

The earl sighed inwardly as he escorted her toward the dance floor. Quite suddenly, he removed her arm from within his and offered her to an eager young hopeful who had been hovering near. "She's all yours, young man. Dance the night away."

"Grandfather, really!" Starlin exclaimed in shocked disbelief.

The earl ignored her pleading look and took a position on the sidelines. He watched as her eager escort twirled her slim figure about the dance floor. Inwardly, he was saddened at the thought of Starlin marrying and leaving Eaton Hall. It would be lonely without her vivacious presence. He did enjoy her fussing over him. Unlike his colleagues at his offices who complained frequently to him that she meddled more of late in his affairs of finance, which he knew should be of no concern to a woman. She needed a strong husband to direct her. Her outspokeness was ruining her reputation. Ice Princess—that's what some of the young bachelors were whispering behind her back. He wondered if Starlin was aware of the nickname, and the thought saddened him.

"Is there not one man in all of England to ease my mind, and sweep a delightful, but very willful young lady off of her feet?" he wondered, his intent gaze never leaving Starlin's face.

Rayne Morgan, The Fourth Marquess of Sontavon, whose companion, Lady Susan Ellendale, had received an invitation to the soirée, sat within the confines of his plush coach contemplating the evening ahead. Due to an unavoidable, and very satisfying, delay between Lady Ellendale's satin sheets, they were late arriving at the ball. He never attended London's pompous affairs, but he knew that this particular one could be of great importance to him. Therefore, when Lady Ellendale had pouted because her husband was away, and said she desperately wished to attend, Rayne had been only too happy to offer his services as her escort.

Susan had cooed over his gentlemanly chivalry until he'd had a difficult time keeping a straight face. Women like her were such complete fools. In the two months that they'd been carrying on their liaison, she'd never once really gotten to know the true side of Rayne Morgan. Not that he would allow her to. He always remained coolly unemotional with his women. It was a hard, fast rule he swore by.

Chivalrous, he thought with an inward, contemptible laugh. Lucifer's twisted tail! If he'd allowed her to know him at all, and that was a big if, she'd have readily assessed the fact that he never did anything for anyone unless he stood to benefit by it himself.

He paused in his thoughts to glance down at the sleeping woman snuggled in the crook of his arm before withdrawing a long dark cheroot from within his waistcoat and placing it between his lips. He lit it, savoring its rich smoothness before leaning his head back on the cushions to think.

His mind drifted back to another woman: his mother April, who had unknowingly taught him a valuable lesson about trusting a woman, any woman. A glimmer of sadness flickered in his brooding gaze.

Even now, after so many years, the memory of her perfidy against her family still haunted him. He wondered to this day how she could have cuckolded his father and had an affair with that lying bastard, who all along had only been after one thing. A valuable clue to a priceless treasure.

Unhappy in her arranged marriage to the ailing lord, Silas Morgan, a man twice her age, young April had been easy prey for the dashing adventurer. And later, when Silas Morgan had learned of the affair and confronted April, her lover had fled, leaving April to her husband's wrath and her children's sorrow. Rayne recalled how she'd pleaded her innocence before his father, swearing that she'd not forsaken their marriage vows. She'd remained true to Silas, she'd sobbed. What others thought did not matter.

But when it soon became known that she'd given him a prized possession, Silas Morgan had shaken the castle walls with his wrath. Their peaceful life at Castle Sontavon was over. Several months later Silas Morgan died in his sleep, from grief, many said. Never, Rayne swore once again, would he entrust his heart to anyone. The price was just too damned high.

He reconfirmed what bloody good fortune it had been to have met the restless Susan Ellendale at the hunt club last month. She had taken to him immediately, and he had whiled away many hours of pleasure in her bed since then. He must have exhausted her, for she hadn't stirred once since they had left her estate.

He glanced down at her out of the corner of his eye, wondered how much longer he'd find her entertaining? Granted, she wasn't hard to look upon and was an appealing wench. However . . . he stifled a yawn with the back of his hand. Women of title tended to bore him so. No matter how good they were in bed, sooner or later he always grew restless.

One tawny brow lifted rakishly. Although, recalling what Lady Ellendale had told him about the Lady Starlin, perhaps it was remotely possible that there was one tempting morsel yet unsampled that would prove far less ordinary and much more satisfying than his usual choices. His interest had been aroused while listening to Susan relate tidbits of Lady Starlin's outspokeness, and her dim views regarding matrimony. Then, to his shock, her last name had been mentioned. Cambridge. A name he wasn't likely to ever forget.

Morgan considered the challenge ahead of him and felt a reckless mood stirring deep inside him that could not be denied. Even now his eyes gleamed as he rolled the black cylinder between agile fingers and stretched out long legs in the narrow space before him. He doubted, if he should so desire, that he would have any trouble in taming the lovely Starlin. He was confident that he knew her kind only too well. Without exception, they were all spoiled and pampered, with little will to do anything but bat eyelashes and prattle endlessly.

From all accounts, the Lady Starlin was just as indulged as her peers, yet there were certain undeniable distinctions.

"Ice Princess," he murmured beneath his breath. "That is what they call you, beauty. Fair, or unjust?"

Lady Ellendale lifted heavy-lidded eyes to search his face. "Mmmm . . . pet names . . . darling?" She stretched like a contented cat who'd been heavily dosed with cream.

He gazed down at her indifferently, his eyes inscrutable, before kissing her lightly on the nose. "Nothing that suits you, you can be certain of that."

"Darling Rayne, I know what will," she cooed, one slim hand slipping within his dark coat to roam at will over his thickly muscled chest. "I'm afraid you tend to bring out the worst in me."

76

He favored her with an indulgent grin, exerting a slight pressure over her hand to stay its movement. "At the risk of sounding crass, dear lady, might I remind you that you love every minute of it."

A provocative smile curved her parted lips as she brushed them teasingly across his. "I love something else even more," she whispered suggestively.

"How well I know that," he drawled, his hands lightly caressing the ivory flesh of her bare shoulders before he crushed her against him with a rough forcefulness that he knew excited her.

"Oh . . . lover," she gasped, then sighed when his hands moved to cup the fullness of her breasts.

He squeezed firmly his long fingers biting through the thin material. He laughed softly at her sighs and squirming motions. With total control he teased and delighted her, torturing sweetly the aroused nipples until she was writhing in passion. Toying at last with the hem of her gown, he slowly brushed seeking fingers up her silk-clad thigh and urged her slim legs apart. Boldly he stroked the heated flesh of her inner thigh, pushed offending garments aside to tantalize her most inviting place. His lips moved enticingly over hers, his tongue filling her mouth with warm, wet delight until she groaned her defeat.

"Don't toy with me, darling," she whispered against his lips. "We have time." She arched her hips invitingly.

With a cool smile he abruptly set her from him. "We're almost there, Susan," he said, "I don't really think this the proper time or place, do you?"

Disappointed and hurt, Susan arranged her skirts and smoothed the material with shaking fingers. She glanced over at him, observed tearfully the indifferent expression now on his face. He could be so cold when he chose to. She was well aware of his reputation as a rake, for there were no end of stories circulating about him.

It was stated he lived a jaded life, and loved every minute of it. Lord of a vast estate since his father's demise, he resided at his seaside castle, rarely coming to London. Although he discouraged visitors, and never invited guests, it was rumored to be a magnificent place. Surrounded by the sea on every side save one, and that moors, it was impenetrable except for a single road that wound through the bogs. The land had been in his family for years. Lady Susan was aware of that, and of the dark secrets that surrounded the Morgans.

She had heard that in Rayne's early youth, he had been quite a decent chap. He had even been captain of the guard in His Majesty's army and was highly regarded by the king. Then, something had happened, an incident so serious that he had been stripped of his rank and had fallen from the king's favor. All talk of the incident had been quickly hushed. But rumor had it that Rayne had gotten into a duel with a fellow officer over the other man's degrading remarks regarding April Morgan. The man had been badly wounded, yet recovered. But that had been the end of Rayne Morgan's career.

Susan quivered imagining her lover's hand wielding his gleaming sword, defending his family honor with his life if need be. He was magnificent. She sighed, vowing that she'd never let another woman take him from her. For even though she was already married, she refused to consider his belonging to anyone else. He was by far the most exciting lover that Susan Ellendale had ever known.

She watched him stare out of the window as they approached the Winfield mansion. She swore she saw a glitter of unveiled excitement in his eyes. She thought he had never looked more handsome. With a practiced eye she studied the savage beauty of the man. His dark bronze hair gleamed in the lamplight; short cropped, wavy, and sunstreaked, he resembled some pagan god sent to earth just to lead astray unsuspecting females. The deep green of his velvet jacket appeared the exact shade as his eyes, and she felt her heart beat faster when he turned to stare into her own.

"Milord . . ." she stammered. "We don't have to stay long, you know. We shall just put in an appearance and then we can go off alone . . . just the two of us." She smiled, hoping he did not notice the way in which her lips were trembling.

"Don't be silly, Susan," he returned, his expression guarded. "You've been looking forward to this for weeks. We may as well enjoy ourselves to the fullest."

"Very well, darling," she conceded reluctantly. "I suppose I will just have to wait until later . . . when we can be all alone in my big bed."

Rayne flicked his cigar out of the window before drawling indifferently, "I never said anything about going back to your place, Susan, did I?"

"Well . . . no, not exactly, but after the wonderful time we had earlier . . . I just assumed."

"Never assume anything where I am concerned, milady," he responded in a callous tone.

Head swirling, Lady Ellendale heard the majordomo announce their arrival. She swallowed over the lump in her throat and observed tight-lipped as Rayne Morgan

79

swung through the open coach door, his sun-brown face and rigid jaw set hard and unyielding. Whatever was going through that fascinating mind of his he had chosen not to share with her. The perfect gentleman when he chose, he offered her his arm. She placed her gloved hand upon the hard muscles encased in velvet, and stepped out to stand beside him. It was then she thought for certain that she heard him murmur almost cynically, "What bloody good fortune that the hunt should bring me here."

Yet, before she could inquire of his meaning, he had swept her into the foyer beneath glittering crystal chandeliers, and the earl was there to greet them.

Chapter Five

The ballroom was filled to capacity. Starlin now stood alone in the foyer receiving the last of the guests. She had noticed that her grandfather was tiring and had urged him to join his friends in the billiard room. The majordomo announced a late-arriving couple. Starlin sighed. Smiling politely, she offered her hand to the tall, elegantly dressed man without glancing up at him. His deep voice dazzled her senses and her gaze flew upward to meet his eyes.

"Lady Cambridge, it is a pleasure," Rayne Morgan said smoothly.

"Likewise . . . I'm sure," Starlin relied faintly. "I am glad you were able to attend."

"I can assure you, I would not have missed it," Morgan responded.

"We've both been looking forward to attending," Lady Ellendale added, glaring at Rayne. She had not failed to notice the spark of interest in his eyes as his gaze had met Starlin's. He never looked at her that way. Anxious to draw his attention elsewhere, Susan fluttered her fan and placed a hand on Rayne's arm. "I would like to dance, darling. You will excuse us, won't you Lady Cambridge?"

"Of course," Starlin replied, trying hard not to stare at Rayne Morgan.

There was something strangely familiar about Rayne Morgan. She was certain this was not the first time that she'd been stared down by those remarkable eyes. Her mind struggled with his image. He was truly a magnificent male animal—all hard muscle and unsettling strength, with a reckless, devil-be-damned air about him that awakened a sense of daring within her soul. Starlin knew that this man was her equal in every way. It was those mocking eyes that jarred her memory.

"Scorpio." The name was spoken softly and without hint of malice.

"I'm sorry?" he returned with a puzzled expression.

Starlin stared at him. "A slip of the tongue. For a moment I thought you were someone else."

He nodded politely, then turned to Lady Ellendale. "You wished to dance, milady?"

"Oh, Lady Starlin, I say, but you are a magnificent dancer. You float like a feather in my arms." Starlin's youthful partner enthused passionately as he whirled her about the dance floor to the lilting strains of a waltz.

"I must say, Lord Courtland, you certainly are the one with the compliments this evening. You flatter me."

"I mean every word."

"I really wish you wouldn't go on so, milord," she returned with a frown.

"Oh, Lady Starlin, if you only knew how much I admire you. You are truly the lady of my dreams."

"Sir, you go too far," Starlin replied, her tone stern. "This is neither the time nor place . . ."

"But, I must say this while I have you all to myself," he cut in.

"Might we just dance?" Starlin found her eyes searching the room for sight of Morgan.

"I just wish you would consent to marry me," he persisted hopefully. "I know all of the other chaps wish the same thing. However, I know that I am the one who could make you truly happy."

Starlin made note of those around them vacating the floor, and whispered in Courtland's ear, "Sir, the music has ended . . . shouldn't we stop shuffling about?"

The young lord turned a deep crimson. "I . . . I did not realize. Forgive me, it appears I lose all sense of reason in your presence."

"No apology necessary," Starlin replied with a tolerant smile. She was relieved when he guided her off the floor.

However, once on the sidelines, Courtland showed no interest in leaving her side and hovered possessively near.

"You are such a rare gem that I know if I part from you for even a moment, some other bloke will surely claim you."

"I'm certain that is true," a male voice agreed, and there came the sound of subdued chuckling.

Starlin and young Courtland looked up in surprise. Lord Courtland was displeased at the intrusion, and even more so when he saw that it was Starlin's chum Paula Allenton and her escort, Terrence Thorpe.

"You have had her to yourself enough this evening, luv," Paula teased, her bright blue eyes dancing merrily as they met Courtland's. "Why don't you and Sir Thorpe fetch us some refreshment before the fireworks begin. Starlin and I will go on over to the stands and secure chairs for all of us." She cast a meaningful glance in Starlin's direction. "You know we girls have to gossip a bit without you men hovering about."

"Yes, please, Buckwald," Starlin added in a plaintive tone. "I am ever so thirsty after so much dancing."

Buckwald Courtland could do nothing but comply gracefully with the women's wishes. "Very well," he agreed reluctantly before his lips took on a calculating smile. "Perhaps it will provide me an opportunity to speak with your grandfather, milady. He has put me off long enough." His golden eyes met hers with a hungry light and his voice firmed. "I do intend to have your hand."

"I wouldn't tarry too long, Bucky dear. Starlin's prince charming just might materialize and steal her right from beneath your ardent gaze," Paula Allenton quipped lightly.

Courtland's fingers reached out to brush Starlin's in a parting gesture before stiffly addressing Paula Allenton. "And knowing you, Lady Paula, I'm certain that you have him secured away in an alcove, and are just waiting for the opportunity to whisk him forward." He managed a curt bow before walking away.

Sir Thorpe shook his head at Paula. "Our lovesick friend just can't win when you're around, my dear. He has set his cap for our Lady Starlin, hasn't he?"

"And far too boldly," Starlin added. It was no secret among the tonnish mob that Lady Paula and Courtland crossed swords at every opportunity. They tolerated each other for Starlin's benefit. Tonight, it appeared their endurance was wearing thin.

Lord Thorpe glanced hurriedly after Courtland's retreating figure. "You ladies go on. I'll go help our boy with the refreshments. We'll be around later."

"Perfect," Paula whispered to Starlin as he walked away. She grasped her friend by the arm and directed Starlin toward the open terrace doors. "Let's take advantage of our freedom while we can."

Starlin smiled knowingly. "You really mean—let's lose our gentlemen friends and give Bucky something else to stew about. You never let up for a moment on him, and it's no wonder he has the disposition of a bear when you're around."

Girlish laughter floated on the wavering night breeze. After they'd managed to weave through the guests on the outside terrace Starlin and Paula meandered along a flagstone path lit by tinted lamps, casting prisms of amber-soft light over the grounds. The weather was lovely, the delicate fragrance of flowers wafting on gentle breezes. Long cloth-covered tables sat about the lawns, silver gleaming in the moonlight, delicious smells wafting from beneath covered dishes. Groups of people were sampling the exquisite fare and chatting companionably. Paula paused, her pudgy nose fairly twitching at the mouth-watering smells. "I just have to have a sampling of that divine food. Do you mind, luv?"

Starlin smiled. "Of course not. But it does look as if a crowd is gathering quickly at the stands. I'll just go on ahead and secure our seats."

"I'll be along shortly," Paula called out as Starlin moved away from the canopy of trees toward the raised platform where many of the guests were choosing seats for a better view of the display.

She climbed the wooden stairs and selected four chairs. She sat quietly to await the start of the fireworks that were always spectacular. It took several minutes for her to realize that she could overhear a conversation that was taking place below the stands. The voices were hushed but distinctly male. She paid little notice until she heard something that caught her full attention.

"Well what do you want me to do, short of murder, that is? I warned you this rogue was no ordinary foe."

"Keep your voice down," the other man snapped.

Starlin peered down between the wooden bench slats and saw two men standing off in the shadows, unaware that she had taken a seat above them.

The first man spoke in a hushed voice. "All was going well until he showed up. I turned my men into pirates to underhandedly destroy my competitors in that area, and had just about achieved my intentions when, quite unexpectedly, I find myself confronted with that bastard trying to do the same to me. He has managed to cripple many of my ships. I cannot delay my stay much longer. I must leave soon."

A cold chill swept over Starlin, and she wondered who the men were. In the blink of her eye, they had moved away. The first gillocks and Roman candles exploded overhead drawing her attention, and she was left to wonder if she had imagined what she'd just heard. She shook her head and promptly waved to

Paula who was approaching the stands.

After Paula was seated beside her, Starlin told her what she'd overheard.

Paula raised her eyebrows. "Intriguing, but I would forget it if I were you, dear. You know how your outspokenness is viewed? Just leave it be."

Yet, even after the two women were joined by Courtland and Thornton, and sat watching the spectacular finale explode colorfully across the dark sky, Starlin found that she was still reviewing that sinister conversation in her mind. She glanced up to find Buckwald Courtland's adoring gaze fixed upon her. Starlin sighed inwardly, realizing that she had serious problems of her own to consider. Courtland leaned over to whisper in her ear that he had found a few private minutes in which to speak to her grandfather. And that he was bloody well elated by the outcome of their conversation.

Starlin managed a smile as she posed the very important question so that only he could hear her. "When do I get to hear what you discussed, milord?"

He squeezed her arm, an intimate gesture that made her flinch.

"Just a few more details to work out, sweet. And then you will be told everything."

Starlin found herself almost mesmerized by those golden, gleaming eyes of Courtland viewing her as if she were a wild vixen that he had at last managed to corner. The fireworks ended. He took her arm and rose to his feet.

"Excuse us, please," he told Paula and Terrence. "Milady and I are going to have one last dance together before the ball ends."

Arm in arm they walked back to the brightly lit ballroom. Courtland did all of the talking, Starlin finding herself far too numb to comment. Had her grandfather seen fit to betroth her to Courtland? Would he do that knowing full well how she felt about such a match?

By the time they reached the house, the crowd was breaking up. The room was less crowded and Courtland eagerly escorted Starlin toward the dance floor.

The earl was occupied with several of their guests on the far side of the room. The Dowager Courtland unknowingly granted Starlin a reprieve when she came to fetch her son to escort one of her prominent friends about the dance floor. Starlin could feel Courtland's eyes watching her as she danced, and she glanced quickly about for a place of refuge until she was able to find a private moment in which to talk with her grandfather. She could see several young men hurrying in her direction, so with a sigh of frustration, she retreated to a quiet corner to untangle her thoughts.

To the casual observer she appeared outwardly calm, yet there was one guest who was quick to notice the tip of her satin slipper tapping in agitation from beneath the hem of her gown. Obviously, there was something very pressing on the lady's mind.

Rayne Morgan noticed her immediately from across the ballroom. And as he'd watched her move gracefully about, slim form held so proudly straight, he thought she looked vaguely familiar. He was intrigued with everything about her. And then it came to him. This was the girl he'd encountered in the cave on Torquay— Lady Starlin Cambridge—his sworn enemy!

Suddenly his emerald eyes narrowed and his full lips

tightened grimly. He had vowed long ago to wreak havoc and destruction upon the blood relatives of Carl Cambridge. He would not, could not, break that vow. He'd have to tread carefully, for there was no doubt the chit was smart. Undoubtedly she would recognize him before long. And he would have to convince her that his transformation from pirate to aristocrat was a sincere one.

Having been a rogue for so many years, even he found it hard to believe he'd resumed his former manner of life so easily. He'd stayed at Castle Sontavon for several months before converging upon London in order to completely banish the rough-edged Scorpio from his actions. With ease, Rayne had fallen back into the way of life that he had been born to. No one in England knew of his other identity, none had questioned his lengthy seclusion at his castle so far removed from London's whirl. And when he'd felt the time was right, he'd come to London and had been unhesitantly accepted back by his peers.

Starlin Cambridge was the only person in England who might reveal him as the pirate, Scorpio. He stared at her in thoughtful silence, knowing that if given the opportunity, and if not handled with kid gloves in the future, that milady would tell everyone what she knew.

Make your move, Morgan, he thought, and make certain you give the lady no chance to gull you.

Starlin was trembling. For some time now she'd been certain that someone was watching her. Like a wild thing seeking a means of escape from an unknown danger, her violet eyes searched the sea of familiar faces for the intruder. She could hear the strains of the last melody begin and noticed the possessive gleam in

Courtland's eyes as he started toward her, but before he could even open his mouth, she boldly cut him off.

"I know we were to have had this final dance, milord. However, I simply must decline your offer for I am wretchedly tired."

His eyes narrowed slightly, but he forced a smile. "Of course. I can wait until our engagement ball for that dance, milady. It will be soon—I assure you."

A formally attired servant bearing a tray of champagne-filled glasses interrupted the tense silence as he stepped between them and offered up a silver tray. "Champagne, Your Ladyship, Your Lordship?"

"Yes, thank you, Bridges," Starlin replied, grateful for the timely intervention. "I think we could use a bit of refreshment at this point."

Starlin accepted a glass, and without another glance in Courtland's direction, moved away from him. Amid a rustle of silk, she circled through the crowded ballroom toward her grandfather. She tried to smile cordially at Susan Ellendale who was standing next to him.

"Are you all right, dear?" the earl inquired with concern.

"Just tired," Starlin replied, wishing that she had found him alone.

"It has been a long evening," the earl replied.

"But such a lovely party," Lady Ellendale spoke up.

The earl turned to her. "Lady Ellendale, have you met my granddaughter, Lady Starlin Cambridge."

"Yes, I've had the pleasure," the woman responded stiffly. She arched a feathered brow at Starlin. "You are truly the belle of the ball, my dear. How thrilling to be so popular."

"The duchess and her husband are recent acquaintances of mine," the earl interceded smoothly. "She made it a point to come to your ball even though her husband was called away on business and she had to ask her cousin to escort her."

"How thoughtful," Starlin replied, her eyes meeting Lady Ellendale's. "Your cousin must be a dear."

"Yes," Lady Ellendale cooed sweetly, "and we were both most anxious to make your acquaintance. I've heard so much about you, and your lovely parties. I can't tell you what an eye-opening experience this has been."

"Thank you," Starlin said. "I hope you aren't disappointed."

"The ball . . . is everything that I thought it would be," Lady Ellendale returned, her smile fixed in place.

In the brief exchange, Starlin was certain she'd observed a glimmer of undisguised envy in the other woman's eyes. She glanced over at her grandfather and saw that he was frowning, obviously aware of the situation. She flashed him a warning glance, and then quickly noticing the furious look Lady Ellendale directed across the room, said, "Your cousin . . . you say?"

"I did," Lady Ellendale returned with narrowed eyes, becoming quite agitated as her gaze riveted upon the tall man before the refreshment table who was conversing with a young woman who appeared enraptured by everything about him. "He's . . . such a disconcerting rogue, that one," she stammered, whisking open her fan and placing it before her terse lips.

The air fairly crackled with tension. Starlin was certain that Lord Morgan, standing with his back to them so aloofly at ease, was something more than Lady Ellendale's cousin.

"I'll have to mention to your husband the next time we meet at the club how nice it was to entertain members of his family in my home," the earl interceded, his voice revealing a hint of underlying mirth.

Starlin almost lost her trained composure. Her eyes met her grandfather's. His were twinkling.

"Yes, well, a very distant cousin, to be exact," Lady Ellendale was quick to add. "On my family's side . . . one that the duke is not too familiar with . . . nor do I refer to him very often." She fluttered her fan nervously. "Ah, he isn't very fond of Lord Morgan, you see, and if you were to mention it to him, Earl, he would be very upset with me for associating with the rascal."

"Morgan?" the earl pondered loudly. "Of course! The rogue who set all of London on its ear some years back."

Lady Ellendale looked as though she might swoon. "One and the same, I'm afraid." She felt Starlin's steady violet gaze upon her and cursed Morgan for having put her marriage in dire jeopardy with his roguish charm. If the truth about her relationship with Morgan ever became public knowledge, the duke would lock her away in her rooms and toss out the key! He chose to ignore her affairs as long as she kept them discreet.

It was precisely at that moment that Rayne Morgan swung about and chanced to glance over in Starlin's direction. Their eyes met, and held.

A shock ran down her body. Surely, Starlin thought, it had to have been sheer chance that had made him turn so suddenly and fix that fascinating gaze upon her.

His eyes, flecked with gold fire, sent a shiver of excitement along her spine. She knew now, beyond any doubt, why Lady Ellendale risked all just to be with him. She found herself completely captivated by that insouciant gaze. It revealed nothing, yet hinted of so much.

Seeing him like this, bathed in soft light, her eyes could not help but study his every feature. He had an absolutely captivating face. Sun-streaked curls fell in unruly disorder over one finely etched brow as he nodded his head in silent acknowledgment. She found herself recalling the fact that this was one man who knew no authority higher than his own. He survived by his own set of rules. What he did, he did because it suited him; what he wanted, he simply took.

She started when she saw he was coming toward her. He moved easily through the crowd . . . circling . . . the confident predator stalking. Before she had time to draw a steady breath he was before her, taking her hand within his . . . and had he caressed her palm boldly before placing it to his lips? Slowly, and accompanied by a lazy smile, he released her hand.

"Lord Winfield, might I introduce . . . my cousin, Lord Rayne Morgan." Lady Ellendale's voice broke through Starlin's silent reverie.

Rayne's gaze took in the lovely woman before him. "It's been a memorable party, milady, although I regret that your legion of admirers kept you so occupied that we had no time in which to become better acquainted."

Starlin favored him with a searching look. "I have this feeling that you and I have met somewhere before. I could have sworn at first glance, that you were an acquaintance of mine that I had not seen for some time." She thought he was undoubtedly a man quite used to female adoration, for he didn't so much as blink one dark eyelash as her gaze raked him insolently from head to toe. "But I see now that I was mistaken. The man I remember would never have possessed such fine manners."

Morgan's white teeth flashed in his deeply tanned face. "A barbarian, this man?"

"Yes, some might say so," Starlin replied with an enigmatic smile.

"And you, Lady Cambridge?" Morgan drawled slowly, "what do you say?"

The earl was entranced by their interplay. Gad! but they made a most striking couple. He was surprised at his distress upon hearing the duchess interrupt their exchange.

"I hate to spoil this charming evening, but I have just developed a beastly headache and simply must go home—immediately."

Rayne was not convinced by Susan's mournful expression. He forced himself to appear concerned. "I shall see you to the carriage, at once."

Lord Winfield had been pleased by the fiery sparks that had been exchanged between Morgan and his granddaughter. It was as if the two of them were all alone in the room and had had eyes only for each other. He knew the marquess was unmarried, and found himself wondering if perhaps he'd simply never found the right lady to complement his discriminating taste and strong nature. He found himself speculating, and almost chuckled. Then, noticing Lady Ellendale's expression, dismissed thought of such an unlikely match. "We'd best allow our guests to leave, Starlin. I

94

can see Lady Ellendale is feeling poorly."

"Yes . . . and I am terribly sorry you must depart so early," Starlin added, holding Morgan's unyielding gaze.

Lady Ellendale cleared her throat, trying to draw his attention away from the ravishing beauty. At last, he took hold of Susan's arm. She almost winced from the viselike grip of his fingers, but she kept her features perfectly schooled until they were safely out of the room and waiting for their wraps. She jerked when he snarled in fury.

"If you ever try that again, I swear I'll call your bluff right in front of everyone."

"Whatever do you mean?" she shot back in her most offended tone.

"You bloody well know what I mean . . . Cousin," he drawled cryptically. "Headache, is it?"

The back of her palm flew to her forehead. "Please, don't snarl like a bear, darling, I feel so wretched."

"I can imagine, with all of that jealousy eating at you."

She glanced about in nervous agitation. "Hush! do you want them all to hear, to know of our true relationship?"

His sharp laugh was instantaneous. "As if you could keep it from them."

"I think that after watching you with that girl just now, they'll be gossiping over your little scene, and wondering how soon you'll have her in your bed."

A searing burst of anger almost overwhelmed him. "Bloody hell, but you push me too far!" he growled, making her jump. He grabbed her cloak from the majordomo and threw it around her shoulders. "You

95

can be a real shrew sometimes, Susan. You'd do well to remember that I don't owe you any explanations." He spun swiftly and walked away, leaving her staring miserably after him.

Susan could feel everyone's pitying gaze. Recovering her composure, she smiled weakly before their startled faces. Gad, but she had never seen Morgan look so formidable! She knew that he would never see her again. They were through. She almost thought of begging him . . . but after meeting Starlin Cambridge, Susan knew it was hopeless.

The realization that he'd never hold her, make love to her, made her cry out even as her ire rose thinking of his callous treatment. Damn him! She should go after him and slap his face soundly in front of her friends. That would show them all how little she cared for him! Yet, even as she longed to do so, she knew she dared not. For one thing was very certain about her dashing lover: he was dangerous, and she was wise to realize it. So she simply raged silently as she quickened her pace to catch up to him.

Starlin turned to her grandfather after Rayne Morgan's departure. With supreme effort she managed to keep her tone light.

"This Lord Morgan, Grandfather? . . ."

"Yes, what of him?"

"Do you know anything about him?"

"Not too much. Rumor has it that he turned his back on London for years following an unfortunate incident—a duel over a slight to his family name—that brought the king's wrath on his head and a dismissal as

96

captain of His Majesty's Guard." The earl frowned. "Too bad, for he was a damned good one." He brushed a light kiss upon Starlin's forehead and drew back in surprise. "Why, you're trembling, dearest."

Starlin took a deep breath to try and calm her racing pulse. "I'm afraid this has been a most unusual night for me, sir. But foremost on my mind is the fact that Lord Courtland is pressing for my hand. And this upsets me. I have not had an opportunity to discuss it with you until now. Could we talk?"

"Of course," the earl assured her, wrapping a comforting arm about her shoulders. "So that is what has my girl so upset?"

He guided her toward a private alcove where they sat upon a velvet-covered settee with tall potted palms affording them privacy.

"We are ill-suited, sir," Starlin tried vainly to point out to him. "Surely you are not blind to this fact."

The earl took a deep breath. "You are both from fine families," he began.

"I don't like the turn of this," Starlin said.

"You know that this has been the primary reason for these lavish affairs. And it is my belief that Courtland will provide you with the stability that you need. And . . . I am seriously considering the idea of betrothing you to him."

Numbly, Starlin shook her head. "You . . . you know how I feel about arranged marriages . . . and I thought that we had agreed I would not be betrothed against my will."

"Starlin," the earl breathed slowly, "you have never quite gotten over your parents' death. We both realize how seriously it affected your state of mind at the time.

97

I firmly believe that it has affected your ability to truly love anyone again. I know it is because you are fearful of being hurt. You are of the belief that anyone you love again will somehow disappear. But I think perhaps all that will change when you have a good man to take care of you."

"It is so hard for me to think of them . . . as dead. I sometimes imagine that they might still be alive, sailing the seas together."

The earl watched her closely before stating softly, "But they will not be coming back. And young Courtland is as concerned for your well-being as I am."

"My well-being is not at the beck and call of some pompous dandy like Buckwald Courtland! I will not marry him! I refuse." She pulled away from him, her eyes flashing rebelliously.

"Darling . . ." the earl began, his words dying in his throat as his distraught granddaughter rose abruptly and stared at him.

"You may as well sentence me to a prison term as betroth me to that man." With that, the distraught girl fled through the terrace doors.

The earl had recognized the glitter of panic in his granddaughter's eyes, and felt certain that it had been prompted by the mention of her inability to give freely of her emotions. Damn! He had thought the worst over with. He recalled having seen her like this only once before. Months after her parents had disappeared, he had tried to get her to exhibit some show of warmth toward a kitten he'd just brought her. At first, she'd not touched the kitten, but had just stared with sad eyes at the mewling ball of fluff beside her on the bed. He'd left them alone, and Starlin had been unable to resist the appealing creature for very long. But he'd never forgotten the look of half fear, half longing, that he'd glimpsed in her eyes when she'd first reached out to hesitantly touch the kitten. That small creature had accomplished what a dozen of the finest doctors had not been able to do. They'd called Starlin's condition post-traumatic shock. The earl shuddered, remembering that terrible time. He'd looked out for her best interest then, and he would do so now. Even if it took his every ounce of strength—and a pompous English husband to do so.

Starlin was indeed upset. The entire night had gone badly, and she was in desperate need of someone to talk with about her feelings. She was far too overwrought to sit still with so many confusing emotions roiling within her, and hurriedly left the patio to walk about the grounds. The young woman immediately thought of one friend who would listen, who would perhaps even offer advice, not judgments. She remembered that Abra had gone into foal earlier in the evening and was certain that Fredrick, the head groomsman, would be attending her. She would go to the stable and perhaps she might find a quiet moment in which to talk with Fredrick.

It was well past midnight as Starlin made her way over the path that led to the stables where the brood mares were kept until they foaled. The night was damp and black, and appeared as unsettling as her mood. Overhead, and just visible through the outspread tree limbs, Starlin caught a glimpse of the moon, the heavy gray clouds rolling past partially obscuring the silver light that aided her steps. In the darkness, every object familiar in the daytime took on unsettling proportions. It was as though she'd stepped into another land, and recognized nothing around her. She tried not to focus on a shadowy form that appeared waiting in the distance, concentrating instead on reaching the stables.

Some memory from the deepest recesses of her mind tried to awaken, yet could not, and remained a wispy tendril of obscurity just beyond her reach.

Unaware, Starlin found herself staring down at the ring on her finger, reviewing so many things, so much of her past. She easily recalled the incident in the cave, recalled every detail, and Scorpio's wrath upon seeing the ring on her finger. Suspicions, frightening and evil, flitted through her mind. For some reason she thought of the sinister conversation between the two strange men at the fireworks display and wondered if it were possible that all of this might be connected in some way? Absurd? Yes, of course it was silly to even consider it, she told herself firmly. Yet, there were so many unanswered questions . . . and staring at the ring she wondered if just possibly . . . it could somehow be a clue?

Key West . . . the ring . . . Scorpio . . . whirled in her head.

An errant shaft of moonlight pierced through the clouds. The stones glittered in the ghostly light. Glittering diamonds surrounding one bloodred ruby. Suddenly, images wafted like dark, somber shadows out of the black night and flashed before her.

Benton, his expression bleak, pleading for her to return to him. Her mother, Carl—appearing faded forms and so very painful to behold. And then, a dark outlaw descended upon her inner visions, tall, threatening, with a gleaming broadsword held in his hand. Starlin blinked, and there was only the darkness before her.

"Scorpio, what links you to this ring . . . and possibly to many other things I have yet to discover answers to?"

Starlin recalled painfully the last day that she'd seen her parents alive. It was the morning of their expedition . . . the day they were certain that their dreams would at last be realized. Her stepfather had come to their special place on the estate—a playhouse he'd built especially for her.

Riches beyond a man's dreams, Starlin, her stepfather had proclaimed as she'd stood filled with unease, and listened to his words. She was too young to go along, she'd been informed earlier, and she was sulking now, saying very little because she was feeling cheated that Benton should be allowed to go. It did not occur to the little girl that Benton was older, and could dive just as well as his father. Two divers were necessary when one was below searching for the riches found on the galleons that lured so many to the reefs off the island Antare.

The fingers of her hand caressed the exquisite beauty of the stones now, grateful for this one keepsake.

She remembered Carl placing the ring on her middle finger as they'd stood there in the playhouse.

Do not tell anyone that I have given you this ring. Keep it for me until I return. His face had grown somber. *And if I . . . do not . . . return, see that your mother receives it.*

Starlin had not wished to answer . . . it was too

horrid to imagine such a thing!

Carl had gripped her shoulders and she recalled even now how intense he'd appeared. *Absolutely no one must know that you have the ring. Promise me.*

She'd nodded numbly.

This ring was given to me by someone. It has enabled me to determine my path in life because of that factor. You must remember—with this ring love will guide you. Tell this to Gwen . . . if it becomes necessary. He'd kissed her. *You are the only one that I can trust.*

Yes . . . and now both of you are lost to me, Starlin mused sadly. Both of you—to death on the bottom of the sea. And the treasure that you were so certain was on that galleon, you never found, for your ship disappeared somewhere off the formidable island of Antare in the lost sea. Only Benton had been saved, tossed into the sea to float half alive for days. A passing schooner finally fished him all but dead out of the sea. Everyone in Key West had assumed Benton had drowned, until several weeks following the accident the schooner had docked in Key West, and Benton had returned home. They had been stunned. Malcom Wells, their attorney who stood to inherit a goodly portion of the business if Benton had been dead, more so than anyone.

The weeks had passed, then months—and Starlin never told anyone of the ring's existence. Of course, everyone had naturally assumed it had been on Carl's little finger when he'd died. Starlin had hidden the precious keepsake. It was years later, long after she'd come to England, that she'd decided to retrieve it from her jewelry case. She now wore it on her forefinger.

The night in the cave Scorpio had been stunned to

see the ring. Would the aristocrat, Lord Morgan, be equally intrigued? Although, it was just a lovely old ring, nothing more . . .

The young woman decided that she must learn more of this Marquess of Sontavon. Everything. But she realized that in order to do so, she would have to expose herself to the other side of the marquess, the dark side—and Scorpio. Caught in the snare of her own unbidden thoughts, Starlin found herself wanting to laugh and scream all at the same time. It was absurd what she was thinking! A marquess, a smuggler on the high seas—linked in some way to her parents' bizarre drowning?

Yet, as unbelievable as it seemed, the man who England proclaimed a titled lord was actually a pirate, and she was intrigued with everything about him.

Chapter Six

Starlin saw the stable looming ahead in the darkness. She hurried toward the sprawling structure, slid back the heavy door, and stepped inside.

Familiar sounds and scents greeted her. The pungent smell of horses and leather mixed with that of sweet straw gave her a measure of comfort. She saw a light in Abra's stall at one end of the immense stable. Thinking of her mare, she forgot her own problems and hurried forward.

Fredrick, the head groom, looked up as she placed a foot between the boards and stepped up to peer into the box stall. "And what would you be doing here this time of night, Lady Cambridge?" he demanded.

"I came to talk—" She halted, and stared down at the laboring mare lying on her side in the straw. "However, it can wait. How is she, Fredrick?"

"She's not having an easy time of it, I'm afraid," Fredrick replied with a sigh, then remembering whom he was addressing, coughed uneasily. "You should not be here during a foaling, it isn't proper."

"Please, Fredrick, this is no time to stand on propriety." Starlin came around to the stall entrance, opened the door, and ventured inside. She knelt beside the mare.

"My lady!" Fredrick gasped, taking notice of her ball gown. "The earl will have my job if he hears of this."

"Nonsense," Starlin responded, authority in her tone. "And besides, he doesn't even know I am here."

"All the more, then," the groom insisted. He wiped the mare's lathered coat with a soft blanket.

"I am staying with Abra until this is over," Starlin told him firmly.

Fredrick's mouth tightened to a thin line, but he knew by the mutinous thrust of milady's chin that there wasn't any way he could convince her to leave.

"So be it, then," he grunted, meeting her level stare. "I don't know whose wrath I'd rather face. By the look in them eyes right now, I'd say it would be the earl."

Starlin's set features softened. "I'll be of great help, just you wait and see."

"The way things are going, I'd say we could use all of the help that we can get." Fredrick's expression was one of concern, and Starlin frowned.

"She will be all right, won't she?"

"I certainly hope so," he replied huskily. "For she's special to me, too." He tried to smile reassuringly at the girl. "I haven't lost a mama or foal yet, you know."

They settled back to wait. And to Starlin, it seemed to take forever. Finally, the groom announced that the birth was imminent. "It's time. You just keep stroking her neck and talking to her like you been doing, milady," he instructed as he worked over the mare. "Abra and the baby are going to be just fine."

106

Starlin held Abra's regal head in her lap, observing with compassion the big brown eyes so clouded with anguish that were fixed upon her own. "She seems to know that we're helping her. I believe she trusts us to do what's right, don't you, Fredrick?"

"I suspect she does at that," he replied, setting back on his heels to wipe his hands with a rag. "Well, it's all up to Abra and Mother Nature now. We've done all that we can."

Both mistress and groom had been so engrossed in their efforts that neither was aware of the silent figure standing off to one side of the stable in shadow.

Rayne Morgan observed Starlin's every gesture like a cunning wolf in pursuit of his prey. His eyes narrowed slightly, his heart beat fast and hard in his chest. He was seeing yet another side of Lady Cambridge. One that sent all manner of ideas churning in his head. He wanted to kiss her soft mouth, taste the heated passion he knew he would find there. Starlin furthered that desire upon lifting one slim hand to brush a few wayward tendrils of damp hair back from her creamy cheek. Watching her, Rayne found his thoughts swaying inexplicably to all manner of ways that he'd like to make love to her.

The wavering light from the overhead lantern played softly about her animated features. Ice Princess? Not when he held her, Rayne found himself thinking. He had found the fire hidden beneath that icy facade, discovered the simmering passion that burned hotter and more intense than any man could have imagined. Just the remembrance of her soft, sinuous body moving so naturally and uninhibited against his, made his pulse leap.

Cambridge—the name still conjured up hatred, but now it was intermingled with desire.

The ring on her finger flashed in the lantern light. Rayne stiffened. The ring—it was at the heart of him and had long ago robbed him of any tender emotions. But soon, he reasoned with firmer control, he'd have the answers—and the revenge. With an effort he concentrated on what must be done. He stood there in silent contemplation, and made his absolute decision. Every Cambridge must be punished for their father's sin. Even this one.

A short while later, Starlin found herself staring in relief and fascinated wonder as Abra's foal entered the world. As difficult as the labor had been, the birth went swiftly. Abra delivered a beautiful, long-legged filly that was perfect in every way. The proud mother took over immediately, rising to her feet to administer to her new baby. The little filly wiggled beneath Abra's persistent ministration, struggling to stand on wobbly, spindly legs that would one day be as long and graceful as her dam's and enable her to outrace the wind.

Fredrick and Starlin sat there for some time. Eventually, they began talking quietly. Starlin conveyed some of the night's events to him and her staunch views on arranged marriages. He listened without interrupting, then commented softly. "Your innermost feelings will lead you, Your Ladyship. Follow them." He rose to his feet with a tired smile. "I think that you are concerned that the earl might be serious about this match between you and Milord Courtland."

"I am," Starlin replied. "You should have seen that stubborn thrust of his chin, Fredrick. He feels he is doing this for my own good." She grew quiet, eyes

108

observing the silent declaration of love that Abra conveyed to her foal. "I do not know what I would do if he decides to force this match. Love is a necessary thing in a marriage, and I can never love Buckwald Courtland . . . never."

Fredrick sighed. "If it's love you're waiting for, milady, then you must accept the fact that it follows its own course. Love is one of the mysteries of life. It just happens, and most often, with the least likely person." He patted her shining hair. "And now, I best see that your grandfather knows where you are."

"No, please, Fredrick." Starlin cast him a pleading look. "You're exhausted, and he's had such a long night. He's probably fast asleep. If you agree, I should like to tell him myself that I was here. He may huff and puff at first, but he'll eventually come around." She smiled enchantingly and Fredrick held little doubt as to the truth of that statement.

"Very well, milady." He stretched his long frame wearily. "I'm ready to call it a night."

"You go on to bed. I'll turn out the lamp in a short while."

"I imagine it will be all right. Just don't stay much longer," he said as he moved through the stall door, closing it behind him.

Starlin listened as he quit the stable. Alone with her thoughts, she decided she felt much better since talking with Fredrick. She would just have to plead her views further with the earl come morning. With a sigh, she reached over to pat Abra's velvet muzzle before lying back in the straw to relax for a moment. Stretching wearily, she closed her eyes. She did not intend on dozing off, only to rest quietly for a while.

Rayne Morgan's devastating image immediately beckoned in the corners of her mind. His unsettling eyes, such an unusual jade and disturbing to her senses, were the last thing she recalled before her fatigued mind gave way to slumber.

Being driven by an inner purpose he chose not to identify, Rayne Morgan moved from the shadows to where the raven-haired beauty lay sleeping.

Something warm and infinitely sensual brushed lightly across Starlin's palm . . . the soft flesh of her wrist. She sighed with intense pleasure.

Something smooth, and ever so intoxicating, caressed her cheek . . . the tip of her earlobe. The scent of sea wind and lime tantalized her senses. She came awake with a start, eyes wide.

He was there beside her, the savage brilliance of those cynical green eyes making her shiver. Her gaze strayed to his slightly aquiline nose, downward to the mocking slant of his full mouth. Slowly his lips descended to the throbbing pulse in her throat. She caught her breath. His head came up and she saw the look of undisguised triumph in his eyes.

Starlin wanted to fight him, longed to slap his face for taking such outrageous liberties with her. But she remembered that other time . . . and how quickly he'd changed from gentle, wooing lover, his actions becoming brutal and unfeeling.

His lips curved upward in a half smile.

"You mustn't look as if you fear being gobbled up, little innocent. I don't intend to do so." Long brown fingers reached out to caress her lips. "Let your fear

110

go, Starlin."

"You do not frighten me," she shot back defiantly.

His smile turned wickedly charming. He appeared able to see into the very depths of her soul and draw her to him. Moving swiftly across her deepest thoughts, he was all-consuming, dominant, feral. Fires were stoked within her. His hands upon her skin were gentle, yet strong and sure, awakening familiar feelings that were so overwhelming, and, indeed, frightening. As her smoke-violet eyes met the heated jade of his, she discerned no mocking laughter in their depths, only passion, undisguised and wanting.

With a small cry, she attempted to roll free of him. "No—leave me alone!"

He caught her easily, grappling to hold her still. Starlin fought wildly. Arms and legs tangled. He flipped her onto her back and held her shoulders firmly against the straw-littered floor. Passion glittered in his eyes. They lingered on the rapid rise and fall of her breasts as he lowered his body over hers.

Starlin could not take her eyes off him. She stared wide-eyed as he raised his hand, one long finger tracing a feather-light path down her cheek, along the slim column of her throat. Realizing his intention, she knocked his hand aside.

With a soft snarl he grasped her chin between his finger and thumb and held her head still. He studied her for a moment, then his lips closed demandingly over hers. All thought of anything but his desire to make love to her left him. Revenge, hate, his need to take her without passion—he forgot it all.

Starlin did not know when she stopped fighting him. She only knew that his lips and tongue were weaving a

111

sensual spell on her reasoning and that it was the most stimulating sensation she had ever experienced in her life. She moaned deep down in her throat and responded to his teasing motions. Her lips parted, welcoming the taste of him upon her tongue. Warmth began low in her abdomen, radiated outward, and soothed shocked nerve endings. With effortless ease, he unlaced her gown, the ribbons on her chemise, and gently cupped her full breast. His mouth left hers to trail downward and capture a sweet nipple between his teeth.

Her hips seemed to move in involuntary reaction to the feel of his hardness where it pressed between her legs. Starlin felt a whisper of cool air play softly across her skin and was vaguely aware that he was removing her gown, then her underthings. She lay naked beneath him. His fingers grew bolder. He stroked her until she was open and ready, her will crumbled; murmuring unintelligible things near her ear that were welcomed, soothing to her startled senses.

Slowly, she relaxed and gave herself up to the wonderful feelings coursing through her. He kissed her there between her legs, tonguing her hungrily, posses- sively. She tried to close her legs to the wild uncontrollable feelings making her twist and arch her hips. He pushed her thighs wide apart, fingers filling her. Then he was naked, poised above her. She closed her eyes. It was hard and hot as fire, searing into her, claiming her as no man had ever dared. His lips stilled her cry of protest, his hands her trembling, and before long, she was moving as one with him. He made love with abandon, as, she sensed, he did everything. Long, slow, delicious strokes that increased in fervor drew her

112

along on a tide of exquisite pleasure. Her nails raked his back with wild abandon and his muscles quivered in response. They surrendered all to passion until the fires were appeased.

"We can never do this again," she stated in a hushed voice when they were standing and he was helping her to dress. She was still feeling dazed.

He was lacing her gown. He didn't respond immediately. He was thinking how innocent she was, and how she did not realize the mysteries or the powerful lure of physical desire. But in remembering how she'd fought him with the fierce determination of a spirited tigress, he knew she was not innocent of any other emotions. She had pride, and until now, an indomitable spirit. It would not be easy to break her, but he had little doubt that in the end he would. She was the best of the Cambridge lot so far, and he was certain she would give him a battle unequaled by any of her predecessors. He almost wished Cambridge blood did not flow in her veins. It was a pity to have to destroy the fire that burned so brightly within her. He turned her in his arms.

"And if I should choose otherwise?" he asked softly.

Starlin was feeling half-mesmerized by stormy green eyes that would not allow her to look away. "You do not deny being a pirate, nor even seem to care that I remember your alliance with those other smugglers. Aren't you the least bit afraid that I might then choose to reveal your . . . other activities?"

His fingers wound into her hair, arching her throat. He viewed her with lazy indifference. "And send me to

113

the gallows . . . is that what you mean, milady?"

Nothing in her dreams of him had prepared her for the man who was here now, in the flesh. His hand around her throat, so gentle but still threatening, reminded her of the uncertainty of her situation. "Do you not fear death?"

His voice mocked her. "Death is a game. And I have managed to cheat it so far. Tonight, I find life more daring."

"You . . . should let me go . . ." And firmer still. "Let me go—*now.*"

"You don't really mean that," he said with a teasing grin.

His tone was like a slap in the face. He appeared so damned smug. She'd been a fool to allow her emotions to overtake her reasoning. "I mean it," she stated heatedly.

"Shall I prove differently?" he responded. She had no time in which to protest before his lips slanted across hers. The feel of him, the scent and heat of him were devastating to her reason. This man was so unlike any other that she'd known! Raw power emanated from his body to hers. She tore her mouth free of his, breathed raggedly beneath his piercing stare. What was behind that untamed look of his that could make her weak with wanting at just one glance, one searing kiss?

"This will not happen again," she said firmly.

"By the look in your eyes now, I think that you believe that. Do you also plan to shout to all of London that Lord Morgan is a lecherous pirate who robbed milady of her most precious gift?" he asked easily, grinning sardonically.

Starlin's eyes narrowed. "I just might—and from

every rooftop!"

"Revenge, sweet?" he drawled. Ignoring her flashing eyes, he suddenly released her. His smile hardened, became cold and calculating. "Should I tag along with you to make it easier for you." He paused. "I might, you know—and then stand back and watch while everyone laughs at your accusation."

She stiffened. "Damn you," she said slowly from between clenched teeth, so filled with humiliating anger that she felt like crying.

"You know, as I do, that your declaring Lord Rayne Morgan a pirate leader will only prompt raised eyebrows and snide whispers behind your back." He felt no regret at his harsh words and even took a measure of satisfaction at the truthful acknowledgment visible in her eyes. "No one will believe that, coming from you of all people. I am titled and greatly respected among the peerage, and can easily prove your accusations absurd." He bowed mockingly before meeting her gaze with a steely look. "While you, milady, are thought of . . ."

"What you are taking such delight in pointing out to me, is that my outspokenness is against me," she cut in tartly. "You bastard! I knew I was right about you from the beginning!"

"Which one of us are you referring to . . . the lecherous pirate, or the titled lord?" he asked teasingly.

Her eyes narrowed to mere slits. "I find both of you despicable! And why I allow you near me I do not know."

"Because nothing you do, can keep me from you," he stated matter of factly.

Watching him closely now, she knew that this man

could slip easily from one culture to the other, and fit any mold that he wished. Some overpowering aura seemed to surround him. It made him all the more dangerous, for one could never really discern the true character of such a man, or his actual intentions.

"Are you cutthroat or titled lord? Tell me, which role are you playing now?" she inquired tersely.

"You decide . . . which suits you?"

"Fie! Nothing about either of you suits me. You are both impossible!"

His long fingers closed over hers. "And you are an equally impossible woman. We are a perfect match, I'd say."

Reluctantly, Starlin permitted him to draw her nearer. He held her so possessively. She stared up at his dark face. "Your bold implication that I will become your mistress shall never come to pass. What took place tonight was not something I wanted. It *will not* happen again."

Her words did not appear to bother him. There was a strange glitter in those emerald eyes. "Don't make promises you won't be able to keep, love."

Starlin felt the awesome lure of him in every thought and action, yet refused to yield. "Oh, but this one I will," she swore with a narrowed glare.

"You can't fight me. I intend to have you whenever I so choose."

She bristled at his insulting tone. "You may fool everyone else, but not me, Morgan. Your accent and your clothes are that of a gentleman, but your arrogance certainly leaves much to be desired. Why is that? Too long keeping company with thieves and murderers?"

Morgan smiled in cynical amusement. "Am I not

forgiven one small mistake?"

She spun away from him and sprinted forward. He only laughed, and caught her to him. An unwanted breathlessness seized Starlin. "Why do you want someone who despises everything about you?"

"Because . . . even though you refuse to admit it, you and I are very much alike . . . tonight went far to prove that."

She laughed contemptuously. "There is nothing about us that could be similar."

He brushed the back of his hand lightly across her cheek. It was an intimate gesture that unnerved her. "Shall I refresh your memory a bit."

She turned her head. "I will resist your every effort." Yet even as she said the words, she knew how hollow they sounded.

He placed an arm on either side of her, palms resting flat on top the rails. "Sweet liar," he whispered huskily.

She breathed a little faster when she felt him draw closer. He lowered his lips to hers, no other part of him touching her, just that wonderful, persuasive mouth moving slowly, drawing away the last defense.

Starlin did not realize that she had moved to entwine her arms around his neck and draw him near, or that her body had molded itself to every masculine inch of him. Heady passion burst forth within her. She quivered when she felt his lips trail a path across her cheek and down to her throat, where he lightly tongued the throbbing pulse to life.

It was a gloriously maddening sensation, but she fought against it. She would never allow him to seduce her again! She pressed her mouth against his shoulder and bit down in an effort to suppress a groan.

Morgan felt her sharp little teeth sink into the hard

117

muscle of his forearm, yet barely flinched. The feel of her, the scent and taste of her sent his emotions reeling.

Starlin slipped further into passion's lure, and caught between a strange sense of terror and exquisite ecstasy, found it impossible to resist. It took the sputtering of the lantern overhead to send her hurtling out of his arms. My God, had she been about to let him make love to her again? What kind of woman was she?

He raised his head, and found he was breathing as rapidly as she was. A current of tension flowed between them, still held them transfixed with each other. The light of awareness shone in her eyes once more. They were narrowed and smoldering, their slightly tilted corners giving her an all-knowing, sultry look that made him begin to wonder just who was seducing whom. Breasts heaving, hair loose and tumbling down around her shoulders, she faced him like a woman who knew exactly how to please a man, and was prepared to do just that. He knew he would never find peace until his need for revenge was sated and this woman put far from his thoughts. A range of troubled emotions added a husky quality to his voice when he spoke.

"You see . . . we have much in common."

"I don't know what it is about you, above all other men, that enables you to sense what I feel, how I'll react, even before I do myself. But,. I know now, that you do . . . don't you?"

He stared back at her through heavy-lidded eyes. "I think that you should go back to the house before I'm tempted to take you away from here with me. He raked his fingers through his tawny-gold hair, wondering why in the hell he should not do just that. Take her away, his inner self goaded. His face appeared grimly set as he glanced up at her. Perhaps the time was just not right yet. And seeing that she hadn't moved, growled, "Go—now! For once listen to someone who knows a bit more than you. Get out of here while you still can, foolish girl."

Starlin stiffened at the sudden change in his manner and the caustic clip to his words. He was such an arrogant, self-assured bastard that he thought all he had to do was crook his finger this way and that and she would jump each time he snarled. "A command or plea?" she stated sneeringly, glaring at him now.

"Whichever suits you," he replied with a shrug of wide shoulders. "It makes no difference, just leave me now."

"I will not take orders from you," Starlin said disdainfully before turning away.

"Women of your nature need a man to tell them what to do," he drawled.

Starlin spun around, face flaming. "What do you mean? women of my nature?"

"Willful, headstrong, and at times, easily led. Need I make it any plainer, sweet?"

Outraged, she flew at him, raised her hand to slap the mocking grin off of his face, only to cry out painfully when he smoothly caught her hand in his.

"Don't." One word. Yet it echoed like a gunshot within her head.

"Release me," she managed to grind out from between clenched teeth.

"I don't think you would like what would happen next if you should persist," he warned tersely.

Starlin wiggled her imprisoned wrist, her eyes meeting his defiantly. "Why doesn't the threat of physical violence from you surprise me?" To her wide-eyed disbelief, he grinned charmingly.

"I might remind you that I'm not the one who instigated it—this time."

"You are despicable, Morgan," she said harshly, her eyes alive with fury, "and you'll always be!"

"In that, at least, I must agree," he replied coolly. "One of my lesser faults, I might add." He dropped her wrist and stood raking her with those all-knowing eyes.

She rubbed her throbbing wrist. "I have no desire to ever again be soiled by your touch. And if you persist in pursuing me, I will most certainly see that you live to regret it." She saw a muscle in his lean jaw tighten at her sharp words, and for a long second they stared at each other without moving.

"You bluff well," he drawled at last, "but your threat sounds hollow."

Their eyes met and held.

"Don't ever underestimate me, Morgan," Starlin gritted.

"You've never truly forgotten me, Starlin. Do you think that after what transpired between us tonight that it will now be any easier. It won't."

"We'll just see!" she cried, storming toward the door.

"Yes . . . we will at that." His easy mocking laughter followed her from the stable and prompted her to slam the stable door soundly.

Starlin sat in front of her vanity watching her maid Mindy gather up the combing cape and brush. It was quiet throughout the house, not a sound or person could be heard. The fire in the hearth crackled cheerily, and she should have been anticipating her bed after such an eventful night, but she was not. Her fingers drummed upon the glass top of the vanity, and the devoted Mindy, thinking her charge impatient to be abed, quickly offered an apology.

"I'm sorry for not 'aving everything ready for you, milady, 'owever, I expected you 'ours sooner, and I must 'ave dozed off waiting. I only woke up when you came in." The woman glanced at the clock on the marble mantel. "'Tis almost dawn," she mentioned pointedly. "You must 'ave been dancing up a storm to 'ave be this late."

Starlin stared after the woman as she offered up the cape for her charge to slip over her dressing gown. "You know full well the soirée ended several hours ago, Mindy." Starlin threaded her arms through the cape sleeves and allowed the servant to secure it at the throat.

"Oh . . . but I was sleeping, I guess, and did not know that at all." She began removing the pins from Starlin's hair. "So, you took a long walk, hmmm?"

Starlin stared at her through the looking glass. "No—I did not take a long walk, if you must know," she huffed at the woman. She was accustomed to Mindy's affectionate concern, for the woman had been looking after her since she had come from Key West. "I went to the stable."

Mindy's fingers plucked several telltale strands of straw from Starlin's thick mane. "By yourself, no doubt," she said drolly, before applying the brush to her mistress's long hair.

"And just what are you referring to?" Starlin contemplated her maid narrowly.

"You know full well what I am getting at, my fine lady," Mindy responded stiffly, the brush stroking faster and harder as if by doing so she might force some sense into her charge's head.

121

Starlin winced several times before reaching up to grasp the arm wielding the brush. "Will you stop that! You are not going to inflict another torturous stroke of that weapon. I've had enough tending to for one night."

Mindy glared reproachfully. "Morning's what you mean."

Starlin wrinkled her nose in irritation at the woman. "Go on to bed with you, and be quick about it. I don't need to have you needling me yet again about my ways."

"Seems it 'asn't done me a bit of good, or you neither." The maid flung down the silver-backed brush with a sigh of disgust. "Whatever do you think of sometimes, a fine lady like yourself." She bit her lip to stem back the tirade she would have liked to heap upon the young woman. She was still pursing her lips disapprovingly even as she touched the girl affectionately on the shoulder before leaving the bedchamber.

Starlin sat there, miserable silence enveloping her. With a dejected sigh, she made her way to the door, deciding to go to the library and read for a while since sleep seemed ever elusive. She was oblivious to the fact that even as she shrugged into a satin wrap and prepared to leave her bedchamber, a figure cloaked in black stood below her balcony waiting for the candle in her room to be extinguished.

When the room darkened, he began climbing the trellis until he was able to swing over onto the balcony. He worked with efficient ease on the lock securing the French doors, and within a moment, he was standing inside her room.

Candle in hand, Starlin made her way quietly

through the cavernlike hallways of the immense house not once admitting to herself that she was, in fact, trying to flee the image of Rayne's sardonic face that had seemed to fill every corner of her bedchamber. With miserable acknowledgment, she entered the vast room, and after selecting the works of Byron, set the candle on a nearby side table and curled up in a plush leather chair.

Angry with Morgan and also herself for allowing him to manipulate her so, she snuggled deeper into the chair and flipped open the book with a determined set to her mouth. She would read until her eyes dropped closed and her mind driven of its demon. In every other word on the page, she found herself arranging the letters just so . . . Scorpio . . . Rayne. After their explosive encounter tonight, and the passion they had shared, Starlin knew it would be best for her to keep some measure of distance between them.

"Scoundrel or lord . . . you're terribly bad," she mumbled as the book dropped from her fingers, "and I must fight this overwhelming urge within that dares me so." Emotionally exhausted, she snuggled into the chair and fell asleep.

Something fell to the floor overhead. Starlin awakened with a start, shaking her head to clear her befuddled thoughts. For several minutes she did not move as she sat listening to the faint stirrings of the household. She peered around her and noticed the pale pink light of daybreak peeking through an opening in the draperies. The sound of anxious voices and hurrying footsteps brought her to her feet. Rushing from the library and out into the hall, she was met by a white-faced kitchen maid.

"Blimey, Your Ladyship, but you've given us all a scare!" She froze as if seeing a ghost.

Starlin felt her heart plummet thinking of her grandfather's frail health and wondering if something had happened to him.

"Annie, what has happened?"

"It's your maid, Mindy," Annie wailed. "She was attacked by an intruder . . . and in your room, no less."

"Oh!" Starlin gasped. "How is she?" She grasped the sobbing Annie by her thin shoulders. "Was she injured badly?"

"Roughed up a bit, she was," Annie sniffled, "with a good thump to the head, poor thing."

"Has the doctor been sent for?"

"Yes, mum, first thing."

"Good," Starlin replied firmly. "Now, I must see to her myself." She started for the stairway.

By the time that Starlin reached the wing of the house where her chambers were and saw the frightened servant huddled on the wide four-poster holding a cloth to her head, she was composed, and hurried to comfort her. She sat beside Mindy on the bed.

"It's all right," she said soothingly. "You're going to be fine." She wrapped a comforting arm around the tiny woman who was like a mother to her.

"I thought the man was going to kill me, Your Ladyship," she breathed shakily, head bowed to hide her tears.

"I'm so sorry this happened," Starlin said softly.

"It wasn't your fault," the maid sighed. "Don't fret none on it. I'll be good as new, I expect."

The earl stepped over beside them, a look of obvious relief on her features as he stared down at his granddaughter. "She'll be just fine, Starlin. The doctor should be here any minute now."

Starlin nodded over the lump in her throat. She enfolded her hand in his. "Why would anyone do something so ugly?"

"Desperate for money I suppose." The earl ran his fingers through his thick silver hair. "Child, I must say you almost scared me to death. We thought that he'd kidnapped you when we first found Mindy in your room, and you nowhere about."

"Oh, sir, I do apologize," Starlin said hurriedly. "I had gone to the stables to talk with Fredrick and see about Abra." Her eyes held a guilty light. "It was impulsive of me, and I am sorry for causing you undue concern."

"My dear Starlin, this is one time I'm glad you acted as you saw fit. For none of us is certain until the police are able to investigate, whether this was a robbery, or something more ominous." He gestured toward the terrace doors. "The intruder must have waited until your light was extinguished and managed to jiggle open the lock on the French doors. With the number of vagabonds roaming about London these days I am surprised that we haven't been subjected to something like this before now."

"That is who you truly think responsible," Starlin asked, "someone who perhaps picked this house with the intention of robbing us?"

The earl frowned. "Don't you?"

Starlin rose from the bed to walk about the chamber. She recalled the shadowy form near the stable. A ghost of memories? . . . Or could it have been? . . . No! She did not wish to confront that possibility.

"It doesn't appear that he had the opportunity to

steal very much," the earl offered, watching the intent expression on Starlin's face in the flickering candlelight.

The sound of her grandfather's voice had faded into the background of Starlin's conscious thought. She could not forget that other time—the night she'd first encountered Scorpio. God, but he'd reacted so violently that night in the cave upon noticing Carl's ring on her finger. What had he said? . . .

How is it you come to wear this ring?

It was the ring that had made him turn so brutal. Before then he'd been of a totally different mind. She shivered even now visualizing that terrifying scene. After he'd glimpsed the ring he didn't appear like the same man. His eyes had hardened, observed her with a calculating light. And he had called her something . . .

"My enemy," she murmured to herself. She vividly recalled his sneering contempt, and his voice, so full of hatred. How could she have been swept away by passion and forgotten the intensity of his enmity for her? She glanced about the room, her heart twisting with painful acknowledgment. How could he have made love to her, and then do something like this?

In confusion, Starlin fought with the part of her that wanted to believe anything that he said, and the rational side, the one that had earned her the title of Ice Princess. He claimed to have changed in the year since last they met. But had he really? She found herself wishing that she could believe he'd abandoned his old ways. Lord Rayne Morgan. The name and family were greatly respected throughout England. Her grandfather had told her that his ancestors had been favorites of the king. Respected, admired, yes, all of that had been said. Henry Morgan had been a distant relative, and a clever pirate whom many had admired. Perhaps this pirating business was something that was just in a man's blood, and could not be purged from some, no matter how hard one might try.

Starlin was convinced that such was the case with Rayne Morgan. She now felt certain that he had demanded to know where she had gotten the ring in an effort to learn more about her background. He had wanted her to relate details about herself so that he might trace her to an address, and, she felt certain now, to a fashionable one at that. He had been planning to find her since their initial encounter—and rob her! For what thief of a pirate could resist jewels? A pox on his stalwart family name!

Her mouth trembled. She felt as if he'd violated her by this act. The room had been thoroughly searched. Personal items were scattered everywhere. It hurt to think of how much she was attracted to him, and how easily he had manipulated her. If she'd dare admit it to herself, he was the one she dreamed of each night who would teach her the ways of love. Love! That was not what they'd shared tonight. Her secret dreams were shattered by the ugly reality of the man.

Starlin peered into the open cache of jewels. She rifled through the contents, and was astounded to find that only a few pieces were missing. Her grandfather's voice broke through her brooding reverie.

"I believe your best pieces were overlooked."

"It . . . it does look that way."

"Lucky for us," Mindy exclaimed.

"He must not have known the value of jewelry, for he left most of the priceless pieces behind. He seemed to have only picked out those that captured his fancy."

Rayne Morgan not know the value of fine jewels? She spun about to face the earl.

"Perhaps he just didn't have enough time to examine each piece before Mindy walked in on him."

Mindy gasped.

"What is it?" the earl queried anxiously.

'My ring! The thief grabbed it off my finger, he did!"

Starlin rushed over to stare down at the woman's trembling hand.

"You remember me wearing a band, milady? My Tobey is gonna be so upset with me. That ring was his mum's."

"Hush now," the earl said in a comforting voice. "I've sent one of the servants to fetch the police. They'll do their best to find your ring."

Starlin sat down beside Mindy once again. "I promise you that I will do everything I can to make certain that you get your ring back."

It was dawn before Starlin was finally alone in her chamber. The servants had straightened everything after the police had finished with their inspection. Starlin lay stretched out on her bed and tried to collect her thoughts.

Not surprisingly, the pirate rogue, Scorpio, and the titled English lord, Rayne Morgan, both intermingled and filled every corner of her mind. And after much soul-searching on her part, she reluctantly had to admit to herself that no matter how she viewed him she still found him absolutely fascinating. Born outlaw, or English lord? That was the question that Starlin was determined to have answered.

Chapter Seven

Shortly after dawn Starlin sat on the padded window seat in her elegantly appointed bedroom reviewing the events of the past night. Wrapped in a thick down comforter to ward off the chill, ever prevalent in a Tudor home of Eaton Hall's opulent proportions, she curled her legs beneath her and stared out over the sweeping grounds.

Generally, she enjoyed the lovely view provided by the expanse of scarlet-draped windows that ran the entire length of one wall. It was a tranquil setting, with rolling lawns shaded by tall, stately beechwood and ancient limes. Trim boxwood gardens bloomed with colorful arrays of spring flowers, and lilac bushes sweetly perfumed the air. However, this morning she barely noticed. Resting her chin in her hands, her mind was busy plotting every conceivable way to place a noose around that pirate's neck. And then, envisioning such a scene, her heart plummeted. The sensation was most confusing to say the least. Why did she cringe at the thought of his hanging? He deserved it for—? Her inner voice halted, and her hands shook. She uttered a choked cry.

"Oh God . . . for what, Starlin? For stealing your jewels—or for making love to you?" Her face grew hot as she recalled his ardent passion, and her response. He was totally crass, and could never love anyone. But then, why should she care? She didn't love him. Couldn't even imagine it! She hated him! Starlin's body shivered with the sweep of emotions surging through her, and her hands clutched the folds of the comforter so tightly that the fine bones were plainly visible beneath her ivory skin. She truly did despise the way he treated her. And she had been a fool to fall beneath his spell last night. Well, no more. Morgan was a hard, distrustful man who cared little for anyone. He only played at being honorable. He was an expert at assessing another's feelings. And when it came to the female species . . . why, he could manipulate a woman's emotions to suit his purpose with effortless ease. Of that she could attest, and would not forget! Her admitted distrust of Morgan sent a horrid thought racing through her head. What if he talked of last night? Her grandfather would hear, and be crushed. Honor meant everything to him. Suddenly, a reckless thought seized her. What if she obtained something of Morgan's to prove he was a pirate? She would then have a means to discredit him if he chose to publicly sully her reputation. It was a crazy idea. Nevertheless, a plan immediately formed in her mind. His ship must be somewhere in English waters. She would find it, sneak on board, and obtain something of his to hold as security should she need it. Only then would she have gained the upper hand.

Starlin knew she must see it through. She resolved to respond favorably to Morgan the next time that they met. Be charming and gracious to him, she told herself, and he will react in kind. And perhaps during the course of conversation if you cleverly pose the right questions, you might learn the whereabouts of his ship. Starlin came quickly to the determination that, however dangerous her daring scheme, she could not fail. She tried not to imagine what Morgan might do to her should he discover her stratagem. He was an aristocrat by birth, and claimed pride, it seemed, in that. She was most certain that he had no desire to have his secret identity and adventurous past shouted about London.

"I shall make him pay if he tells anyone what transpired between us last night," Starlin murmured with renewed confidence, "and I will never fall prey to him again." She tested this new inner fortitude against his awesome image by closing her eyes and mentally envisioning him. As always, to conjure up his taunting image would send her heart pounding in her breast and a rush of lusty heat through her veins.

"No!" she gritted. "If you allow his mental image to overwhelm you, Starlin, how in the world do you think that you can hope to succeed at this seductive mind game that he plays? Disgusted, she sprang from the window seat and rang for breakfast.

She hoped everyone was back on schedule and the household running efficiently again, for she did not wish to tarry long attending to guests and details. She had much to set into motion today, and the sooner the better. Starlin released the bell cord and crossed over the plush Persian carpet to peer in the oval gilded mirror above the rosewood bureau, taking note of the slight shadows beneath her eyes, evidence of the long night just passed. She would have her maid apply a touch of rice powder, for it would not do to look worn before she'd even begun. Yet it wasn't any wonder she could scarcely keep her eyes open this morning with so little sleep.

It had taken ages for the household to quiet down after the inspector and his men had finished questioning the staff and overnight guests, and had finally departed in the wee hours. It had been their final conclusion that it had simply been one of the many thieves of the city who had chosen the Winfield mansion as his night's work.

"Oh, milady, I knew you wouldn't get any sleep in this room. I don't know why you insisted on staying in here all by yourself."

Starlin glanced up, startled from her reverie to see the upstairs maid, Clara Turner, standing in the room holding a covered tray. She set the offering on a console table.

"Did you sleep at all?"

"No," Starlin admitted.

Clara shook her head. "I figured as much. But to tell you the truth, I can't say as I blame you. I keep thinking about that unfortunate girl, and how she might have been . . . you."

"I feel just awful about the whole thing. How is Mindy this morning?"

Clara poured steaming tea into a china cup. "Much better, mum. It wasn't your fault, and things are back to normal. I took Mindy her breakfast earlier and she polished it all off right quick, she did." She picked up the cup and offered it to Starlin. "Drink this, and then have some of this hot food."

Starlin accepted it and took a sip of the soothing brew. "Clara, please send someone to help me dress. I think I shall ride this morning."

The maid smiled. "Of course, and I'll leave you to enjoy your breakfast. I'll just come back for the dishes later." She paused in the open doorway. "And after tea, why don't you have a long nap before you go off to Almacks this evening."

"I almost forgot that this is Wednesday and I'll be expected to attend the temple of the *beau monde.*" Starlin sighed.

"I believe Lord Courtland is escorting you."

"Yes," Starlin replied with little interest, lifting the lid on a silver bowl. "He left me very little choice. He's so persistent."

It was an hour later before Starlin left the house and waited at the back for the groom to bring her horse from the stables. For mid-June the morning had turned bleak and cold with a lingering mist hovering in the tall sycamores and droplets of crystallike dew blanketing the crisp lawn. Murky streamers of sunlight filtered through low-lying clouds, trying vainly to add a measure of warmth to the day.

Starlin was glad she'd dressed in her warmest habit. It was her favorite. Of the softest rose material with a collar and cuffs trimmed in sable, it enhanced her ivory complexion and added a bloom of color to her cheeks. The slim cut complemented her willowy form. Her lustrous hair was swept beneath a feathered black hat placed at a saucy angle on her head.

Catching sight of the young stable boy rounding the

path with the sleek hunter Rue prancing flashily beside him, Starlin waved, impatient to be off.

Once mounted, she glanced down from her lofty position to inquire of Fredrick's whereabouts. She was anxious to discuss last night's events with him.

The boy told her that Fredrick had gone off to the small lake on the far tip of the estate to fish. Starlin thanked him and directed Rue toward the path that led in that direction.

Rue took all of her concentration to keep him firmly in hand. He was a big gelding who liked to play the trickster by taking the bit in his teeth and running with the wind.

Starlin was holding him easily. However, she had little time to enjoy her surroundings, and she was scarcely aware of it before they were almost out of the copse of trees and upon the lake. She could see the blue water in the distance, and just barely discerned Fredrick moving about on the boat dock, a long slender pole in his hand. As she drew closer she saw him draw in his line and unhook a good-sized fish. Even in the worst weather, Fredrick could always be counted on to catch something.

She observed him fondly, recalling the previous year, and his arrival at Eaton Hall. He'd been broke and without reference, but beyond doubt a kindly soul who knew his horseflesh and how to easily make friends. A bond had quickly formed between Starlin and the groomsman. He'd taught her everything about horses, and she offered up advice on catching fish. In the interim, she found that he was a good listener as she talked of her dreams for the future. They'd spent many companionable hours together, and not once had their difference in station ever intruded upon their closeness.

Fredrick had been especially comforting to her after he'd learned of the manner of her parents' untimely demise, and of the long, hard road she'd had to follow just to keep from losing her sanity because of it. For the first time, she'd found she could discuss the incident in the Devil's Triangle that had been so bizarre and tragic. Treasure, fie! she'd fumed to Fredrick, and he had agreed. Even now she thought there wasn't a one worth risking life and limb for.

Starlin was brought up short upon reaching the woodsy fringe of trees. The groomsman had disappeared, though his fishing gear still lay about. Once again she heard the sound of two deep voices conversing quietly, just beyond a shelter of trees.

Two men were conversing . . . one voice belonging to Fredrick, the other . . . to Morgan? Perplexed, Starlin dismounted. Suddenly, without warning, a large black wolfhound bounded through the grove at her, his fangs drawn back in a snarl. Heart pounding, she froze, watching apprehensively as the nasty brute sniffed at her. Immensely relieved, she saw a young man race through the trees, stopping short when he saw her.

With a shrill whistle he brought the sleek animal immediately to heel at his side.

"I apologize, madam, I had no idea that Merlin was going to tear from the park and onto your property. He isn't as fierce as he appears. Did he scare you?"

"Yes," Starlin managed shakily. "I wasn't expecting such a beast."

"He's a good sort, actually." He clamped a long strap to the dog's collar. "It won't happen again, I assure you. And, now please excuse me."

"Wait," Starlin said.

He turned, his rich gray cloak swirling about his long legs. He appeared very familiar. He stood smiling, even white teeth piercing the gloom.

"Can I be of some service?" he queried expectantly, his accent cultured.

"I thought perhaps . . . you might have noticed an older gent wearing a slicker? I had thought I heard conversation between the two of you."

"Oh, the groomsman," he replied without hesitation. "Yes, we were talking back there." He reached one big hand downward to pat the wolfhound on the head. "Merlin here startled the gent same as you. He's a fond habit of making fun for himself that way. I expect your man will be along shortly."

Starlin glanced over as Fredrick's familiar figure appeared from the trees. She felt relieved to see him.

The young man's dark-lashed eyes flickered over her once more before he bid her good day and turned away, the wolfhound beside him. Starlin watched him leave, then hurried toward Fredrick.

"You are certain that animal did not hurt you?"

"No, not a bit," he returned with a reassuring grin. He led the way back toward the lake. "Think no more about it. The fish are awaiting us—let's turn our thoughts to a great catch."

Malcolm Wells, the attorney for Cambridge Salvaging and Storage, watched a young woman of great beauty and distinction approach the house from the expanse of glass windows that made up the conservatory along the back of the house. There was no doubt in his mind who she was. Starlin Cambridge. Her willowy figure drew a slow half-smile to Malcolm's face, brightening his intense features. He was remembering her as a child in those ridiculous boyish clothes she always insisted upon wearing, with her wild mane of hair a riotous black mantle that fell to her waist, and her feet bare of any shoes. Yes, she'd been a little scamp, always adventuring along the most isolated stretches of the Key West shores without remembering to tell anyone where she was going.

And now? He wondered what she was like now. He wished he could find some way to talk with her. He had so many things to ask her. Of course, he knew it was impossible. The earl, and time, were against that ever happening.

The earl had told him in the beginning he must never communicate with Starlin, and that he must do everything in his power to keep her stepbrother away from her. The earl did not want to risk exposing her to bad memories. When he had first brought the girl to London he'd had the best doctors examine her. She had been in a subdued, unnatural state, and unresponsive to anyone. The doctor had advised the earl to keep the girl sheltered from anything associated with her past. It was vital to her emotional stability. So, the earl had kept Malcolm on retainer, and Malcolm had kept Benton Cambridge from Starlin. It had not been too difficult a task, until now.

Time—it came back to him sharply. His business in England must be concluded this week. He had to return to his practice in the Keys, and, of course, Benton. He withdrew his pocket watch and checked the time.

Damn the earl! If he didn't stop dallying, Malcolm was certain he'd force him to miss his meeting in London later. He snapped the watch cover closed, his thoughts concentrating on the task ahead.

The exotic array of plants and bright-blooming flowers that bedecked the room went unnoticed. He was anxious to get his confrontation with Lord Winfield out of the way. He had arrived at Eaton Hall a short time ago and had presented his card to the butler at the front door. The very proper Bridges had looked down his nose at the attorney, gauging by his manner of impatience that he was an American, and had told him in a cool voice to please wait in the foyer until milord had received his card.

Leaving off his hat and gloves, Malcolm had expected to be ushered directly to the earl. However, upon the butler's return, he had been surprised to hear that he was to wait a few minutes longer.

"Milord wishes for me to inform you that he will see you just as soon as he has concluded the business he is attending to at the moment." He bowed curtly before swiveling about on his heel. "Now, if you will follow me, please, I think that you will find it quite pleasant to wait in the conservatory where it is private."

The attorney fumed inwardly. So, the old boy does not wish me anywhere near his precious granddaughter, he thought darkly. He was being led like a stray through the out-of-the-way hallways of the house to avoid any possible confrontation with the girl. As they walked through the halls of the great house Malcolm could not help being impressed by the obvious show of wealth that he glimpsed as they passed various rooms. Drawing rooms extended in vistas on

138

either side, with impressive mantelpieces graced by ancestral portraits. The furnishings were of cherry wood, expensively designed and upholstered. Thick carpets stretched luxuriously across the expanse of floors, and vases of delicate cut flowers graced various tables. Money was plainly evident—and Malcolm could hardly refrain from whistling his awe. The attorney, while he lived with a certain degree of refinement and elegance in the unusual cosmopolitan community of Key West, had never in his forty-five years seen anything as opulent as his present surroundings.

At last, the butler entered to announce the earl.

Malcolm looked up as the Earl of Eatherton strode into the conservatory gripping Malcolm's card in his clenched fingers, his thunderous expression bespeaking a foul mood, Malcolm noted. He drew up several feet short of the attorney and stood glaring until he heard the butler close the door behind him.

"So—a matter of utmost urgency has brought you all the way to London posthaste, eh, Wells?" He waved toward a pair of highback chairs with overstuffed cushions. "This is a definite breach of our agreement, I might remind you. Come, sit down quickly and tell me what could not be relayed to my solicitors."

Malcolm Wells took his time in making himself comfortable. He fussed with the cuffs of his shirt, tugged negligently at his stiff collar, then glanced coolly at the earl whose face was mottled with rage. "You look well, sir. The years have been kind."

"I have no desire to exchange pleasantries with you, Wells. My granddaughter is due back from her ride at any time. I do not wish the two of you . . . to borrow an

American expression . . . to bump into each other. Now—get on with it."

"Crass of me to forget how lowly I appear to a man of your station," Wells replied with no hint of expression. "In thinking of your granddaughter's welfare I overlooked the fact that I am just like the rest of the hired help—your hired help, I might remind you, Earl."

"And I hope you know that you are jeopardizing the monthly retainer that I have deposited in your American account?" the earl shot back.

Malcolm formed a steeple with the tips of his fingers and peered over the point at the distinguished-looking earl. "Benton wishes to see the girl again. And if you do not allow him to do so, he has threatened to come after her himself, and without delay."

"Is he mad?" the earl thundered.

"Yes, quite frankly. His drinking has ruined his emotional health as well."

"Good Lord, I knew he was unstable since the accident, but I had thought his only concern was the fact that he had to split the inheritance with Starlin."

The attorney shrugged. "It's been coming on for years, actually. He drinks incessantly. And there's been a sudden turn of bad luck with the salvaging business."

"This disclosure must never reach Starlin. She is not to know, or for certain, she will insist on going to Benton's aid." He pointed a rigid finger at the attorney. "And you must not allow Benton to contact her. I am warning you, Wells."

The attorney did not so much as blink. "I am doing my very best. However, when Benton is drunk he is uncontrollable. He is liable to do anything, even come to England. I was supposed to have written you a letter some time ago to inform you of his legal rights."

"He has no legal rights!"

"You forget yourself, milord, hmmmm?" Wells returned.

The earl suddenly looked very old. He rose to his feet and crossed over the gleaming tile floor to stare out of the windows. "He must not be allowed to go any further with this. You and I both know what will happen if he does."

"That is why I came. You have paid me well to keep Benton under control. I may not be able to do so much longer. If he challenges the will in court, it may be discovered that it is a forgery, and that Benton is truly Starlin's legal guardian."

The earl's shoulders slumped. "How I have cursed myself for not reconciling with my daughter before her death. I know she would have stipulated that she wanted me to have Starlin and not Benton."

"What do you wish me to do?" the attorney stated somberly.

"I want you to keep him in America. Return to the Keys at once and watch him every minute. I am doing what is necessary at this end to ensure my granddaughter a happy, productive life, although I doubt very much whether she sees it in that way."

"You can rest assured I will do everything in my power to meet your request." Wells rose from his chair and took his leave.

"I bid you Godspeed on your return journey," the earl said. "And hasten your departure, for time is of the essence, as you well know."

Wells was just stepping out into the hallway when

Starlin's voice drifted down the long hallway from the kitchen. The earl waved the attorney onward with a frantic motion of his hands. The last thing that he wanted was for Starlin to see the Cambridge attorney here at Eaton Hall. The earl proceeded toward the kitchen, pausing just before pushing the door inward to take a deep breath.

Starlin glanced up at the creak of the swinging door. "Grandfather, I hope you were at last able to get some rest after all of the fuss earlier?"

"Yes, I was, thank you." He requested a cup of tea from one of the maids. "And no sugar, please."

Starlin also accepted a cup. "Why don't we go into the study, sir. I think we have a matter of last evening to discuss further."

The earl and Starlin made their way to the large, darkly paneled study and took seats in comfortable lounging chairs. Starlin's gaze traveled over the handsomely furnished room, the shelves lined with several rows of morocco volumes that the earl was fond of reading each day. She tried to keep her voice calm as she addressed him.

"Grandfather, have you had time to consider what you are asking of me?"

"What . . . exactly are you saying?"

"This proposed marriage to Lord Courtland. It is not of my choosing, nor will ever be."

The earl's chin sank upon his collar and he appeared to stare at the shiny buttons of his waistcoat for a time before answering. He raised his eyes to meet hers.

"My dear, I have done nothing for years but consider your feelings—and your dreams. And I have waited patiently for this one special man to come into your life and declare his overwhelming love for you. But frankly, darling, that is a girlish dream that should be relinquished. And you know it too, Starlin," he posed gently.

"It is not, Grandfather! My mother found it with Carl. She did not have it with my father, I am sorry to say. And that was an arranged match, I might remind you," she stated most directly.

Becoming annoyed by his own desperation to see her safe from Benton Cambridge, he said irritably, "I will not allow you to continue having your suitors dance a jig to suit your fancy. You have been gossiped about long enough and have continually turned aside many a fine English lad." He paused to draw an even breath. "It's time for me to take a stand regarding your future. These alliances are a part of our life-style, Starlin. And unless the man of your dreams turns up very soon you shall wed Buckwald Courtland.

To his astonishment, Starlin issued a quiet but profound statement that left him staring after her quite speechless.

"Perhaps this man has entered my life, Grandfather."

She had uttered the words simply to put an end to this stubborn notion of his to see her married to the foppish Courtland. Now, after hearing them aloud herself, she found herself wondering if she had stated them for another reason as well. One that she did not wish to admit as yet. Not even to herself.

"Well . . . do you wish to share his name with me?" the earl blustered, clearly taken aback by her words.

Starlin fidgeted uncomfortably, wishing she had bitten her foolish tongue instead of saying something so absurd, and untrue.

"He . . . he doesn't even realize how I feel about him yet, sir."

"This is astounding news," the earl responded. "Although it pleases me no end to hear you have taken an interest in someone." And then he said nothing for a moment, merely sat staring off into thin air as if he could picture quite clearly the face of the man his granddaughter had been referring to.

"What are you considering?" Starlin probed hesitantly.

His gaze shifted to hers. "A matter of time?"

"Time?" she echoed with a puzzled frown.

He smiled patiently. "Bluntly, dear girl—I was thinking to myself how long I should hold off on announcing my decision to betroth you to young Courtland."

A deep silence fell into the room. Starlin knew she was trapped like a fox, but she could be as clever as one when cornered. "Just a short time . . . that is all I am asking," she stated softly, rising to walk over to the bay area of the study to view the expanse of green lawns in the distance.

"A reprieve, Starlin, or the chance to win your Prince Charming's favor?" the earl inquired quietly, walking up behind her to place a calming hand on her shoulder.

Starlin felt her brief feelings of hostility leave her. She turned around to hug her grandfather lovingly.

"No matter what happens, it will never destroy our special relationship. I shall always love you . . . remember that."

The earl stroked her head tenderly, beginning to

144

wonder if perhaps there was something more to his granddaughter's words than even he knew. "You have your reprieve, darling. But only for a short time. If this man you have spoken of does not seek your hand in marriage, then you will be affianced before the year's end to Buckwald Courtland. Is that understood, and agreed upon?"

Starlin nodded, having barely heard the last of his words. The only thing that she could think of at the moment was that she had won her freedom for a while longer. And as for this dream man? . . . Where she was to find him, she did not know.

Chapter Eight

"The earl doesn't know who he's pushing around, but he will soon . . ."

With a series of muffled oaths on his lips and fury within, Malcolm Wells hurried at a brisk pace through the twisted cobblestoned streets of the underbelly of London's city life, a section vastly different from the fashionable district he'd just left. Hyde Park far behind, this was a menagerie of humankind: common souls of the working class who strived daily to seek out an existence in the netherworld of the underprivileged. He passed a wretched beggar turning an organ for hope of a ha'penny. So engrossed in his own concerns, Wells failed to see the tall, cloaked figure following behind him in shadowed pursuit, or the beggar thank the man for his toss of coin. A wolfhound sprang forward on command to tread on silent paws behind Malcolm, his dark nose sniffing at the attorney's heels.

Damn the earl! He'd guarded the Cambridge chit so closely that Malcolm had not had opportunity to say even a word to her. He'd felt driven, ready to throw caution to the winds in order to obtain his objective: Carl's journal, filled with notes that he was certain would reveal the location of the galleon lying on the reefs in the Sargasso Sea.

His dark eyes glazed with greed thinking of the legendary riches that awaited him. It was something Carl had talked of, and plotted to find along with Malcolm. Carl's ship had reportedly sunk while cruising the lost sea. Malcolm knew he'd been searching for the treasure! And he'd departed without telling Malcolm of his plans.

Through the years, Malcolm had questioned Benton Cambridge many times regarding that fateful expedition. To no avail. Benton had told the attorney that he'd been sleeping on deck when the ship had hit a reef and recalled little of the accident, only his rescue. And what he could recall, he wished to forget. Was Carl's son seeking to cover up something? Did he have knowledge of something more than he let on? Malcolm was forced to accept the fact that the only surviving person of the expedition appeared to know nothng of the treasure. Even the liquor Malcolm kept supplying to him, had failed to loosen his tongue.

Christ! All those years wasted on Carl Cambridge and his salvaging firm, working behind the scenes for Carl as his solicitor, waiting for that one big find, only to discover he'd been left with innumerable debts and holding the bag.

Carl had left his son and his firm's attorney with very little. And for whatever reason, he appeared to have left only Starlin with knowledge of the fortune beneath the sea. And what made Malcolm even more livid was that it had taken him so long to uncover the fact that the girl was perhaps the only living person with knowledge of the journal.

It was Benton who'd unknowingly directed Malcolm's thinking. He'd been drunk one night, raving deliriously about Starlin and his father sharing so many hours together in the playhouse that love had built. Malcolm had known then why he'd searched everywhere and had never found the journal! At first he'd feared that Carl had taken it with him on the expedition and it was lost at sea. But then he'd reasoned that Carl would have wanted him to think just that. He was now of a mind to think that the girl knew where it was. But why hadn't she produced it as yet? Surely, she knew . . . she had to!

Malcolm had come to England to seek out the truth, or the journal, if the latter could be easily obtained. Obviously, it could not. It was hidden well. He knew a more foolproof plan was needed, for his hired thug had gotten word to him that no journal had been found. And the oaf had almost been caught in the girl's room. Gad, that's all he would have needed. A string of ugly epithets streamed from Wells's lips as he turned a corner and entered a streetside pub. The attorney was so intent on his own concerns that he did not pay heed to those around him. A man had followed him inside the pub to merge with the crowd, picking an out-of-the-way table where he could silently observe Malcolm Wells.

"Ova here, guv'nor!"

Malcolm stared in the direction of the gravely voice and strode through the smoke-filled room to a secluded table where sat a bedraggled man.

"'Av yourself a chair," he said, his ratlike eyes

gleaming brightly.

"I understand things didn't go as I'd hoped?" Malcolm queried with a sneer, sitting down and resting his elbows on the table.

"Could'na be 'elped. The Cambridge girl came in while I was searchin' the room. I roughed 'er up a bit to keep 'er from screaming 'er 'ead off and then got outta there 'fore someone caught me." He paused to watch Malcolm closely. "I was in her room all right. And to prove it, I brung something back of 'ers to show you."

The man stank so bad from sweat and unwashed clothes that flies hovered about him. Malcolm was forced to withdraw his handkerchief and swish it about. The thief's meaty hand dove into the pocket of his coat and withdrew a dingy, grayish handkerchief. "'Ere . . . look at it yourself."

Malcolm glared at him. "Keep your voice down. The last thing I need is for someone to hear you."

"I wrapped it up real good for you so's I wouldn't lose it," the thief whispered as he unfolded the ends of the cloth to reveal a gold band set with a tiny chipped diamond.

"This proves nothing, you idiot," Malcolm scoffed, his gloved fingers playing an irritated tattoo upon the tabletop. "Couldn't you tell just by looking at this piece that it is not even worth a ha'penny." He gingerly plucked it from the handkerchief and held it before the thief's narrowed eyes. "What tonnish young woman would wear such a cheap thing?" He plopped it disdainfully into the thief's hand. "Robbie, you have brought me back nothing more than some kitchen maid's wedding ring."

The thief scowled. "I was there, I tell ya. I did

150

everything that you told me. There weren't no journal to be found. And I think you knew that all along. You just wanted someone to make sure, that's all."

"Oh, shut up," Malcolm hissed, considering the thief suspiciously. He reached in his pocket and tossed the thief a handful of coins. "This should keep you in rum for a few days. And consider our business concluded. I no longer have need of our association."

An evil leer appeared in Robbie's gleaming eyes. "Not so fast with you." He grasped Malcolm by the arm. "You promised me more than this. And if'n I don't get it I just may 'ave to split your 'ead." He doubled up his fist threateningly.

With a muttered curse, Malcolm brought his cane down sharply on the man's wrist. "Release me at once, you fool!"

The thief howled in pain and jumped to his feet clutching his injured limb. He stood glaring malevolently at the stern-faced attorney. "You shouldn't 'ave gone and done that. Robbie don't like being hit."

"If you'd take time to use that brain of yours before reacting, you might make out better in life, my lad."

Robbie thought he would have liked nothing better than to have flashed the jewels he'd stolen from the room before the attorney's eyes. That would show the blowhard who the real fool was. Robbie Brent knew how to take care of himself just fine, he mused triumphantly, thinking of the riches in his pocket and the gold that he'd have when he sold them off. He didn't need this American to tell him how to get along. He knew how, very well.

After a few more heated words, Malcolm Wells departed, knowing that if he wished positive results, he would have to seek them himself. He'd been thinking about that since his discussion with the earl. If it were ever discovered that the will he'd drawn up for the earl to claim guardianship of Starlin was a false one, Malcolm knew he'd find himself in serious trouble. He realized now what a mistake it had been. But at the time he'd considered it a stroke of luck to have an opportunity to get rid of the girl and leave Benton the only Cambridge to deal with. It was time to act. And within a week.

From his sources, he knew that the earl enjoyed a leisurely ride every morning on his hunter, Krager. With all of the groomsmen about, it shouldn't prove too difficult to slip in as one of them and alter a cinch strap a bit. He smiled coldly. A bad tumble could put an end to one obstacle, leaving the other easy prey. He turned up the collar on his cloak and hailed a passing hansom.

"The West End Highway, half flash," he called out to the burly driver before bounding into the vehicle.

He glanced behind him as the vehicle sprinted forward, breathing a relieved sigh when he saw only a black dog who appeared the only living thing intent on his departure.

He really felt no guilt for his ugly plotting, and even now, an icy sardonic smile graced his thin lips as he reclined comfortably against the cushions and anticipated certain victory.

First the earl, then later, Benton. Callous?—not really, he mused. He'd worked long and hard through the years, and had received nothing but a paltry salary for his efforts. He had been all ready to step in as administrator following the boating accident that had reportedly claimed all the Cambridges' lives, save Starlin's. And then, several months later, to his astonishment, Benton had returned to Key West.

"Benton Cambridge may not know of the journal, but Starlin does," Malcolm murmured to himself. "She's the only one left. Waiting somewhere in the Triangle is a treasure that Carl had decided, should none of them return, would one day be the girl's legacy."

The wolfhound came to heel at a sharp whistle, his tail wagging happily at the pat on his head.

"Big brother was absolutely right, wasn't he, fella," Ely Morgan murmured beneath his breath as he stepped from the tavern to observe a hansom cab disappear around the street corner. "The attorney is involved in more than legal affairs for the Cambridges. His sort would not venture to this area just for a bit of ale." He turned back toward the tavern that Wells had spent the last hour in. Just before reaching the entrance, he quickly glanced around, then with several loud hiccups and stumbling feet, he resumed his charade of drunken reveller before he burst back through the tavern door.

The huge beast cocked his head to one side, puzzled, it seemed, to see the sudden change in his master. He sat down just outside the entrance to await Ely's return.

"Listen up, all you seadogs!" Ely shouted in a voice slurred by drink. "I've been a long time at sea, and now that I've wet my whistle proper, I'm ready to do me a bit of celebrating." He reached inside his cloak and withdrew a small leather pouch. He shook it. At the sound of gold pieces jingling, the proprietor favored him with a hearty grin.

"Seen you over there all by yourself earlier a-talkin' to no one," the barkeep said. "Guess you was just windin' up, right, lad? Come, pick yourself a wench and have another mug. Both will do wonders for ya, me boy."

There were loud guffaws as Ely accepted the proprietor's invitation by grabbing a smiling doxy and tossing her, squealing in delight, over one broad shoulder. Grinning widely, he swatted her upon her ample behind before perching her on the edge of the bar. "All drinks are on me, lads!" he shouted boisterously, and made room for the rush to the bar.

For the next hour, Ely Morgan drank his ale and sang bawdy tunes with a goodly number of seamen who were in a state of alcoholic bliss and therefore did not notice he was not drinking as much as they were. Ely stumbled about from table to table, laughing and raising a ruckus as all men do who have just returned after long months at sea. But out of the corner of his eye, he watched the shifty eyes of the beggarly wretch sitting at a table off in the corner of the room. A comely strumpet strolled past Ely and giggled shrilly when he grasped her about her waist and staggered over to the lone man's table.

"No use in you sitting here by yourself, friend. Mind if we join you?"

The man's gaze narrowed, and he sized Ely up one last time before kicking out a chair next to his.

"Take a load off your feet, mate."

Ely sat down after sending the girl to fetch mugs of ale.

The afternoon wore on, and by early evening the occupants of the tavern were well into their cups, save one who played his part well. Ely leaned back in his chair, regarding those around him. Many were in a drunken stupor, their heads resting upon tabletops, loud snores penetrating the murky corners of the taproom. Ely made a show out of checking the dwindled contents of the leather pouch. He grinned crookedly at the besotted man sitting across the table.

"Still got me a coin or two left. Mayhap I'll buy me something real nice to take home to my darlin'."

His companion's eyes glittered. "Could be, mate, that I 'ave something for ya that might be better'n anything you could find in any shop around 'ere."

Ely's eyes had fallen closed, but one now opened slowly to peer at the man. "What might that be, friend?"

The man leaned closer to Ely and whispered in a raspy voice, "Somethin' real special for your special lady when you returns to your 'ome port. She'll give you a proper welcome after you give 'er these, she will."

Ely swayed a bit in his chair. "Sounds like you know the way to a woman's heart is with baubles. Aye, and I wish I could afford me some to make her pretty little face light up when she saw them." He watched from behind narrowed eyes as the man dug into his grimy coat pocket and produced a ragged handkerchief.

"'Ave yourself a look at these." He held the handkerchief close to him. "Them's the real thing, too."

Ely stared down at the sparkling jewels in the tawdry setting. "Blimey! Those are truly something." He fingered them carefully before favoring the man with a suspicious glare. "But how do I know that these are

155

real, mate? You could be trying to sell me nothing but colored glass."

"No. They're real sure enough. They come by way of a fancy lady. A *real* lady, I might add." He grinned meaningfully.

A look of dawning awareness appeared on Ely's face. "I see. In such a way as to present problems for you if you don't dispose of them right quick, is that it, friend?"

"It could at that," he man replied. "And more so if they get traced back to a certain prominent gentleman that I know. I done a job for 'im." He favored the young man with a conspiratorial wink. "You know what kind I'm talking about? They're good stuff—I swear."

"You make it mighty tempting."

"I'll give them to you dirt cheap, but you must keep them 'idden until you ship out again, matey." His face bore a hopeful expression. "Deal?"

Ely looked a bit doubtful. "It just might be that I don't have enough to buy them even for that." He jiggled the pouch once more before tossing it down on the table. Being a man to drive a pretty mean bargain himself, he was determined not to part with any more coin than he had to.

The man licked his lips greedily. He glanced at the pouch lying so temptingly near his fingers. "I figure you got enough for me, sport. I'm not 'ard to do business with. A man like me don't need much to see to 'is comforts."

Ely slid the meager bag of coins toward the thief. The man reached out and grasped it like a dog after a bone. He was smiling when he handed Ely the jewels. "A good buy you got for yourself. The little lady's gonna be right 'appy with you after you give 'er those."

"Yes," Ely replied as he rose to his feet. "I think so, too."

Ely left the tavern and went directly toward the waterfront district. His stride was even and smooth and his whistle was merry. He was sober as a judge on hanging day. Merlin loped alongside his master, pausing only once, nostrils flaring, to sniff at an organ grinder's monkey who screeched in fright when the big dog came too near.

"Come, Merlin," Ely called back to the dog. "We have much to do yet and little time left."

Man and beast continued onward, and when Ely saw the topmasts of many ships ahead in the distance, he knew they were almost at their destination. He grew extremely cautious. This particular section of London was its worst, a haven for thieves, muggers, and derelicts of every sort. His hand slipped inside his gray cloak, his palm resting upon the hilt of a sheathed knife. Ely did not intend to become a victim of this night. He ducked into a shadowy alleyway and paused before the side door of an inn. He glanced at the faded letters of the sign. It read The Green Parrot Inn. Not the sort of place he was accustomed to. For this venture, however, he had to agree it would serve the purpose well.

"You Morgan?" the night clerk inquired just as soon as he entered the building.

"Aye," Ely responded.

"The man you want is upstairs in fourteen." He regarded him over the top of his newspaper.

Ely nodded at the coarsely dressed innkeeper who appeared to have been told to watch for his arrival. "Make certain no one is following me," he told the man. "And if there is someone, stop them." He reached in his pocket and withdrew a coin to toss at the clerk before bounding up the stairs two at a time and turning down a dimly lit hall. He viewed the water-stained walls, the threadbare carpet, and shrugged. It wasn't Rayne's usual style, but then, it suited the purpose well enough. Upon reaching the correct room, he rapped lightly on the door with his knuckles.

"It's open" came the deep reply.

Ely swung the door inward and stepped over the threshold. He was met with the sight of a gleaming broadsword leveled at his stomach.

"Jesus Christ! It's me, Rayne!" Ely yelped, instigating some fancy footwork to evade the deadly weapon.

Lazy laughter filled the room and Rayne Morgan dropped the sword to his side. "It never hurts to be cautious, Brother."

Merlin bounded snarling into the room. Ely viewed him with a dry snort.

"A lot of good you do me bringing up the rear, you overgrown lap dog. I could be skewered by now."

Rayne grinned. "Little chance of that. I was almost certain that it was you by the sound of your footsteps." He motioned for the younger man to sit down. "I take it all went well?"

"Aye, better than we imagined." He sprawled easily into an overstuffed armchair, draping one leg over the padded arm.

Rayne walked over to a side table and picked up a bottle of port. He poured two tumblers and returned to hand one to his brother. "Well, don't keep me waiting. Were we correct in our assumptions?"

Ely sipped at his drink. "I was summoned by our man to Eaton Hall after Wells was seen arriving at the mansion earlier today, and was admitted. Presumably, to speak with the earl. He did not stay more than a few minutes and was back out again and left in a cab. I had just gotten there myself and remained inconspicuous in order to observe him. By his expression, it didn't appear to have been a social call. I left Eaton Hall right behind Wells. He took a cab to a tavern on Grover where he met up with the sort of bloke that one would hire to do dirty work for them. After Wells left, I managed to spend some time with the hoodlum, and also bought these from him." He withdrew the jewels from within his cloak and handed them to Rayne. "Nice, aren't they?"

"Yes, and expensive. Where did he get them?"

"There was a break-in at Eaton Hall last night. They're Starlin's."

Rayne's long fingers brushed across the gleaming gems. There was a sapphire brooch and matching earrings, and a diamond necklace with a single drop diamond in the center. The lot was worth a fortune. He regarded Ely with a dubious expression. "Wells was not interested in the jewels?"

"Let's suffice to say that I believe Wells sent the man there for only one thing," Ely said.

"He did not find it—just as we'd suspected all along."

"You still believe the girl knows more than she's letting on, don't you?"

"She's wearing the ring."

Ely pondered seriously Rayne's statement. "And

whoever wears it is supposed to hold the key—"

"To a treasure of riches beyond a man's dreams," Rayne finished.

"So you intend to protect the location of the treasure by keeping the girl as close to you as possible?"

"Yes. It rightfully belongs to April. It was her great-great-grandmother whose dowry provided much of the treasure. And from stories handed down through the years, dear Grandmother does not take kindly to having her final resting place converged upon by greedy treasure-seekers."

Ely favored him with a dubious expression. "You believe those ghost stories?"

Rayne shrugged one shoulder. "The Triangle never treats interlopers too kindly." He sipped at his drink. "I believe that anything can happen there."

"In view of this . . . do you think that there is a chance that Carl Cambridge might be alive, perhaps keeping a low profile until he can make his final, triumphant move?"

"I've thought of that."

"There are some who think they've seen him around his estate in the Keys, you know—sort of keeping an eye on things."

The tumbler lifted slowly to Rayne's mouth. "Maybe someone else is prowling about . . . looking for something?"

"I think perhaps in order to protect the secret, you are going to have to set aside all thoughts of revenge, Brother, and concentrate on keeping the girl from falling victim to Wells's scheming."

"You are probably right, Ely," Rayne agreed. "We still have much to learn about him. And soon, I think, it is time for us to leave England and make our presence known in Key West once again."

"And leave milady unprotected?"

Rayne laughed softly, wickedly. "I think not. She shall have my undivided attention from this day forward."

"And how do you propose to do that if you are across the ocean from her?" Ely posed.

"That is your conclusion—not mine," Rayne replied dryly.

"What goes on in that head of yours, Brother? I am beginning to think you seek to punish the girl for her father's sins."

"You are the one who pointed out to me how the lady requires my constant presence in her life."

"I said she needs protection," Ely said tightly. "You have taken it upon yourself to exact vengeance. But you can leave me out of using her, Rayne."

"One and the same thing. In order to protect her, I must be near to her."

"She appears to be so innocent, Rayne," Ely could not help but mention. "Must she be made to suffer for something she has no knowledge of?"

Rayne's face darkened and his green eyes flashed fire. "Vengeance is an emotion not easily set aside. I have agreed to do so only for a time. The girl is a Cambridge, and in the end shall also pay."

Starlin knew he was there before he even stepped into her line of vision. She was standing in the crowded ballroom of Almacks chatting with her friend Paula when she heard his husky voice speak her name. She glanced up to find Rayne Morgan before her. Her heart raced.

"I never thought to see you here," she stated calmly.

"Do I detect a note of gladness in your voice?" he said in an indulgent tone that made her instantly grit her teeth. He nodded toward Paula, then swung his gaze back to Starlin. "Where is your gallant escort, the ever-persistent Lord Courtland?"

"He will return soon, and he should not find you monopolizing my time," Starlin stated testily, wondering how the man could irritate her and fascinate her all in the same instant.

He looked at her with that surprisingly patrician air, which suddenly changed to that irrepressible grin. They stared silently at each other. His elegant black attire fit his tall frame and wide shoulders perfectly, the white shirt and lacy jabot at his throat only serving to enhance his darkly tanned face.

"Such sharp claws," he teased infuriatingly.

Starlin's back went rigid and her cheeks burned, for she knew her friend Paula was enjoying this immensely. "When one senses predators about, yes," she shot back, her violet eyes beginning to show anger.

Paula chuckled. Starlin suppressed the urge to jab her with an elbow.

"Are you implying that I'm stalking you?" he said silkily.

She placed her wineglass to her lips, studied him over the rim. "Do you deny it?"

"Not at all," he replied bluntly. "I am stalking you, milady, and I think you are enjoying it."

Paula's blue eyes peered owlishly from her chubby face to observe this display of fireworks. They were a couple quite unlike any other that she'd ever seen. She did not think her friend was aware of it as yet, but Paula felt certain that Starlin's long reign as Ice Princess was soon to end. Gore, she wished a devil like Morgan would look at her in such a way. She would follow him to the ends of the earth with not one question asked.

"It seems you have forgotten what I said the other night, milord," Starlin said coldly, controlling her fury with an effort.

His smiled widened, devilish lights in his jade eyes.

"On the contrary. I remember it only too well," he returned, raising his champagne glass to his lips, his eyes never once straying from hers.

"You are a most uncooperative man, aren't you?"

"Sometimes," he drawled, "when I think the end result will be in my best interest."

Her violet eyes were stormy, but she managed to keep her voice hushed. "You're looking for a lot of trouble, Morgan, if you persist in this fashion."

"I'm not the one causing trouble at the moment," he said dryly.

"Yes you are. I didn't give you permission to court me," she persisted, "and that is what everyone is going to think if you keep showing up wherever I am."

"Perhaps I'd like to court you."

Starlin stared at him as if he'd lost his mind.

Paula's extravagant sigh was cut short when Starlin stepped on her slipper. Paula muffled a gasp and blushed scarlet.

While Starlin would have liked nothing better than to shout to everyone that he'd stolen her jewels even as he'd seduced her, she knew that would never do. She had vowed to best him. There would never be a better time than the present to begin weaving her silken web about him. He was even going to make it easy for her. But oh how she longed to smack that arrogant, self-assured smile off his face. The haut monde were listed in Almacks' exclusive guest register. She would show them how easily Starlin Cambridge resisted his charm. And how ardently Rayne Morgan pursued her. Starlin flashed a brief, alluring smile.

"You love saying things to shock people," she stated softly.

Music wafted over the din of voices, a lovely waltz that was a favorite of hers.

"May I have this dance?"

Her eyes flew to his face. Before she could protest, or even think what to say, he'd taken the glass from her stiff fingers and handed it, along with his, to a passing butler.

"Oh go on, Starlin," Paula urged. "I'll be happy to occupy Lord Courtland for you."

Starlin's blood raced through her veins as Morgan swept her in his arms. Holding her much too close to him, he didn't make a move for several heartstopping seconds. His handsome mouth lifted at one corner in a rakish grin, and he caressed her mouth with his eyes. And just when she felt certain every pair of eyes in the room must be turned upon them, he swept her gracefully onto the center floor and stole the last of her resistance away with the touch of his body.

It was a wonderful, glorious sensation to twirl breathlessly in his arms as they moved round and round beneath the multicolored prisms of crystal globes. She was filled with heady delight, and at the same time wondering what had gone wrong? He was the one who was to fall beneath her spell. Looking up into his bold face, feeling the heat of him pressed so intimately against her, she felt her firm resolve slipping away and saw his mouth quirk ever so slightly.

"You cannot fight me, Starlin," he whispered smoothly.

Starlin's heart began beating in her breast and she leaned her head back, her eyes drawing his. She had to admit he intrigued her more than anyone she'd ever met. He was all dare and passion, terribly wicked, and set on having her. The risk to share just one night with him at this instant was almost worth taking; he was that captivating.

"I wish you wouldn't talk as if you have the right to order me about," Starlin said quickly.

"You need watching after," he stated matter-of-factly, and was surprised when she didn't argue. His arms went about her waist, pulling her even tighter against him. Together their bodies swayed and floated, moving over the dance floor as if they were the only two people in the room. He was an expert dancer, smooth and light on his feet. It was madness again, she reminded herself. But this time, there was no full moon.

People whispered around them, eyes staring, some smiling knowingly. Starlin did not even hear them. Rayne sensed their watching and her surrender.

"Come outside with me for a breath of fresh air, if you think you might find the nerve to slip away from your escort?" he challenged. Before she had time to protest he was sweeping her through the crowd with a graceful flourish toward the open terrace doors.

Once outside with him and walking through the

dimly lit gardens surrounded by the privacy of the high hedges, Starlin began to relax. He chatted companionably as they meandered along beneath the swaying limbs of silver-leafed birches silhouetted in shadow by the moon. Around them came the soothing night sounds. Crickets with their persistent song, an owl seeking his mate, and fireflies, glowing amber-gold before her eyes, soon lulled her into a sense of calm.

After awhile, she found herself conversing with him as though they'd known each other all their lives. They talked about many things, and if he was surprised at her knowledge of political events he gave no indication. He listened to her views on world matters: the tragedy of war, her abhorrence of bloodshed. He never once scoffed at her womanly concerns, but offered in lengthy detail his own thoughts on these issues.

Starlin was amazed to discover his distaste for killing, and his total absorption with everything that she said. He seemed genuinely interested in everything about her. As they paused beneath a rose arbor heavy with perfumed blooms, the moon caught them in its penetrating aura, and she found herself listening enraptured to his words. He stated that sometimes killing could not be avoided and was necessary. It was never easy to take a human life, he said, though at times, for love, honor, and defense of one's self and one's country, it was necessary.

"But that still does not make it right," she replied quite seriously.

"Nor wrong." He cocked his head. "Just unfortunate . . . like many things." At these last words he reached forward and lightly touched the becoming

166

blush of color on her cheek.

They both fell silent.

Starlin stared up at him, wishing she could read the message in those magnetic eyes. A hot rush of searing heat consumed her, making her lost and eager when he reached forward to pull her against him.

Her arms went about his neck as their lips met. The tip of his tongue teased hers then slipped into her mouth and out again to brush with fire the inside of her lips. He kept this up, teasing, drawing away her every restraint, so when she felt his fingers free her breast and cup the fullness, she made no move to stop him. The lush peaks swelled to meet his touch.

Starlin could feel the heat of him through her gown and longed to shed the clothes that lay between them. She wanted nothing but that magnificent hard body of his moving over hers, claiming hers in the way he had that first time.

Boldly she met the thrusting motion of his tongue with her own, her hips moving suggestively against him. There was a rustle of silk and a flurry of petticoats and his fingers were caressing the silken splendor of her thigh, teasing inside the drawn waistband of her pantalets.

"We can't do this," she breathed against his lips.

His lips moved downward, tongue flicking across a quivering nipple. "Shall I stop?" he murmured.

"No," she gasped.

He raised his head, a hint of a wicked smile barely evident. "Don't stop or don't continue? Which is it, Starlin?"

Starlin tried to withdraw from his arms, but he held her tightly.

"Tell me what it is you want," he murmured, taking her chin between his fingertips and slowly coaxing it upward.

Her violet eyes went wide, half mesmerized by stormy green depths that clouded her reason. "I . . . I . . . please don't ask it of me."

He gathered her close in his arms, his hand moving over the smooth flesh of her stomach, teasing her with feather-light motions. She could not stop the moans that came from deep inside her as he dipped lower, yet never quite low enough. He knew just the motion to drive her wild, and with each thrust of his tongue the heat soared. It was bliss. Penetrating . . . withdrawing . . . working her nerves into a frenzy of desire and making her forget everything but the delicious sensations spiraling through her.

Unwilling, Morgan knew, yet so innocent of desire that she was eager in his arms and yearning for that heady fulfillment he promised with his touch. Why not take her now, you fool? his inner voice goaded. She's ready, you have Carl Cambridge's sweet young thing right where you've wanted her. Take her—here with her skirts hiked up to her waist and false promises on your lips. Strip her of all pride, like he did to those you love. She's the enemy . . . and to destroy all of the awful memories you must seek your revenge on his flesh and blood until there is nothing left for them but their shame.

He lowered his mouth to her breast, capturing a rosy-tipped nipple between his teeth to nibble the hard bud. Suddenly he drew back his head.

Starlin's breath was coming in short gasps. She knew if she did not break free of him that her reputation would be ruined for certain. She was aware of approaching footsteps. Her eyes widened. She tried to protest, to resist his caresses, but her limbs felt as if they were weighted. She was losing control, succumbing to her desire for this man yet again.

"Bloody hell," Rayne cursed softly as he set the raven-haired beauty from him. "This is not the place for a lovers' tryst, milady." He straightened her clothing, his face a cold, hard mask.

Starlin's body trembled with emotion. She brushed his fingers aside and adjusted the bodice of her gown. She did not wish to meet his eyes.

"I don't believe it's a good idea for us to be seen together again," she said.

To her intense mortification he laughed.

"Do you honestly think that I will honor such a request?"

"I am not your property," Starlin shot back, her back going rigid with indignation.

"Aren't you?" he drawled.

Her hand shot forward to slap him soundly across the face. He grabbed her and yanked her back into his arms.

"I was your first lover," he said fiercely, "and your last."

A pair of steely eyes glinted challengingly at her.

Starlin tried to regain her composure. She tilted her head to study him closely. "You will never own me, Morgan. I am not one of your cheap whores who you can order about and buy with gold coins. And you insult me with your presuming manner."

"You aren't the kind of woman who lets very much unnerve her. I am what I am. And that's what excites

169

you, beautiful. Because I'm just a bit different . . . the rogue you swear you hate."

He released her and stood back to study her closely, admiringly. Starlin noticed another couple pass by in the shadows. They nodded politely at Rayne and Starlin and continued onward.

Starlin frowned. "Why is it, that whenever I'm with you, I feel that we are trying to best each other?"

"It's the nature of people like us, I expect. I admire that in a woman."

She sighed and clasped a shaky hand to her throat. Suddenly, the ring flashed a glittering reminder in the moonlight.

He took hold of her hand. "Your ring. From the first, it has reminded of another. One that would have been worn by my wife if I had ever married."

"Is there someone—?" Starlin felt compelled to ask.

"Was, and is no more—just as the ring." His tone was flat.

For some insane reason Starlin felt gladdened by his reply, and was stunned. She had experienced a fleeting stab of jealousy visualizing another woman in his arms. More than ever, she knew she must guard her heart against his ardent assault. There had been someone very special to him. Possibly, he'd even return to her. She vowed never again to become a willing victim of his game of passion.

"There is so much about you that I don't understand," she said.

"I could say the very same thing about you. You're the only woman who has ever intrigued me."

A dainty brow arched. "I'm glad you find me so amusing."

170

"You misread everything I say," he returned, giving her a measuring look. "The only thing you understand, it seems, is the mutual attraction between us."

Her eyes blazed with sudden and absolute understanding. She was just turning away when he grabbed her. His head dipped forward. Her rational thinking became threatened and she fought frantically with her self-control. He made no move to take her into his arms but simply lowered his lips to kiss her trembling mouth.

To his surprise, he experienced a brief stab of regret for the necessity of bending her willful spirit to his own. She was so young and innocent in her passion, and absolutely unaware of how her emotions would eventually betray her. His lips persuaded hers to part, to accept the hot thrust of his tongue hungrily exploring the sweet warmth she offered.

Her breath came in short gasps, her body melded against the seeking hardness of his. In her heart Starlin told him of her secret longings.

In his, there was no room for love, or a woman who expected it. But tonight, he had decided not to think of anything but Starlin, and how good it felt to lose himself in the sensual promise she offered him.

Chapter Nine

Starlin left Rayne in the garden and went in search of Courtland. She found him in the ballroom and, pleading illness, persuaded him to leave earlier than usual. He was disgruntled to say the least. As soon as they reached his carriage he turned ugly. He'd looked everywhere for her, he had said, and demanded to know where she had been. When Starlin told him it was none of his business, he had flown into a rage. When they reached Eaton Hall, Starlin hurried from the carriage, Courtland in fast pursuit.

"Where were you, Starlin? I looked all over, asked everyone if they'd seen you. You were gone a long while," Courtland ranted behind her. "I have a right to know. After all, you will soon be my wife."

"There is no betrothal as yet," she replied over her shoulder.

Courtland stiffened. "You don't care if you make a fool of me. Well, I won't stand for it any longer."

"I am extremely tired," Starlin said as she opened the front door. "And I have no desire to discuss anything more with you tonight. Good night, Buckwald." It was while she was peeking through the parlor window, watching Courtland stride angrily away, that she saw another carriage parked off in the shadows. It was some distance down the street, but Starlin did not fail to notice the coat of arms on the vehicle.

"Morgan," she breathed, her hand going to her throat.

She watched the door swing open, and saw the interior was softly lighted and very intimate. She held her breath upon catching sight of long lithe legs elegantly encased in clinging black breeches. He stepped out of the vehicle and stood there in the street staring up at the mansion. Had he come back planning another break-in? Her breath came in excited gasps. She saw him turn suddenly and say something to the driver, then climb back into the carriage. To Starlin, it appeared he had been looking over the grounds. It made her furious. She was seized with a wild idea. Suppose she followed him. Perhaps he might lead her to his ship. She would then go to the authorities and inform them where the pirate Scorpio could be found. Even though she did not wish to face the truth, she knew she must. Morgan was a dangerous, unpredictable man. And somehow, she had to stop him. Grabbing up her velvet cloak, Starlin secured it about her.

Slipping through the terrace doors, she hurried toward a hansom cab that was parked beneath a streetlamp. It was unoccupied, and the driver was more than happy to comply with her wishes. When Morgan's carriage finally departed, the hansom followed at a discreet distance.

When they stopped sometime later, Starlin peered cautiously out of the window. She did not recognize the area.

The cabdriver leaned over the side. "The other vehicle halted up ahead. A gent got out and walked toward the pier."

"I'd like to get out, Driver," Starlin said.

"Here?" the man queried with an astonished look.

"Yes, and be quick about it, please."

The driver turned up his nose. He'd seen his share of fine ladies who came to the docks after dark. They were looking for some rough seamen with whom to have a bit of fun. The driver swung down and opened the door for Starlin. She quickly handed him several coins.

After the hansom had rumbled off, Starlin glanced around her to find she was standing on a secluded waterfront pier. Before her in the foggy night loomed the masts and figureheads of many ships. Even at the late hour the Thames was busy with river traffic: barges, laden with barrels and crates, tugboats, towing the heavier craft to the pier, and, in the distance, the tall masts of brigantines and clippers moored in the bay. Up ahead, she saw Morgan conversing with several seamen who were lounging about. He appeared to know them quite well.

The group laughed abruptly, as though sharing a joke, and then Morgan continued onward toward a waterfront tavern. Starlin became alarmed. She'd assumed he'd go to his ship. She heard the raucous sounds of the river and of the taphouses that lined the pier. Boisterous voices of drunken rowdies and the shrill laughter of painted women made her shudder. She'd heard of the rooms above these shanties, and of

175

the things women did there with complete strangers who could pay their meager fee. Unease settled within, and she was just about to turn and flee when she saw two drunken sailors weaving their way in her direction and quickly ducked behind several large crates.

Rough hands immediately grabbed her.

"Well . . . would you look at what just stepped into my path," a gruff voice rasped.

Caught off guard, Starlin felt herself being spun about.

"Looking for a man, are you, darlin'?"

She found herself staring up at the biggest man she had ever seen. He was dressed in coarse clothes and had long dark hair and a scraggly beard. He had dark, expressionless eyes and a feral smile. "Take your hands off of me," Starlin demanded.

"Now you know you don't mean that," the man chortled, running his hands up and down her arms. "Fine lady like you comes here for only one reason. And I promise you that Hector Deacon can show you a night like you've never dreamed."

Alarmed by his implication, Starlin began to struggle. She kicked and scratched, but the blackguard held fast to her.

"One of them that likes to fight . . . hmmm," he grunted, shaking her like a rag doll. "We'll go someplace private, and have us a good time. I know where there are no curious innkeepers with sharp memories. No one will disturb us."

"You oaf . . . let go of me!" Starlin raged. "I wouldn't go anywhere with the likes of you."

The man scowled at her. "Fancy lady . . . don't want Hector," he grumbled under his breath as she

176

continued her desperate fight. He shoved her beneath a streetlamp and stared down at her. "Too ugly for a beauty like you. Well then . . . that's all right, too, for I can make a tidy sum off you. Now what do you think about that?"

Her startled, questioning gaze met his. "What do you mean?"

He laughed jeeringly. "A scant measure of time, lady, and all of your questions answered." He put a hand to the small of her back and gave her a firm push. "Go on with you now, and if you try and bolt, I'll make you real sorry."

All of her instincts warned her to escape. This man was the lowest kind of vermin. She did not like to think what he was planning. She tried to dash away, but he grabbed her and twisted her arm behind her back. A desperate cry escaped her. Her eyes widened when they approached a brightly lit taphouse. He leaned over her shoulder.

"There are men here who will pay a lot for a beauty like you. We may as well both get satisfaction this night."

"You must be joking," she hissed.

"Put on your fancy airs if you like. But I know what you really want."

Starlin's heart began to thud painfully, his fingers aware of the erratic beat as they settled beneath her breast. He pulled her against him.

"Got you excited now, ain't I?" he cackled. "That's good . . . I like that."

A bubble of a sob rose in Starlin's throat as the man shoved her through the open door into the room. The air was thick with smoke and whiskey fumes. There were men of questionable character standing along a wooden bar and sitting at various gaming tables. Painted harlots in gaudy dresses hovered about a table where sat several men dressed in fine clothes. Starlin had heard stories of such places, but never dreamed she would ever be in one. How could she have been so stupid to have gotten herself into such a predicament. Hector forced her to follow him. They paused beside a table where a group of men were playing cards. Hector leaned over one fellow's shoulder.

"In for a bit of sport tonight, lad? How about this sweet darlin', and no questions asked?"

The sailor eyed Starlin closely, assuming that the fine lady was playing along with the scheme. Even when she begged him with her eyes not to listen to her captor, he thought it part of a role. The man turned to his companions.

"Hector says he'd like to give us all a chance to win this fine beauty here. How about playing a game of chance—the man who comes up with the highest hand wins her."

"Sounds real good to me," a sailor at the table said with an eager grin.

There were murmurs of agreement all around. Starlin noticed one of the finely dressed gentlemen at the other table eyeing her closely. She shot him a pleading look, but he only averted his eyes.

Hector took a chair at the gaming table and gave a rude jerk on Starlin's wrist that brought her to her knees beside him. She glared hatefully up at him. He took the belt from his breeches and bound her wrists securely to his chair. She spat at his feet. He wanted to deck her, but he played it to his advantage.

"Plenty of sass, as you can see, chums." Hector grinned. "She likes to play a bit of hard to get, but she'll do whatever you tell her if you show her who's the boss." He fixed threatening eyes on her and grabbed a fistful of her hair. "Ain't that right, darlin'?"

"I'll have your head for this," she ground out through her pain, forced to sit on the floor next to him.

"Do you mind if I join your game?" a deep voice inquired.

Starlin's head flew up and her eyes stared in disbelief. Rayne Morgan stood over her, not a flicker of emotion visible in his eyes. He tossed a heavy pouch in the center of the table. Coins jingled. "My stake, gentlemen."

Hector grinned widely. "Get yourself a chair, mate."

Rayne sat down next to Starlin, yet barely paid her notice. She was smart enough not to say anything, but her eyes fixed on his every move, told him exactly what she thought of him.

The game began; the cards dealt to each player. Starlin found herself holding her breath. She wasn't certain if she felt safer knowing Morgan might win her, or afraid that he would. At the turn of each card, she cringed.

One hand, winner take all. Several men folded. It was only Rayne and two sailors left to turn over their final cards. When it was Rayne's turn, Starlin watched as he took his time, leaning back in his chair and dragging slowly on a thin black cigar. Favoring her with a cool, assessing look, he drawled softly, "Are you afraid?"

Scared to death, she felt like saying, but would have sooner bitten off her tongue. "Not at all," she said with haughty disdain, chin held high. She had thought he might smile in that arrogant, infuriating manner of his, but he didn't. His gaze returned to that one last card. With a quick flick of his wrist he turned it over. And won. Amidst the grumbles of disappointment he leaned over her. She tried to draw away but was held fast by her bonds.

His fingers caught in the windblown strands of her hair, tilted her head backward. "It looks like you belong to me, my beauty. I hope you'll be worth what it cost me."

Before she had time to think clearly, he untied the belt and grasped the end. He stood up and favored her with a commanding look. It was clear that he did not expect her to defy him in any way. Glancing around her at the surly group of men, she decided it was to her favor to comply. Her wrists were aching from the tight binding, but she dared not complain. Morgan gave a short tug on the belt as he took his leave. Starlin could do nothing but follow along behind him.

By the time they'd walked down to the end of the wharf, secured a sloop and sailing for the open sea, she was windswept, recovering her composure and swearing that she would make him pay for his humiliating treatment. There was bitterness in her voice, but he acted as if her discomfort meant nothing to him.

When the distinct outline of a three-masted ship rose suddenly before her startled eyes, Starlin's knees nearly gave way beneath her. The waves surged in frothy peaks against the sloop's hull as it was piloted smoothly alongside the larger ship that lay in anchor, secluded by a curtain of misty darkness.

Careful to conceal the alarm from her features, Starlin met Morgan's penetrating eyes. "Your ship?"

"The *Tempest*."

She viewed the sleek, smooth lines, built for speed and a firm hand, just barely able to discern the figurehead of the dreaded Scorpion. Huge guns appeared trained upon them. It was an ominous reminder of the man as he really was. Deadly, and very unpredictable. "It suits you, Morgan," she stated, "both in name and structure."

"Aye, she does at that."

A bit hesitantly, but nonetheless determined not to appear afraid, Starlin allowed him to lead her on board and walked the broad sweeping decks of the *Tempest* at his side. It was a beautiful vessel, all flowing lines and burnished teak, with tall masts and furled sails. The ship looked nearly deserted, most of the crew obviously enjoying themselves on leave in the city

Only the watch high above them witnessed their silent exploration and his captain's quick step to the helm. Rayne unbound her wrists then left her to brief a sailor at a position by the great wheel. Turning back to the small figure who stood proudly defiant before him, he took her hand within his and drew her along behind him toward a companionway.

As they disappeared below deck, Starlin heard the anchor being hoisted, and shortly thereafter, the ship canvas snapping stiffly overhead, caught by the sighing winds that would take them out to sea. What was he planning? In view of her predicament, she wondered how she'd ever assumed she would gain the upper hand with this man.

They walked down a dimly lit companionway until at last he halted before a dark-paneled door situated directly under the quarterdeck. He turned the brass handle and swung the door inward.

"After you, milady," he bid her.

Starlin stepped hesitantly into the chamber, and slowly examined the tastefully appointed cabin. Her eyes were immediately drawn to the focal point of the room: a large comfortable berth. It comprised much of the area, and was covered by a dozen or more luxurious furs, their dark color and richness intensified by a single brass lantern swaying gently above the structure. More furs were scattered on the floor beside the berth. She swallowed, her eyes hurriedly sweeping beyond it, touching briefly on teak-covered walls where hung gleaming weapons: sabers, knives, and cutlasses. Expensive leather-bound books were tucked into wood shelves that lined one wall, and maps littered a corner desk. There was a marble-topped washstand with an ivory-encased comb and brush, engraved in gold, lying upon it. It was an elegantly furnished cabin—and not at all what she had envisioned. Did all pirates live in such a grand manner? She knew no others to compare.

Her violet eyes widened upon noticing a red damask couch, a large black wolfhound lying in the center of it, watching her every move. She froze, for he looked ferocious even in repose. Good heavens! Was it not the very same animal that had wandered onto her property the other day when she'd been searching for Fredrick? Blister it all, but there were so many unanswered questions where this man was concerned. His presence never failed to scatter her wits, and her best intentions! And why did he always seem to know what she was feeling, even before she did!

"I have seen that dog before!" She whirled to face him accusingly.

"It's possible." Rayne issued a short command and the great animal bounded off the couch and disappeared through the open door. "He's my brother Ely's hound. Sort of the ship mascot." Starlin heard Rayne swing the door closed, then come up behind her. She trembled slightly when she felt him remove her cloak.

The cabin suddenly seemed very confining. He was clever, and very self-assured. And she? She was beginning to feel like a vixen at the end of an arduous chase. She sought a diversion, anything to sway his intentions elsewhere, and perhaps buy her some badly needed time. Frantic, her eyes searched the cabin. An object caught her eye, stood out vividly against the dominant male aura of the room. A dainty Oriental music box of bright red lacquered wood sat in the midst of masculine items on a shelf next to his wide bunk. She turned to watch him closely, questioningly.

"A family heirloom," he offered simply and unemotionally as he shrugged out of his own cloak and laid both aside.

Starlin walked over and picked it up. "How lovely." The delicate tune it played when she opened the lid brought a smile to brighten her intense features.

"Yes, it is, isn't it," he commented, regarding her delicate-boned profile in the wavering light.

She spun about to face him.

"Why don't you explain to me how you got yourself into that predicament back there?"

"That awful man accosted me!"

"You were in the wrong part of town, Starlin. You know it and so do I. You followed me from your house, didn't you?" He was glaring accusingly at her.

"So what if I did?"

183

"It was a stupid thing to do."

"I hope I don't have to listen to this much longer," she snapped.

"Would you have preferred to have stayed with those other men?"

She glared at the half grin curling up one corner of his mouth. "I prefer to go home now."

"Oh no. You have a debt to pay back first."

"I'll see you get your money back after you take me home."

"I don't want your money, my beauty."

Starlin drew back warily. "You can't mean? . . ."

"You followed me, remember. So you have only yourself to blame for the situation you're in. Those men were ready to pass you around right there in that tavern." He drew her against him. "It was either the lot of them . . . or me."

"From the frying pan into the fire," she sneered.

His eyes glittered. He lowered his head to kiss the side of her neck. His body moved with hers to the clear, melodious notes of the music box filling the room. He was luring her to him, wooing her with the motion of their bodies. She felt that bold assessing stare, those ever-smoldering cat-eyes observing all from behind smoky lashes.

Her own spiky lashes fluttered upward, lavender eyes meeting the high passion in his. She could feel every hard, driving muscle in his body yearning for her to touch him closely, to surrender everything for just this one night. She felt herself succumbing to an emotion that only this man could evoke.

His lips brushed against her hair, her closed eyelids. She tried to force the memory of his lovemaking from her mind. But she could not. He made her feel so good . . . so much a woman. Her breasts were pressed against his hard chest, aching and longing, her thighs in sinuous motion with his, weak and trembling. She knew she wanted all of him, everything. Later, she would deal with the consequences, but not now . . . for it was impossible to think with his lips so near.

He held her close to him and she was afire. Starlin felt the world spin away as he led her through the steps, arousing her like nothing she could have imagined, or dreamed. She tilted her head backward, her slim body supported by his arms, her long hair cascading like a riotous waterfall about her shoulders, almost touching the floor. Through her lashes, she viewed the flickering play of candlelight on the ceiling. Spinning shafts of molten gold that danced in a kaleidoscope of flaming desire, flitting about before her lazy-lidded eyes, drawing her into a whirling vortex of passion. His lips were slow and deliberately gentle, yet growing ever heated as they moved across her cheek, her nose, downward to press against the throbbing hollow of her throat. Whisper-soft, he touched the velvety flesh with the tip of his tongue, swirling in tiny circles, prompting her to gasp her pleasure.

"Kiss me . . . everywhere . . . like that other time," she said breathlessly.

Supporting her slender frame easily with one arm about her waist, he deftly unfastened her gown. Before she was even aware, it drifted downward, a shimmer of ivory satin cascading to the floor. An indrawn breath, a quiver of uncertainty, and her body was revealed to his gaze. Naked and unbelievably beautiful lying back over the circle of his arms, Starlin had no idea how devastating the first glimpse of her was to Morgan.

Slim, alabaster curves, sleek golden thighs, and full, rose-tipped breasts narrowed his gaze and brought his breath into his throat.

"You're perfection, goddess." His eyes, ablaze, followed the fluid lines of delicate beauty from her finely arched brows to the graceful turn of trim ankles. Half smiling, he traveled the return path and met the sultry heat of her eyes. His head bent forward, his lips pressing against her breast, his tongue, warm and wet, circling the rigid peak that trembled at his touch.

Dark memories threatened to tear her away from him. Stubbornly, he fought against them with the fierceness of a predatory animal. Dammit! She was his for this night. For a few short hours he wanted just to make love to her. He held her against him, and thought that he must be losing his mind for having even brought her here like this. The risk he was taking was great, but not as great as his desire. Something had transpired between them earlier. Unplanned, unmotivated, but too heady to deny. He knew he was taking all manner of chance to have brought her here. In all of his thirty-three years he had never known another woman who made him feel like this one. She was enchanting in her unassuming innocence, yet all fire when he awakened the woman within.

Starlin moaned in his arms. She wanted him, oh how she longed for that moment when his body would at last join with hers. The high, hard passion of him pressed against the vulnerable joining of her thighs, taught her once again the motion that would claim her.

"Undress me," he commanded softly, and she complied, slender fingers moving swiftly to untie the lacy jabot, unbutton his shirt, then hesitate and stand shyly away from him. He understood, and silently cast aside his boots and unfastened his breeches. She did not take her eyes from him, yet could not help but suppress a shiver when he shrugged out of the last garment to stand like a bronzed god before her. Wide, assessing purple eyes roamed over his gleaming, muscular torso, and could not help but stop and stare in wonder at the proud, jutting staff between his legs. He was big there, she thought, her heart beating crazily, and faster when she thought of how soon he would be inside her. Her tongue ran across dry lips. Would there be much pain like the first time? she thought, frantic.

He sensed her fear and held out his arms. "Come here, Starlin." She eagerly went to him and buried her face in the curve of his shoulder. "You're trembling," he said, placing a kiss on top her head. He tilted her chin up to meet his eyes. His lips came forward to brush across hers. "I promise you, there will be no pain."

Her arms went about his neck, clenched in tawny curls as he seared her lips in a burning kiss. Her mouth opened, drew in the taste of his as their tongues touched. His hands were everywhere, teasing, stroking, awakening a raging inferno within while thoughts spiraled and tumbled in tempo with her emotions.

The night breeze sighed through the open portal, a sibilant sound treading softly through her innermost thoughts and taunting her with all of the things she longed to hear him say. Only in her mind, in her dreams, did he answer. She knew she could not go on like this with him, for beyond a doubt, she was losing herself to him. She desperately tried to recall her firm resolve to win over him at no matter the cost.

The plaintive sound of soaring nightbirds drifted on the breeze, sounding lonely, as if calling for a mate's return. Pressing closer to him, against those long, knowing fingers that were causing her such exquisitely sweet torment, she abandoned her will and gave herself up to the magic of his hands.

"I want to take away all of the pain that I caused you that long-ago night, my fiery beauty." It was a ragged statement as his hands tangled first in her wild mane, then cupped her face, raining kisses along its petal smoothness. His hands slid down her back, over her rounded buttocks, and molded her against him. Their eyes held, his hot and now very definite.

Somehow, she knew before he'd even spoken the words what it was he was going to say. She was already complying, springing upward in a lithe, catlike movement, aware of strong hands supporting her.

"Put your legs about my waist." Their gazes smoldered as her slim legs wrapped unhesitatingly about him. Her fingers laced around his neck and held fast. Her eyes opened wider when he nestled instinctively against her womanly charms. She sighed in the wake of unbelievable ecstasy upon feeling the pulsing heat of his passion touching her so intimately. He moved his hips, the throbbing length of him sliding up and down her satiny splendor, readying her for his possession.

She was moaning through gently parted lips, head thrown back, eyes closed to the unbelievable sensations awakening there. Between her legs, she softened and surrendered, hips writhing now against his, unaware when he shifted her just enough so that he felt her moist acceptance. With a possessive snarl he grasped her beneath the arms and up, so that her breasts were now level with his ever-seeking mouth. His lips sought her breast once again, suckled the aroused bud until she was drowning in a sea of passion. His tongue laved the delicate flesh, first one, then the other.

"Ohhh . . ." she purred raggedly, feeling him slide her body downward, across his hair-roughened chest, his lean belly. His large hands beneath her coaxed her limbs wide, just before his hips thrust forward. Then he was completely sheathed inside her. She moaned in mindless desire upon feeling the delicate flesh yield swiftly to his possession. Still she was unable to comprehend how so much of him could fit there without tearing her asunder. Her body trembled with emotion.

"Are you all right?" he whispered in a voice thick with desire. He held her unmoving, allowing time for her to recover. He watched her face closely.

She could only nod, for she, too, felt overwhelmed by the feelings coursing through her. With a tenderness that surprised her, he began to move in a beautiful, satisfying rhythm that drove everything from her mind but the exquisite pleasure he was giving her.

"Starlin . . . Starlin . . ." he murmured, "you are more wonderful than I remembered." Their bodies still joined, and while kissing her hungrily, he carried her to the bed of furs and gently eased her back into the enveloping luxury.

He thrust deep inside her, burying his face in the warmth of her neck. She clung to him, raining kisses along his chest, driving him to heights of incredible passion with her wild, unhampered movements.

Unbridled lust like she'd never imagined surged through her. Intense, driving strokes, so hot she felt on fire inside, drugged all of her senses. She arched upward in unrestrained response, her fingers grasping his sweat-slick shoulders as shudders of ecstasy encompassed her body. She wanted him to love her forever and never let her go.

His lips captured hers, hard and demanding as his arms tightened around her like inescapable steel bands. She grasped his buttocks, felt them quiver beneath her touch. He groaned her name again and again, relinquishing his firm control and soaring with her to blissful fulfillment.

Chapter Ten

"Wake up, Starlin, it's time for you to leave."

Sleep-dazed, she turned over to stare up at the dark face hovering over hers, recalling then their shared intimacy. Her body went rigid as she met his eyes. They held no warmth for her. "The debt has been paid. I'd like to go home now."

He didn't protest, or say much of anything. "All right. I'll see to it." She saw a muscle quiver in his lean jaw.

"And that finishes things between us, Morgan," she stated firmly. "I don't ever want to see you again." She fought vainly not to express even a fleeting glimpse of emotion. She did not draw back when he reached outward to cup her chin in his hand.

One large hand lifted to grasp her damp hair and entwine it about his fingers to draw her close. "Do you honestly believe that?"

"I never say anything that I don't mean."

"You tell me how much you hate me, and expect me to believe you, yet I sense something else when I hold you in my arms." His voice held a mocking tone. He easily dodged the wild slaps she aimed at him.

Starlin was furious. "Your arrogance is insufferable!" she snapped, trying to roll away from him before he could catch her.

He reached out and grabbed her about the waist. Starlin screamed in outrage when he tumbled her back onto the bed. Rational thinking became difficult with her naked body pressed against him, yet Morgan knew he truly had only one mistress—revenge. It had claimed him long ago. And until her flesh and blood were made to suffer as his had, there would be no room in his heart for anyone. Beloved enemy, he thought holding her, how I wish it did not have to be so. Mentally, he shook himself free of her sinuous silken threads that threatened to bind him.

"The hours have all been claimed away from us, Starlin. But you will never forget me, no matter how hard you may try. I will be leaving England and returning to the sea. So you can rest assured that I won't come near you again."

His lips hovered over hers, and Starlin fought against the flame of desire that had ignited within her as soon as he'd touched her. Damn you, she thought. Why do you affect me like you do?

The air was charged with emotion, and for a moment, looking at her, he wanted to never hurt her again.

"Love and hate, so similar, and both so consuming," he murmured softly, lowering his head to kiss her hungrily.

When he lifted his head she was breathing as rapidly as he was and her eyes revealed her desire. If they shared nothing else, he knew they were perfectly matched in their passion. She was magnificent. Not surprisingly, Starlin calmed once she was in his arms.

"Where will you be going, Morgan?" she queried huskily, feeling an odd little twist in her heart thinking of his leaving.

He placed a finger to her lips. "Enough talking . . . more than enough. Just know that by leaving, you'll be free to go on as before with your life." Even as he heard his own words and realized that he was seeking to keep her safe from his own vengeful wrath, he cursed his stupidity and her. Starlin was very close to destroying all of his carefully laid plans, and he had made it so easy for her. He'd gone willingly into her arms, been drugged by her kisses and caresses, and he should not have allowed it. At the moment, he was fighting himself more than he did her. He did not like that.

"Why don't you talk about yourself to me?" she asked quietly.

He stared at her. "There are things, that if I were to tell you, would tear you from my arms and heart, and send you running as far from me as you could." His tone had turned hard, and she immediately stiffened. "No more need be said. Just recall my words later, months from now when you hear of me again, and you will better understand." He reached up to unclasp her hands from behind his neck and roll away from her onto his back. He stared blankly up at the flickering shadows on the ceiling. "Get dressed. I'll see you safely back to Eaton Hall."

Starlin did not like the sick feeling of despair inside her. Why did she feel as if her heart were breaking? Could she possibly care for this man more than she was willing to admit? Foolish girl, her mind defended, this is not how love is. Passion is the only thing that is

193

between you. His cold, heartless declaration —as if their lovemaking meant nothing to him now—surely revealed his true feelings. Love is trust, sharing, never wanting to part. The remembrance of his heated love words whispered in the throes of his passion had made her blood sing, but they had been merely breathless words, easily spoken in the heat of fiery desire. Lord, but they'd had that. Coming together in a tangle of sleek, golden limbs and searing passion that had consumed them both. She could not stop herself from blindly reaching out to him.

With a soft cry, she rolled over toward him, sable tresses whipping around her shoulders to flare across his lean belly as she placed her cheek against corded muscle. His clean male scent tantalized her senses. When she was so near him like this, she felt as if she wanted to absorb all of him, had to have everything: his flesh, his thoughts, his emotions to seep inside her through her pores and hold him there, forever.

Seemingly of its own accord, and without her conscious thought, her mouth pressed against his lean bronzed flesh, felt it quiver as her lips brushed over the whorl of damp hair so enticingly near. Strong fingers laced through her tangled curls, tightened almost painfully.

"Starlin . . . you witch," he rasped hoarsely, even as his hips pressed closer, his desire hard and urgent against her dew-soft cheek. He watched her through barely slitted eyes that gleamed golden green like that of a tawny jungle cat.

She glanced up at him with heavy lidded eyes. Burying her face against the hollow of his hip, she fought against rational thinking. She felt his hands, gentling, stroking the back of her head soothingly.

Slowly, her lips worked their magic upon him, kissing, tongue lapping lightly along the fine line of fur that traced down his belly, along the curve of his hip, tantalizing his heaving stomach, the gentle roughness of her tongue nuzzling him everywhere, knowing full well where he really wanted her, there between his thighs, where his desire rode high.

Impatient, his hands tightened around the back of her head, urged her to bolder motions. A moan burst from him. He was on fire beneath her teasing lips. Sharp little teeth nipped along the inner curve of his thighs, drove him into a frenzy of mindless desire. "You won't win, Starlin, I can never let you." Cries of exquisite pleasure escaped his half-parted lips to drift on gentle breezes through the open casement windows where it wavered above the dizzying surf and echoed across the night.

Later, neither of them had dared speak until they were both fully clothed once again. Already, the shadows in the room were lessening. She allowed him to wrap her cloak around her.

"We'd better go now," Starlin said calmly. She could feel his eyes watching her closely from behind those long, dark lashes.

"Ice Princess . . ." he murmured. "You play your part so well. One moment, all fire, the next, so cold and distant."

"What do you want from me, Rayne?" she countered, her voice rising a note. "Do you want to strip me of all pride, have me cry over your leaving, and perhaps even beg you to marry me and ease my shame?" She gave a brittle laugh. As if dismissing him, she moved toward the door. "Can we go now, I am really very tired and wish to go home."

She appeared so matter-of-fact, and he stood there caught by the inexplicable desire to take her into his arms and force her to admit she cared for him. A frown marred his handsome countenance.

"Don't talk like that," he said tersely. "It doesn't become you."

There was a sudden knock on the door.

"Yes, what is it?"

"We've docked, Captain. I thought you'd be wanting to know."

"Aye, we'll be right out," he replied in a flat tone.

She was almost blinded by hot tears as she followed him above deck. Bravely, she fought them back. There were no whispered words of desire this time, or torrid kisses as he escorted her to his waiting carriage. And if she was surprised that he climbed in beside her, she did not show it. She had assumed he'd send her on alone. His nearness drove her crazy. She sat staring out of the window at the brightening of the sky, nails digging into her palms to keep from screaming. Why did he confuse her emotions so? He had told her so many things in his passion. But she knew there was not a word of truth in anything that he said. She thought of her earlier decision to win at any cost, to expose him as Scorpio. In her pocket she had his personal diary. In her clenched fist she held a gold chain and medallion. Somehow, it had come unclasped during their love-making. It bore the likeness of a scorpion. She tucked it away. A memento . . . or would she use it against him?

The entire trip back to Eaton Hall was spent in cold silence. Yet, just before the carriage had come to a stop beneath a canopy of concealing tree limbs and she'd stepped out, he'd taken hold of her hand and kissed her palm.

"Sweet witch, I won't forget you." His voice held a smoky quality.

No longer able to control herself, and feeling the tears come in a rush, Starlin wrenched free of him and ran along the path toward the dark house. She did not know that another stood watching her in the shadows, and her tears blinded her to his identity when he quickly stepped out to confront her.

Starlin felt arms going around her in a possessive embrace. Taken unawares, she had little time to react and could only gasp weakly, "Who are you?"

"You lying, deceitful jade," a male voice snarled. "Who have you been sneaking around with behind my back?"

Fingers like talons bit into the flesh of her upper arms, and then he was shaking her until she was certain she might swoon. Dimly, she recognized his face contorted with unbridled fury.

"Courtland! Let go of me," she cried. "You're hurting me."

"I saw you giving Morgan the eye tonight, and the way you allowed him to hold you while the two of you were dancing. He's the one you've been seeing on the sly, isn't he?" he growled, making no move to release her. "I bet you weren't cold as ice with him."

"Take your hands off me!" she burst out angrily.

An anguished sob escaped her as he grabbed her hair and yanked her head backward.

"Look at you!" he raved. "It's obvious you were doing more tonight than just talking and holding hands—which is all you've ever allowed me." He laughed cruelly. "Your lips look ravaged, beauty, your eyes dazed by passion. But you were the one taken in tonight, my darling." His words seared through her haze. "He made a boast to several of his chums how he would thaw the ice around your heart and have you in his bed. He did exactly that, didn't he?"

Starlin struggled feebly. "No . . . no, you are jesting."

Courtland only sneered. "No longer the Ice Princess, I would be willing to bet." His mouth came down on hers in a bruising kiss.

A deep voice, carefully controlled yet hinting of fury, came out of the shadows and froze Courtland where he stood.

"Unhand the girl."

Startled, Courtland spun around to find himself staring down the point of a long gleaming sword. Rayne Morgan's voice crackled like fire in the night.

"You don't hear very well. I said release the lady."

Courtland hesitated, knowing the moment he freed Starlin that he might very well feel the full force of that steel searing into him. He observed one of Rayne's tawny eyebrows arch upward, and felt the tip of his blade sting his flesh.

"Is dying more to your liking?"

A shudder encompassed Courtland. "Morgan, please don't . . . this has nothing to do with you. She's made a fool of me once too often."

"This has everything to do with me, you son of a cur." Rayne's tone was deadly, his jaw rigid with fury. "The girl is mine. To insult her is to insult me. Starlin and I have decided to marry."

Starlin's shaking fingers clawed at Courtland. He stood there slack-jawed, too stunned to comment.

"Morgan, you mustn't . . ." she stammered. Neither man paid her notice, they were so intent on each other.

Courtland released his hold on Starlin. She stumbled and would have fallen if Rayne hadn't reached out quickly and caught her against him. She was shaking badly and too overcome by the events to protest. She could only cling to him.

"Starlin agreed to marry you?" Courtland ground out.

"Yes. Therefore, her whereabouts tonight are none of your business. She is mine now. Do I make myself clear?"

Courtland was furious. He had always placed her upon a pedestal, been content with her chaste kisses in hopes that things would change once they were engaged. Now, that was never going to happen. She had willingly, and easily, given herself to Rayne Morgan.

"Damn you, Starlin," he gritted from between clenched teeth. "You have cost me everything."

Morgan saw the change in the other man's eyes, and knew before Courtland's hand even dropped to the hilt of his sword what he was intending. In the blink of an eye, he'd shoved Starlin to the side and swiftly parried the first thrust of Courtland's blade.

"You shall pay a price for her, Morgan!" Courtland growled, his eyes alive with fury as he advanced toward him.

The clashing of steel upon steel broke through the quiet.

"You fool," Rayne snarled, the curve of his blade slashing a cut on Courtland's arm. "No woman is worth your life." Like a graceful dancer he moved, making it all appear to Starlin, who watched from the sidelines in horror, as if it were another game that he participated in simply because it suited his purpose. It was not because of her honor that he crossed swords with Courtland. No woman was worth risking his life for, he'd openly admitted it. It was to defend his own honor.

The thrusts of gleaming swords rang sharply in the night, brilliant blue sparks igniting where steel crossed steel. The two men fought determinedly. Courtland was a surprisingly good swordsman, but it was easy to see that Morgan was just toying with the man, giving him the chance to vent his anger for the slight to his proud family name. Starlin determined this by the relaxed way in which Morgan gripped his sword, the casual indifference he directed toward his combatant. He was sharply alert, and Starlin was certain he was doing his utmost to contain his actions. He had only pricked his opponent once, although the wildly pressing Courtland had left him several opportunities to thrust his sword home.

Sweat poured down Courtland's face and into his eyes, blinding him at times to Morgan's quick sideways movements that left him without a target and fuming in outrage. Countering every one of the man's lunges, Morgan at last grew weary of the contest and decided to encourage an end to it. He stepped quickly backward as though retreating, and then swiftly darted forward on bended knee meeting Courtland's advance with ease and sending the surprised man's sword flying from his hand.

Morgan placed the point of his blade against the stunned Courtland's heart. "Do you accept quarter, sir?" he asked with narrowed eyes.

Courtland stared over Morgan's shoulder at Starlin's face. He felt like everything he'd ever truly believed in had been taken from him this night. And it was her fault. Somehow, it was not right that she just walk away. But he did not wish to die. Morgan was right about that—no woman was worth death.

Sighing tremulously, he rasped, "I do."

Morgan lowered his sword to his side. "Good. Now, leave here and don't come back."

Courtland glared at Starlin as he walked by her, hissing beneath his breath so that only she could hear, "Life with him will be far different from what you would have had with me, Ice Princess. But seeing the two of you together tonight . . . somehow I have to agree you are well matched. He's a cold bastard, and you, his heartless bitch."

She flinched but said nothing in her defense. She had never loved him, but she was sorry that she'd hurt him and caused this humiliation. Tears glistened in her eyes as she watched him stride away, a seemingly broken young man.

Morgan walked over to her. Brooding silence hung over them.

"It is a high price for a night together, isn't it?" he said, standing over her.

Starlin swallowed with difficulty, suddenly feeling sick inside. Surely he was not inferring that they should really marry? She would not have it.

"We can manage to keep it quiet, milord," she said coldly. "I will talk with Buckwald after he's had a chance to regain his composure. He . . . he will listen."

"No he won't, Starlin. His pride won't allow it."

"What are you saying?" A strange dizziness washed over her and weakness settled in her limbs.

"There can be only one way to salvage your reputation."

"No . . . I refuse," she gasped before slipping to the

ground in a dead faint.

Rayne glanced down at the still form in his arms, a queer sensation overcoming him for a moment. He felt as if he were her protector, wanted to be, in fact. He tried not to notice the way in which her lips trembled slightly, or how good her arms felt wrapped about his neck. He thought that he'd never seen her look so lovely. Breathing deeply, he forced himself to remember she was his enemy, and how with little conscious forethought, he now had the key to all of his plans. Unknowingly, the means had come to him. If he so chose, retribution was close at hand. As he brushed past the sleepy-eyed butler who answered his knock and snarled for him to show him the way to Starlin's room, the demons of vengeance began playing havoc with his emotions.

Starlin would fit nicely into his plans after all. His possession, that he could break whenever it so suited him to do so. He laid her down on the bed and stood staring at her delicate beauty in the diffused light. Strangely, he could not fathom actually hurting her.

"You would weaken me," he said softly, his voice unsteady, "and that I can never let you do." He spun on his heel and left the room.

Lord Winfield was stunned to say the least when he was awakened by his butler and told that his granddaughter's intended wished to speak with him immediately. The earl wasted not a second, but hurried to the library, his hair uncombed, his spectacles barely on straight.

At the sight of Rayne Morgan standing before the fireplace, snifter of brandy in hand, he hesitated.

"This must be some kind of a practical joke," he muttered, eyes staring wide and disbelieving at the tall man who had not bothered to formally acknowledge his presence.

Rayne slowly turned toward him, his features a polite mask. "No it is not, sir. Your butler informed you correctly. Your granddaughter and I plan to marry at once. We have been together for the better part of the evening, and I thought you should know of our plans."

"I . . . I assumed she was with Courtland this evening?" the earl queried, looking terribly confused.

"Yes, well, let's just say her plans changed quite unexpectedly," Rayne replied with a stiff smile. "I had you awakened, sir, because I felt it only right to let you know posthaste. And there is much to do, and very little time to see it accomplished."

"You, Lord Morgan, and my Starlin . . . to be married," the earl breathed, sinking into a chair. "You did not speak with me of this, sir. This is highly irregular."

"It is no joke, Earl, and I must caution you not to try and do anything to prevent our marriage. It would not be advisable."

Time appeared to stand still as both men stared at each other, their eyes hard, unyielding. The earl read the message in Rayne Morgan's, and paled.

"It is not for love . . . nor is this something you wish, is it?" There was no reply, but in the silence, the earl received his answer. "Dear lord in heaven . . . I had hoped that you were the one."

"I'm sorry?" Rayne replied a bit confused with the earl's last statement.

"Something my granddaughter said to me when she found out I was considering a match between her and Courtland."

Rayne only nodded. "He was waiting for her tonight. I had to intervene to save her reputation. As it is, the lad will tell enough."

"Oh, merciful heavens," the earl sighed. His eyes held Rayne's. "I've always wanted the best for her, a strong man who could look after her and give her fine children. She has ridiculous notions for a woman, I know that. But she's smart, and beneath that ice-cool exterior there is a real flesh-and-blood woman. She needs the same kind of a man." He assessed Rayne closely.

Rayne felt edgy listening to his words. "The wedding, sir, would you like it here?"

"Yes, certainly. And you may invite anyone of your choosing, of course. Your family, close friends."

"There is no one I wish to invite" came the laconic reply. "My only wish is to have all of the arrangements taken care of at once. I will secure a special license myself." He placed the empty brandy snifter on a side table and prepared to depart. "My bride and I will leave London soon after. If there is a child . . . leaving will be for the best."

"Yes, I agree." The earl nodded, praying that he was doing the right thing by agreeing to let Starlin marry this man. For a long time after Rayne Morgan departed, he sat and sorted out his feelings. He was sad, yet, for some reason, not displeased about the marriage. True, he would have chosen another, less notorious man for Starlin if he'd been allowed any say. He was well aware of English law. Starlin would be Morgan's chattel after they married. Her wealth would become his. Yet, he knew for certain that Morgan was not marrying Starlin for her money, for his wealth as a

204

marquess far exceeded that of an earl. Starlin would become a marchioness, with prestige in the aristocracy, vast holdings, and a strong-willed husband to guide her.

With a sigh, he rose and shuffled from the room. Rayne Morgan and Starlin? Who in the bloody hell could reason a woman's mind, and least of all a fiery-tempered one like his granddaughter?

"I'll not marry Rayne Morgan!" Starlin raved later that morning upon rising and hearing from her grandfather that wedding plans needed to be discussed.

The earl's voice brooked no denial. "This time, Granddaughter, you left yourself no choice, nor me. You will marry the marquess, and immediately."

Starlin's eyes widened, and she gripped the back of the dining room chair. She stared at the earl as he sipped at his morning tea. "He . . . told you? . . ."

"Not exactly. It was rather evident. And he is doing the gentlemanly thing. I admire him for that. He could have easily gone off and left you to the gossip-mongers."

"Admire him! He took advantage of your grand-daughter, and you have the gall to say such a thing!" she interjected.

The earl viewed her calmly. "Starlin, I love you more than anything in the world, and if I thought for one minute that Morgan truly took advantage of you I'd call him out myself." He peered hard at her. "But I know that is preposterous, there isn't a man born who could make you do anything that you don't have a mind to. Not even a dashing blade like Morgan. You're far too strong-minded a woman for any chap to seduce

205

you with flowery phrases." He viewed her closely. "If I am wrong, tell me, and I will see that Lord Morgan is dealt with."

Starlin could see this was one battle she was not going to win. She plopped disspirited into the chair and sighed. "Can't I just go away, I don't have to marry to resolve this mess. The talk will calm down eventually."

"What if there is a child?"

"No, there won't be!" she gasped, thinking how foolish she'd been not to think about becoming pregnant before now. "Can't . . . be . . . for don't you see, he doesn't care a fig for me, Grandfather. He is only marrying me because he feels he must. Please, don't ask me to marry a man out of obligation."

"And what of honor, Starlin? Our family has always prided themselves upon it?" the earl queried gently.

"I am being bartered for honor's sake," she said bitterly.

"I believe it is an even exchange on both sides. You both possess noble dignity and position. And, whether either of you is willing to admit it, something drew you two volatile people together. And by the look deep in your eyes, I'd say you've found more than you know."

Starlin bristled and hurriedly rose to her feet. "Hardly! But I will meet my obligation to our family since I am the one who has brought shame upon it. Yet, no matter what you might think, Morgan and I are ill-matched. He is not the gallant that you think he is. He is scheming, ruthless, and does not know the meaning of the word love."

The earl smiled faintly. "Whether you'll admit it or not, my dear, he's found the fire beneath the ice. You have always wrapped every other lad around your finger, and you are smarting, I think, because with him you cannot."

Starlin didn't see Rayne Morgan until the following day when he arrived in his carriage and informed her that they were going for a drive through Hyde Park. He checked his elegant timepiece and then replaced it in his brocade waistcoat.

"It's almost five o'clock. The usual tonnish mob should have congregated by now and I feel that we should be seen together at once." When he glanced over at her and saw that she hadn't paused from her needlepoint and was obviously ignoring hm, he walked over to boldly remove it from her hands and toss it aside. "You might wish to change from your day gown, madame—or—wear what you have on. Either way I don't give a tinker's damn. But you are coming with me."

She did not see the wicked amusement in his eyes as she had shut hers tightly and was swearing softly. "God's blood, but you are a bully of a man. It's bad enough that you stormed into my life and made a shambles of it, now you have taken to ordering me about—and I have not even consented to marry you."

"But you will," he stated evenly. "For you know neither of us has a choice." He pulled her up from the chair and into his arms. "I have already put in a request for a special license, and I have no doubt that it will go through. And when it does, you will become my wife."

"You really mean to see this through until the bitter end, don't you?"

"Yes, and deep down you are glad of it. After all, what if you are with child."

A trembling began inside her, and she paled. On

impulse, he kissed her, ignoring the gaping servants that passed by. "It is something neither of us considered in the heat of passion, but now we must. And honor is the only thing that has guided me all of these years. It means everything to me."

She studied his serious expression. "And if I am not expecting?"

"You may then have the marriage annulled if you wish," he replied without hint of distress or a shred of emotion.

Her words came in only a whisper. "Yes, of course . . . for there will never be any love between us . . . never."

"But there is honor, and possibly, our child." Gently he set her from him. "Go on and change, Starlin. All is not as bleak as you imagine."

A sort of numbness settled within Starlin that saw her through the hectic time preceding her wedding day. She allowed no emotion of any kind to penetrate the hard shell of indifference that surrounded her. Inwardly, when she was alone and could not will her mind to stop thinking, she felt she might go mad. For surely she was not truly going to marry a man without love. She refused to acknowledge, even in her heart, that they had shared anything more than passion.

Over the next few days, he made certain that they were seen together in all of the right places. One evening, a party in the West End, the next day, a concert at Vauxhall Gardens, and that night, a ball in honor of Queen Victoria.

And of all the people that they had to literally bump into as they were dancing: the duke and duchess.

Rayne's ex-mistress, Susan Ellendale.

The duchess had smiled sweetly over her husband's shoulder. "Why, look who is here, Duke, none other than the earl's little granddaughter and Lord Morgan. Hello there!" she called.

Just by her honeyed tone, Starlin knew what to expect next. Rayne nodded curtly in their direction, but it wasn't enough to satisfy Susan.

"Milord, I heard from Lord Courtland that you quite literally stole that darling girl right out from under his nose, and that now wedding bells are surely going to ring," she exclaimed loud enough for those nearby to hear over the orchestra. "You always were the trampler of innocent hearts, weren't you?" She tittered shrilly. Her husband attempted to guide her from the floor, but she refused to follow his lead. He was forced to shuffle about or make a worse scene.

"Are you speaking from experience, my dear duchess?" Rayne replied coldly. "Or merely quoting hearsay again?"

The portly duke grasped his red-faced wife by the arm and directed her toward the club entrance.

By the end of the week, all of London was buzzing with the news of the devoted lovers and their impending marriage. Close friends dropped by at Eaton Hall to extend their best wishes, and congratulatory notes from distant acquaintances began arriving daily.

Yet Starlin could not help feeling like a helpless pawn. One brief night had set a course of events into motion that could not be altered.

True to his word, Rayne secured a special license that would enable them to marry without a lengthy waiting period. The earl and his staff were finalizing the plans for the ceremony which were to be held in the gardens at Eaton Hall the following week.

And just as soon as she was certain there would not be an innocent child made to suffer, she would see to the annulment. She might then take her evidence to the authorities and tell them where a pirate ship could be located. She hadn't had time to read the entire diary as yet, but there was reference in the first pages to his activities, and his life in England. She hadn't wished to read any more. Somehow, she felt closer to him with each page. That was something she could not handle. A series of shudders ran through her upon envisioning that bronzed, lean frame swinging from a British yardarm.

"Damn you, Rayne Morgan," she gasped despairingly. "But I don't think I could bear that—even though it would serve you right."

Confused and upset, yet ever thoughtful, her fingers found their way to the gold chain bearing the likeness of the scorpion that she kept carefully hidden beneath silken undergarments.

Strange, she wondered, that he hadn't mentioned the diary or the necklace having disappeared. Perhaps he did not think she would have taken it? Perhaps the thief was always the last to realize when he had been taken himself? An enticing dimple appeared in her cheek as she smiled ever so secretively.

"Something old, something new, something borrowed . . ."

With little enough time for the wedding, Starlin was at least spared having to endure a large, formal engagement ball. There was an intimate dinner given in their honor by Rayne's good friends at their London townhouse. She had managed to smile and converse graciously with those in attendance. There were looks of envy from many of the women when they saw the diamond and amethyst ring that Rayne had given her to officially seal their engagement.

The ring was made of a large teardrop diamond nestled amidst a cluster of purple stones. It was saved from being ostentatious by the smoky violet stones.

"I was at the jeweler's and when I saw those stones I knew instantly that I wanted them for you," Rayne had said, his mouth twisted up at one corner in a mocking half-smile as he'd slipped it on her finger before they'd departed for the dinner.

She stared down at the ring. "Are you ever going to tell me why you are really marrying me?"

"I've already explained it all to you."

"Do you expect me to believe that nonsense about marrying me to save my honor?"

"I did not lie to you."

"No, only leave out what you do not wish for me to know," she returned sarcastically, her gaze meeting his.

His voice had turned harsh. "I do not like to think I will be spending the rest of my life facing the condemnation in your eyes each time you look at me."

"You know I never wished to marry a man who did not love me. I cannot be expected to change my feelings."

Something hard and cynical gleamed in his jade eyes. They penetrated her forced reserve. "Am I to be condemned for accepting the invitation that I saw in your eyes?" The slant of his chiseled mouth warned her what was coming next, but it still cut deeply. "If it will make you feel any better, I have cursed myself a thousand times over for that one foolish night, but, you see, I was bewitched by a lovely, desirable woman that night. I was blinded by my need."

"With luck, there will be no need for us to stay married for very long," she spat furiously.

"Aye," he'd snarled darkly, "with luck, madam, you will be married and free of me before the summer's end. And with even a bit more good fortune, your Lord Courtland will not object to accepting my leavings."

The fires guttered in her eyes and a flash of pain she could not hide flickered, then was quickly veiled by long lashes. He yanked her roughly into his arms, the very idea of her longing to be free infuriating him.

They stared at each other: loving, hating, condemning, their damnable pride coming between them.

"Of one thing I am most certain, my beautiful Ice Princess. I have never come close to possessing your heart, and shall not even try, for it lies within a barrier of cold, cold ice that not even the most loving of men will ever melt."

She didn't realize that she'd been holding her breath, a part of her fervently hoping that he would not say anything more that would drive those lancelike words any further into her.

"You will vastly regret what you have said to me this day," she hissed.

He reached out and drew a finger across her lips, his caustic tone defying his gentle touch. "Don't allow vengeance to become your willing master, my love, for it will only serve to enslave you."

He was striding away from her before she had time to respond. She felt like screaming at the walls. It was not the first time that he'd left her feeling in such a way.

Chapter Eleven

"What do you want, Susan?" Rayne inquired coldly. He had just departed his club and climbed into his carriage. Lady Ellendale was waiting for him.

"After seeing you the other evening, I realized how much I've missed you, darling." Susan pouted prettily. "Life has been so dull without you."

"Oh really," Rayne drawled. "From what I've heard, you're busier than you've ever been."

She stiffened in indignation, but was careful to mask her anger. "I must keep busy. If I don't, sad memories overwhelm me."

Rayne's jade eyes danced with amusement. "I had no idea the duke had passed on."

"The duke is fine, and you know it," Susan snapped, losing her self-control. "I was referring to the wonderful memories that you and I once shared. I can't forget the times we shared . . . the love I thought was ours."

"A few lusty tumbles is hardly love," Rayne stated coldly, looking directly into her eyes. "There was never any love lost between us."

Susan's eyes grew round and tearful. "Oh, how can you be so cruel? I truly imagined that you would marry me one day. Just as soon as the duke passed on, that is." She dabbed at her tears with a lace handkerchief.

"You never believed any such thing," Rayne snorted. "You've left a legion of scorned lovers behind you, without once looking back. You're only miffed that I left you first."

Susan's manner changed abruptly. Her face contorted. "And for that little Cambridge miss! Well, I won't stand by and let you humiliate me this way."

Rayne grabbed her arm. She winced from his biting hold.

"Starlin Cambridge is going to be my wife, and she is more woman than you could ever hope to be."

"And just what will she think when she hears of my . . . little problem?" Susan said with a tight smile.

"What are you talking about?"

"I'm carrying a child—yours, to be exact."

"You'd like for me to believe that," Rayne countered, his voice perfectly controlled.

"The duke can't father children. And I am pregnant."

Rayne's face became grim. "How many months have you been with child?"

Susan's face flushed scarlet. "Such a question to ask a lady."

"It's a reasonable question, and you are no lady. Now, tell me damn it!"

"About . . . two months." Susan looked away from him out of the window.

"Are you certain?"

"Yes!" she snapped, turning to stare up at him. "And

I'd like to know what you intend to do about it?"

Rayne swore softly.

"I have thought of . . . another way," Susan said calmly.

"What are you planning?"

"I can go away, have the baby, and then return as if nothing happened."

"What about the child?" Rayne asked incredulously.

"There is a family I know in the next county who will take it," she replied with seeming indifference.

Rayne's eyes were cold. "I won't allow that."

Susan's eyes flared. "Then you'd better break your engagement, darling, for I don't intend to face the duke's wrath alone. I won't hesitate to go to your Starlin and tell her the truth."

A dark look shone in his eyes. "If you know what's good for you, you won't open your mouth." He studied her tense features. "I'll have to think this through."

"Very well," Susan agreed. "But don't keep me waiting long. Time is my enemy now. Only your support can see me through this, and keep me from talking to Starlin." She opened the carriage door and disappeared into the night, leaving Rayne to ponder the unexpected, and unwelcome, turn of events.

The household was in a constant state of disruption with plans for Rayne and Starlin's wedding. Miss Eggie and the staff were all in a dither preparing the house for the ceremony and reception afterward. Several hundred people of the aristocracy had been invited. The earl left all of the arrangements to Miss Eggie and Starlin, and had taken to riding every day with Rayne

215

to escape the hubbub. The two men appeared to get on famously. Their newfound relationship irritated Starlin.

On one particularly sunny morning, several days after her betrothal to Morgan, Starlin stood at the windows in the music room observing her grandfather striding over the lawns in the direction of the stable. She knew he was going to meet Rayne and experienced an odd little twinge. Even though she hated Morgan, he still was the only man who could make her heart skip a beat just by entering a room.

"Damn him" she sighed. "He no more wishes this union between us than I do, yet he will cling to stubborn pride and meet his obligation, and make the both of us miserable."

With a forlorn sigh, she sat down at the pianoforte. Unconsciously, her fingers began playing the haunting tune she remembered from the music box. Awake or asleep, it was always with her.

She did not know how long he had been standing there, listening, watching her. She had been so involved in the emotional piece that his voice startled her.

"You never cease to surprise me, Princess. I would have thought you'd never wish to hear that melody again."

Her fingers froze on the ivory keys, then dropped self-consciously to her lap.

"Don't stop on my account. I rather like that song myself."

She turned around slowly and was not fooled for one minute by the calm, unassuming look in those expressive eyes. Lounging negligently against the doorway, blocking any means of passing him, he stood studying her, arms crossed over his broad chest.

"Grandfather has already left for the stables," she offered evenly, "I suppose he thought you were detained elsewhere this morning." She plucked nervously at the threads of her velvet skirt.

"I know exactly where the earl is. I came to tell you to stop avoiding me. This is no way for two people who are betrothed to act."

Her eyes hot fire. "I detest the thought of marrying you. And I refuse to act happy about it, or to spend any more time with you than is necessary."

His eyes roamed insolently over her. "It seems I'm marrying a child as well as a woman."

Furious, she jumped up from the piano stool. "I will not allow you to manipulate me further, Morgan! If you insist on marrying me, I will make your life miserable."

"You are a brat, you know," he stated slowly, moving toward her, purpose in each step, drawing her wary eyes to watch him closely. "But at least when you act like this I know how to treat you."

"Don't come near me." Starlin pierced him with a withering glare.

He kept coming.

Damn the man! she thought, trying to calm her racing heart. Why did he have to look so handsome, so virile, and be such a villain? She dropped her eyes to keep him from guessing her thoughts. It was then his hand snaked out and yanked her to him. He sat on the piano stool and jerked her across his lap. Her mouth fell open in surprise as the first hard smack was delivered to her bottom. Even through her voluminous skirt it hurt. She began to struggle, her skirt and petticoats rising as she squirmed. He held her legs between his, refusing to release her. The next stinging blow fell across the rounded curves beneath silken pantalets, and Starlin could not contain a sharp yelp.

"Stop it, you brute, that hurts!"

"It's supposed to," Morgan said blandly. "Maybe you'll learn something from it."

"I'll never marry you now!" Starlin cried, tears forming.

"Yes you will," he said sternly, suddenly pulling down her skirts and setting her upright on his lap.

Her head snapped backward and their eyes met in a clash of wills. When she was like this, so brazenly defiant and spitting like a cat, Morgan thought she was quite easily the most exciting woman he'd ever encountered. She gave as good as she got. His mouth widened into a rakish smile.

"While I am fully aware of how much you hate me and abhor the prospect of becoming my bride, we are still obligated to put on a believable show before everyone." He kissed her pouting mouth long and hungrily before she could turn away, then released her so abruptly that she stumbled backward and grabbed the edge of the pianoforte for support. "Try to be a good girl for just awhile longer, will you? Your grandfather is looking forward to all of this so much."

"You've managed to take them all in, haven't you, with your false words and your facade of an English lord?" she said crisply. "I wonder more and more of late, just what you stand to gain from all of this?"

"I have a distinct feeling in my gut, madam," he said softly. "that I will live yet to see you make me regret that night of heaven with you."

"You are no true gentleman, Morgan. To live the life of one for very long would bore you to death." She drew back her head as if to study his every feature most astutely. "I, better than anyone, know that other, dark side of you. Hear me well. Don't ever think to best me, for you will not. I am your equal in every way, and I will not hesitate to prove it before everyone if you try and force my hand."

"I am just a merchantman, and the *Tempest* is used for legal commerce. I have nothing to fear."

"So you say, milord pirate," she responded in a cutting voice, "but remember my words well. I'll destroy you without conscience if you push me too far."

He gave her a long, hard, calculating look. "You've got the diary . . . I know that. It takes a thief to know one, my dear. And I swear to you now, if you ever say anything to anyone, you may rest assured that I'll break your pretty neck." Before she had time to move, his head bent forward and his mouth came down on hers with demanding force.

Starlin knew he was seeking to show her how easily he could dominate her if he so desired. She fought him, hitting him with her fists, trying hard not to respond. There was no want or passion in his kiss. It was hard and hurtful, and it frightened her the way he could be so cold. His hands roamed over her lush curves as his tongue ravished her mouth. A curl of desire stirred within her. Unable to resist him, she whimpered unconsciously and wound her arms about his neck. He held her away from him and stared down at her. Then he turned and strode from the room before she'd even opened her eyes.

It was precisely then that Starlin realized how dangerous he was to her. It seemed no power on earth could keep them apart, or eliminate the desire that constantly drew them together. Yet she felt sure they were charted on a disastrous course. Sooner or later, one of them was bound to destroy the other.

All of London soon had news of the betrothal of Starlin Cambridge to Lord Rayne Morgan. Over the next few days they began a social whirl. One night, Rayne informed her that they were going to Her Majesty's Theatre in the Haymarket to hear the incomparable singing of Jenny Lind. It was an Italian opera, one that Starlin had longed to attend for some time. She remembered having mentioned this before one of her friends in Rayne's presence. Had he secured the costly tickets to please her? Starlin could not contain her excitement at the prospect of an evening of fine music. If nothing else, she and Rayne did share a love of music and dance. As she stood patiently waiting for Mindy to finish fastening her gold satin gown she wondered if Queen Victoria and the prince would be in attendance.

Rayne and Starlin arrived just before the curtain and were shown to the Morgans' private box situated but a stone's throw from the royal box. The hall was packed with over two thousand people in anticipation of seeing the queen and hearing the famous singer.

When Queen Victoria and her husband arrived, the hall grew perfectly still. Starlin, who admired the queen very much, was surprised when Victoria's eyes met hers and she smiled at Starlin as if she were attempting to assure her in some way.

Paula, who was sitting in the box next to Starlin, leaned over and murmured, "The queen has heard of your forthcoming marriage. I understand that she has given you her unofficial blessing."

Starlin's pulse quickened. "She is aware of the circumstances?"

"She is wise, Starlin, and is not disapproving. After all, her own marriage is an arranged one. And yet, it is said she adores her husband."

Starlin was still looking in the queen's direction when the curtain rose and the entertainment began.

It was during the intermission, when they were sipping champagne and conversing with several well-wishers who had dropped by their box, that Starlin became aware of rude tittering in the box behind theirs. It was the Dowager Courtland's voice.

"He's only marrying her because he is bound by honor to do so, you know. I understand from my son that he is still wild for his mistress."

Starlin looked down at her hands which were clenched in her lap. The circumstances of their marriage were well known, it seemed. As was Rayne's continued affair with Susan Ellendale. Why did the thought of his holding that woman in his arms make her feel like scratching his eyes out. She was startled from her brooding reverie by Rayne's drawling voice near her ear. "Dammit, keep your chin up. You've nothing to be ashamed of."

She stared at him with bitter regret. "Is it true what she said?"

"You're staring at me as if you believe that it is."

"Is it?" she ground out tersely.

"By the look in your eyes, I'd say that no matter what I say, you're going to believe what you want."

"I don't appreciate being made a fool of over your mistress," Starlin said in a cold, suppressed fury.

"Do I detect a note of jealousy in your voice?"

Starlin's cheeks turned pink. "I will not stay here another minute with you. I want to leave."

"No" came the biting reply. "I will not allow those biddies to have the pleasure of seeing you flee. Stay put, and show all of them your fine spirit."

"Why should you care one way or the other?"

"Because we're in this together," he said flatly, "until the bitter end. Now stay where you are."

Starlin was forced to endure the rest of the evening feeling like a wild thing caught in a trap.

Starlin and Rayne were included in every prominent social gathering. After three days of activities, Rayne was weary of parties and formal dinners and looking forward to sharing a private dinner with Starlin that evening. Somehow he had to manage a way to retrieve the diary that she'd taken. He didn't think she could have read the entire thing, or she would hate him even more than she already did.

Settling deeper into the plush cushions of his carriage, Rayne considered his plans. He was on his way to pick up Starlin, anticipating taking her to one of London's most popular supper clubs. It was the first time they'd been alone in several days. He was doing his utmost to ease the tension between them. But while Starlin's body yielded to his touch, he knew her response was purely reflexive. She still remained as stubbornly self-possessed as ever.

Suddenly, his driver's voice brought his thoughts back to the present.

"There is a coach up ahead that is broken down, milord. Should I offer assistance?"

Even though they were on a particularly lonely stretch of road frequented by highwaymen, Rayne told George to stop. When his man didn't return after a few minutes, he stepped out of the vehicle. The world appeared to explode around him. Fists came from everywhere, beating him, pummeling his face and driving into his body. Rayne did his best to defend himself, but he guessed there were a dozen men surrounding him. The fight was brutal, but Rayne would not fall easily. His eye swelled shut and his mouth tasted like blood, but still he remained standing. It took them a long time to beat him down.

A blurred face hovered over him and said in a jeering voice, "This is a pre-wedding present from your fiancée, Morgan. She thought it well deserved."

The pleasant evening was shattered. Starlin heard the sound of voices in the foyer and hurried from the parlor to see what had happened. She found the butler trying to restrain an angry Rayne Morgan from seeking her out. Starlin was shocked by his appearance. His face was battered and covered with dried blood.

"What happened?" she demanded.

Rayne tore free of Bridges.

"As if you have to ask," he snarled.

From behind Rayne, George's eyes met Starlin's

wide ones. "We stopped to investigate a carriage on the side of the road," he explained. "Men came out of nowhere. They jumped us. We didn't have a chance."

Starlin choked on a sob as she stared at Rayne. "Why would anyone do this?" She glanced up at George's bruised face and saw the answer there in his eyes. She swore in a very unladylike fashion under her breath, but her features remained perfectly controlled. She knew there was no sense in trying to explain her innocence. Someone had tried very hard to make it appear that she was behind the attack.

Rayne swayed on his feet. "Madam . . ." he slurred, shaking his head to clear it. "I only came here to tell you that your men didn't frighten me, you deceitful jade." He wiped at the blood streaming in his eyes, never even aware when he slumped over in Starlin's arms. Immediately, George took him from her.

"Take him upstairs to an unoccupied bedroom," she ordered crisply. "And go easy, he might have some broken ribs."

Starlin was relieved that her grandfather was out for the evening, and most of the servants ensconced in other wings. She did not wish more gossip. It certainly seemed that their marriage was going to start out with enough problems.

By the time that Rayne regained consciousness, Starlin had cleansed his face and applied antiseptic to the cuts.

"I think we'd better send for the doctor," she told him as his ice cool eyes fixed upon her. "It doesn't appear that you are as bad as I first imagined, but we can't be certain."

"No," he said. "I don't want a doctor."

"Very well," she said stiffly.

"Where are my clothes?" he demanded, looking around the room.

"You'll get them back in the morning."

"This is the last place that I wish to be tonight."

"I understand," she replied coldly, "but you're the one who came here. And I think you'd better stay. But please leave early enough so that I don't have to . . ." Her words trailed off and she began gathering up the soiled rags. He caught her hand.

"Explain my appearance to the hired help," he finished for her.

"I had nothing to do with what happened," she said suddenly.

"You expect me to believe your word. I wonder why the same was not applied in my case," Rayne stated bitterly.

"It wasn't the same," she breathed softly. "The evidence was damning." She saw the condemnation in his eyes and found herself longing to see anything but that.

"It always is, isn't it, Starlin?" he said cuttingly.

She turned away. "You can't have your clothes. You're in no condition to travel. Now try and get some rest." She quietly left the room, feeling his eyes stabbing her in the back.

Starlin passed the remainder of the night wide awake in her bed. When morning came, she went down to breakfast. Passing Bridges in the dining room, she quietly asked if Lord Morgan was awake yet.

"Awake, and gone, milady," he replied solemnly.

The earl glanced up from his newspaper. "Unpleasant business. He needs you, Granddaughter."

225

Starlin took her place at the table. "He doesn't want to believe anything that I say."

"He's a good man," the earl returned without hesitation. "You've treated him horridly. And now, this. What do you expect from him?"

"What about my feelings?" Starlin shot back. "And this other woman . . . how do I know that he doesn't really love her. Nor can I forget that he's only marrying me because honor dictates it."

"If you truly believe that, then you are a poor judge of men, my dear," the earl stated evenly, his eyes returning to his paper.

Starlin felt more confused than ever. She didn't know what to believe. She could only pray that the next few days would pass quickly and her wedding day arrive. For then soon after, came the annulment. And an end to their uneasy alliance.

The early morning sun shone brightly through the trees and upon a black wolfhound loping along beside two riders who'd just reined their mounts onto the trail that wound through Hyde Park.

"Have you managed yet to win my fiery granddaughter over to your way of thinking?" the Earl of Eaton queried the brooding man who rode beside him.

A short laugh rang out in the still air. "I mean no insult, sir, but Starlin is not the sort of woman who is easily persuaded to do anything she does not wish to. Marrying me is not something she's doing willingly."

"And you, how do you feel about marrying her?"

"My feelings haven't changed."

"Good," the earl stated heartily. "I was afraid after

226

what happened, that you'd change your mind."

"I'm trying to believe that she didn't set those men upon me."

"She isn't capable of plotting something so brutal." He caught Rayne's eyes. "But I know there are several people who are."

"I've thought of that. And I'm investigating the possibility. You need have no fear. I will meet my obligation."

"I wish your sole purpose for marrying my granddaughter was not to save her reputation," the earl said with a sad sigh.

"There is no love lost between us, sir," Rayne said. The bruises on his face were fading, but would not be completely gone in time for the wedding. "Starlin fights me at every turn because she believes that she will lose something precious by marrying me."

"And what is that?"

"Her freedom." Rayne considered his answer, and could not help but remember the night that had set this chain of events into motion.

Surprisingly, it rankled him to think that the only reason Starlin was marrying him was because she was being forced. She'd made it clear she did not love him, so what could he expect? He recalled once again the night he'd made love to her in his cabin. Starlin . . . the temptress, glorious in her passion, fiery in her contempt, and everything that he could ever long for in a woman. And the only one he had ever known who truly did not want him. The thought was sobering.

Lord Winfield expelled a long sigh. "Freedom . . . something I have allowed Starlin too much of, I fear. All of this could have been avoided if I would have applied a firmer hand. And now, it is too late."

"Due to many things that were beyond your control, sir." Rayne touched his heels to the prancing hunter's sides. The animal leapt forward eager to run. Raw emotion was too near the surface. He urged the horse faster, toward a series of jumps that stood beside the trail.

Too late for all of us—my mother, my father . . . and Starlin.

Immersed so deeply in his own thinking, it was some time before he realized the earl was not behind him. Something flashed ominously through his thoughts and prompted him to wheel his mount around and send him into a full gallop. He felt danger and death, yet gave no thought that he was racing head-on to meet it.

Chapter Twelve

The cloaked figure hurried from behind the trunk of a towering elm and approached the earl's sprawled form lying still as death on the ground. Blood from a wound on his head was already staining the green lawn a sickly brown.

A queer, mad glitter entered the man's dark eyes, and he smiled coldly. Malcolm Wells bore a pleased expression with just a hint of malice. "He looks quite dead actually," he murmured to himself. Yet just to make certain he squatted down beside the earl's body and felt for the pulse in his neck. He scowled blackly. "Damn! he's still breathing." He shot to his feet, thoughts scurrying frantically. Quickly he raised his cane over his head with every intention of striking the earl. "And now . . . the final coup de grace shall be my pleasure."

With cold-blooded intent he slashed downward with the cane, only to jerk backward at the sound of an approaching horse. A streak of black fury sprang at him, jaws snapping, tearing off a piece of Malcolm's billowing cloak. Malcolm swung the cane in self-defense, catching the dog a glancing swipe. The animal yelped and darted aside, fangs drawn back in a menacing snarl.

"You wretched beast . . . get away," Malcolm spat, hastily retreating. He realized that there was no time to spare. Rayne Morgan would be upon him in a matter of minutes. The wolfhound stood fierce guard over the earl. With a grunt of dissatisfaction Malcolm hurried away from the grisly scene. At the early hour the park was fairly deserted. He was able to slip away with only the wolfhound watching him escape.

"Milord!" Rayne shouted in alarm when he saw Lord Winfield's crumpled form. He noticed that Merlin appeared extremely agitated as he sniffed about the area where the earl lay. Leaping from his horse, he knelt beside the inert body. Carefully, he rolled the earl onto his back and muttered a coarse oath when he saw the ugly, gaping cut on his forehead and the trickle of blood that oozed down the side of his face.

Lord Winfield moaned softly, but his eyes did not open. His skin felt cold and clammy to the touch and his breathing was very shallow. Rayne did a brief examination of the gash, assuming by the shape of the wound that the earl had been grazed by one of Krager's hooves as he'd lost his seating and fallen to the ground. Rayne swiftly unbound the scarf from his neck.

Noticing a fountain nearby, water trickling from a stone nymph, he hurried over and wet the scarf and returned to press it to the earl's head. In the confusion, he had failed to notice that Merlin had dashed off.

It took some doing, but with care and slow going Rayne finally managed to lift the injured earl onto his hunter and walked the horse back to the estate grounds.

Fredrick saw them coming and threw down his fishing pole. He ran toward them.

"What in the world happened?" he asked, breathing heavily. He walked beside the horse making certain that the earl's body did not sway from the animal's back.

"Damned if I know," Rayne returned with a frustrated growl. "One minute we were riding along having a conversation, and the next we were heading for the jumps and I noticed that Lord Winfield was not behind me. I found him some yards back." He peered over his shoulder at the earl's inert form. "How is he doing? He doesn't look too good, does he?"

Fredrick checked the earl's pulse. "It's weak, and he's lost a lot of blood."

"We must get him to his room and send for the doctor immediately."

"There isn't a moment to spare, I'm afraid," Fredrick commented grimly.

Rayne heard the sound of running footsteps. Starlin was racing toward them, a look of horror on her face.

"Starlin, go back to the house!" he ordered.

She ignored him. "What happened?" she cried in anguish, reaching her grandfather's side and seeing the blood soaking the makeshift bandage.

"An accident, Your Ladyship," Fredrick stated.

"He must have lost his balance on the jump," Rayne said.

"But he's an expert rider," Starlin said incredulously, striding with them toward the house. Her hands kept going to her grandfather, touching him, reassuring herself that he was still breathing.

"I didn't see him fall, Starlin," Rayne said.

"This was no accident!" Starlin cried. "It was undoubtedly precipitated by the Duke of Claybourne's men in retaliation for Morgan's dalliance with his wife!"

Fredrick sighed forlornly as he reached for the earl's crumpled form. His eyes met Rayne's. "She does not know what she's saying."

Rayne's face remained grim.

Starlin raced up the stairs ahead of them, calling out for someone to hurry for the doctor.

Starlin sat outside her grandfather's suite of rooms, waiting. She had been forbidden by the earl's physician to remain with her grandfather. She cast Rayne Morgan baleful looks.

"If you'd have stayed out of my life this wouldn't have happened," she hissed, her nerves at their peak.

"You're distraught right now, Starlin. We can talk about this another time." Rayne was attempting to soothe her somehow, but was meeting stony silence and hatred in those alluring violet eyes. She simply refused to listen to anything that he had to say. "Believe what in the hell you want. I'm tired of explaining myself to you."

"And I'm sick of wanting to believe you," Starlin choked, realizing that what she said was true.

"You've never really tried, and we both know it."

Her back was as straight as a broomstick. "I don't know why I sit here and listen to you. You haven't a shred of decency. If you did you would get out of my

232

life and leave me alone."

"You're really no different from me, Starlin."

His words shook her. She wasn't like Morgan! He didn't care what anyone thought of him. She was not like that. "I would sooner be compared to the devil than to the likes of you!"

He reached her in two strides and grasped her shoulders to yank her upward into his arms. For several long seconds their gazes locked.

"All you're doing is trying to convince yourself that you don't want me—" Rayne said, his eyes strangely shadowed. "—that you couldn't possibly want someone as awful as me. But you do . . . and that's what really drives you crazy."

"No . . . no," she defended, shaking her head furiously. "You make me want you . . . force me to succumb to your advances."

Starlin saw at once the uncompromising slant to his lips. "Do I really?" he asked softly. "Or is that the way you salve your aristocratic conscience?"

She wanted to turn away from him, not to respond when she saw his mouth dip forward. But already her eyelids were fluttering shut and her lips half parted, waiting for the inevitable touch of his. Their kiss was searching, filled with passion and emotions that neither wanted to accept.

Tilting her head back, Rayne's persuasive lips moved over her cheek, her throat, and the warm silken flesh between her breasts. She was yielding to him, warm and passionately. He teased her with light kisses.

"You can never deny me, Starlin. For it was you who drew me to England, and even in the cave you wanted me to take you."

233

"Whatever else that you believe, Morgan, know that I'll always hate what you are," Starlin murmured between kisses.

"Perhaps," he agreed absently, "but then a real gentleman would bore you to death."

Starlin felt the blood leap in her face, humiliated by his crude insinuation that she could possibly welcome his coarse advances. He was trying very hard to control her thoughts, her dreams, her entire life, for that matter. She knew she must not let him. Pulling free of his embrace, she turned her back on his magnetic eyes.

"I will not marry you!" she blurted in exasperation. "Your affairs are the talk of London. Your current mistress flaunts herself before me every chance she gets. I would find less shame in bearing a bastard then in becoming your wife."

"You'll marry me," he stated tersely.

"Not even if you beat me," she stated with more bravado than she felt.

"If you value your precious family name, you'll marry me," he told her with a hard edge to his voice.

She laughed scornfully. "It doesn't matter to me like it does to Grandfather, Morgan."

"You do not care about anything but yourself, Starlin," he returned flatly. "I promised your grandfather that I would marry you to keep your name from being denounced in society. It was an agreement between gentlemen. I intend to do so—even more so now that the old gent is in a bad way."

"What do you, a man who was once an outlaw on the high seas, care for honor. You traded that before, didn't you—for monetary gain?"

His features totally impassive, he replied, "I would

not expect you to understand, for, after all, you are only a woman and cannot be expected to know what a high price a man sometimes has to pay because of honor."

She wrenched free of him, quite aware of his implication and smarting from it. "My being a woman does not enter into this at all."

"Your being a woman has everything to do with this entire situation." His mouth twisted. "And that, you cannot deny."

It was at that precise moment that the earl's doctor opened the bedroom door and stepped out into the hallway.

"He's holding his own," he offered immediately, closing the door quietly behind him. He motioned for them to be seated and proceeded to explain the earl's condition. "He took a nasty spill. There appear no broken bones. However, I am almost certain he suffered a concussion. He has been failing in health for some time."

"Will . . . he live?" Starlin posed.

"He is stubborn, and has been determined to cling to every last drop of life until he could see you properly wed. He has not wanted to burden you." The physician patted her arm and glanced at his timepiece. "Time, milady, holds all the answers."

"He might . . . die?" Starlin asked shakily.

"He's tough, and he'll fight," Rayne said quietly.

"Yes, he is doing that," the doctor replied, wiping his brow with a handkerchief.

"Has he regained consciousness?" Rayne inquired.

"No, and I don't know for certain when he will. Why don't the two of you go downstairs and get a cup of hot tea. You look as if you could use it."

"I think the doctor has some sound advice," Rayne said, reaching out for Starlin. She deftly avoided him and stepped around him and walked toward the stairs; dismissing him. Like hell, he thought, and quickened his pace to catch up with her.

Outside, Fredrick milled about the grounds waiting for some word of the earl's condition. He saw the wolfhound loping across the lawns and walked toward him. Merlin trotted over. It was then he noticed that the dog had something in his mouth.

"What have you got there, fella?" he said, bending to remove a ragged piece of cloth from the dog's jaws. He examined it carefully. It looked like a piece from a gentleman's cloak. He turned it over in his hand. It was ragged around the edges, as if the dog had snatched the cloak in his teeth and the man had tried to pull away. "You were with Rayne and the earl in the park, weren't you, Merlin?"

Without another word, Fredrick rose and hurried to the front door. He pulled lightly on the bell cord. When the butler opened the door, he requested that Lord Morgan be summoned at once to meet him in the stables.

"The cinch strap is absolute proof," Fredrick said, observing Rayne Morgan examine the piece of burgundy material and then the severed leather strap of the earl's saddle.

"It appears to have been sliced just enough to bear

the earl's weight for a short time."

"Until stress was placed on it, and then it snapped," Fredrick added.

"Someone is going out of their way to bring harm to this family," Rayne intoned coldly.

Fredrick eyed the tall man, and replied slowly, "Aye, it does look that way."

The two men stared at each other.

"I do not strike behind men's backs. And the earl is not a Cambridge."

"But his granddaughter is."

"I have my own method of punishment, Uncle. It will come about all in good time."

"Leave these people out of it. I took this position because I knew that you would come sooner or later. Once you saw that ring on her finger there was little doubt."

"And as soon as you saw it, you knew who should rightfully be wearing it, didn't you, Uncle?" Rayne's narrowed eyes met Fredrick's.

"Yes," Fredrick replied softly.

"My mother."

"Yes."

"And you still say that I should leave Starlin out of this?"

"You don't know for certain how Carl Cambridge came into possession of April's ring, for she was never able to tell you."

Rayne was overwhelmed by black memories. His mouth tightened. "No . . . she was not. She is lost to all of us forever, I am afraid."

"As I wish the ring would have been."

"The girl is the reason you left the *Tempest* shortly

after the incident on Torquay, isn't she?"

"I could not allow myself to remain a party to this vendetta any longer."

"I am beginning to think that even Ely is ready to abandon our cause."

"He has been troubled since the incident in the cave. He discussed his concerns with me. After I heard him describe Starlin's ring, I suspected she was a Cambridge. We've carried this hatred long enough. It is going to destroy all of us if we continue."

"You are growing soft, Uncle," Rayne sneered.

"Nay, only wise," Fredrick replied. "Please listen to me, nephew. Your parents would not have wished this."

Rayne scowled, his eyes sulphurous. "Don't bring them into this. What I do, is for them. What I have become, is because of Carl Cambridge."

"I'll do my best to protect the girl, Rayne," Fredrick warned. "I've grown fond of her. There isn't a mean bone in her body."

"Don't get in my way, Uncle," Rayne warned.

Fredrick faced his sister's child with a stubborn light in his eyes. "As you, I must do what I feel is the right thing." His expression softened. "There has been enough sorrow and heartache. Do you have to destroy her?"

Rayne scowled darkly. The time was near for him to make a choice. Honor and vengeance—or Starlin? "I decided this long ago, and I must see it through until the end."

"Even if it costs you Starlin?"

"She hates me. I take no chance in losing her love," Rayne stated bitterly.

"You are a fool if you truly believe that," Fredrick returned with a hard look. "There is something that binds the two of you to each other. You can not sever it. You have been drawn to this girl from the beginning." He peered at Rayne intently. "Did you ever stop to think that the past, no matter how painful, had to occur in order to secure the path of the future?"

"You sound like Bettina."

"Starlin needs you in her life," Fredrick said with the first real stirrings of hope. "And I think, deep down, that you need her, too. If you exact your vengeance and then leave her, and the earl should not recover, what will become of her? She will be at the mercy of this fiend that struck today."

"I never said anything about leaving her," Rayne replied, turning away and steeling his heart. "She will help me to lure the last—Benton Cambridge."

Fredrick's ire could not be contained. "By all means," he yelled after his nephew's retreating figure, "uphold the family honor at all costs, for a Morgan's pride means everything to him."

"Don't force my hand, Uncle," Rayne flung back over his shoulder. "Let it be enough that I vow not to kill her."

"Yet you'd break her proud spirit!"

Fredrick Morgan stood for a long time after Rayne had left the stable. For too long now Rayne had harbored this hatred, and it was embittering him more every day. Furthermore, a pirate on the high seas could not elude capture forever. And when he was finally brought to justice, he would be hanged. Fredrick did not think that the brash Rayne Morgan had ever stopped to consider the effects on his family if that should ever come to pass.

Several days later the earl regained consciousness. Weak, his eyes shadowed by mauve circles, he gazed up at his anxious granddaughter who'd rarely left his bedside. She was astounded and displeased at his first words.

"Bring him . . . to me," he was barely able to whisper.

"Grandfather—you are awake!" Starlin wept tears of joy and hugged him close.

The earl frowned with impatience. "Starlin," he said more firmly. "Get Morgan, at once. There is no time to waste."

The young woman drew back with a look of utter disbelief. "Why, sir?"

"Don't stand there asking questions, just do as you're told," he said with a faint pat to her hand. "I . . . I must speak with him at once."

Starlin whirled about, her eyes filling with hot tears. It was a great shock for her to hear her grandfather ask to see Rayne Morgan. Why he would wish to talk with that man she did not know. But she knew one thing, she wouldn't allow Morgan to remain alone in the room with the earl. She had no concrete evidence to back up her claim that Morgan had caused all of their misfortune of late, but she didn't trust him just the same.

She summoned a footman and gave him word to seek out the Marquess of Sontavon.

The footman searched the favorite haunts of the gentry, and finally discovered Lord Morgan at the gaming tables of The Solarium, an exclusive club for gentlemen of leisure and finance. He handed Lady Cambridge's card to the doorman and made certain the man realized the matter was of great urgency.

If Rayne was surprised to have Starlin summon him to Eaton Hall, he did not reveal a hint to that fact. With casual indifference, he rose from his chair and collected his winnings. There were groans from his colleagues, but he only shrugged.

"Sorry you're feeling the pinch, gentlemen, but I understand that there's been a change in the earl's condition. I must leave for Eaton Hall at once."

"Is the old chap coming out of it?" an acquaintance of the earl's inquired.

"I can only hope so, sir," Rayne replied, accepting his cloak and hat from the footman.

Upon reaching Eaton Hall, Rayne was ushered immediately to the earl's bedside. Starlin was also in the chamber. After barely glancing at her, he turned his attention to the frail figure upon the bed.

"You sent for me, sir?"

"Promise . . . me," the earl's voice was barely above a whisper and Rayne had to bend his head in order to hear his words, "that you will marry my granddaughter. Do not let this deter your plans. Now more than ever, it is imperative that you marry . . . and protect her."

Starlin stood off to the side, her face pale. "I'll not marry him," she insisted. "You're going to need me, Grandfather!"

The earl scowled at her. "Hush, child, a gentleman's agreement has already transpired between Lord Morgan and myself as to your marriage." He pointed a thin

241

finger at her. "You will not bring shame to my family and go back on it. The wedding will proceed."

Starlin blinked her eyes. Her lips parted to speak, but already the two men were further engaged in conversation and it was more than apparent to her that they no longer acknowledged her presence. Overwhelmed by frustration, the girl fled the room and hurried to the sanctity of her private chambers.

Upon hearing Starlin's bedroom door slam shut, the earl winked at Rayne and propped himself up on his pillows.

"She'll not go against my wishes, lad. I hate having her worry about me, yet I feel that nothing must deter you from marrying Starlin and leaving here."

Rayne shook his head, smiling. "You old fox. I am delighted to see that you are feeling . . . decidedly improved. And while I can see the wisdom of your plan, if Starlin ever finds out about your ploy she'll be furious with both of us."

"She doesn't have to know—unless you tell her."

"Not me. You may rest assured about that."

"Very good." He motioned for Rayne to have a seat in a chair beside the bed. He held Rayne's eyes as he spoke. "I have not been immune to the gossips. I know what is being said about you and that Ellendale woman. Is it true?"

"Lady Ellendale is no longer my mistress, sir," Rayne replied without hesitation.

The earl beamed. "I didn't think so. But you understand, I had to ask. Starlin is riled I know, but you must continue on with the wedding, and immediately after, take Starlin away as you'd planned." An oppressive silence followed, then the earl continued. "I

242

say this because I'm certain that someone tried to kill me by severing Krager's cinch strap. I felt it snap right before I took the spill."

"I know, sir. Your groomsman discovered the cut in the leather and brought it to my attention."

"Starlin must not know, or she'll balk even more at marrying you. She's a protective little thing. Just go . . . and know that you have my blessing." His voice wavered. "And keep her safe from harm."

Rayne could not find the words to reply. He had never been in a more frustrating situation in his life. Part of him was triumphant that his plans were all about to be realized, and the other wished that, somehow, things could have been different between them.

Secluded by the London fog, two men on horseback waited in a moonless hollow for Lady Ellendale's coach to leave the inn. They were dressed like highwaymen, in dark clothes and concealing cloaks. Their eyes met as a couple left the inn, embraced, then went their separate ways. After waiting until the duchess's coach departed, the horsemen hurried to overtake the man's vehicle. Pistol shots reverberated through the night. One of the bandits leaped from his horse to the carriage and overtook the driver. He then brought the team of wild-eyed horses to a halt.

Buckwald Courtland's face was a mask of fear as he was dragged from his carriage to face two fierce-looking bandits.

"Take whatever you want, just don't hurt me," he blubbered.

The taller of the bandits stepped out of the mists, a cold, mocking smile directed at Courtland.

"You!" Courtland gasped. He turned to flee, but the man lunged forward and brought him easily to the ground. With a murderous snarl Courtland's attacker tossed him onto his back and straddled his prone form.

"Fancy you Lady Ellendale's new stud," Rayne Morgan snarled, his fist poised above Courtland's face. "And no doubt, the one behind her clever scheming. I wasn't certain until you pulled that sneak attack the other night. It was you who attacked me, wasn't it?"

"Don't hit me, Morgan!" Courtland screamed in fear, thrashing about, shielding his face with his hands. "I'll tell you whatever you want to know."

Rayne sprinted to his feet jerking Courtland with him. He threw him roughly against the coach. "You spineless jackal. Did you think I would allow that spiteful bitch to keep me from what I want?"

"You don't love Starlin any more than I do. You're after her wealth just like the rest of us," Courtland ventured bravely.

Rayne shook the frightened man until Courtland was sobbing. "Tell me—who is the father of Susan's unborn child?"

"Susan told you she was pregnant to try and get you to break your engagement with Starlin. She isn't pregnant!"

Rayne glared at him. "You're telling me the truth?"

"Yes! For God's sake, please . . . let me go."

"Not so fast, sport. Were you one of those who jumped me?"

Courtland nodded miserably. "She . . . she made me."

Rayne clipped him on the jaw. Courtland sagged against the carriage, but was quickly hauled back into Rayne's grasp. "I owed you that one, Buckwald."

"You and Susan make the perfect couple," Courtland rasped, wiping his bloodied mouth with the back of his sleeve. "She's also a manipulator who will stop at nothing to get what she wants."

Morgan's fist connected with Courtland's jaw once again. This time the man reeled and fell to his knees. Rayne reached for him.

"Rayne!" Ely shouted from his horse. "Let him alone. He isn't the sort to stand up to a beating."

Long legs splayed arrogantly, Morgan stood above the dazed Courtland. "Don't say anything about this to Susan. I'll handle her in my own way. And if you do anything further to try and stop my marriage to Starlin, the next time I'll kill you."

He spun on his heel and swung onto his horse, leaving a shaking Buckwald Courtland to take refuge in the fact that he was still alive.

Chapter Thirteen

It was her wedding day. Nothing she said had changed the earl's mind. Starlin recalled how she'd gone to his room yesterday in a last effort to convince him to call off the wedding. He would not listen.

"This is one time I cannot allow you to have your way, darling. We both know that I will not live forever. Now, more than ever I need to know that your future is secure. You must promise me that you will see this through."

Secure! With a bloody pirate, she'd felt like blurting back at him, wishing he were well enough to listen to her suspicions about Morgan, even read some of the passages in the diary. But fear of Morgan's wrath kept her from doing anything. She could never love that man. She recalled Courtland's sneering words. How Rayne had bragged openly of adding her to his list of conquests. Physically she was bound to him. Want, desire, yes they had that. But never love. Morgan might control her treacherous body, but he would never capture her spirit.

She'd viewed the earl's tired face with concern. "Very well, sir. I'll marry Morgan. But there is absolutely no one who will tell me where I am to live. I intend to live here after the wedding. And I expect no contest from you."

Lord Winfield had not looked pleased. She'd caressed the side of his pale cheek. "You won't change my mind. I love you too much to abandon you when you need me most."

To Starlin's surprise, the earl had not tried to persuade her differently. Despairingly, he'd shaken his head. Starlin had quietly left the room.

With amazing efficiency, Rayne Morgan saw to the last-minute planning. The day of the wedding was warm and sunny, with a faint breeze stirring the treetops and birds singing merrily.

A lovely arbor, shaded by towering elms and ancient limes, would serve as a makeshift chapel. The surrounding rose gardens, their heavenly blossoms perfuming the air, would provide the two small children who would precede the bride with rose petals to strew before her path. Baskets upon baskets of white roses had been placed about the wisteria-entwined arbor where the couple would exchange their vows, and more decorated the grounds beyond. Silver ribbons and bells festooned the trees, and elegant tables amass with silver dishes gleamed brightly in the streaming sunlight.

Servants bustled about seeing to last-minute preparations, arranging buckets of iced champagne and heaping platters of gourmet food. The final touch was the wedding cake, an elegant confection of whipped eggs and cream that had been created by the finest of chefs. It took a half dozen servants to carry it to its place of honor on the bride's table, for it towered over five feet and boasted sugared doves, fresh baby's breath, and a replica of the bride and groom on top.

Starlin stood on her balcony overlooking the area and observed the proceedings with growing unease. She knew it was natural for a bride-to-be to have jitters before the ceremony. Yet this was decidedly more than that. She had so many confusing emotions warring inside her. She had always said she would not marry until she met a man who loved her.

"I wished no bonds upon me," she murmured to herself, "and a man to love me as his equal and share my life. Morgan controls me with his deceitful kisses and whispered lies."

As the hour of the ceremony approached, Starlin dressed solemnly in her finery and went to her grandfather's room to see him one last time before the ceremony. He'd been waiting for her, it seemed, and appeared cheery as she twirled about the room in her flowing gown for his appraisal.

"You are a vision of breathtaking beauty, Starlin dear, and I'm sure your intended will agree when he sees you." The earl was far too weak to leave his bed, but the servants had received permission from his doctor to make a comfortable place for him on the balcony so that he could observe the proceedings.

"I have looked forward to this day for so long," he'd said as Starlin had kissed him before departing. "Try to be happy . . . for me."

Her mood had lightened a bit when she'd seen the

misty look in his eyes. He'd looked so pleased and had been smiling brightly. The earl's last words as she'd closed the door had disturbed her. It was almost as if he were saying good-bye, a prospect that Starlin could not bear to think about.

"Never think that I don't love you, and know that whatever I do is for your benefit, my darling girl. Even when times appear darkest . . . remember that."

How could they possibly get worse? she thought as the fingers of one perfectly manicured hand picked unknowingly at the seed pearls adorning the satin material of her wedding gown. The beautiful dress fit her to perfection: an exquisite creation of ivory satin, tucked in at the waist and billowing downward in yards of French lace. The sleeves were Grecian-style, and quills of silver ribbon and more seed pearls had been hand-sewn over the lace overlay that draped the gown. A diamond tiara secured a white veil in place. Between her breasts nestled the gold medallion with the figure of the scorpion. She closed her eyes and swallowed with difficulty upon hearing Mindy's voice call to her from the bedroom.

"You'd best come inside, mum. It's time. The guests are all beginning to arrive and the groom is prowling restlessly in the foyer."

Smiling encouragingly, she settled the wispy veil over Starlin's face, attached the flowing train, and handed her the bouquet of roses and white orchids.

"Thank you, Mindy, you've been most helpful to me."

"Good luck to you, mum. And much happiness."

A knock sounded on the door and Starlin took a deep breath. It was the signal from Miss Eggie that all

250

was in readiness.

Brilliant sunshine greeted her as she followed behind the entourage of attendants all resplendent in pale blue as they stepped through the terrace doors and into the gardens. Her eyes looked past the sea of faces, to meet his. Her uncle gave her hand to him. Oh, Rayne, Starlin whispered in her heart. Do we really know what it is we are doing?

He stood unmoving, his features perfectly controlled, revealing not one hint of emotion. She thought he looked terribly handsome in an elegant jacket of deep wine with black lapels and a white, ruffled jabot gracing his bronzed throat. She felt those penetrating jade eyes watching her closely, never once straying from hers. The force of those eyes, and the truths she read in their depths, almost made her turn about and flee. And if not for the disgrace she would bring on the earl whom she knew was watching with pride, she would have done so—and never once looked back. For she knew that Morgan did not love her, he was marrying her to keep her good name from disgrace.

An unwanted bride, and soon, an unwanted wife. She stood beside him, staring up into his diamond-hard gaze. Very shortly, after a brief exchange of vows, that obligation would be met.

"Your fingers are like ice, Princess," he murmured. "Don't look so grim, it's not as bad as all that."

"Let's just get this over with, shall we," she whispered tightly. "And then once you've made certain that I can hold my head up in society again, you shall be free to pick up your life where you left off." She saw his gaze rivet upon the gold medallion beneath the lace at her breasts.

251

"I did not think that I had lost it." He stared down at her with steely calm. "A souvenir . . . or trophy?" Something flickered in his face and a cold shaft of fear gripped her heart.

"Security," she replied unemotionally, and was rewarded by discerning a flicker of unease in his eyes. It was then the clergyman began the ceremony, and they turned to face him.

Their vows were repeated in hushed, forced tones, neither of them quite certain if the other would complete the entire ceremony. But, in the end, they did, and before Starlin could shake herself free from her dreamlike state, he'd slipped a wide gold band on her finger and his lips were brushing hers in a cold, unfeeling kiss. There was no love or appreciation in the steely look he bestowed upon her as he raised his head. He appeared almost gloating, as if he'd finally won a long, hard-fought battle. His fingers entwined about hers and she couldn't suppress a shudder. He favored her with a half-smile which failed to quite reach his catlike eyes.

"You're mine now, Lady Morgan, for better or worse . . . until death us do part."

Later, when they were dancing at the reception that boasted every prominent citizen of London, he'd pulled her against him and kissed her cold lips.

"You haven't said very much all afternoon."

"I've been thinking, that's all."

He looked down at her, then raised one tawny brow. "How soon you can make yourself a widow without drawing suspicion?"

"Don't put ideas in my head," she flung back, tossing her head.

"All right, then tell me what you were pondering so deeply."

Her blood was beginning to run hot in her veins with her body pressed against his. "How we could pledge love and fidelity so easily and then both of us stumble over the word obey?"

"We're both very independent people, Starlin. It's only natural that we'd hesitate over a word that hints of shackles and lack of freedom."

"Yes . . . I suppose so," she whispered against the warmth of his throat as he gently kneaded the tense muscles along her spine. She did not protest when she felt him reach up and loosen the ivory pins from her hair. They scattered about their feet on the polished floor, all but forgotten.

His long fingers toyed lazily with the curls tumbling down her back. She did not see him close his eyes as the sweet scent of it filled his nostrils. He remembered all too well the feel of her satin skin, the taste of her, and how erotically she moved in her passion. A hot surge of desire shot through him.

"You make a beautiful bride, Starlin. Every man in this room must be in envy of me right now."

Starlin heard the husky quality of his voice, and leaned her head back to stare up at him. "I doubt that they would envy you long if they knew there was to be no wedding night."

For a long moment he stared into her upraised face before smiling cynically. "Ah yes, the reluctant bride. Very well, I will not touch you if that is what you wish."

"It is," Starlin returned firmly. "And remember, I am only your wife until we find out whether I am with child."

"I forgot for a moment how much you loathe me—or claim to." The last was added with a hint of arrogance.

Starlin was finding it difficult to breathe. She did not know why her pulse was beating so, or for that matter, how she could explain the queer flutter of her heart. She should be feeling nothing but resentment. But the longer she was in his arms the more her senses felt drugged by that overpowering aura that was so much a part of him. He only smiled at her black expression, that innocent half-boyish grin of his that drove her to seething anger. Her violet eyes narrowed and she suddenly longed for the night to end.

"Stop holding me so tightly," she demanded. "I can hardly draw a breath."

Almost as if he wanted to prove his dominance of her, he ignored her protests and forced her to remain close in his arms. She could feel the solid muscle of his body, his long, lean legs, and a quiver of desire in his touch. She trembled with reminders of how good he could make her feel.

"You don't hate me near as much as you'd like me to believe." He lifted a finger to trace it along the graceful arch of her nose, down over her moist, pouting lips.

Starlin gave a breathless murmur that was lost in her uncle's request for a dance.

"I say, Morgan, give the rest of us a go, will you?"

Her mouth trembled as Rayne bowed low over her hand and whispered, "Until later, Lady Morgan, where there will be only the two of us."

Starlin's uncle beamed as he swept her about the floor. "It's obvious to everyone how much you two care for each other by looking at the blush on our little bird's cheeks."

She longed to tell him that it was not a bride's blush

254

on her cheeks, but a stain of seething anger because of an insufferable rogue who thought he controlled her emotions with ease.

"Can't tell you, my dear, how happy your aunt and I are that you've finally come to your senses and married, and a fine chap, too."

"Yes, I've heard the very same comment from several others today," Starlin stated with forced calmness. She felt tears of rage pricking behind her eyelids and wondered forlornly how she was going to make it through the entire evening. Her uncle was clucking soothingly at her.

"Just nervous jitters . . . they'll pass come morning, pet."

Starlin could only sigh. She was to lose track of her husband as the long evening wore on. She was growing tired and irritable, and was ready to slip away to the suite of rooms which had been prepared for the newlyweds in the east wing. Although she planned on retiring at once to her own bedroom and locking the door behind her, she knew that she could not leave until her husband came to claim her. And he had simply disappeared.

She remembered having seen Rayne and Susan Ellendale talking earnestly at the side of the room. Her eyes searched the sea of faces. She thought she caught a glimpse of Rayne leading Susan Ellendale out into the gardens. Damn him! she fumed. Why did he have to humiliate her by flaunting his mistress in front of their wedding guests? She hadn't wanted to invite the Ellendales, but the earl had insisted, reminding her that protocol demanded it. A sick feeling gripped her.

*   *   *

255

Susan was glaring accusingly at Rayne as they stood in the gazebo.

"You pulled a nasty trick on me, Rayne darling. And now I'm just going to have to spoil the honeymoon, I'm afraid."

"Underhanded of me, wasn't it?" he drawled.

"You can rest assured that it will be your last—"

His sharp laugh cut her off. "You never give up, do you, Susan? Now will you just calm down? I have everything under control."

"You . . . do?"

"I couldn't give you an answer sooner because I had an obligation to fulfill first, and now that it's done, I'll take care of you, you can be certain of that."

Starlin had heard her husband's voice coming from the direction of the gazebo. Intending on confronting him, she had just approached the gazebo when she heard Rayne and Susan discussing plans . . . and the woman's pregnancy!

Starlin spun around and walked quickly deep into the gardens in an effort to flee her own thoughts. Images began taunting her—and every one of Susan Ellendale in Rayne's arms, smiling, gloating, and loving her husband.

Rayne didn't give Lady Ellendale a chance to say another word before he was propelling her toward the ballroom, his hand splayed against her back. To her mortification, he directed her before her startled husband and promptly congratulated him on his impending fatherhood. Everyone standing around began to offer their congratulations. The duke and duchess both stood in stunned silence and accepted the well wishes.

Rayne could not help grinning when he saw the duke grab his wife's arm, a very unpleasant smile on his face. He leaned over and whispered something in her ear. Susan went pale.

Starlin sat dejectedly in the garden. Her marriage was over before it had begun. She didn't know why that thought upset her so.

Suddenly, she was grabbed from behind and a hand clamped over her mouth. Kicking and thrashing, she was dragged away from her home. Something dark and soft fluttered down over her head and was swiftly wrapped about her entire body. Steellike arms banded around her. She struggled wildly, but to no avail, and she almost had to laugh at the ridiculous picture she must make being abducted in her wedding gown.

"You'd better calm down, little spitfire," a deep, raspy voice warned, "or I'll have to get rough."

Starlin almost laughed. God forbid he get any rougher. And then fear took over as she felt herself being lifted and carelessly tossed over a broad shoulder. There was a coiled tension in the muscles that met the touch of her body. Like an animal stalking, he moved stealthily through the night. Leather boots crunching on gravel, night creatures calling and . . . were those whispering voices that she heard? Jingling harness and the muffled snorts of horses drifted through the confines of the cloak. And even though not a word has been spoken Starlin realized that some horrible fiend was kidnapping her.

Rayne! her mind screamed. Help me! Mentally, a vision of her husband holding Susan Ellendale crossed her mind. He had sent someone to kidnap her so he could go off with that woman. Terror sprouted inside. This was her worst nightmare realized. An anguished sob escaped through the confining cloth.

Completely disoriented, she could only assume that her abductor had reached a carriage by the wayside and had dumped her rather carelessly inside and slammed the door. A sharp whistle, the crack of a whip, and the vehicle lept forward with a creak of hinges. Beside her, she heard a chuckle of triumph. They were rumbling over cobblestoned streets at such a furious pace that Starlin was bouncing about on the cushions. A dog howled in the distance, a lonely, plaintive sound. She tested the confining garment and found she could not manage to work her arms free. Where were they going? And what were they planning on doing with her? One thing was definite: Rayne Morgan was most certainly behind this sinister plot. No wonder he hadn't seemed disturbed when she had told him there wouldn't be a wedding night.

An hour—or hours—passed. Starlin had been lifted from the carriage and carried a distance. She now felt a violent rocking motion that made her fear she might be sick. Thunder rumbled ominously in the distance. She whimpered slightly as the cloak was removed. It was totally black here. She couldn't see a thing.

"If you scream, I'll gag you," the barely discernible voice warned.

She kicked out with her foot.

"I'm getting real tired of this," he growled as he grabbed her.

A blindfold was quickly secured over her eyes. She wondered if she'd possibly heard the sound of the docks, smelled the salty air of the sea. The distant echo of crashing waves drifted to her, confirmed her suspicions. Her abductor was taking her out to sea! Perhaps to sell her into slavery!

"Why are you doing this?" she said raggedly. There was no reply.

Her hearing strained to pick up any sound that might give her some indication who the man was. She heard nothing, only his steady breathing.

The floor beneath her feet seemed to roll. Weak-kneed, Starlin felt as if she might fall. She didn't know if her senses were still in confusion from the wild carriage ride, or if her body was truly swaying, forcing her to search with outstretched hands for anything solid to cling to.

A bed, she thought, as her knees bumped the wood frame. With relief, she sank down upon it and clutched her arms about her.

"I know you're there, you bloody cur. And while I have no idea why you've done this thing, I can assure you my grandfather will find me and you will pay!" She was gasping for breath, the stays of her corset biting into her.

Hands came out of nowhere to touch her. Starlin gave a cry of alarm and attempted to tear at the blindfold. His strong fingers were relentless as they captured hers. Terrified, she kicked forward and felt brief triumph when her satin slipper connected with his shinbone. It was like a kitten swatting at a mountain lion. He didn't so much as flinch, just laughed down deep in his throat.

Starlin did not want to beg. But she could not help the pitiful sob for mercy that escaped her upon feeling long fingers slide along her arm.

"My grandfather will pay you if you do not harm me . . . I swear . . . anything."

"I didn't spirit you away for money."

His voice was so gravelly Starlin could barely understand him. And the blindfold dulled her senses.

"Then why?"

"All in good time. If you do exactly as I tell you."

It was so hot in the stuffy room that she could feel sweat trickling down her neck and between her breasts. She was growing light-headed and she wished now that she hadn't allowed Mindy to lace her stays so unbearably tight. Her struggles cost her badly needed oxygen. She felt faint. She floated backward, could feel his warm breath on her cheek. The back of his hand brushed lightly across her cheek, slid downward.

Lord, please no, she cried inwardly, hands and feet flailing in every direction to stay him off. Growling softly, he held her down, then wiped her face with a cloth. His fingers skimmed along her shoulder, then downward to curl in the low neckline of her dress.

Starlin tried to twist out of his grasp, and in doing so, his fingers tightened instinctively on the material, ripping her dress to the waist. His breathing quickened at the sound of tearing cloth and she knew she could do little to stop him from doing with her what he would. He made short work of the imprisoning stays, and great gulps of air burst into her lungs. Revived, she could only dwell on being in the arms of this brutal stranger clothed only in a thin, satin chemise.

With a primitive yowl, she bent forward and bit him on the forearm. Even through the cloth of his jacket, she knew she'd managed to inflict some pain, for he

260

grunted harshly before grasping hold of her. Wisps of silken hair cascaded about them as she tossed her head and bared white teeth like a cornered vixen.

"You'll not have me without a fight, you Satan's son!" she raged.

"You're making this a helluva lot more difficult, lady." His hands threaded in her hair and she automatically winced, expecting him to jerk roughly. But he only gave a slight tug toward him, and she knew then what it was he wanted. Frantically, she tried to resist by pulling the opposite way. He tugged harder this time, slowly drawing her across the tangle of sheets. With a rough jerk, she found herself sprawled helplessly between his spread legs.

By her position, and his muscular thighs wrapped about her, she could tell he was sitting on the edge of the bed. He tightened his long legs and immediately had her upper body pressed intimately against him, her hands laying flat upon his thighs, her knees resting on the floor between his boots. Both of them were breathing hard.

Trembling beyond control, Starlin shook from head to toe. She prayed that he would not hurt her and would be quick. Instinctively she closed her eyes when she felt him slip the straps of her chemise down her shoulders. His fingers kneaded the tense muscles. Starlin simply could not relax.

"Loosen up a bit . . . that's right, let your mind think of nothing but how good it feels."

Starlin could not believe that his words calmed her, his touch even more so. A primitive throbbing began, pulsed deep within her, demanding, coiling tightly in a sweet ache. What was happening to her?

261

How could she be enjoying this, Starlin wondered frantically. She should be fighting him—to her death if need be—before she'd allow him to take such liberties. Yet strange as it seemed, there was something oddly familiar about the hard, lean body pressed so close to hers. She found herself caught in the same emotions that had enslaved her that explosive night in the cave.

In bittersweet despair, she envisioned a dark, ruggedly handsome outlaw who still held her in his powerful vise even though it was another man now who appeared to have every intention of making love to her.

His hands slid down her arms, kneaded the rigid muscles beneath the dew-soft skin along her arms. Outside, the wind had increased, sighing forlornly against the porthole, shaking the craft around them until Starlin imagined them at hell's gates. A sudden strong gust blew the porthole open, cool air swirled about her naked shoulders. He shielded her nakedness with his body. More than anything Starlin longed to tear away the blindfold and confront her captor. Yet even though he hadn't been especially brutal as yet, she still did not trust him.

She could feel the heat of his gaze sear her, and knew exactly what he had on his mind. To her horror, her nipples rose impudently against the wispy material of her chemise. She heard him inhale sharply, but he did not touch her again. Desire spun and whirled in the room, making them both tremble with the intensity.

Starlin would not be able to recall later who it was who made the first move that brought her lips to his. She only knew that her limbs were no longer able to resist, feeling suddenly drained of all energy. She was helpless against him. She knew she should shout vile curses, rake his face with her nails, but in a tiny part of her darkest soul, an answering need was betraying her. She stirred against him, loving the feel of him and hating herself because of it. Her lips parted freely beneath his sensual probings and her tongue eagerly entwined with his.

Right or wrong, her hands slid eagerly from within his grasp and upward to clasp about his neck.

His mouth seared like a brand upon hers. Again and again his tongue plundered her mouth, her cold lips brushed across her teeth. Instinctively, she responded to the startling warmth of his kiss. She moaned softly, desire igniting within her. He knew women well, of that Starlin had no doubt. His touch was heaven, his kisses lingering. He sought out every warm, intimate place within the trembling hollows of her mouth, kissing her ruthlessly, drawing her to him.

The sea breeze eddied about the room tantalizing her nostrils and bringing with it the faintest scent of lime. She thought surely she must be imagining it, certain that she was wishing it so. A sudden chill coursed down her spine.

Self-reproach replaced passion, and brought tears to her eyes. You stupid fool, she chastised herself. Can't you see what this man is doing, what Rayne prompted him to do? He's playing a game with you—sport for his kind—clearly in retaliation for all the contempt you previously directed at Morgan. No doubt her husband was back in England spending their wedding night with his ladyship, Susan Ellendale. She recalled the conversation she'd overheard in the gardens. Starlin's mouth curled in bitter contempt and she tore free of her captor.

"My husband is behind this horrid scheme, isn't he?" she lashed out.

There was nothing but tense silence. Starlin took a tremulous breath. "You don't have to answer me, I know he is. And I imagine he encouraged you to enjoy your perverse game to the fullest. Well, I say bloody hell to you, and him!"

A husky laugh danced on her ears. The wretched beast found her an amusing plaything, did he? she thought with rising ire. She swung outward with her closed fist, missing him, but feeling some measure of satisfaction when she heard him take a step backward. Her mistake was in reaching upward to grab the blindfold. Her wrists, first one then the other, were immediately grasped between strong fingers. She tried to resist but her strength was no match for his. With persuasive pressure he slowly spread her arms wide, and held them there. Neither of them moved for several moments. He stood so close to her that the heat of his body seemed to envelop Starlin's in dark, sensual promise. He wanted her. She could feel his desire in the room, reaching out to her . . . drawing her to him.

One hand released her wrist, trailed long fingers across the soft skin of her inner arm.

Burning . . . luring . . . Starlin jerked backward.

"Don't touch me!" she cried.

He ignored her plea and grabbed her wrist again.

She felt his gaze and knew just by the iron grip of his fingers that it would be arrogantly commanding. She sensed those mysterious eyes moving over her, dwelling on slightly parted lips, the pulse throbbing rapidly in her throat and lingering heatedly on the rounded outline of her breasts visible, she knew, through the delicate ivory chemise.

Starlin thought desolately that she had goaded him too far, and that he would take her now, completely, and with little mercy. Desperation pumped through her veins and made her body tremble.

A plaintive message, unspoken yet somehow understood, seemed to pass between them and suddenly he made a harsh sound under his breath. Before she could think to draw away from him he'd spun her slight form about and bound her wrists behind her back with some sort of cloth. She flinched as he tied the knot, and although snug, it did not bite into her flesh. He led her over to the bed, sat her down, and methodically removed her shoes and stockings. When he'd tossed them aside, he nudged her.

"Lie back," he demanded in that whispery voice that gave her goose flesh.

"No!" she replied.

Her body came in contact with the mattress so fast that she gave a startled gasp. A firm hand held her there. "You do what you're told with me, my dear," he said harshly.

"If you try and . . . and . . ."

"Fight me again, and I might," he warned in a threatening voice.

Starlin swallowed over her fear and slowly lay back. She gave a strangled yelp when he flipped her rather indifferently onto her side. Something comforting fluttered down around her. A cover—tucked in around her legs and gently draped about her shoulders.

"Get some sleep. You're going to need it."

She heard him moving away. The door opened then closed. At last, she was completely alone. And with that, came the doubt. A frightening sensation assailed her. It reminded her of how she'd felt after her parents had disappeared. Visions wavered like somber ghosts behind her eyelids, intensifying her despair.

As the hours slowly passed, she mulled over her predicament a thousand times, yet found no solution. She was his prisoner—bound on a journey she knew not where. She was filled with hurt and confusion, and just before she fell into a troubled slumber, she thought of how ruthlessly her husband had betrayed her. He had not wanted to risk the chance that she might be pregnant, an annulment out of the question. Now he was free.

Her captor saw to her every need. For the next day or so she did little but doze fitfully and try to guess by the monotonous motion of the ship how far out to sea they'd traveled.

Whenever she could summon the strength, Starlin worked at the knot securing her bindings. To little avail; it held fast.

Endless hours went by. Night or day? She had no concept. He had brought her two day's worth of meals, she thought. After she'd promptly thrown the first plateful in the direction she thought him to be, he kept her hands tied and fed her himself. It was not a time either of them appeared to enjoy. She would eat only what he could pry into her mouth, and could not know that with each spoonful he would move backward a step or two.

Although the blindfold stayed over her eyes, he allowed her to pace when he was in the cabin. He didn't converse with her, only ordered her about. She assumed he only sat with her then because he didn't want her bumping about the cabin without someone to look out for her. Bruised flesh did not bring as high a price as a creamy, unmarred body. By this time, Starlin was certain this was her fate.

She would be sold, might have been already, to the man who now sat across the room from her.

When was this nightmare journey going to end? she brooded angrily. She spun about a bit unsteadily to face the direction she felt his eyes watching . . . watching . . . always staring.

"You really are the worst kind of coward, you know," she could not help but snap at him. She cocked her head, a tumbled mass of raven hair falling over one shoulder to spill across her heaving breast. "Are you afraid of me? Is that why you keep me bound so securely?" When there was no response, she goaded further, fury pumping through her.

"I believe you've rightfully earned your place in hell for this evil thing you've done—right beside my husband."

Starlin almost regretted her words, certain he meant to snap her neck upon feeling those now familiar fingers close around the back of the slender column. He tightened his grip and propelled her foward. Just as abruptly, she was stopped short, a firm hand clamping on her shoulder.

The binding around her hands was removed, her stiff wrists chafed by his competent fingers before he whirled her around and she felt those eyes once more.

She was pleasantly surprised to feel a cool, wet cloth upon her arms. It was soothing, and must have been

267

scented by attar of roses, for the pleasing scent wafted about her.

"I thought you'd like this," he said throatily.

"The bath, yes. Your hands upon me make my flesh crawl," she retorted bluntly.

He chuckled, seemingly unaffected by her insult. "We both know that's a lie."

"You—"

The soapy cloth touched her lips. "Ah-ah, ladies shouldn't use bad words! And stand still, or I'll leave the rest of you unwashed."

Seething, yet willing to bear his hands upon her if it meant she would feel clean again, Starlin gritted her teeth and submitted to his brisk ministrations without protest until she felt his fingers on the ties of her chemise. Her hands immediately came upward to clasp his.

"No." She put her volatile emotions into the single word, and he must have understood how strongly she felt, for he did not force the issue.

Instead, she felt him take her hand and fold her fingers around the cloth. "Then you do it," he said in that muffled tone.

"I'd like to." Eagerly she allowed him to lead her, dip her hands downward into a cool bowl of water. It felt divine.

With a sigh she splashed some on her arms. She used the cloth to scrub every inch of her that she could reach without having to remove the chemise.

Down her arms once more, over the tops of her breasts, her throat, and unable to bear thinking of leaving her bare feet dirty, accepted his hand on her upper arm as an anchor so that she might wipe them clean, wiggling her toes and smiling for the first time.

It wasn't until she'd quickly swiped along her calves upward over her legs, the cloth disappearing beneath the hem of the chemise, that he released her with an indiscernible mutter and grabbed her hand. It was rigid as steel and his breathing uneven.

As though anxious to leave, he quickly rebound her wrist and sat her upon the bed. Starlin smirked when the door slammed. The knot was loose. She began working on it frantically—and was still tugging on it when night fell.

It was the low, rolling sound of thunder and the gentle patter of rain overhead that awoke her. She couldn't recall when exhaustion had claimed her, but she had fallen asleep.

Certain they had sailed into the depths of hell and envisioning all manner of wretched souls prowling about, she jerked upright in terror at the sound of the door crashing open against the wall. The wind rushed into the room.

"Who's there?" she murmured breathlessly.

She sat up, ears straining to pick up any sound. To her amazement, Starlin realized she was very much alone.

As the tempest moaned and the wind howled, she envisioned a fierce storm that would certainly dash the boat upon jagged reefs, leaving her to fend for herself trussed up like a Sunday goose! The blackguard! he was probably busy saving his own neck. The least he could have done was send someone to untie her.

She struggled with her bindings, and eventually

undid the knot.

With a vengeance, she tore off the blindfold and sat blinking in the shadowed room. There was no light, only that which spilled through the doorway and porthole. Scooting quickly off the mattress she sprinted toward freedom.

What she was going to do once she reached topside she had not contemplated. But surely, she thought, there would be someone on the boat who would help her. And if all else failed, perhaps she could bribe them with promise of money. The floor lurched beneath her bare feet. She was tossed about like a feather in a windstorm and several times she bumped into furniture. She stifled an outcry, the fresh sea air luring her onward. A quiver of hope ran through her upon reaching the door. And then, without warning, her body came up against a hard, immovable object.

"Going somewhere?"

The voice was not muffled. It was distinct. And she was dazed by the sound of that all-too-familiar drawl. Some inner voice had been telling her all along who it was that held her prisoner, and why his touch should instill such burning desire within her. Every muscle she possessed suddenly froze. She found herself staring down at dark Hessian boots that gleamed even through the shadows. Her wide eyes traveled slowly upward, over thickly muscled legs in tight-fitting breeches, skimming past a broad chest covered by snow-white linen, coming to rest on a granite hard face. Her eyes widened.

"Morgan! You . . . you bastard!" she hissed.

"I take it you're not exactly thrilled with my little honeymoon surprise," he replied dryly.

270

"I should have known only you could do something this despicable!"

Before she could think to move, he'd taken her chin between unrelenting fingers and gripped it tightly.

"Enough, Starlin," he ordered gruffly. "I don't have time to listen to any of your childish tirades. I have my hands full just trying to keep us secured in this cove until the waters calm. I only came down to make certain you were all right." He whirled her about, a lean finger prodding her between her shoulder blades. "Go back to bed. It's the safest place for you right now."

She turned on him so quickly that he almost looked surprised.

"As if I would do anything you told me to do, you bloody pirate! I have no intention of staying down here . . . and I insist that you return me to my grandfather this instant!"

"You may insist all that you want. But it's not likely to happen," he replied in a cold, dispassionate voice.

"You no good conniver," she hissed, her eyes rounding in fury.

One of his thick eyebrows quirked upward. "If I were you, I'd think about curbing that sharp tongue, my dear. If you don't, I just might have to gag you again."

Starlin's eyes darkened to smoky violet. "I don't have to do anything! You and I are finished, and I never want to see you again." She glared at him like some wild untamable siren bent on destroying him.

"You haven't realized yet, have you?"

"Just what is that supposed to mean?" she glared before searching the room frantically for some clothes. She thought about wrapping up in a sheet if she had to. "I'm getting out of this cabin, and then I'm certain I'll

271

find at least one person on this vessel who will listen to my plight and help a lady in distress."

His mouth twisted upward in a broad smile. "I rather doubt that."

"If I offer them money, they will. For undoubtedly they are all just as corrupt as you and can be persuaded by the promise of gold," she told him with a look of triumph.

"That might have been true if . . ."

"If what?" she demanded tersely.

"If there was anyone else on board this boat but you and me."

Chapter Fourteen

Starlin stared up at her husband's face. Tense emotions quivered through the room.

"We are alone?" Her voice was hoarse with dread.

His mouth curved into a nasty smile. "The happy couple sailing off to begin their new life."

"What is that supposed to mean, Morgan?"

"It's quite clear I would think. It's just you and me, and miles and miles of ocean."

There was no stopping the fear that gripped her. She had suffered all of this because of him!

"I have never hated you more than I do at this moment." She was almost weeping with frustration, and to add to her agony, Starlin observed his handsome features come alive with amusement.

"By your tone, dear wife, am I to take it you are disappointed to find it is your husband who you've allowed to sample your delectable charms?"

"I never consented to your vile touch!" she said defensively, a telltale blush staining her cheeks. "And for you to think that I was enjoying your disgusting actions only proves once again how crude a man you really are."

Insolently, he looked her up and down, his easy expression slowly fading. His eyes smoldered now, twin beacons of fire in the dim room. "Believe what your conscience tells you. But know this. In the beginning, I had no intention of touching you. Your desire reached out to me, drew me to you."

Starlin clamped her hands over her ears. "No! It's not true!"

"You know it is," he growled. Before she could protest he'd cupped her face in his hands, his lips searing down upon hers so fiercely that he took her breath away. She wanted him to go on kissing her forever, yet knew she could not. He was only playing games with her emotions again, cold, cruel games that she must make certain he did not win. She had to protect herself, place a barrier of ice around her heart as she had always done, and never again allow him to penetrate it. She was terribly frightened at the moment by the intensity of her need for him. Even blindfolded, her body had known his touch, had surrendered to it unhesitantly. Starlin fought against the overwhelming desire inside her. It was useless.

She molded her body against him, seeking more of his warm mouth and those sure, stroking fingers that were sending shivers of delight wherever they touched. With a move so sudden her head snapped backward, Rayne broke the kiss.

Her eyes slowly opened and met his. She saw his flash with triumph.

"So you don't want me," he drawled in that mocking tone she hated.

"I'd rather die than suffer your lovemaking again," she stated emphatically.

A grin slanted his mouth. "You can stop the melodramatics," he said with quiet firmness. "And when I decide to make love to you, you know you won't stop me."

Her hands curled into claws and she swiped outward to catch him along the side of the neck.

"No man has the right to my bed unless I want him," Starlin cried.

His eyes went black with fury. "I have the right. I am your husband."

Having almost forgotten their bizarre wedding day, which at the moment seemed like part of a dream, Starlin's heart twisted in acknowledgment. She was his chattel to do with as he chose.

"By law," she said tightly. "But it does nothing to alter my feelings of hate and contempt for you. You are a liar, a womanizer, and if my suspicions prove correct, a thief. If you bed me against my will, I shall hate you forever."

"I have challenged men for slurs to my name that were less than yours."

"You do not frighten me any longer." Her words were brave, yet seeing his mouth tighten and a nerve pulse in his jaw, she felt her courage begin to fade.

A thin smile split his lips.

"That is the last thing that I wish to do," he said tauntingly. "I prefer to elicit other emotions far more pleasant to the senses. And when I take you, Starlin, it will not be by force."

"You told me there would be an annulment!" she lashed back.

275

"I lied." Mesmerized by the creamy vision of femininity before him, Rayne was not prepared for the hot rush of desire that suddenly overwhelmed his common sense. He met her wide gaze with cool eyes.

"I despise you," Starlin hissed.

He was upon her again, so fast that she only had a moment to cry out softly as he yanked her to him.

"You planned all of this from the beginning, didn't you?" she gasped.

"I know that's what you want to believe," he returned, eyes glittering in that way which made her feel as if a storm had just raged through her.

Rayne suddenly wished an end to the bickering and longing, wished for the fury to turn to passion, the night to be spent making love. His hand slid down her arm to grasp her waist, tug gently.

"Stop fighting me, will you?"

Her eyes sought his, searching for truths there but seeing nothing. She bit her lower lip, a trace of hurtful tears in her voice. "What do you expect? You've taken me away from everything that I love. I have no idea where we are going, or why? And I can't help thinking how easy it will be for you to . . . get rid of me when you become bored. And you will . . . I know it."

"I'm not so sure of that," he said softly, surprised that her tears should bother him.

She swallowed with difficulty, looking up into his face. "For sooner or later the passion will die, and we will be left with nothing."

He shook his head slowly. "That is the one thing that we will always have." He was watching her closely.

The room was suddenly confining to Starlin. She could not stand his nearness, or the way his eyes

276

caressed her in a way they'd never done before. Or was it just that she'd never truly taken notice before? What was the depth of feeling she saw within that jade gaze? And how could he expect her to choose, or why should she even want to so desperately when she knew that there could only be one answer. The words formed on her lips, trembled there. She was struggling with herself, torn between the truth about him, and the desire to forget it all and surrender to his touch. Yet, macabre thoughts danced in her head, and brought to light something she'd not considered until this minute. Her lips tightened to a thin line.

"You'd like for me to fall into your arms, wouldn't you? My money, my properties, and if I fall in love with you, assurance that I will never tell anyone that you are the outlaw, Scorpio."

Frustration, not rage, darkened his features. "I never planned this marriage any more than you did—and I don't recall ever requesting your love, madam. As you've told me time and again, love may be the one emotion that I can never feel. But for whatever reason, I did marry you—and you now belong to me. Moreover, as your husband, I did not kidnap you. I spirited you away in such a fashion in order to save myself a scene much like this one."

"Forgive me for mentioning that one word that you so detest," she said haughtily. "I'm quite certain that when it suits you, you will tell me what really prompted you to marry me—and kidnap me."

Rayne laughed in bitter contempt. "My beautiful Ice Princess, if you only knew how much you really need me." He halted momentarily, then added deadly soft, "And how easily I could have destroyed you at any time . . . if I had chosen to."

"You're right about yourself, you don't have the ability to love anyone, for if you did, you could never have done such an awful thing and have left my grandfather to wonder what has happened to me."

"Did you ever consider the fact that perhaps he is not wondering?"

His calmly spoken words shocked her immensely. She shook her head fiercely from side to side. "He would never have agreed to this! He loves me more than his own life!"

"Yes, he does. And perhaps when a person cares that much they will go to any lengths, or make any sacrifice, to protect those who mean everything to them."

"You expect me to believe that this bizarre scheme was enacted to protect me?"

"The earl wanted you away from England for good reason. He asked me to see you someplace safe, and knowing how you would protest, I devised a scheme that would catch you off guard and attract little attention. The servants and the guests were simply told that the happy bridal couple had slipped away quietly to begin their honeymoon. It was all done without a fuss, and with no interference from you."

"I know that Grandfather's spill was no accident. And I'm puzzled that you truly seem concerned over it." Her eyes were glacial. "Who is responsible?"

"There are several who stand to gain much if he is out of the way."

"You included," she said bitterly.

He gave a mirthless laugh. "Your admirers tagged you proper, milady. You are a cold-hearted temptress if ever I've met one." His eyes stabbed her. He bowed

278

mockingly. "It appears we have nothing more to say to each other. You may have the cabin to yourself. I shall bunk elsewhere, for I have no intention of taking an unwilling woman to my bed."

She pierced him with a malevolent glare. "Especially when there's a very willing one waiting back in London. You've tricked me, lied to me! I know you can hardly think of being shackled to me when you really long to go back to her."

"You have goaded me too far this time," he thundered, fury in his eyes. "And at this moment I damned well feel like saying what is on my mind. I regret having married you as much as you loathe being shackled to me. You may be the most beautiful woman I've ever seen, but never have I known a woman who is such a shrew."

Starlin trembled from the roiling emotions inside her. How could anything ever be right between them? He was heartless and unfeeling, and felt nothing but contempt for her. "God help me if I should be carrying your child," she said woodenly. "For I don't honestly know what I will do if I am."

The look in his eyes was almost demonic. "Nor I. You are right—I don't love anyone. But I do protect what is mine, and you do belong to me. I suggest you get used to it."

Rebellion pumped through her. "I knew there was something darkly dangerous about you the first time I saw you. I won't be a victim of your scheming. I'll find some way to get away from you."

"No," he drawled, "you won't."

"I will find a way!" she screamed. Eyes flaring wildly, Starlin bolted around him and made a mad dash for the door, never once looking back as she ran headlong up the narrow stairs not even considering that there was nowhere to go.

Rayne strode after her. With her bare feet and the deck slick with moisture, Starlin could very well be racing straight to disaster.

Even anchored within a sheltering cove, the tiny sloop, which bore the name *Ice Princess,* tossed and rolled in the angry sea. Up ahead, sprinting ghostlike across the top deck through the light drizzle, Starlin sought any means of escape from the man who had humiliated her so terribly. The small craft lurched crazily in the wind-whipped sea. Her bare feet slid this way and that on the slick teak and she had to fight to maintain her balance, hands grasping frantically at whatever was near in an effort to remain upright.

Starlin couldn't see through the gloom. It was black as the depths of hell and just as frightening. Overhead, the wind moaned a siren's song through the rigging. The sound of booted feet hurrying behind her drove her onward in desperate flight. There wasn't any way she was going to allow him near her again. She would brave death before she'd stay on this boat with him.

"Starlin!"

Rayne's voice reached her over the wind and she had to laugh at herself for thinking he sounded concerned.

Unexpectedly, the ship careened wildly and she was flung up against the rail. Her fingers gripped it like a lifeline. She spun about, eyes wide with expectation, knowing what choice she must now make. Through the fine gray drizzle she could barely discern the outline of the far shore—the English shore. Glancing back to the stairs, she saw him advancing toward her.

His golden hair was damp from the mists and clinging to his scowling brow. His white shirt was open to the waist, the full sleeves plastered about his thick, muscular arms. He looked like the pirate she remembered from Torquay, untamed, and dead set on breaking her.

"Don't come any closer, Rayne, I warn you!" she yelled, watching him warily.

He advanced cautiously. "Don't do anything foolish," he warned, yet by her wild eyes and tensely poised form, he knew that she was desperate enough to do just that.

He slowly extended his hand.

"If you so much as make a move . . ." she threatened, glancing furtively over her shoulder first at the sight of land in the distance then down at the sea lashing angrily at the sides of the boat. They appeared to be anchored in some kind of cove. Lightning zigzagged across the sky, the rigging snapping and cracking over her head. She was scared to death. If she only had a minute to think she could consider how far she would have to swim to shore. But he was closing in on her, and she had no time to reason anything but escape. She was a strong swimmer, she could reach the beckoning shore.

"You'll not make the distance with the waves," he warned.

She lunged upward to swing her legs over the rail and sit on the narrow ledge. Her fingers gripped the rail tightly behind her.

Slowly, carefully so as not to frighten her, he moved closer. "Starlin," he called huskily. Her head swung around and their gazes locked. She regarded him with uncertainty. Against the explosive brilliance of the storm-lashed sky, she had never looked more beautiful.

Eyes of smoky violet spewed hatred at him. Her small chin lifted defiantly. Water ran in rivulets over her bare shoulders, her long hair clung wetly to the enticing curve of her breasts.

"You can't keep me prisoner. I won't stand for it."

"Even if I let you go, you'll still be my prisoner, and you know it."

Her eyes were enormous as her proud spirit struggled with the implication. She did not wish to acknowledge it, refused to. But still a little voice inside her would not be still. *He has a powerful hold on you, and if you allow him to touch you one more time, you'll be lost.*

"Damn you, Rayne Morgan, for ever coming into my life!" she blurted in frustration.

His face lay in shadow, but his voice was strong and sure. "Stop this, Starlin, and for once in your life, give in to someone else."

"You know we're no good for each other," she persisted, eyes imploring him. "Just let me go."

"All right! Jump if you're so all fired set on doing so," he snarled suddenly, tired of it all. Inwardly he reasoned how quickly it would all be over with then. Revenge would be his. All that he had to do was stand back and let her jump. He saw her move, and lunged forward. Damn! The little hellcat was going to do it.

Starlin wasn't prepared for his quick movements. She screamed in frustration as he'd caught her about the waist in an ironlike grip and pulled her over the rail into his arms. Her anguished sobs echoed across the crashing waves.

"No! Don't touch me . . . don't hold me," she

panted. "We're poison to each other." Bare wet legs, lithe and shapely, tangled about his thickly muscled calves in an effort to stay his movements.

Even when the schooner began to pitch, threatening to toss them both over the side, Starlin continued to struggle. But there was no breaking his grip. Suddenly, Rayne's head snapped up and his point of concentration fixed on the motion of the vessel. He was certain the wheel had broken free of the line he'd tied fast and was now spinning freely. If he did not secure it they would end up battered on the rocks. Geysering spray boiled upward over the side of the boat and pelted them with its stinging lash.

"I must reach the quarterdeck and secure the wheel," he told her. He forced her along with him.

She did not go willingly, but at last Rayne was able to reach the helm. He quickly grabbed hold of the wheel and gripped it firmly. The schooner ceased to lurch violently.

Rayne drew the exhausted girl into the curve of his body where she fit perfectly against him. She was rigid at first, but after a while her head lolled back onto his chest and she dozed.

Dreamily, she felt the sinewy muscles flex beneath his shirt each time that he spun the wheel through his fingers, and tried hard not to envision the agile movements of those well-remembered hands. But in the end, she did exactly that. Her eyes flew open. She watched him play the wheel with effortless ease, and her body responded.

Strangely, the recollection, and the feel of him pressed so near was not unpleasant. She nestled further into his arms, arched her buttocks against hard,

283

unyielding flesh. He felt wonderful, even smelled wonderful. The scent of him was so very familiar to her now.

Standing behind her, Rayne bent his head close to hers to shield her from the wind.

"Are you cold?"

"No," she replied softly.

She could not see him smile. In spite of everything, he thought she was the most exciting woman he had ever met.

The storm eventually blew itself out to sea, and by the time a few sprinkling of stars could be seen in the sky, Rayne had maneuvered the schooner deeper into the cove next to towering bluffs.

A shaft of moonlight pierced a lingering cloud and suddenly it seemed to Starlin as if there had never been a storm at all. How strange the tempests that blew in from the far oceans: intense, violent, they would rage as though they might tear the world asunder and then pass with the same unexpected swiftness and all would be calm, a night of uncommon beauty left in its wake.

The girl emitted a small sigh of pleasure as she watched the scene unfold. The waves ceased to pummel the boat, the wind shifted, and the air warmed. A moist breeze caressed her face and stirred her cascading mane, fine tendrils of her hair curling in wisps about her forehead and cheeks, the sweet perfume of it like a drug to Morgan's senses. She watched his every move as he left her just long enough to tie off the wheel once more, and then he was enfolding her within his arms and urging her body against his. A thrill shot through her as her slim thighs came up against the hard muscle of his.

"We'll be fine now," he said huskily near her ear.

"I have been standing here remembering the night I first saw you. It was you who guided the ship so easily into the cove at Torquay, wasn't it?"

"Were you watching the entire time?" he asked in surprise.

"I couldn't have turned away if I'd wanted to. It was as if . . . you had somehow known I'd be waiting there for you."

"Perhaps I did," he whispered into her hair.

She wasn't certain whether she willingly turned in his arms or if he drew her around to face him. Suddenly it no longer mattered who had made the first move, or that only a short while ago she'd been trying to escape him. The only thing at the moment that truly mattered was that he was looking at her in the way that made her knees feel all watery.

She eagerly reached upward, her hands clinging to his broad shoulders. A gleam of desire was there behind those long dark lashes that shadowed emerald eyes staring hotly into hers. Starlin felt a need so great within her that it brought a small moan to her lips. Fully aware of what she was doing she laced her fingers behind his head and drew his lips slowly down to hers.

"I want you . . . now," she murmured throatily. She felt a quiver race through his body.

"Do you know what you are saying?" he asked, his voice hoarse with suppressed desire.

There was no need to reply. Starlin kissed him with all of the pent-up longing inside her. Hazily, enfolded in passion's warm glow, she pushed aside the fact that he had a mistress he planned on returning to after their annulment.

She knew he'd take her whenever she let him. And that she wanted to let him—again . . . and again . . . and again.

And even knowing that he would leave her in the end, did nothing to dissuade her from his arms.

Hands that would always capture her will with effortless ease moved with exquisite delight up and down her spine, gripped her rounded buttocks, and pressed her hips to his. She could feel the heat of him luring her through the thin satin of her chemise and moved her hips feverishly against him.

Her uninhibited passion surprised him and banished all thoughts save one from his head. Ally or enemy? Of a sudden it no longer mattered. He knew it should. He wanted it to. But there was something about this woman that made him lose all sense of reason each time she was near. Damn, her witch eyes had surely cast him in their spell. Deep within the dark recesses of his soul primeval passion awakened and all thought of everything, including revenge, vanished. Just looking at her was enough to make desire flare within him. She was a beautiful temptress who threatened everything he believed in. And he knew that soon he would have to let her go. They were only together to protect common interest. When all quieted in London, he would leave her.

But here tonight, far from civilization, bounded only by a canopy of stars and the restless sea, Rayne's tenuous control had snapped, and with a muffled groan, he surrendered to the coiling fire in his loins. His lips moved over hers, his tongue pillaging her sweetness, seeking the honeyed warmth within. Sleek limbs molded to his broad form, drove all sanity from his mind. He wanted her, like he'd never wanted another woman.

Just as mindlessly, Starlin returned his heated passion, wanting so to drive all the demons from his soul, and needing more than ever just to hear him say they were not enemies. She returned his ardent kisses, her tongue entwining with his, hands exploring him boldly, making him think then of taking her here, wildly and passionately beneath the stars with the dark cloak of night around them.

She did not protest when he slipped the straps of her chemise down her shoulders. A breathless sigh and a slight tremble and the chemise lay in a wisp of ivory satin at her feet. Her body quivered as his lips found that erotic place at the base of her throat that set her soul on fire.

"I want you so damned much," he murmured against her satin skin.

She placed a finger to his lips. "Shh . . . don't tell me . . . show me."

His lips slanted hard across hers. Desire rose in sweeping waves to blot out every other emotion save for one. Here, far from the crush of responsibility and what was right and wrong, he was free to express himself. This was his element, where he felt the greatest peace—and he would at last allow her a glimpse of the man he'd once been.

Chapter Fifteen

The storm had abated, but within the two lovers a storm of desire raged. Rayne was kissing Starlin passionately, his hands moving over her curves, tantalizing her with delicious promise. The sea breeze whispered through the rigging, lulling her drugged senses. She felt the balmy caress of the ocean wind, like warm velvet against the coolness of her skin. She shivered in anticipation. He raised his head slightly and asked huskily, "Are you cold . . . we can go below?"

"No," she replied in a throaty whisper. "Out here, with only the sea and the sky to shelter us I feel free. And for the rest of this night that is how I wish to be."

Unable to resist her intoxicating allure and innocent beauty, Rayne felt his soul accept her sweet surrender.

Her eyes met his, smoky colored from desire, before her thick lashes dropped and she hid her deepest feelings from him.

He studied her with leisure, pleased that she made no move to stop him, but stood, shoulders held proudly, rose-tipped breasts so perfectly formed, beaded with droplets of sea spray and inviting his lips to taste of them. She tossed her head proudly, as if impatient, sending her riotous mane spilling over her shoulders, a night-black veil shielding the twin mounds, prompting his fingers to reach forward and brush it aside. His eyes feasted upon her.

"You take my breath away with your beauty." His voice was soft and husky, his hands so erotic as they gently stroked her breasts.

Starlin shuddered when his thumb began a slow circle around each aroused peak. Her back arched, bringing her body up against his. Whenever he was near like this, she could find no way to resist him. He was a master of seduction, and she his willing slave. Yet this was her decision. She knew if she but whispered one word of protest that he would stop. But she did not wish him to draw away. She wanted him—all of him—and was trembling from the force of her emotions. As always, he seemed to know exactly what she was thinking. There was no need of words, or questions, only eyes that met and understood.

His mouth plummeted down upon hers, invading the trembling fullness of her lips, tongue seeking, conquering. Their wet bodies melded and clung, their hands eager to caress and please. Passion rose higher than the waves that tossed the sea, drawing them into a blaze of ecstatic delight, setting their battered hearts free from stormy waters for just a while, and drawing them into each other in fiery passion. They had denied themselves this closeness for so long in anger and pride that they were consumed by their need.

Mindlessly, Starlin writhed against his seeking

hands, ensnared by the hot, heady desire that swept through her. The sensitive peaks of her breasts grew taut beneath the sureness of his fingers. He rolled the eager buds between finger and thumb and Starlin felt searing flames lick deliciously between her legs. His lips trailed along her cheek, her chin, nipped lightly at the graceful curve of her neck, tasting of her silken splendor before moving downward to take a quivering peak in his mouth.

Fires that raged turned liquid and white-hot as they rushed through her body. She groaned down deep in her throat and attempted to shield her most vulnerable place as his hand dipped lower, caressed her trembling fingers.

Starlin bit into her lip as his hand moved over hers. His mouth hovered inches above hers, those alluring jade eyes glittering in the moonlight like diamonds ablaze. Her gaze met his and held, then widened as she realized his intention. His hand encompassed her own, began a devastating motion that pressed her flesh against herself. A spasm of hungry desire surged through her and her knees almost buckled from the intensity of it. Suddenly, with a low, keen cry she tore free of him and shielded herself from him.

"I am frightened of the way I feel . . . the things that you can make me do so easily." Her voice shook. He reached out for her and she attempted to shrink away, only to feel the hard surface of the wheel at her naked back and knew that there was really no place to run. Her eyelids fluttered closed.

"Don't deny me now, love." His fingers gently pried her crossed wrists apart, long fingers stroking her wet sleekness. "You're warm and eager," he whispered huskily, "and you want me to take you now—here. Tell me, Starlin. Say the words."

She was gasping for breath, and ready to do anything just to obtain that wonderful starburst of ecstasy that he was leading her toward. "Yes! Yes, I want you so badly I hurt from it!" she said.

She felt the smoothness of teak press into her spine and struggled only briefly. His hands urged her legs apart and his mouth traced a path of fire over her cheek, nipped gently the throbbing points below her ear, making her blood sing through her veins. He cupped her slender buttocks with one hand and brought her to him.

Without further protest her arms went about his wide shoulders, slim fingers skimming over sleek bronzed skin—perfection, she thought, except for a long saber scar that curved down his spine. He groaned as his pulsing need was slowly encased in hot flesh. Smooth slim legs wrapped about his as hips melded and thrashed, their rhythmic thrusts increasing fevered desire.

The wheel was their mainstay, an aid to trembling legs that were weak with wanting and threatened to fold beneath them. Sounds drifted on ocean breezes and were soothing to the senses. A night bird calling to its mate, the wind playful in the rigging, and their throaty whispers of passion, soft and husky, all blended as one.

Starlin felt his hands slip around her to cushion her spine against the hard wood as his body moved so beautifully against hers. He was everything that a woman could want in a lover, she thought. He was all strength and rippling muscle, a steellike body with a touch of velvet in his fingertips. But his ardent words she could not listen to . . . for she knew they were only whispers of desire. The only truth between them was the intense passion that held them spellbound.

Slowly, he teased, thrusting in and out, drawing her ever closer, then faster, deeper, making her want to match his hard driving rhythm, hips arching wantonly in pace with his. She was moaning softly, a primal sound of lusty pleasure that lured him ever closer to that final crest of pleasure. Exquisite agony held him suspended, then melted into liquid heat, pulsing through his body to every one of his nerve endings. He felt her nails digging into his back, her heels into the hardness of his buttocks, and lost himself completely within her burning heat.

Starlin was glorious in her uninhibited passion. Every part of her clung to him, moved with him, and sought the same sweet release. At last, it came . . . bursting upon her, a maelstrom sweeping through her, filling her, consuming her, and when it was over, leaving her feeling strangely bereft.

He was quietly holding her, his own passion sated, his breathing ragged.

"Did I hurt you?"

His soft words brought her plunging back into the real world. She was surprised that he appeared content to hold her against him, and, indeed, was supporting her entire body against the length of his.

Reluctantly, Starlin moved out of the circle of his arms. "No."

Rayne felt her withdraw from him. With that one word, she was all ice once again.

His hand reached for hers. She eluded it. "Don't turn

away from me, Starlin," he ordered brusquely.

"Another command, milord husband?" she returned sharper than intended.

Before she could protest he'd swept her up into his arms and was making toward the stairs. "God's wounds, if you persist, I swear that I will bind your mouth this time instead of your eyes."

Starlin stiffened in indignation, but she did not open her mouth.

Upon reaching the tiny cabin, Morgan deposited her on the bunk, and when she made no move to scoot over and share it with him, slipped a hand beneath her rump and made room for himself. He stretched out beside her and casually drew the covers up around them both.

"Sleep well," he said pleasantly. After a contented sigh, he turned over and presented his back to her. He grunted upon feeling a finger poking his ribs.

"Are you going to sleep . . . here, with me?" she asked, surprised.

He rolled over. One tawny brow arched and a glittering emerald eye fixed upon the lovely vision leaning over him. "Do you object?"

"I . . . just thought that perhaps you would seek other quarters now that you are . . ." Her words trailed off upon realizing what she had been about to say.

"Done with you," he finished for her.

"I wasn't going to put it quite so bluntly."

"Say what you mean." He stifled a yawn with the back of his hand. "That way there's no reason for anyone to misunderstand your intentions."

At that moment she was glad she had stifled any passionate endearments.

"I can't sleep with another person," she blurted.

"I . . . I've never had to before."

"Well, you have to now," he shot back, "unless you'd prefer to sleep on the floor. Sweet dreams, Princess. And try not to lie there too long thinking of ways to get even with me. Daybreak comes early out here. We'll be setting sail."

There was total silence, and then Starlin could contain herself no longer.

"To where?"

"You have to know absolutely everything, don't you?"

"When it concerns my welfare, yes," she returned, unruffled by his gruffness. Shapely calves entwined about his rock-hard ones and left him short of breath and suddenly very wide awake.

Starlin never ceased to amaze him. Any other woman would have sailed to the ends of the earth with him, and have asked no questions. Just accepted her place in his life. But this one . . . He glanced over at her—she was of an entirely different mind and spirit. He sat up, folding his arms across his knees.

"I think I'll take you to Antare."

Starlin was shocked. "The island . . . in the Triangle?"

"You'll be welcome. And I did promise your grandfather that I would take you somewhere safe."

"For how long?"

"I can't answer that. I have business to attend to elsewhere. You'll stay until I return."

"Business?"

"Something I have been neglecting of late."

Starlin went cold inside. She did not even feel him enfold her fingers within his and gently caress them.

Was he going to abandon her on some godforsaken island and leave her there forever? Was this the plan he'd been discussing with his mistress in the gazebo? He could return to England without fear of exposure and even proclaim her dead, lost at sea in a tragic accident. Not if she could help it, she vowed. He could find physical satisfaction with any woman. She was a fool if she thought for a minute that he felt anything more for her.

"I must know something, Rayne."

"Must we continue talking?" He moved to kiss her shoulder.

"Yes." Starlin drew back from him.

He frowned. "Don't push too hard, Starlin," he warned quietly. "My business is my own. I realize you are accustomed to meddling in your grandfather's affairs, but you will not stick that pretty nose of yours into mine."

"There is something you should know before you follow through with your plans for me," she said quietly.

"I'm waiting," he said tightly.

She swallowed. "I know, Rayne . . . everything."

He was still and silent. Starlin forced herself to continue.

"I heard you talking with Lady Ellendale in the gazebo. But I warn you, if I should mysteriously disappear your diary will be exposed."

His eyes hardened until they were almost black. "Susan Ellendale has nothing to do with my taking you to Antare. As for the diary, you must not have read very much of it, or you'd know there is nothing in it to link Scorpio with Rayne Morgan." He leaned forward slowly, his face inches from Starlin's. "I'm not that stupid, my dear."

She turned her face away. Was there no way to best this man?

He appeared to have read her thoughts.

"I'm leaving you on the island for your safety, Starlin. There's been trouble in the Keys. Many of my friends are being forced out of business. The mayor is an old friend. I've offered to help, and he has accepted." He made no mention of the rumors abounding that the pirate Scorpio and his crew were the very ones accused of the evil deeds, and that he was going to Key West primarily to settle an old score.

He could not tell her that he would seek out Benton Cambridge for their final confrontation. And after? What would he do with Starlin then? He pushed the thought aside.

"I have this feeling that you won't be coming back," Starlin said.

Rayne lay back on the mattress and flung one arm behind his head. He stared up at the ceiling. "You have to admit you've given me enough reason not to return."

Starlin moved away from him. Immediately he reached a hand toward her. "Enough! Come here," he said huskily.

Starlin saw that he was of no mind to talk further, and despite her firm vow, found she could not refuse him. The pleasure he gave her with his body was like a drug to her senses. She allowed him to pull her down beside him and mold her pliant form against his. She could forget everything when he held her like this. Thoughts of future nights almost made her smile. Until she realized they didn't have a future.

Rayne was given to wonder, even as he held her with a fierce possessiveness against him, why thoughts of honor and revenge hadn't been nagging at him so much of late. Starlin stirred beside him, nuzzled her head beneath his chin. A tentative but bold finger traced the taut line of his flank, the hard ridges of his belly, then dipped with a feather-light touch to tantalize him with stroking motions. He writhed and arched against her seeking hands, and thinking became impossible. Starlin—beautiful, passionate, as fresh and innocent as the new morn, yet, when it suited her, unpredictable and luring as the darkest shadows of night.

Her mouth, when it sought his, was burning with passion and eager to please. He rolled over her and caught her roughly against him. Almost desperately, he made love to her once again.

She gave him so much that night, and so unselfishly, that he reconfirmed in his mind what he already knew. To keep the fires of revenge burning, he had to put distance between himself and Starlin. He could not allow it to continue.

Sunbeams, warm upon her face and scented by the sea, teased lazy-lidded eyes open slowly, a delicate hand lifting to shield their violet depths. Lazily, Starlin rolled over and stretched sleek limbs. She lowered her hand. Her gaze swung to the open porthole where a hint of blue sky and clean, crisp air beckoned.

Rayne was not beside her, but then she had known that instantly, even before she'd opened her eyes. They had slept closely throughout the early morning hours, their bare limbs entwined intimately, covers draped in an unconcerned tangle about them. She'd first awakened several hours ago when he'd slipped out of bed. When he'd seen her regarding him through barely slitted eyes, he'd leaned over and kissed her, telling her not to get up just yet, that he would see the schooner underway, that she should sleep in.

He'd idly laced his fingers in her hair and had drawn her against him. The cover had fallen away, her bare breasts pressed against his broad chest. The kiss had deepened, become demanding and searching. And even though she'd been exhausted, her body had instinctively responded. Her slender form had arched upward into his arms. He made love to her with abandon. And she returned the same.

Starlin smiled dreamily and sighed with contentment. This seductive pull of forces between them was something she could no longer deny, or hope to banish. His lovemaking thrilled her in a way she had never thought possible. It was absolutely wonderful, beautiful beyond the physical sense.

She had only one thought as she rose in one lithe movement to drape the sheet about her and pad with bare feet toward the aft hatch. A sense of peace had settled within her.

Starlin passed through the hatch opening to stand for several minutes blinking in the bright sun. The day loomed large and spectacularly before her.

The sky was a bright blue and the sun warm, glistening off the brass fittings of the craft and drawing her eyes to an image reflected there. Rayne, his back to her, a wavering symmetry in motion standing before the massive wheel.

The magnificent vessel was skimming lightly over

the waves with the breeze, the hull slicing cleanly through soaring waves on a straightforward course with its only master at the helm.

Starlin's breath seemed to catch somewhere in the region of her throat as her gaze shifted, riveted now on his tall, bold form, the long lean muscles playing beneath that sun-browned back. His hair accepted the playful wind's caress, the thick tawny-streaked mane like spun gold in the sunlight, and a flutter of butterfly motions erupted in her stomach. She stood motionless clutching the thin cover to her breast. She kept reminding herself as she looked at him, that this man would never love her. Willing to accept that for now, she trod lightly across the cool teak deck to stand behind him.

He didn't acknowledge her presense. Tentatively, she reached out one hand to run her fingers along the jagged saber scar on his back. It surprised her to feel sorrow because of it. Lord, but she'd never guessed passion could make one feel this peculiar inside.

"How do you feel this morning?" he asked, eyes still fixed on the water before him.

"A bit light-headed from lack of sleep."

He half turned to meet her eyes. "But it was worth it, wasn't it?" he teased.

She thought he looked so different this morning. No longer did he appear the English lord, but more pirate once again. The dark breeches he wore were dampened by sea spray and clung to every masculine inch of him. Turned-down jack boots encased his lower legs. The night they first met came back to her. Her pulse raced. She sought something in his gaze to reassure her. He gave her nothing. Starlin sighed inwardly. There was that same savage light and restless desire in the emerald gaze.

"Yes, it was," she replied a bit breathlessly.

He held out a hand to her. Starlin came eagerly to him. His lower arms were glistening with droplets of water. She laid her head back against his chest and felt the sway of his body against hers. There was something about the way he moved that could convey what he was thinking and feeling to her. A sort of language, she thought, and smiled, knowing that they certainly had that. She had learned the meaning of it last night.

"Are you hungry?" he asked.

"Starved."

"Can you boil water?"

She tilted her face upward to meet his eyes. "And if I couldn't?"

He brushed back a silken tendril of her flowing hair that had caught in the wind and wafted about his cheek. "I suppose I'd have to let you man the helm while I went below and fixed us some breakfast." His smile was devastating.

"I can manage a few things," she admitted, matching his smile and noticing the fires deep within his gaze flare as he watched her.

He patted her bottom. "Good. For I could use something hot right now." His hand lingered, caressed.

Starlin resettled against his solid frame. "I would have thought after last night . . . that you might wish something a bit cooler this morning," came her suggestive voice in his ear.

Rayne nudged her toward the aft hatch. "You are a lusty wench, Lady Morgan."

"We're a perfect match I'd say," Starlin moved away

from him, her hips swaying provocatively beneath the thin cover.

"Be about your task before you brew up something more here than just a cup of tea," Rayne stated with a wicked gleam in his eyes.

All was quiet after she went below. There was nothing but the sun, the deep blue water, and the wind that sighed her name. God's blood, but she was some woman, Rayne found himself thinking. And envisioning the long days and nights that they would have together before meeting up with his ship and crew, he found that for the first time in his life, he wasn't irritated by the thought of spending considerable time with the same woman. He lifted an ironic brow. Rayne Morgan feeling the first stirrings of contentment? He snorted. Not a chance in hell. It was her delectable body that made him think of her with a smile.

The wheel shifted in his grip. He sent the little ship winging in the direction of an isolated cluster of islands that were a day's sailing from them.

Chapter Sixteen

Their clothes lay discarded beside them. The sun was warm on her bare body. Starlin felt almost decadent lying beside Rayne beneath the canopy of blue sky without a stitch to protect her skin from turning golden brown. It was an unthinkable thing she was doing, she chastised herself, stretching sensuously.

At first, he'd said they would be staying only a day, but they'd already been here a week. And they hadn't fought once, she was to think, moving closer to Morgan's powerful form, snuggling into the crook of his arm when he urged her to him. She enjoyed his automatic response to her closeness, even though he was dozing peacefully and was not aware of her touch.

Wild and uninhabited, the small grouping of islands had looked rather desolate to her when she'd first sighted them from the quarterdeck of the *Ice Princess* and had turned questioning eyes toward Rayne.

"I think you'll like this place," he told her over the crashing of the sea breakers battering the hull.

"What place?" She had looked at him quite puzzled.

His smile was mysterious. "You'll just have to wait and see."

She had liked it. They'd spent idyllic days here, lost somewhere in the Atlantic. She liked to dream a bit of how it might be if theirs had been a normal marriage based on love. Yet, if it had, she doubted very much whether she'd be here with him like this. They would still be in England, she, governed by society's dictates for a marchioness. Perhaps it was to her advantage that Morgan was so unorthodox. At least life was not dull.

Rayne had even been willing to teach her to guide the schooner about the calmer inlets that graced the islands, taking the time to explain the rigging, the different sails, how to read the clouds and wind, and, with infinite patience, show her how to carefully stitch a flat seam along a torn bow-sprit sail. Starlin knew few men who would teach seamanship to a woman—and then take pride in her accomplishments.

Glancing over at Rayne, she sighed with pleasure, reveling in the delicious intimacy she shared with this man. He alone evoked feelings within her that at first had been as foreign to her as their island fortress. He proved a constant source of guidance and understanding as he taught her so many things, but foremost allowed her to experience complete freedom without society's mandates.

Starlin was a willing and apt pupil. Where once he had thought her bold, he now found that very same boldness challenging, and quite different from any other woman he had known. She embraced his lifestyle with the same enthusiasm and confidence that she did everything.

Tentatively, in the beginning in only fragments,

Rayne talked about his life with her. They were lying in bed one night, completely relaxed and content just to talk and share a glass of wine. If Starlin was surprised that he appeared willing to discuss his family of a sudden, she did not show it.

Later, when she had expressed her opinions on political matters, she thought she had seen a spark of admiration for her in his eyes. It was the only time any man had looked at her in that way.

Rayne shifted on the blanket and Starlin glanced over at him. His hair had grown rakishly long and streaked with blond from the hours he spent in the sun. It lay in a honey-gold tangle about his forehead and ears. His features were relaxed, almost innocent in appearance. The tiny lines around his eyes had deepened just a bit, evidence of their sojourn here where the days were always hot and bright, and the many times he'd smiled of late—because of her, she hoped.

He was terribly handsome. But then, she'd always thought so, even that first night. His head came to rest in the curve of her shoulder, his hand automatically seeking her breast. A trusting gesture, she thought with pleasure—yet knew that sleep had initiated it. With a tiny sigh, she held him close and dozed off.

It was the clearly definable sound of something succulent being eaten, and enjoyed, that awakened her.

Starlin slowly opened her eyes and stared upward, her mouth already beginning to water.

Rayne was standing looking down at her, a pear in one hand. The rapidly setting sun backlit his powerful form, but she could see that he had dressed in dark breeches and a linen shirt open to his waist.

"I didn't realize you'd awakened," she said throatily. "Why didn't you rouse me?"

He only smiled lazily as his eyes roamed over her curves. "Why do you think?"

She stretched sinuously. "Because you know that our fresh fruit supply is about exhausted," she replied with a teasing gling in her eyes, "and you wished to enjoy your treat without having to share."

He shook his head slowly before planting one booted foot on either side of her hips to stare down at her.

"Whatever I've got is yours." He offered the pear.

Starlin felt desire awakening. "A tempting offer, sir."

"Are you accepting?"

"I don't need the whole pear, a bite will do." She smiled softly, feeling pinned beneath that heated look and the warmth of sun-kissed leather boots touching her skin. She prepared to rise, and was surprised when he preemptively obstructed her movements. Starlin froze on one elbow as he hunkered over her.

"Since this is our last piece of fruit, I insist we share it." His smile had given way to a piratical grin.

Starlin stared him directly in the eye, self-assured, almost cocky, and definitely brazen. "If you wish." She reached for his outstretched hand and took hold of his wrist. He allowed her to draw the piece of fruit within inches of her mouth, yet made no move to relinquish it. She felt like they were the only two people in the world. Woman . . . the seductress Eve luring Adam. The tip of her tongue parted her lips, moistened their fullness.

Fires lit in his eyes. He jerked back gently. "I did not say that there would not be a price to pay for the sharing."

She felt hard muscle press to her skin as he reclined

on one knee. She arched one dark eyebrow. "Ever devious, aren't you, Milord Captain Pirate?"

"You know me well enough by now to realize that I always demand a price in everything, and from everyone."

"I have very little. What could you possibly want of me?"

His voice dropped to a husky murmur. "Something you have not given me yet."

"And what would that be?"

"You've told me very little about yourself. I wish to know of your past. Everything there is." He traced a finger down her cheek.

"I have told you more than I have ever told anyone."

"Only certain things."

"I'm afraid the rest would bore a wordly sort such as you."

Starlin trembled as she felt the brush of his lips across her fingertips.

"You're not the sort of woman to bore a man very easily."

Slowly Starlin drew his wrist toward her until she had positioned the fruit right where she wanted it. Watching him, she saw his jade eyes darken and smolder as she bit down, sucking gently, drawing the sweet, refreshing juice into her mouth. With wicked delight in her eyes, she moistened the tip of his fingers with her tongue, teeth nibbling lightly, the taste of him mingling with the ambrosiac flavor of the pear. She raised her head, chewing the piece of fruit in a very precise manner before swallowing.

"As I said . . ." Rayne breathed raggedly, "you could never bore me." The breeze whispered soft sighs around him, urging him to touch her, hold her, make love to her.

Bright, amethyst eyes stared up at him from behind dark thick lashes, shielding her innermost feelings from him, but revealing her desire.

His eyes held hers, hot and demanding. With a shrug of broad shoulders his shirt slid down his arms. Starlin's gaze narrowed as his jackboots and breeches were carelessly tossed aside.

Seemingly of their own accord, her eyes drifted shut. She felt his hands tangle in her riotous long hair, arching her head backward. Slipping one hand behind her neck, he slowly drew her lips to meet his. The kiss deepened, became urgently demanding. He never seemed to grow weary of making love to her. She was so lovely, how could he? He drew back to study her closely, follow the path of his hands with his eyes.

One finger traced downward, along her nose, her dew-soft lips, feather-light upon her throat. When he swirled that long tanned finger across perfect rose-tipped mounds a moan of pleasure escaped her, and his heart soared.

He bent his head to swath the firm crests with his tongue, nipping at the aroused buds until they grew hard as pebbles. He heard her whisper softly, urging him for something more. Head thrown back, she wooed him with the sensual movement of her hips to shift lower . . . touch her there where the heat was most intense.

Lazily . . . deliciously . . . his lips moved a bit lower, exploring the smooth satin flesh stretched tautly across her stomach, the hollows on either side of her hip bones, teeth nibbling the soft skin of her inner thighs before kissing her finally where she burned hottest for him. He made the fires flare even higher with that masterful, feathery touch swirling across her moist flesh until the very world seemed to explode in brilliant color all around her. Liquid warmth surged through her, seeped into her bones and brought a cry of fulfillment to her lips.

Grasping the curve of her hips, Rayne thrust deep inside her to seek his own sweet release in a powerful driving rhythm that sent her pulse racing out of control. She held him a willing prisoner with her flesh. Squeezing . . . releasing . . . drawing him ever deeper into her, almost as if she truly longed to become of one body and soul. Hips arching to meet his, she clung to him in wild, mindless abandon. He took her with him on that pleasure ride, neither of them in control any longer, their soft cries mingling as one when they reached the very peak.

After their breathing had quieted, she nestled to him automatically. He curled one arm about her and kissed her bare shoulder.

Starlin was so tempted to tell him how wonderful he'd made her feel these past few days, but when she tried to, the words would not come. Just as well, she thought, for she was certain he really didn't care how she felt about him. It would be the last thing he would want to hear.

Awake the next morning before Rayne, Starlin dressed hurriedly, grabbed up a thin shawl, and padded topside to sit in quiet reflection on the deck and stare down into the water. The *Ice Princess* bucked against

309

her restraints, tossing and bobbing about the whitecaps as though anxious for an end to the idleness.

Their time together was nearly over. Rayne was growing restless. Starlin sensed it in him. There was something nagging at him, something he wouldn't talk about. She wondered if it could be the possibility of her carrying his child, but Starlin was beginning to suspect that she was not. Although there were no definite signs as yet, a woman has a certain intuition about these things, and Starlin felt nothing inside her. Surprised to experience a moment of regret, she fought back tears.

"You silly fool," she murmured. "He is on the verge of leaving you behind, don't allow yourself to care now."

Rationally she knew she could not trust him, but her heart would no longer allow her to believe he was responsible for the break-in at Eaton Hall, or her grandfather's accident.

Was it possible the macabre incidents were somehow linked in some way? And why did she feel so strongly that Rayne was involved?

She buried her face in her hands and breathed deeply. Just a while longer, please. Last night they'd lost themselves in passion's promise, yet this morning she knew they'd soon be like strangers once again.

Admitting it, free of his heady presence, Starlin had to acknowledge it was purely false hope that she harbored. There was no security in this marriage. It was a mockery. An unwilling bride who had suddenly, but too late, become all too willing. She had forgotten the future while they had been here. But now it loomed large and without promise before her.

*   *   *

Rayne knew instantly that she was no longer beside him. He felt as if half of him was missing without her. The realization did nothing for his mood. He scowled darkly. Assuming that she was attending to private needs, he stretched his lithe frame, placed his hands beneath his head, and waited patiently for her return.

The sun streaming in the porthole glinted on his gold necklace that she had tossed on a table beside the bunk. He suddenly remembered the stolen jewels that Ely had recovered and that Rayne now had secured away in his cabin on board the *Tempest*. He wanted Starlin to have them back. However, he did not want to provide explanation.

This brief escape had yielded him far more than he could have dreamed. It had gone well, but it had cost him, too. He had learned much about Starlin, even discovering that she had no idea of her important link to the treasure. But he was not the kind of man to settle down. It was time to move on. And even though Starlin was everything a man could want in a woman, Rayne was very much aware that their time together was at an end. Now it was time to take everything from the Cambridges that his family had lost. He would not forsake his family honor for Starlin. Remembering his mother, and her confinement in her rooms at the castle, he felt renewed anger. She would never again be sane. She was mad! Carl Cambridge—the bastard—had driven her insane!

When Starlin did not return after several minutes Rayne slipped into his breeches and went above deck to look for her. Immediately his eyes were drawn to her sitting near the rail, feet dangling over the side of the schooner.

"May I join you?"

She did not turn to look at him. "Yes."

He grasped the rail and slid in place beside her giving her a long considering look. She had dressed hastily in a pale blue blouse and long skirt, and he knew there were no petticoats beneath it. She didn't wish her movements hindered in any form or fashion. Risqué for some, but so befitting for Starlin. It silhouetted her long, sleek legs to his appreciative gaze at least a dozen times a day.

"Is something the matter?" he asked.

"No," she stated emphatically.

"Look at me." He went to touch her face and she turned her head away.

"I came up here to be alone for a while." She was irritated by his cool unaffected manner this morning when her emotions were in such turmoil. "Does that bother you?"

He gave her a sharp look. "In that case I'll just leave you alone and go below and see if I can find us something to eat. We're beginning to run low on food supplies so don't expect anything fancy."

She turned abruptly to find herself staring into his eyes. "One excuse is as good as another, I guess." There was a taunt in her voice.

"Now what does that mean?"

She shrugged slim shoulders. "The honeymoon is over, right?"

"So that's what has you so upset."

"I'm not upset," she quickly replied, trying to keep a steady voice.

"Without food, we have no choice," he said.

"You don't have to make excuses, Rayne."

He stood abruptly and started to walk away. "I don't

312

want to argue with you. I'll go see about that breakfast."

"I just want to ask you one thing," Starlin said, confused and strangely frightened.

He stopped dead in his tracks. "What?" He turned to face her.

"Are you planning on leaving me there forever?" she asked point-blank.

To her surprise, he favored her with a wolfish grin. "Not unless you want me to."

"I don't find that the least bit amusing," she said, eyes flashing.

His hand reached out to her. Slowly, moving as if she were hypnotized, Starlin found herself drawn into his arms. The warmth and comforting nearness of his body was the only security she had. Rayne turned her face upward and their lips met. The kiss deepened, became searching.

Starlin pulled free of him. She knew if he made love to her just one more time she would make a fool of herself and say all the things she didn't want to say and that he wouldn't want to hear.

"Shall we have breakfast?" she said thickly.

He looked at her assessingly. "Sure. I'll be right back."

Their supplies were low, but Rayne managed to put together a passable breakfast of sea biscuits, salt pork, and hot tea and brought them up on deck. He found Starlin sitting on the stairs that led to the helm.

"Here, it's good and hot." He hunkered down beside her to hand her a mug of tea.

313

She accepted it, watching him through long lashes tinged gold on their curling ends. "Thanks." The next words slipped out. "Will we be leaving today?"

He studied her closely. "Yes, we will."

"I thought as much."

He remained still, sipping quietly from his cup, avoiding her eyes.

"What happens now?" she asked softly, hesitantly.

"What would you like to happen, Princess?"

"Don't call me that," she shot back, lowering her eyes. "It . . . it isn't proper-sounding." And it has become like an endearment to me, her inner self cried, and I cannot hear that from you at this point and remain strong.

He reached for her.

"Don't touch me," she said quickly.

"I can't seem to please you this morning," he commented wryly.

She looked at him through night-black lashes. "Take heart, with luck you'll soon have your freedom and we'll each go back to our respective lives."

His lips twisted and he made a harsh sound. "It won't be that easy. There can no longer be an annulment."

"What . . . are you saying?"

"We made love . . . That makes a simple dissolution of the marriage impossible," he said. "Surely, you knew."

But she hadn't! She'd thought it a matter of whether she was with child or not.

Rayne could see from the expression on her face that she hadn't. He ran his fingers through his hair. "Don't worry . . . we'll find some way to dissolve the marriage without your tonnish friends hearing of the details," he said coolly.

"Yes, of course." Her voice was low. Her eyes caressed the harsh lines of his face, the rigid jaw covered by a dark stubble. Caught by the possessive gleam in those stormy eyes, she whispered, "I have to know Rayne . . . will I be going to your island as your lover, or your prisoner?"

He didn't even blink, but asked quite calmly, "Which would you prefer?"

"I couldn't stand to be confined again," she said with force. "I'll do anything to avoid that."

"Even warm my bed," he said crisply. His gaze was penetrating. Something was visible there. A warning, or some undefinable emotion that Starlin could not interpret? She quickly averted her gaze, staring out to sea. At first, when she caught sight of a tiny speck on the horizon she thought she was imagining it. Looking closer, she knew she had not. It was a ship, barely hoved into view, but definitely there. Its point of destination was uncertain but quickened Starlin's pulse nonetheless.

Rayne's gaze was upon her; he hadn't seen the ship. For some unexplainable reason, Starlin had the sudden urge to turn and kiss him. Just one more time before . . . before I signal to that ship, an inner voice said. She knew she had to do it. She could not stay with him any longer. She was falling more under his spell with each passing day. And if she went to Antare she would never get free of him. She turned to Rayne and handed him her cup.

"May I have more?"

"Certainly." He added teasingly, "You won't jump ship on me while I'm below, will you?"

If he had not turned away at that given time, Starlin knew he would have seen what she was planning in her eyes. But he did, disappearing through the hatch, and leaving her only minutes to put her plan into motion.

Methodically, she removed her cream-colored shawl and rose to her feet. She walked determinedly toward the mainmast. She did not know how to say good-bye. She could not play this game like the master. He had won her heart. Now she must leave him. She reached the rigging and slowly looked upward.

Starlin was not afraid of the perilous climb. She had watched Rayne clamber agilely up the mast above the sea, shim aloft on the windward rigging, and cross to the leeward without faltering.

Utterly without fear and yet filled with despair. Starlin began the dangerous ascent.

Chapter Seventeen

"What the hell are you doing?"

"Go away!" she yelled.

"You're going to kill yourself." His voice was gruffly commanding.

Not daring to look down, she continued upward, body moving in fluid motion with the ships. Hand over hand, seventy feet or more above the pitching deck, her only thought was on self-preservation. She grasped one rope, held it tightly while reaching for the other. One hand for yourself, another for the ship, she had heard Rayne repeat often enough.

Ignoring the square openings in the top platform—the lubber's hole for fools—Starlin climbed the ratlines running over the top platform and continued onward on the short out-leaning shrouds to her destination.

Finally she was able to scramble onto the small platform. She noticed the ship on the horizon drawing still nearer. Waving the shawl overhead, the young woman prayed frantically that they would see it. She had no idea whether they were British, Spanish, or

American. It didn't matter. She only wanted to escape.

Rayne had seen the approaching ship, still too far away to make out her colors. He knew he could climb the mast and stop Starlin, but it might also prove risky. If she struggled with him at all, she could slip from her precarious perch to the deck below. But if he allowed her to bring that ship in, he was taking a considerable chance. She might have decided it was time to do an awful lot of talking. That was something he couldn't allow. Not now. He was too close.

Grabbing up a two-sectioned spy glass, he raced forward to bound effortlessly up the ratlines. Agile as a cat he climbed, hand over hand until he'd reached a high enough point. Looping his arm around a line, he peered through the glass. A mysterious smile broke the tense lines of his face. The impressive, black brig with fore and aft sails stretched full by the wind was making a good four knots judging by the slight bow wave round her prow. She would be upon them within a short time.

Starlin kept signaling, her face set grim and determined. A flash of light from the ship sent her pulse racing. Her signal was being returned! She chanced a quick look below.

Rayne was waving her down with his hand. He looked terribly fierce, and filled with deadly purpose. She shook her head.

He began climbing upward toward her. Starlin couldn't think what to do then. She hadn't considered this!

He stopped several feet below her.

Starlin kept her eyes on him like a chick watching a hungry hawk.

318

"Just what do you think you're doing?" He was scowling. "Let's climb down together before you slip and hurt yourself."

"No!" she shrieked over the wind.

His face went dark with fury. He was not accustomed to disobedience in the face of danger. "I warn you, girl, if I have to fight you on this, punishment will follow."

Mutinously Starlin set her jaw. "I'll fight you every inch if you but lay a finger on me." She kicked outward with her foot as he reached upward. She very nearly lost her balance.

Rayne froze.

"Don't move," he said in a low voice meant to calm her. "Stay exactly where you are."

"You too, Morgan!" Starlin lashed back, her slight body swaying in the wind.

"I'll not force you, Starlin. I'm climbing downward and I suggest you do the same."

"I should trust you, Morgan?" she said with contempt. "You'd think nothing of tricking me!"

"I'm going down," he said.

Starlin eyed him skeptically. She watched his quick, agile retreat until he was once more standing on the deck. She glanced once again at the approaching ship. It would be upon them soon. He was watching her. She began her descent.

When her feet were planted firmly on the deck before him, she stared defiantly into his eyes, daring not to breathe, or even blink. He was madder than she'd seen him in a very long time . . . since that very first night when he'd come into her life like a whirlwind and turned it upside down.

Hands on his hips, he said softly but tautly. "Do you know what you've done?"

"Yes," she replied without hesitation. "I've gained my freedom from you."

"Have you?" he queried with a hard edge to his words.

"I'm leaving, Rayne, and you won't stop me this time," she said firmly.

Before she had time to react, he yanked her along behind him to sling her roughly against the rail.

"Take a good look out there, my clever wife," he growled low, "and tell me what it is that you see."

Starlin felt her limbs go weak.

"Well, what do you see?" he persisted in a sarcastic voice.

The craft was close enough now for her to see the black piece of silk waving like a proud banner in the breeze.

"A . . . a ship," she stammered at last. Her eyes darted to meet his.

He was smiling coldly.

"Look closer. What kind of ship?"

Starlin's heart plummeted. "A . . . pirate ship."

"And you have brought her to us."

After a moment of chagrin, Starlin said brusquely, "Can we outrun them?"

Rayne threw back his head and laughed. "So—now you wish to sail with me, do you?" He released his grip on her arm. "Perhaps we might barter with them." His eyes glittered wickedly. "Pirates love to dicker—and especially over beautiful women."

Starlin paled.

"You brought in the wrong ship, Starlin," he drawled.

Together they stood at the rail. An eerie hush settled over the ship, the only noise the creak of the rigging and the ever-restless water shifting beneath the hull.

In full view, the brig, black-hulled and sleekly designed, drew ever nearer. Gilt-touched trimming glinted brightly in the sun, a figurehead plunging downward into the waves then thrusting upward in plain view. Starlin stared at it. It was the configuration of a deadly scorpion.

The reality of her situation made her turn pale. "Damn you! You tricked us all!"

Rayne turned on her, his voice simmering with bitterness. "And what of you? You knew what you were going to do all along. So don't pretend innocence with me."

"You took that, too, remember," she said. "You've taken everything from me, or tried to. But I will not give you what you desire most. My pride remains intact." Her blazing eyes held his. "Are you going to turn me over to those men?"

His voice was cutting. "I should. Your shrewish tongue is becoming wearisome."

"I think that you have been after something all along," she said. "I've tried not to believe it . . . but I must now."

Hard jade eyes pierced her.

"And what could you have that I might possibly desire?"

She could not help shivering as he spoke each word with cold, unfeeling contempt, but her eyes stared into his with open hostility.

"The ring," she breathed, glancing down at the bloodred stone on her finger. "I knew . . . I just didn't want to face the truth about you."

"You can't begin to know," he cut her off bluntly. "Or you would have run as far from me as possible as soon as you learned my last name was Morgan."

Starlin felt sick at the pit of her stomach. She stood looking up at him and wondered how she could have thought she cared for this cold, unfeeling man. She had sensed all along that he was dangerous—that he was using her, that he was her enemy. The sound of men's voices turned her attention to the ship drawing nearer, almost beside them now.

Men were scurrying over her deck, up the mainmast with effortless ease to knock the wind from the sheets and secure the sails by gaskets. Guns bristled from two tiers. The black flag drew her eyes. The anchor rushed through the hawesehole and splashed into the sea. Grappling hooks sailed across the distance of water separating the vessels, men already making ready to swing across to the *Ice Princess*.

Desperate now, she said quickly, "I'll barter my freedom, Morgan." She slipped the heavy ring off her finger and held it out to him. "Take it—you paid a high enough price for it."

Rayne made a swift, reflexive movement that had the ring within his hand before she had time to even blink.

"It must be given in love . . . and accepted . . . for the secret to unfold," he said.

"How do you know this? Where did you hear it before?" she asked.

"From the one person I truly did love," he responded in a husky voice.

Starlin's breast felt heavy and tears blurred her vision.

"Stop it! Just take the godforsaken thing and get out of my life." She swung about just as the first intruder scrambled over the rail to be followed by several of his scruffy comrades.

"Whatever secret it bears you are all welcome to! I curse the day I came into possession of it." She swung past Rayne's astonished brother Ely, yelling angrily over her shoulder, "You may even give it to that bitch who waits for your return in England, for I no longer give a damn, about you or that ring!"

Ely favored Rayne with a look of total confusion.

"Wherever she is, she brews trouble," he said, grinning. "And here I thought you'd have her tame as a kitten by now. I've heard you boast many times of the women who fairly scrambled over each other to do your bidding."

"Don't goad me, Brother," Rayne growled menacingly. "I am not in the mood at present."

Noting Rayne's scowl and tightly clenched fists, Ely waved the men away. They fell back grumbling, for they had been eager to greet their captain.

"See to loading my brother's possessions," Ely instructed one burly fellow. "All save one, that is."

Starlin lay upon the bunk that she had shared with Rayne in miserable silence. Not very long ago he had lain here with her, loved her, whispered so many things that she had wanted to believe. She was the most desirable woman he had ever known, he'd told her—his dream temptress who had lured him to England's shores.

Liar! Damned liar! Tears streamed down her face.

She heard footsteps over her on the deck retreating, and knew that he was making ready to leave her. She was alone again. She should be happy that they were leaving her behind. She gave no thought to how she'd get home, nor even cared at the moment.

Frustrated anger prompted her to throw his pillow forcefully across the room.

Suddenly, the door burst open. The feathered missile landed with a soft plop before booted feet. Starlin scrambled to a sitting position quickly wiping at her tears with her sleeve.

Rayne stood in the doorway, his eyes blazing emerald fire.

"Are those tears of joy . . . or of sorrow?"

His voice was so jeering, as if he despised her.

Starlin held her chin high. "I don't owe you any explanations. I thought you'd be long gone by now."

"I'd forgotten something."

She looked about the tiny cabin, feigning an air of indifference. "Take whatever suits you. I want nothing left here to remind me of—"

Before she had time to finish her sentence, he was beside her, grasping her arm in one agile movement and slinging her upward over his shoulder. Without another word he strode back the way he had come.

"Just what do you think you are doing?" she sputtered. She grasped at any fixed object as he sprinted up through the hatch.

"Claiming what is mine."

He strode purposefully across the deck toward the side rail. Starlin's eyes grew round as saucers. Good lord! He'd grabbed a remaining grappling line and leaped effortlessly onto the edge of the rail!

324

'Hang on tight."

Those were the last words she heard before she pierced the air with a shrill scream as Rayne swung fluidly across the expanse of open sea. She grasped fistfuls of his billowing shirt, feeling the wind whip through her hair and whistle in her ears. The breeze blurred her vision, but she glimpsed a sparkling flash of blue . . . the fleeting swoop of a bird over the water . . . before they landed effortlessly on the wide polished deck of the *Tempest*.

She could only gasp that he release her and was ignored. She found herself bouncing along over his broad shoulder, her stomach lurching and her head still spinning sickly, as he made his way across the main deck. Loud guffaws greeted their arrival. The sound of the men's laughter stung her pride, and she swore with all the gusto of a sailor. Rayne's flat palm immediately swatted her rump in retaliation.

"Show some respect in your captain's presence, or you shall feel my hand again."

Starlin wanted to scream, yet considered his words and thought better of it. She dangled at his mercy, silently promising him every form of retribution.

He bounded down the stairs and through the shadowy parallel gangway toward his cabin. He opened the door and entered. With a backward kick of his boot, he slammed it closed. With several quick strides he reached his bed, and bending one shoulder, dumped her onto the covering of soft furs. She landed in a sprawled heap, her teeth gnashing together.

He stood observing her coolly, breathing easily, as if the arduous trek he'd just undertaken was something he did every day. Hooking his thumbs negligently in his

325

belt, he stated flatly, "This is going to be your new home for a while. Get used to it. I'll not have you out and roaming about the ship unless you have permission from me." He placed a hand on her shoulder when she attempted to rise. "Listen well, Starlin, for I'll tolerate no disobedience from you."

"And just what will you do if I choose not to listen, Captain Scorpio?" she sneered. "Heave me to the sharks?"

One tawny brow lifted. "I had not thought of the sharks . . . it bears consideration, I think."

Starlin's eyes narrowed dangerously, but still he stood unmoving, a mocking gleam in his emerald gaze.

"I will not forget what you have done to me—ever," she said solemnly.

"It did not have to be this way," he told her with a trace of regret in his voice. "You are the one who refuses to give quarter."

"Give quarter!" she spat back, her cheeks rosy with anger and contempt. "You've been using me no better than a whore! Nothing is sacred to you . . . not even marriage vows."

He towered over her. "Whore?" he snarled. "Is that how you think I treated you?" He stared at her, then in one lightning-quick move, grabbed hold of the neckline of her blouse and with a vicious jerk, ripped it from top to bottom.

Starlin screamed in furious indignation and clawed out at him. He easily caught her wrist in one hand. She struggled in vain. A bubble of a sob rose in her throat.

"Now you know exactly how it feels for me to treat you like a whore," he growled, thrusting her away from him with disgust.

Starlin collapsed back on the bed and curled her arms and legs into her body.

"Damn you," she heard him sigh raggedly. "Why do you always bring out the worst in me? Do you purposely goad me to it . . . Aye, I think so. You push everyone beyond their limit, even yourself."

She wanted to tell him that she could not play any more games, that she was tired of fighting him and herself. Suddenly he regained his cool composure and was viewing her as if she were merely his chattel to dispose of however he saw fit.

"You are to do exactly as I tell you every second that you are here," he commanded in a steel-edged voice. "And I swear to you, if you defy me before my men I'll punish you in a way that will have you wishing you had not." He spun about and strode to the door.

Starlin was so overwhelmed with misery and a need to strike back that she gave no thought to what she was doing. She scrambled to grasp up the nearest object, the little music box next to the bed, and threw it at him.

It missed the back of his head by inches, smashing against the wall in front of him to crash to the floor, the melody wafting sickly through the sudden silence.

Rayne stared down at the shattered music box, the dancers severed in two, and felt as if he were foreknowing something of his own future. His upper lip curled into a sneer.

"Nothing of mine warrants your respect, does it, Starlin?" After a moment's pause he opened the door and was gone without another word.

Starlin lay too exhausted to even think. She closed her eyes against the bright sun streaming through the glassed casement windows. With a small cry she turned over to bury her face in the pillow, small fists beating angrily into the mattress on either side of her.

It was hours later before she finally summoned the strength to move. She rose from the bed and began pacing the room. Stiff and weary, she longed for a decent meal and a good soak in a hot tub.

A bath would do wonders to restore her spirits. Bathing on the schooner had consisted of a dip in the sea. She looked down at her rumpled clothing. Had he thought to bring their trunks on board? She certainly hoped so.

She took a minute to search through a huge sea chest sitting on the floor at the foot of the bed. It was filled with expensive garments that were obviously Rayne's. The clean scent of lime wafted from the trunk and she felt a tug at her heart. Reaching into the chest, Starlin's fingers touched lightly upon a leather jerkin, caressed the soft leather before fingering a white linen shirt. The rich quality of the garments did not surprise her. Rayne liked nice things. There was nothing there of hers. Perhaps he hadn't meant to bring her along after all, but had planned to leave her on the island. Angrily, she slammed the lid shut and sat back on her heels.

She hated him so. He trampled on people's lives and emotions as though they meant nothing to him. She was his slave, and at the moment, there was nothing she could do about it.

Chapter Eighteen

A knock sounded at the door. Starlin got quickly to her feet and darted around the chest to sit on the bed.

"Come in," she called, and was astounded to see a huge bear of a man lumber through the door, a tray balanced in one great hand.

He smiled, revealing a sweep of pearly teeth in his swarthy face. "Beggin' your pardon, but I thought you just might like a spot of tea and some biscuits to hold you over until supper."

She stared mutely at him.

"Well, missus?"

Starlin swallowed.

"Oh, tea . . . that is very thoughtful of you," she stammered, regaining her composure. "Just put it on the table please."

She stared in wide-eyed wonder at the flashily dressed rogue. He was living testament to the true and numerous buccanneers who had once sailed the seas. Towering well over six feet, he wore a flowing gold shirt, dark pantaloons, and had a scarlet cloth tied around his head. A golden hoop earring dangled from his ear and a sweeping black mustache graced his generous mouth. Starlin found him striking in a wild, primitive sort of way. She noticed his black eyes twinkling at her. He offered her a mug of steaming tea.

"Have a cup of Chevaz's tea and you'll be feelin' fit in no time."

Starlin accepted the cup, her fingers wrapping about the warm pewter.

"Are you the cook of the ship?"

"Aye, I am Chevaz, and I be the best cook and swordsman combined to be found in the seven seas," he proudly boasted.

"And you love this life, no doubt," Starlin said dryly.

"It is a good life for a man. And Scorpio a fair captain," he returned without hesitation, watching her closely.

Starlin took a sip of tea. The breath promptly stopped in her lungs and she gasped chokingly, "What in the world is in this besides tea?"

"Added just a bit of Grog," Chevaz returned. "It will help keep up your spirits, and your health."

"I . . . I've never heard of putting such a thing in one's tea before," she choked.

"It's my own recipe." He offered up the pot. "I'll leave this for you."

Starlin did not argue the point. When she had caught her breath, she inquired how Chevaz had come to sail under Scorpio. She hoped he might provide her with some clue as to why her husband willfully sailed the seas as a pirate leader when he had a title and family in London.

"He intercepted a slaver ship bound from Morocco

330

to the colonies. Scorpio set the captain and crew adrift in longboats and freed the lot of us who were being held prisoner in the hold."

"And so you all became pirates together?"

"Pirates? Is that what you think of us?"

"I'd say it is rather evident by everything that I've witnessed."

"You haven't looked close enough," Chevaz said, appearing miffed.

Starlin stared at him, then replied, "What other reason would you have for sailing the seas in this particular guise?"

"You should talk with your husband, not his cook," Chevaz replied.

Starlin felt a flare of embarrassment. "You must know that is impossible at this time. I'm his prisoner— or have you forgotten how he brought me aboard ship?"

Chevaz gave her a long, measuring look. "Perhaps in seeking the reason you are here, you'd do better to search your own heart well," he said cryptically.

"I have no illusions about that," she snapped. "I hate the man with a passion."

"Scorpio is not a man easily understood. He is fierce when crossed, and not one you'd wish for an enemy. But he is a fair man," Chevaz said. "He only seeks vengeance upon those who destroyed something very precious to him. We have all sworn allegiance to the same cause, for most of us owe him a great debt."

"And how do you know that I am not one of the people he seeks vengeance upon?"

"You are a part of him now," Chevaz replied with an odd light in his eyes. "To destroy you would be to destroy himself."

Somehow, his words had not made her feel any better. Chevaz turned to leave.

"I'll bring you dinner later."

"What about the captain's dinner?" she asked hesitantly.

"I'll tell him that I have sent his dinner on to his cabin," Chevaz replied with a grin.

"You are a kind man, Chevaz. I feel as though I have found a friend."

"No one on this ship is your enemy," Chevaz replied before departing.

The sun was just setting through the stern windows when Rayne Morgan entered the cabin. Starlin was busy setting out the covered dishes that Matthew the cabin boy had delivered. The food smelled heavenly, and Starlin could only hope that Chevaz did not take to lacing his food with spirits the way that he did his tea.

Rayne went straight to the basin, stripped off his shirt, and proceeded to wash. There was a distinct change in him since the island. No longer was he the laughing, carefree lover she'd spent so many idyllic hours with. He was as distant as a stranger. Starlin began filling a plate with food, but found it difficult to concentrate on her task while facing the sight of his bronzed back. Muscles rippled in sinewy splendor each time he moved, and Starlin could not stop her heart from racing.

"Rayne?"

"What?" He did not turn around, but sluiced water through his hair with his fingers and then shook his tawny head like some great beast, droplets of water splaying out around him, glistening diamond bright in the setting sun gleaming through the windows.

At last he took a seat at the table. There was a tautness about him, an air of pent-up emotions. He reached for a biscuit and bit into it. It appeared he had no intention of making the meal an amicable one. Bristling at his scornful treatment, Starlin snatched his filled plate from beneath his nose before he'd time to take a bite.

Angry jade eyes were nearly black with fury as they met the fiery violet orbs challenging him.

"You have a choice," Starlin managed to say levelly. "You may dine here, and treat me with the respect due your wife, or you can choose to eat in the galley with your men."

One large fist came slamming down so hard on the table that the dishes were sent a good inch into the air. Starlin didn't move an eyelash.

"I am tired and hungry," he roared, "and I seek only a few minutes of quiet in my own cabin and to share a bite of food with you—and this is what I'm faced with!"

"Share! Did I hear you say that word?" Starlin shot back, arching one ebony brow.

"You've made your point. Now, please, sit down so that I might eat before one of the men seeks me out for one thing or another," he retorted gruffly, shifting uneasily in his chair.

Starlin remained stubbornly unmoved. Rayne glared daggers at her.

"Oh for Chrissake." He rose to his feet and held out her chair.

She sat down without another word, put his plate

333

before him, and waited politely for him to sit back in his chair. He sat stiffly, waiting for her to serve herself a portion of food. When she picked up her fork, he resumed eating. She bit back a smile.

"By God's wounds," she heard him grumble between mouthfuls, "if I haven't saddled myself with the most stubborn female to be found in any port."

The meal continued without incident, and although conversation was minimal, at least they spoke civilly to each other.

After they'd finished the meal, Starlin stacked the plates on the tray and retrieved a bottle of port from a cabinet. She caught the brief flicker of surprise on Rayne's face as she offered him a glass.

"Grandfather always enjoyed a glass of port after dinner."

"Thank you," he said rather dubiously, accepting the tumbler.

"Would you care for a cheroot?" she said casually, pausing in straightening the table.

He stared unbelievingly at her. "Why, yes, I think I would."

Starlin could feel his eyes watching her as she withdrew a long, black cheroot from a box on his desk and crossed back over the room to hand it to him. She even lit it for him. By that time he was at a loss for words and wondering what Chevaz might have put in her food to make her behave so.

"What's going on?" he asked suspiciously.

Starlin stared after him and wondered what she should say. When they were together like this it was easy to forget their stormy relationship, and even dream what it might be like if things were different

334

between them. But just as quickly she dismissed such an absurd notion. It wasn't going to change.

"I'm merely tired of being alone."

Dusk was gathering the natural light from the cabin, the single lantern on the table glowing warmly in the room. He studied her closely in the wavering light. He liked what he saw.

"I think it's more than eating alone," he said huskily.

His eyes were searching as they moved over her face.

Starlin clasped her hands together. "I can't go on like this . . . not knowing. Tell me what your plans are for me?"

"I told you once before that I am taking you to Antare." There was no warmth in his voice.

She nodded and stared at the ring on his finger. "Yes you did. But now that you have what you were seeking, are you going to abandon me there and return to England?"

He knew he could not tell her that he manipulated the ring from her in order to protect her. She would ask too many questions then.

"You do have plans, I know you do."

"I'm taking you to Antare because I feel it is the safest place for you right now. I can't stay because I have a job to do."

"Can't—or don't wish to?" she bit out in return.

"I'm not abandoning you for the love of Christ," he said curtly. "I'll return."

Starlin was desolate. She felt certain that he had every intention of abandoning her. And to add to he misery, she was fighting an overwhelming urge to throw herself into his arms and beg him to hold her, that she was afraid of being alone, afraid of losing him.

But her pride would not allow it.

He stood up to leave then, their gazes locking. "I must get back on deck." Starlin recognized the heated look in his eyes but could not bring herself to ask him to stay.

She sat for a long time after he'd left thinking bleakly about the future.

By the end of that week Starlin had settled into the routine of the ship. Although Rayne still refused to allow her to wander freely above deck, claiming that it wasn't proper, her being the only female on board, he did take her for walks. They had formed an uneasy alliance.

Starlin was content for a time. She took morning and evening strolls with Rayne and kept busy with simple chores the rest of the time. But after five days, she began to feel stifled by her confinement and her curious nature would not be contained.

On one particularly fine morning, she finished her breakfast, and after a leisurely toilette, dressed in a yellow and white striped day gown and began tidying up the cabin.

She hadn't seen Rayne that morning. He had been called to the hold at dawn to check on minor damage caused by several barrels that had shifted because of rough seas the night before. It didn't take her long to complete her tasks, and she soon found herself staring longingly out of the stern windows at the beautiful day. Golden sunbeams glistened on vivid turquoise water and danced on the windowpanes. Starlin longed to feel the breeze in her hair and the sun on her face. The seemingly endless hours stretched before her. Then and there she decided that a short stroll about the deck was exactly what she needed.

She snatched up a shawl and stepped out into the companionway. After a quick glance down the passageway, and seeing no one about, Starlin swiftly made her way up the stairs and out onto the deck. The fresh salt air was delightful, and she breathed deeply. Several of the men were working about the area and smiled in greeting to her. The entire ship appeared alive with activity.

High in the rigging, a good hundred feet above her, Starlin saw fleeting movement. She craned her head back to observe agile seamen scrambling about the ratlines checking the lines and sails. These were the topmen, a fearless lot who spent a large amount of their time aloft the ship at the "tops." This was one task Starlin was not of a mind to take on. She remembered her climb to the top on board the *Ice Princess*. Once had been enough. She was content to be an "idler"—one of those who spent their time below carrying out their duties.

Thinking it best not to draw undue attention to herself, Starlin walked over behind a longboat and paused at the rail. Shielded by the boat, she was blocked from curious stares, content to watch a school of dolphins play off the starboard bow. She was surprised when Ely Morgan unexpectedly joined her.

"I thought it was you I saw from the quarterdeck." His tone was solemn.

Starlin turned to smile up at him.

"Good morning. I was wondering when the two of us might find time to meet. I was beginning to think that you might be avoiding me."

An odd little smile curved his lips.

"My brother will not be pleased to learn you were above deck alone."

Starlin's eyes flashed. "And I suppose you will waste precious little time telling your brother of my insubordination."

Ely shot her a piercing glare, hesitant, deciding what he should do.

"Go right ahead. He'll rant and rave for a little while," she cast Ely a meaningful look, "and then all will be forgiven."

"You sound awfully confident of that."

Starlin didn't blink. "I am." But in truth she was not at all. She was envisioning being locked in their cabin until hell would freeze over. She could only stare at Ely who, it appeared, was suddenly seized by a fit. He threw back his head and laughed until he nearly choked.

"I knew the first time I laid eyes on you in the cave that you were a little hellcat," he chortled almost gleefully, "and that you would give my brother something to lie awake nights thinking about. What a fine lady he has chosen for his bride." His eyes sparkled as they met hers. He extended his hand. "Welcome to the Morgan family. You shall fit in very nicely, I think."

Starlin, surprised, shook his hand. "I must say I did not expect you to be happy about the marriage." She thought he looked very much like a younger version of Rayne, except he was not as devastatingly handsome—charming was more the word to describe her brother-in-law. His smile was warm, his manner open. She

338

thought they would get along famously if given the opportunity.

"I would have come to your wedding, Starlin. However, circumstances muddled things that day."

"You don't have to pretend, Ely," Starlin stated softly. "Rayne did not wish any of his family present." She felt her cheeks burn. "I think he is ashamed of the circumstances that led to our marriage."

"No, that is not the reason at all," Ely hurried to assure her.

Starlin curved her hand across her forehead to block out the brightness of the sun glinting off the water. "You know why, don't you?"

He sighed, staring at her intently.

"I wish we had time to talk," he stated huskily. "This is not something one can explain in a matter of minutes."

"Tell me what haunts your brother," Starlin urged. "Is it a woman he once loved?"

Ely leaned on the rail and stared out to sea, his eyes narrowing against the sun. "It is true that a woman haunts him, but not a lover. April—our mother— haunts Rayne. You have to help him, Starlin. And I'll help you if possible—for I believe you are the only one capable of reaching him. This horrible nightmare must come to an end. I am sick to death of sailing the seas myself."

Starlin was surprised. She saw the look of unguarded anguish on his face and knew that he meant every word.

"Even when he told me that he was through with this life, I knew that would never happen," she said.

"He wants to be," Ely replied.

"But I wore that ring, Ely. How can he ever trust me completely?"

"You know?" He appeared surprised.

"Most of it. I have been piecing it together since our first encounter. Although I really don't know what the ring had to do with your mother, or how Carl came to have it in his possession."

"Neither do we. But Rayne will never rest until he knows the truth. It eats at him constantly." He sighed with dismay. "Has Rayne ever told you anything about our father and mother, the life we led before that ring disappeared?" He turned to search her face, a piercing look of inquiry in his eyes.

"No he hasn't," Starlin returned.

"It isn't anything either of us likes to remember, but it is something we're not likely to ever forget."

"Are your parents dead?"

"My father is dead. Rayne never could forgive my mother for her part in our father's death. She is very ill and cannot tell us anything."

"Did something terrible happen between your father and mother?"

"There was talk of an affair. My father believed it, and since Rayne was the oldest, he suffered more from the gossips than I did." Ely paused, his eyes shadowed by grief. "He swore if he ever found April's lover that the man would pay dearly. He swore to kill the man."

Starlin recalled that first night the pirate Scorpio had come hurtling into her life. "In the back of my mind I suspected something like this. I didn't want to accept it, but it explains many things. The vendetta, the dark looks Rayne sometimes cast me when he thinks I am not aware—and the bitterness between us." Her eyes searched Ely's. "And the ring that I wore . . . it was April's?"

Ely nodded grimly.

Starlin recalled the ring that Rayne now wore on his little finger—the clear red ruby with the strange, black swirling design within the stone. "Carl gave it to me just before he disappeared in a boating accident along with my mother. He was off on some wild search in the Triangle." She swallowed. "Carl had told me the ring had been given to him by a very special person—that I should remember love would always guide me, as it had him."

"You realize what that means, don't you?" Ely asked quietly.

"Yes, that Carl was your mother's lover—the man my husband swore to kill." Starlin sighed despondently. "To think the ring belonged to your mother."

"It did," Ely replied solemnly.

"Yes." She thought back aloud. "I knew the ring was the key to this mystery. Yet, when I once asked him about it, he replied that it reminded him of another— one he would have given to his wife if it had not been lost to him."

"And now you are his wife," Ely stated quietly.

"Yes, but I have no right to wear it. Don't wish to, in fact. He cannot truly love me—he wants me only for revenge. It's obvious to me now."

"I think you're wrong," Ely stated emphatically.

Starlin was suddenly most grateful for this man's sincere gesture of friendship, and it was just after he took hold of her hand to squeeze it gently that she noticed the tall, dark form of her husband stride unexpectedly around the bow of the longboat. She

341

could not help her guilty expression even though she had done nothing to feel ashamed.

Rayne favored Ely with a brief searching look, his eyes turning to ice upon fixing on Starlin.

"Get below," he ordered curtly.

"I beg your pardon," she returned icily, hating him for trying to bully her in front of his brother. "I like it here." Her eyes were bright with threatening tears.

"I wasn't trying to steal your wife," Ely said lightly. "We were just getting to know each other a little better. After all, she is part of the family now."

"I do not blame you, Ely." Rayne faced Starlin. "When are you going to learn to do as I ask?" he inquired tersely.

"Perhaps when you learn to ask properly," Starlin lashed back.

"I have tried, yet you still defy me at every turn."

Starlin's eyes glittered with indignation. "If being bullied about by you is your idea of how to treat a wife, then might I suggest you take a few lessons from your brother!"

Starlin spun on her heel and stalked off.

Ely's lips twitched suspiciously.

Rayne glowered at him, then whirled about to storm off in the same direction as Starlin.

Turning back to the expanse of deep blue sea, the humorous expression on Ely's face faded to one of thoughtfulness. He reviewed the conversation he'd just had with Starlin. He was confident he'd judged her feelings accurately. She loved Rayne—he was certain of it—and his pig-headed brother loved her. It was good that he'd told her some of the story. He smiled. Well, he had done what he could to force Rayne and

Starlin's true feelings to the surface. And thinking of Malcolm Wells and his interest in the devil's treasure, Ely felt certain that it was best Starlin no longer had the ring in her possession. Obviously she had no idea the ring was a link to a treasure. He hoped that would help to keep her safe.

He was relieved that their ship was bound for Antare. Starlin would never be discovered there. At first, he'd thought Rayne meant to take her with them to the Keys. A quiver raced through him. Key West—and the final confrontation. The end was near. He was glad.

Chapter Nineteen

Starlin reached their cabin and slammed the door behind her. She shoved the bolt home. "You have tried to bully me for the last time, Morgan," she said angrily. "I won't stand for it."

"Starlin—open this door."

"I will not," she called out bravely.

"I warn you, madam."

"Don't try to browbeat me, Rayne. You have tried from the beginning to break me . . . strip me of my pride as punishment for something you believe my family did to yours. Well, it's time you realize that I am not to blame," Starlin yelled back at him.

Silence prevailed for a moment and then Rayne swore even louder.

"Open the door, or I swear by all that's holy I will kick it in!"

"It is your door," she returned with icy disdain.

She immediately jumped backward as the door was delivered a vicious kick, then another, splintered wood flying as the door swung violently inward to bang against the wall. Rayne stepped into the room, obviously in a furious temper.

Involuntarily she moved backward. Tensely, they eyed each other. She was not surprised to notice the expression in his eyes change, become smoldering and heated, their silent message quite clear. He closed the door, then advanced slowly toward her.

"Get away from me!" He advanced another step. "I will not stand for it." She meant what she said, yet even as she heard herself utter the words, she felt her limbs grow weak and the first stirrings of desire awaken inside her.

The hard, chiseled slant to his lips gave way to a sensual smile. "I think it's time we straightened out some misunderstandings between us," he murmured silkily, a strong surge of lust rushing through his loins.

Her back came up against the table, one hand automatically reaching out to grasp for something, to make him stop for just a moment so that she might think. Her fingers touched something smooth and cold.

"Don't come any nearer!" she commanded.

His dark menacing face bore a wolfish smile. "Or you will do what—stop me?"

"Yes!" she cried in desperation, swinging her hand forward to point a knife at his chest.

Surprise flickered momentarily in his eyes, then vanished. "The cabin boy was careless when he cleaned up after our breakfast." He reached out one hand. "We both know you cannot stab me. Now hand it over like a good girl."

"First you must listen," she said. "This personal war you have been fighting against my family is destroying us, don't you see?"

The cabin became deathly quiet.

Rayne's eyes narrowed. "How much do you know?"

"Can't we talk about it like two sensible people?"

"Who told you? It was Ely, wasn't it? That was why you had your heads together. How much did he tell you?"

"He is so worried about you, Rayne. He does not wish to see you come to harm any more than I do."

"It is not me that you fear for. It is your brother Benton, and yourself."

"I am concerned for him, yes. But for myself, it is a totally different kind of fear."

He stared at her with that cold, ruthless look glittering in his eyes that she remembered so well from the time in the cave. She had been foolish to believe she could sway the pirate leader in him from his quest.

"Use the knife, then, if you can. But you'll have to kill me to keep me from you," he said menacingly.

She thrust the knife forward an inch, her grip on the handle light but dangerous, earning grudging respect from him.

"I am impressed by your obvious skill."

"I was taught years ago how to wield a knife as good as any seahand."

"Is that supposed to scare me?"

"I doubt that anything I do would accomplish that."

"Put the knife down. You know I'd sooner cut off my arm than harm you." He was watching her face intently, the expression in his jade eyes shadowed by thick lashes.

"I won't submit to you again," Starlin ground out.

The hard slant of Rayne's lips curved upward in that

taunting smile. "Is that what you call your response—submitting?" His mouth twisted mockingly. "When we are in each other's arms, Starlin, you give everything to me. Everything. You hold nothing back."

"Damn you! Can't you see how you seek to belittle me?"

Rayne moved so swiftly that she had little time in which to react. Starlin knew she didn't want to hurt him, but blind instinct made her strike out. The sharp blade caught him on the forearm, slicing through his shirt-sleeve. He yanked her into his arms.

"I never thought you had it in you," he murmured just before his lips crushed down upon her half-open mouth, kissing her, drawing from her as if he were a drowning man seeking her as his lifeline.

Starlin tried hard to deny him—and the need deep within her body that made her ache for him. Stubbornly, she fought him and herself, sobbing with frustration, yet unable to use the one thing that would keep him from her. She gripped the knife tighter, determinedly raised it upward behind his back. One small part of her threatened to send it plunging downward and end this torturous agony once and for all. It was then, with the tip of the blade poised, that she realized even if she killed him she would never really be free. He would always be a part of her, even in death. She dropped the knife.

The slender legs beneath her tangled skirts ceased to thrash, became supple and clinging. Her blood sang through her veins and her heart beat with excitement. Her hands moved over him, stroked him, and told him what was in her heart.

Lost in the throes of passion, Rayne thought he had

never wanted her, needed her, more than at this moment. He lifted his head, and through slitted eyes watched the play of emotions on her lovely face as he slipped his hand inside her dress to cup one full breast, tease a silk-soft nipple with a calloused palm. It rose hard and impudently, seeking the pleasure to be found in those long, stroking fingers.

"My beautiful Ice Princess," he whispered, his lips inches above hers. "No matter if you flee to the ends of the earth to try and escape me. You never will, for I'll find you."

His heated words, softly spoken, sent the last of her will rushing from her.

"Make love to me, Rayne, I need you so," she moaned, caught in the grip of mindless desire from which there was only one escape.

He was quick with the fastenings on her gown. The cloth slid with a whisper down to the floor. A sudden jerk of his wrist left her naked body shivering in his embrace. Her breasts responded to the coolness of the sea air, her nipples taut and eager for his touch. His gold medallion was the only thing that she wore and it gleamed like his own personal brand against her skin. His warm lips moved over her face. Every fiber of his being was inflamed by her sweet surrender, wanting so to join his flesh to hers and lose himself within the silken warmth between her legs. Sweeping her up into his arms he carried her and tumbled them onto the bed of furs.

Wild, uncontrollable pleasure seized Starlin. With a moan of submission she came fully to him and knew she could deny him no longer, even knowing each time he made love to her that she died a little more inside.

For although he was a skilled and ardent lover who pleasured her completely before seeking his own, Starlin knew there could be no love for her in his heart. It was only physical hunger for her body and his relentless pursuit of revenge that drew him. As her arms went eagerly around his strong neck and her fingers brushed the tawny curls long against his collar, she thought perhaps she had one last weapon that she might yet bargain with—to save her stepbrother's life, and the soul of the man she loved with all of her heart.

Harsh, angry words were forgotten and whispered words of desire filled the room. Slowly, sensuously, she undressed him, kissed lightly each area of bronzed skin that she uncovered. She nipped at him, tasted him, and at last moved over him to impale herself upon him and become one with him in the most beautiful way that a woman can make a man part of herself. Her sleek golden legs held him prisoner, her hips moving in an age-old rhythm.

Breathless, quivering limbs and feverish lips sought in every way to please. Furious, wild abandon gripped them both and drew them into each other. Bending over him, cloaking him in a maelstrom of rose-scented hair, she whispered huskily in his ear, "Show me with your body what you cannot put into words," she whispered, sensing what he held within.

Moving her hips in an erotic motion that brought a soft cry of exquisite pleasure to his lips, Starlin arched and swayed . . . faster . . . faster, seeking to draw everything from him and force him to face the truth.

His hands reached out to touch her breasts, squeeze the high, firm flesh so perfectly sculpted it took away his breath just to gaze upon them. He felt her pleasure, heard her speak to him of love, even though no words were said, and knew it would always be this way with them. In every way, they were lovers.

It wasn't until much later, when the fires within them had cooled and they lay peacefully at rest within each other's arms, that Starlin fully realized what had passed between them. He had given all of himself to her this time. Never would he share with any other woman what they had shared this day.

As they neared the Bahamas, moist tropical breezes hinted of an approaching storm. The smell of rain hung heavy in the air. Starlin was standing on the quarter-deck near the wheelhousing chatting with Ely, who was splicing strands of rope together. Rayne was at the great wheel, his full attention on guiding the *Tempest* safely past the ship-eating reefs so prevalent in the area. He no longer appeared to mind the friendship Starlin and Ely shared, nor cared that she spent considerable time with him, the two of them laughing like children most of the time. She seemed to enjoy Ely's seafaring tales, and the stories of their childhood and family.

Yet Rayne did not mind. In the past two weeks he had felt an easing of his bitterness. Starlin was teaching him how to live again. And how to be gentle. He remembered how tentatively, and yes, with fear in her eyes, she'd told him yesterday that she was not to bear him a child.

"I had thought as much," she had murmured with a catch in her voice. "It was just the upheaval of late that made my time overlong." Her shining eyes were misty. "I will not hold you any longer. You are free, if you so desire."

"Free," he groaned, pulling her slender form into his arms and laying his chin upon the top of her dark head. "I can never be free of you. You have bewitched me from the first day I laid eyes on you."

He had gone to tell her that he would be staying on Antare with her for a while to see to necessary minor repairs for the ship. Starlin had been elated. They had shared an intimate supper and a long bath, and he refused to believe that her freely given love was perhaps only a ruse to gain her freedom.

A sharp cry from the crow's nest commanded Rayne's attention.

"Land ho! Off the starboard bow!"

Starlin hurried to stand beside Rayne. "Antare?" she questioned in eager anticipation. Rayne had told her that many of the crewmen were married, and their wives and children were living on the island. She was looking forward to talking with other women. She had been too long in the company of men.

Rayne had described the cottage that he maintained on the island. It sounded like paradise. She could hardly wait to see it.

Rayne held the wheel steady on course. "It will be an hour or more before we arrive. Why don't you go below and pack what we'll be needing."

"All right, darling." Starlin smiled. "I'll have us ready to go with time to spare."

"Then go to my cabin and gather my things, will you, Starlin?" Ely called out in a teasing voice.

"One man is enough for any woman to look after, Ely. Sorry, but you'll just have to find yourself a wife," she chuckled just before she descended the narrow stairs leading down from the quarterdeck.

Once inside their cabin, Starlin set to work gathering up their belongings, packing their bags. Setting what she wished to take ashore by the door, all accomplished with little effort, as if she'd been a sea captain's wife for years instead of just weeks. She was humming a jaunty tune that she'd heard Ely sing while he worked about the ship. Deciding that she'd best take Rayne's leather jerkin, she walked over to the sea chest and lifted the lid. While she was leaning over the chest, one of her earbobs came loose and fell down among the garments. She knelt and rummaged through the contents. It was then her elbow struck the side of the chest and a secret door fell open.

She was almost afraid to look. Something inside her warned her to slam the lid on the chest and forget what had happened. But she could not. With her heart beating rapidly, Starlin reached her hand inside the compartment and drew out a black cloth pouch with a gold scorpion on one side. With trembling fingers she loosened the drawstring and dumped the contents out on the floor.

Jewels, brilliant and glittering, lay before her eyes. And all were very familiar.

"They're all mine," she gasped in disbelief, and knew with a sickening sense of loss that she must have been right about her husband all along. He was the one responsible for all of the awful things that had happened! And she had been such a fool to allow him to sway her thinking otherwise.

She remembered her vow of several months ago to learn everything there was of the Marquess of Sontavon. Well, she had almost accomplished that. But she had not even begun to scratch the surface when it came to Scorpio. And what did he really have

353

planned for her? Perhaps he really was going to take her to Antare and keep her there forever, make her family and friends think that she had died at sea? She sat back, devastated.

Starlin gathered up the jewels and put them into the pouch, then placed it back in the secret compartment. Her fingers closed around another find—a jeweled dagger, slim and deadly looking. She shut the secret door and closed the lid on the chest before rising to her feet, still holding the dagger.

"You haven't bested me yet, you black-hearted devil," she hissed softly. "Just you wait and see."

Starlin would always remember her first glimpse of the island Antare. She stood on the quarterdeck beside Rayne and viewed the lush, tropical paradise through the haze of amber mists swirling around it. White sand formed a crescent beach up to the thick, green foliage and jagged seaside cliffs. Colorful, exotic birds swooped about from tree to tree and the air lay heavy with the scent of perfumed flowers.

"Breathtaking, isn't it?" Rayne asked as he adjusted the black baldric over his shoulder on which rested the broad sword.

"Like nothing I've ever seen before," Starlin replied.

Under topsails alone the *Tempest* sailed toward the island. They went in slowly due to the deadly reefs prevalent in the area. The leadsman chanted each change of depth.

"Ten fathoms!"

"Keep her on course!" Rayne yelled to Ely, who was at the helm.

"Anchors all clear, sir!"

The ship was buzzing with action and excited voices. Home port for the crew. A tropical prison of a sort for Starlin. Less than a mile from shore, Rayne gave the order to drop anchor.

"Aye, aye, Captain" came the eager reply, and soon after, the topmen were busily furling the sails as the anchor cable roared into the sea.

"We'll be climbing down the rope ladder," Rayne explained to Starlin. "It isn't dangerous if you take your time. I'll be right beside you."

As Starlin stared up at him searing anger surged through her. Right beside her, he'd said. Of course, he would not wish to lose the prisoner he'd worked so hard and sacrificed so much to capture.

She had dressed in a pair of the cabin boy's breeches and a faded blue shirt. The breeches molded to the fine lines of her legs and rounded derriere and were secured at the waist with a dark sash. She had also confiscated a pair of Matthew's knee-high boots that were a tad big, but would protect her feet better than satin slippers. Around her ebony hair that the damp air prompted to curl in riotous ringlets around her face, she tied a piece of scarlet cloth. She also wore the gold scorpion medallion on a chain around her neck.

Rayne had taken one look at her and grinned appreciatively.

Across the expanse of crystal blue water a crowd of people were beginning to gather on the shore. She could see them waving and laughing gaily. Rayne's hand at her elbow prompted her forward.

"I'll go over the side first. You wait until I'm on the ladder then it's your turn." At her nod, he swung easily over the rail and motioned her to follow.

Starlin copied his actions, earning a nod of approval from him as she began the descent on the rope ladder. Midway, she somehow lost her footing, and before she knew it she had slipped two rungs and was dangling by her fingertips. Rayne swung behind her, a protective arm wrapped around her waist. She could feel his heart beating rapidly against her. Had he been alarmed by her near fall, she wondered? No, just afraid he would lose an important pawn.

"Now—slowly this time," he ordered in her ear, his warm body pressing close against her. "One step. Good . . . that's better."

She grumbled beneath her breath, grateful that none of the men, or Rayne, could see her flushed face. Somehow, she must learn these barbaric ways if she had any hope of surviving to ever see England again.

Once inside the longboat, Rayne saw to her comfort, then took a position at the fore of the boat, one booted foot braced before him.

Starlin stared at the proud set of his broad shoulders, the fluid way his body moved in perfect timing with the sway and dip of the rowing craft. His tawny hair, long and rakish now, stirred in the light breeze. Since finding her jewels behind the secret panel in the trunk, he appeared once again, the stranger. She was more certain than ever that he was intent on something, something so awful she feared to even contemplate what it might be.

Chevaz and the two other men put their backs to the six oars, and it wasn't long before the boat ran lightly across the ivory sand of the shore.

Rayne leaped onto the beach and offered his hand

to Starlin.

"Watch your step."

His expression was unreadable but his reference plainly understood.

Starlin allowed him to take her hand, but she barely felt the touch of his fingers. She was staring unbelievably at the familiar sight of the schooner *Ice Princess* moored in a sheltered cove.

"Rayne, how is it the *Ice Princess* is here ahead of us?" she could not stop herself from asking.

"A better sailor than any on board *The Tempest* brought her." He glanced over toward the cove.

"Who is this mysterious person?" Starlin persisted, her brow creasing slightly.

"Not now, pet," Rayne teased, with his usual charm, deftly changing the subject. "Come greet some of the villagers who no doubt are most anxious to meet the captain's new bride."

"And how did they know that you had taken a wife?"

"There are ways" was all that he said before turning away, leaving Starlin continuing to wonder who it was who had piloted the *Princess*. Her attention was drawn to several women who stepped from the crowd to hand her a bouquet of colorful flowers.

"Welcome, milady. We hope that you will be happy here."

Starlin could read nothing but kindness in their eyes. They seemed genuinely pleased by her arrival.

"Thank you. I must say your thoughtfulness pleases me." She smiled. Everyone certainly seemed to be going out of their way to make her feel welcome. The women were gracious, and the children curious. Starlin did not realize that the entire island was in awe of the woman who had managed to capture their captain's heart. Everyone, that is, save one.

Bettina stood aloofly distant from the throng of well-wishers, observing the scene with narrowed eyes. With a hiss of rage, she spun about and left the beach for the thick covering of trees.

Starlin quickened her steps to catch up with Rayne, following him along the path of crushed shells that wound through a sweep of coconut palms.

They walked through a lovely village that contained rows of neat cottages and several shops, all well kept, the grounds surrounding them immaculate and colorful with wild tropical flowers. By the time that they climbed the steep mountain trail to the whitewashed cottage nestled in the hillside, Starlin was weary and longing for a hot bath. She followed Rayne up the stairs onto the veranda, impressed by such elegance in the primitive surroundings.

"Like it?" he asked her softly, pride gleaming in his eyes.

"It is not at all what I expected," she replied, then glanced around him at the sound of the door opening.

"Scorpio! At last you have returned!" a female voice exclaimed happily.

Starlin could only stare dumbstruck as a young girl hurtled herself into Rayne's outstretched arms. Rayne swung her around in circles seeming to delight in her joyous giggling.

Chapter Twenty

"It's good to see you, Jamie. I've missed you," he said, his eyes regarding the young girl warmly.

"I'm so glad that you had a safe journey," Jamie replied, eyes shining brightly. "You'll be staying for a while, I hope?"

Rayne released her. "I'm afraid I can't stay very long." He saw her blue eyes glance furtively over his shoulder. "Although I think that it is someone else that you wish to see more than me . . . hmmm?"

"Well, maybe just a bit," the girl admitted with an impish grin. At that instant her gaze fell upon Starlin. With a sheepish expression, she stepped away from Rayne into a quick curtsy. "Excuse my manners, it is a pleasure to welcome you, milady."

"My wife Starlin, Jamie." Rayne performed the introductions and then turned away to give instructions to the man who had just appeared with his sea chest.

"It's a pleasure to meet you, Jamie." Starlin smiled warmly.

"I hope my enthusiastic welcome didn't offend you," Jamie said, looking somewhat sheepish. "It wasn't very ladylike, I know. But sometimes I tend to forget to do things as I should."

"I understand perfectly," Starlin replied, laughing softly.

"You are not at all what I expected," Jamie said on impulse.

"My wife is full of surprises, I assure you," Rayne's voice cut in.

Starlin cast him a look designed to let him know that she did not find his remark very amusing.

Jamie glanced back and forth between them, appraising the two volatile people. She saw a muscle quiver slightly in Scorpio's lean jaw, a hint of rebellion in Starlin's eyes. Why was there such a strained relationship between the captain and his new bride? She wondered if Bettina had welcomed them as yet. Jamie knew her sister was seething because of Scorpio's marriage. And when Bettina was unhappy about something, everybody knew it. When word of Scorpio's marriage had reached Antare, Bettina had thrown an enormous tantrum.

"The servants have everything ready for you," Jamie said. "You both must be exhausted and hungry. Why don't you go on inside, there is time enough to talk on the morrow." She met Rayne's eyes, and asked quietly, "Did Ely go to the village?"

"Aye, and most likely wondering why you have not come to greet him as yet," Rayne told her, smiling briefly.

Jamie smiled back at him, her dimples flashing. "If you both will excuse me, I think I'll leave you to your privacy."

With a flurry of ruffled skirts, the young girl hurried off the veranda and disappeared along the path that led down the hillside.

Rayne held the door for Starlin.

"Whatever you wish while you are here, you only have to ask. Anything and everything is at your disposal."

Starlin went inside, and was pleased by what she saw. She glanced around her in amazement. While the outside of the cottage had been well maintained, she had not suspected the inside would be so comfortably elegant. She was standing in the entrance hall, a drawing room to her left and a dining room to her right. Both were expensively furnished and tastefully appointed. Dark wood beams supported the ceilings in each room. There were thick carpets covering the floors in a pale moss green. The windows were long and without draperies, small panes partially obscured with white shutters that could be closed to shut out the afternoon heat. They were half open at the moment to allow the breeze to circulate throughout the house.

A servant dressed in a flowing white shirt and baggy pants came forward to greet them.

"We were told you would be arriving any day," the silver-haired man stated with a welcoming smile. He nodded politely at Starlin before turning his attention to Rayne. "I trust you had a good journey, sir?"

"Better than expected," Rayne replied, casting a meaningful smile at Starlin. "Romani, this is my wife. Lady Starlin is to have anything that she wishes, with one exception—" His eyes held Starlin's. "A boat, or access to one."

"Very well, sir," the servant replied, sounding a tad perplexed. "It shall be as you say."

Starlin was affronted. She ignored Rayne's steely gaze and addressed the servant.

"Romani, might I be shown to my bedchamber. I am really quite weary and would like to have a bath and rest before dinner."

"Of course, mistress. There is plenty of time. Dinner is at eight o'clock."

Romani hurried ahead of her down a hallway papered in grasslike silk, the walls adorned by watercolors of the island. Starlin followed behind the spry little man, having to quicken her pace to keep up with him.

Entering a large room at the back of the house, Starlin was delighted to see that it was bright and airy, with wide louvered doors that opened out onto a veranda. Romani saw that she was pleased.

"I am glad that the chamber meets your approval, mistress," he said. "My wife and I did our best to make the room presentable after hearing that the captain had married and was coming home."

"Your wife?" Starlin exclaimed, glad that there was another woman living in the house. She walked about the room, admiring the furnishings, running a hand over the satin coverlet of deep rose on the large canopied bed. Rose silk panels wavered in the breeze on all sides of the bed. "I'll look forward to meeting her."

"Maria should be returning soon. She went to the village to purchase some items that she needed for the dinner this evening." A speculative look gleamed in his dark eyes. "The captain sent word that everything must be perfect when you arrived."

Starlin didn't wish to discuss Rayne. She deftly turned the conversation.

"Which of the rooms belongs to you and your wife?"

"My wife and I do not live in this house. We live in the village. We arrive just before sunrise, and leave after the house is quiet for the night. The cottage has only this one bedroom."

"I see. We'll have the house to ourselves then?"

"Completely."

"How like the captain," Starlin murmured under her breath.

"Pardon, mistress?"

"Everything is very nice." Starlin told him. "Tell your wife I am pleased."

After the servant had left, promising to return with water for her bath after she had rested, Starlin wandered over to the armoire which covered half the space of one wall and opened the door. She was astounded to find an assortment of gowns in every color of the rainbow hanging within. Silks and satins, from the palest pink to the deepest blue—all the same size, and by their appearance, made for one particular person.

"They're all for you" came a husky voice.

Surprised, Starlin whirled around. A tall, voluptuous woman with flowing dark hair and assessing eyes was standing just inside the doors off the veranda. She was dressed in a colorful print skirt and blouse. Several gold chains were around her neck and a thin gold chain was secured around one trim ankle. She was sunbrowned from hours spent in the tropical sun. Everything about her exuded sexuality. Starlin knew immediately that this woman had been Rayne's mistress. She could see it in the woman's eyes as they traveled the length of her—calculating, comparing.

"You are Starlin," the sultry beauty said, her dark eyes sweeping over Starlin in a manner that immediately forewarned the girl that this was not going to be a pleasant encounter.

"And who, might I ask, are you?" Starlin inquired.

"I am Bettina. I take it you have not heard of me, hmmm?"

"From your tone, I suspect that you thought I might have," Starlin returned after a brief pause.

Bettina stared unmoving at Starlin as if she could not quite believe what her eyes were telling her.

"I was right all along. I knew you would look exactly as you do," Bettina's husky voice whispered.

A shiver raced along Starlin's spine. "What do you mean?"

Bettina stared into Starlin's violet eyes and saw the truth of her words so many months before. "I told him all about you, you know. He knew as soon as he laid eyes on you what you were to him."

"You talk as if you had somehow predicted our meeting," Starlin said, a note of disbelief in her voice.

"Perhaps I did," Bettina returned.

"That's preposterous," Starlin scoffed. Yet Rayne's own words the night of their first meeting had not been forgotten by her. A chill swept over Starlin. "How could you have known?"

"It was the ring that drew him, but love is the only thing that can hold him," Bettina stated calmly. "And I do not think that you can give him that."

Starlin was astounded by the statement. She felt

trapped by the woman's penetrating eyes. "And I wonder why you should even care?" she said dryly.

Bettina narrowed her eyes as if to take better measure of the young woman standing in front of her. "But you're worried that I do, aren't you? I see the answer in your eyes. Hear me well, Englishwoman. You and I will never be friends. For I know what will soon follow—what must transpire before he can be at peace within himself. I only came here to tell you not to fight the events. It will only bring more pain."

Even though she thought the Gypsy's words ridiculous, Starlin could not stop the quivering of apprehension that raced through her. Forcing her voice to sound calm, she said, "I don't need your advice, Bettina. I think you'd best leave now. I don't wish to hear any more of what you have to say."

Bettina shrugged indifferently.

"You'll never hold him," she said as she left. "If you were wise, you'd admit to yourself why he is so obsessed with you."

Placing a hand to her forehead, Starlin sank onto a nearby lounge chair and stared up at the ceiling. Her hand crept to the gold medallion around her neck, her fingers tracing over the outline of the scorpion. More than ever now she felt that she must find someway to escape him. She wondered how it could be possible to care about someone, even though you feared that they might destroy everything you held dear. Tired from the long journey, Starlin slept for some time before she was awakened by a knock at the door.

"Come in," she called out groggily.

Romani entered the room followed by two young boys carrying buckets of steaming hot water.

"For your bath," Romani explained, gesturing to the boys to pour the water into a tub behind the silk screen. When everything was in readiness, he turned to leave. "Can I do anything else for you, mistress?"

Starlin shook her head.

He bowed his head. "Very well. Dinner will be served in one hour. The captain has secured a girl from the village to help you with your toilet. She will be here shortly."

As soon as Romani closed the door behind him, Starlin stepped eagerly behind the screen and began to disrobe. After securing her tumbling curls on top her head with several combs, she stepped into the steaming water and sank down into the tub. The water smelled heavenly. It was scented with attar of roses. Coincidence, she wondered, or had Rayne ordered her favorite scent especially for her? A large sponge and a bar of soap floated on top the water.

She washed herself with long, luxurious strokes that gave her skin a soft pink glow. Feeling totally relaxed, she rested her head back against the ornate copper tub, allowing the cares of the past weeks to slip from her mind. Several raven tendrils curled becomingly about her face and forehead, giving her an innocently provocative look that was heightened by the sleepy, lazy droop of ebony lashes.

The night air wafted into the room, jasmine and hibiscus a delight to the senses. The sounds of the night on Antare drifted over the island. Starlin listened to it all, and it was then she heard the click of the door as it opened and closed. She sat up quickly and reached out for a towel.

"Looking for this, Princess?"

366

Her eyes met Rayne's. She did not move, willed herself not to, even though she would have liked to cover her breasts—the nipples rigid and glistening with moisture—from his disturbing gaze. He leaned forward to drape the towel about her shoulders, making no move to touch her. Starlin watched him closely. He was dressed in a black silk robe that was tied at the waist. He turned to pick up two glasses of wine from a tray he'd set on a side table. Starlin's eyes watched his every movement, were drawn to the gold scorpion emblazoned on the back of the robe.

"I must say this room certainly seems to draw its share of people," she said stiffly, all of the sudden afraid to move with his eyes watching her so intently.

He extended a glass to her. "This is excellent wine. And I thought you might like some."

"I would like for you to leave me to my bath."

"Have some wine," he urged.

"Will you leave then?"

He smiled tantalizingly. "No."

"You stretch your husbandly rights to the limit, sir," Starlin said tersely.

The smile widened. "Aye, and without hesitation, my love. I enjoy looking at you." His eyes smoldered. "You were meant for a man's admiration. Correction—for my admiration."

Starlin clutched the towel around her nakedness. She accepted the offered glass and took a gulp of wine.

"Savor it, Starlin . . . slowly," Rayne cajoled.

Starlin glared at him. "You are making jest of all this and loving every minute of it, aren't you?"

"I do not jest in the least where you are concerned."

The lazy humor in his tone belied his words, and

367

Starlin felt extremely uncomfortable beneath that penetrating gaze. In one lithe movement, she was to her feet, and setting the glass of wine on the table, she moved to step out of the tub. He blocked her retreat.

"You haven't finished your wine."

"It's what you want again, Rayne, always what you want. You'll never change."

He answered her with deliberate slowness. "I have never taken anything from you that you were not willing to give me."

Starlin gripped the towel so tightly that her knuckles turned white beneath the skin. "Oh no? And did I give you my jewels which I saw with my own eyes—hidden away in your sea trunk?"

Rayne towered over her naked form, a black scowl on his lean features. He grasped her arm and shook her, sending the combs tumbling from her hair, loosing the thick mass about her shoulders.

"Do you always form your own conclusions without first hearing my side of things?"

She drew back to look at him with lingering suspicion. "It proves all of your words false ones, Rayne. I want no further explanation from you." Even furious with him, she was unable to tear her eyes away from his lips that were close, and appeared so unyielding. Now, Starlin, she found herself thinking, use his desire for you to your advantage. Thanks to his expert tutelage you have the means to escape him.

"I offer no explanation other than whatever I do, is to free us both in the end." His lips were drawn closer to her own, poised inches above her mouth. "I have decided there is only one jewel that is worth obtaining, and keeping."

Starlin was drawn into his arms, the towel slipping unheeded into the bathwater. What was between them, she could not deny. She would use it to survive. Then thinking became impossible as his lips touched hers.

Starlin pressed her hips against him, straining to be as close to him as possible. The entire hard length of him felt wonderful, and she knew without any doubt that he wore nothing beneath the robe. She did not protest when he swept her into his arms and carried her to the huge bed. Laying her gently on the coverlet, he drew the rose panels of silk around the bed before joining her in their private world.

Her raven hair cascaded about them both, ensnaring him in rose-scented bindings, her lips searing him with eager kisses. He felt himself being gently persuaded by stroking fingers to lie back upon the bed and allow her to work her magic upon him. With a sigh of expectation, he stretched out full-length and drew her over him.

Rising up on her knees, Starlin took the initiative, certain of how she wished to please him and intent on leading the way. She untied the sash to his robe and pushed the satin hindrance aside. Her breath caught in her throat just to look upon his lean, muscular form. He was perfect in every way. Leanly muscled and ruggedly male, no woman could ask for a more desirable partner. Dark tawny hair covered his long body, starting at his chest, tapering downward to form a thin line, then darkening when it met the whorl around his thick manhood. Her lips came forward to brush across his chest, nip the taut muscles, tongue the slight saltiness of his skin.

As always when they made love, a sense of belonging

drew her ever closer to him. Each knew what brought the other the greatest pleasure and would not hesitate in the least to provide. it. She kissed him everywhere, her tongue flicking, mouth moist and eager, driving him wild for her. His lips reclaimed her sweet mouth, his tongue seeking and enjoying.

She had become a skilled and exciting lover. But instead of letting her take the lead, he grasped her firmly in his arms and tumbled her over onto her back. She began to protest, but he kissed her harder and deeper, and she soon relented. Lifting her hips, he eased inside her with deliberate slowness.

Starlin felt his entry with every nerve she possessed. Slowly . . . tantalizingly . . . he slid up into her. Their eyes met, a soft groan escaping her as he filled her completely with his hot flesh. Neither of them moved further, just lay joined. Rayne allowed her the time to adjust to him. "Move, sweet," he ordered softly, "set your own pace . . . that's right . . ." he whispered near her ear, inflaming her beyond rational thinking.

Burning with need, Starlin arched her hips against him. His fingers digging into her hips, Rayne felt her draw him deeper into her. She was driving him mad with her movements, and at last he matched her motion. Caressing, kissing, between whispered murmurs holding each other close, they sought to share their feelings in the only way they could. Recklessly and completely, they loved and together reached sublime rapture.

Sometime later, the girl arrived from the village. Rayne was dressed for dinner and smoking a cheroot on the veranda just off the bedroom. Starlin was sleeping soundly. He told the girl to awaken her and see to her toilet, that he would wait for his wife in the parlor.

Less than an hour later Starlin appeared in the parlor looking ravishing in a gown of pale lavender taffeta. Rayne came forward to greet her, his eyes telling her everything.

They shared an intimate supper in the dining room. The smoked fish and wild rice were delicious, and afterwards, they sat outside on the veranda and enjoyed the beautiful evening. Ely and Jamie soon joined them, and Starlin found their company refreshing. She had grown fond of Ely, and thought Jamie a charming companion for him.

"Do you have a house nearby, Ely?" Starlin inquired.

"Yes, but nothing as lovely as this one," he replied, dragging deeply on his cigar.

"He needs someone to look after his place, give it a woman's touch," Rayne intervened with a roguish smile.

Ely squirmed in the wicker chair and avoided meeting Jamie's eyes.

"I've told him that myself at least a dozen times," Jamie chimed in, her blue eyes taking on a hopeful light. "It is a nice house really, just a bit in disorder, that's all."

Ely glared at his brother. "I find it meets my requirements. And just as soon as you have a woman poking around the place she starts fancying it up with frilly things that provide no other purpose beyond gathering dust."

Starlin and Rayne laughed, but Jamie only smirked.

A twinkle in his gray eyes, Ely said to Jamie,

"Someday, my pet, I shall take a wife and settle down with the girl of my dreams."

"I shall believe that when I see it," Jamie stated incredulously.

Starlin and Rayne smiled at each other. It was obvious to both of them that Ely was quite taken with Jamie, and she with him. But love seldom is acknowledged easily, Starlin mused. And for some people, that acknowledgment never comes.

Seemingly from across the sea, a haunting melody suddenly pulsed through the shadows. The foursome grew quiet, the sound of tambourines intermingling with wildly paced violins appeared to charge the very air around them with sensual rhythms.

Starlin had never heard anything like it before. "What in the world is that?" she asked in a hushed voice.

"Gypsy music," Rayne offered solemnly. "A celebration of night."

Jamie hastened to her feet and grasped Ely's hand. "The dancing has begun." She appeared eager for them to follow her. "Come—all of you. They will be dancing in honor of Scorpio's marriage. I heard talk of it earlier."

Rayne caught Starlin's wary eyes. "Do you want to join them?"

"Oh, please say yes," Jamie urged Starlin. "It is really quite exciting. You must see it."

Prompted by Jamie's urging, Ely rose to his feet. "Lead the way, pet. I shall dance with you."

Starlin agreed to go, too, but told them she wished to change into a casual dress.

"You go on with Jamie, Ely," Rayne told his brother.

"We'll be there shortly."

Starlin would never forget her first sight of the Gypsies. She had followed behind Rayne, who escorted her along the path sheltered by towering trees out onto the sandy beach. He held her hand within his. She thought of the other times they had danced together. It was a fond remembrance. Whenever they danced, it seemed they could forget their differences and just enjoy the moment, and each other. She stared at the scene before her.

The entire beach was alive with colorfully dressed figures leaping and whirling about the perimeter of a huge bonfire glowing bright orange against the velvet black night. Sea breakers crashing behind the dancers added their own bizarre accompaniment.

Rayne sensed her awe. "I felt the same way the first time I saw them," he said. His eyes roamed over her appreciatively, admiring the off-the-shoulder blouse and flowing red skirt that she wore. He remembered having chosen it with a night such as this one in mind. He could not believe that she was actually here with him like this, eager, appearing unconcerned, her body already swaying to the melody. He smiled challengingly at her. "Can you dance in such a fashion, do you think?"

Starlin tossed her head, her flowing hair a blue-black cape around pale gold shoulders. "Can you keep up if I do?"

He was already pulling her along with him to join the dancing Gypsies' celebration. Starlin did not hesitate, but followed in carefree abandon. His darkly clad form beckoned her ever closer, lured her with fiery eyes and suggestive movements.

She was mesmerized by the sight of him, the lean muscled strength of his arms reaching out to her, drawing her against him. They danced so closely that she felt as though they were one. His movements became hers, their feet never once falling out of step or losing the beat of the music.

His teeth flashed in his sun-brown face. "I should have know not to underestimate anything about you."

Starlin favored him with a sultry smile. "You would do well to remember it."

Bettina watched their every move from across the bonfire. Knowing that fate had drawn the couple together did not help to lessen the ache inside her. But she knew, too, that soon fate would intervene once more. And then, perhaps there might still be a chance for her.

Chapter Twenty-one

Ely was waiting for him on the beach later that night. Rayne had seen Starlin back to the house and had immediately left again. He didn't say a word as he joined his brother, but Ely knew how he was feeling. Rayne was a man possessed by two demons: love and revenge. Which of the two was stronger Ely did not know.

"The men are waiting below the cliff. The *Tempest* has taken on supplies and fresh water. I guess we are as ready as we'll ever be." Ely spoke simply, but his eyes revealed unspoken thoughts of depth. "It's not too late to turn back, Rayne. We can deal with Wells and forget about this vendetta of yours."

Caught firmly within the grip of black, brooding anger, Rayne glared at him. "Suddenly, it's all my vendetta, is it? I won't let Starlin stand in my way. I swore on my honor to avenge the Morgan name. And I shall." He strode off down the shoreline, ignoring his longing for Starlin twisting so painfully inside him.

Ely quickened his pace to catch up to him. "You

won't admit how you really feel about her, will you? Because you care about her more than you ever thought possible. And she loves you, very much. If you go to Key West in the frame of mind you're in, you're going to lose something very special."

"We've been all over this before. But I won't rest until I've had my revenge."

"The trouble with you is you've always found it so easy to bend women to your way of thinking," Ely blurted with narrowed eyes. "This one is different. She is as strong as you, every inch your equal, and you cannot stand the thought of Starlin Cambridge having captured your heart when you wanted to hate her so badly."

Rayne whirled about, his fists clenched at his sides. His expression was livid. "Shut up or I swear I'll deck you!"

"Go ahead if you think it will make you feel any better," Ely sneered, yet making certain to keep a goodly distance between them.

They had reached the bluff and were on the winding trail that led to the opening of the cave beneath it. Rayne glanced back over his shoulder.

"We'll have to settle this another time. The men are waiting. We have much to discuss before we sail." He stepped into the midst of his crew and immediately set about explaining the voyage they were about to undertake.

Starlin did not stay at the cottage as Rayne had ordered. After making certain that Rayne was far enough ahead of her not to notice that she was following, she slipped away into the darkness and kept to the shadows. Envisioning Bettina's sultry features, and remembering the way the woman's eyes had followed after him all evening, Starlin began to wonder about that message she had read in Bettina's eyes. Did her husband have women in every seaport? Of course he did. It was the nature of a man like Morgan.

Upon reaching the high bluff overlooking the moonlit shore, she was brought up short by the sound of Rayne's voice. Cautiously she peered over the edge and saw the familiar faces of the crew sitting around a campfire listening to the words of their captain.

Then she saw the *Ice Princess* riding at anchor out in the small bay and a long figure milling around on the deck. He appeared familiar to her, but was too far away to clearly discern his features. Her attention was drawn back to the scene beneath the bluff by the sound of men's voices raised in discussion. She saw Rayne hold up his hand and the group quieted.

"If all goes as we've planned, men, this will be the last journey of its kind. Tomorrow at dawn, the *Tempest* will sail for Key West, and the final leg of our quest."

Starlin observed the first mate stand up, indicating that he wished to speak. Rayne nodded at him.

"Something on your mind, Riley?"

"You said that the mayor accepted your help to go after the pirates that have been attacking the salvaging ships and stealing their goods."

"I did."

Riley ran one hand over his bushy red beard, appearing thoughtful.

"Out with it, man," Rayne said impatiently.

"Well, ain't we taking an awful chance, Captain . . .

with us doing a bit of that in them waters ourselves?"

"It bears some risks. But you all know that I only seek to put an end to one—the Cambridge salvaging firm. The other attacks on ships in the area have been perpetrated by individuals seeking to place the blame on Scorpio and his crew. As you know, our previous attacks upon the Cambridge ships have done much to mortally wound their entire operation. But we're not through yet." The flickering firelight cast shadows across the harsh planes of his face. "You know of the vow I've made to see the Cambridges pay dearly for the pain they caused my family. Carl Cambridge sought a treasure that rightfully belonged to my mother. Save for her ring that I'm certain he took without her knowledge, and a journal that he compiled, he would never have sought out the treasure. He almost found it. But he disappeared before he could obtain it. He is presumed dead, lost at sea, mayhap a victim of his own greed."

"Or the lady of the galleon," Chevaz intervened. "Many of us have heard the stories of the ghostly apparition of a woman that appears through the mists and leads ships to their destruction on the reefs."

There were murmurs of agreement.

"Mayhap Carl Cambridge met his death in such a way?" Riley posed.

Rayne did not seek to deny this statement. "Since his family claims they have never heard from him again, it could be true. The only thing I seek to do is discover the truth, and in the interim, prevent the vultures from disturbing my ancestors' final resting place. If anyone is entitled to the treasure it should be my family. Yet, we have chosen to leave it undisturbed. The dowry that my grandmother was bringing with her to the New World should be left where it rests."

"We all agree, Captain," a crewman said. "The area is cursed. Everyone knows of the mysterious occurrences in the Devil's Triangle. Leave be what you can't explain."

Rayne held up his hand, the ring gleaming in the firelight. "The ring I now have back in my possession. It is a clue that no one else has now, save me."

Another crew member spoke out. "You're not entirely certain that this Cambridge fellow is really dead, are you?"

"Perhaps he's not," Rayne said. "It could be he's just waiting until things quiet down again before resuming his search for the galleon. We've all seen the strange occurrences that have taken place here. The spinning of compasses, the lost ships we've sighted that were aimlessly drifting, seemingly with no one on board. Could be Carl Cambridge was one of those who survived such an event, and used it to his benefit. I don't know."

"But seek to find out," Ely said.

"Aye, I do," Rayne said fiercely. "Vengeance has yet to be mine. Soon, it shall be, and then I can live in peace once more." His eyes scanned the group of faithful followers. "You all may rest easier knowing that the *Tempest* will not attack the other salvors or burn any of their warehouses. We'll concentrate solely on Benton Cambridge." Rayne's words rang with truth, and the men did appear easier.

Unaware that a figure stood in shadow on top the bluff listening to their words, the men continued their open discussion. Much more was said, plans were reconfirmed, the route they would take was discussed, and then, suddenly, the man she'd seen on the deck of the *Ice Princess* strode into the circle of seamen. Starlin felt sick to her stomach but could not turn away. Even knowing that she had been callously duped, worse, degraded, could not prompt her to turn away. Absolutely stunned as she stood their in the mist-shrouded darkness and listened to their words, she stared astounded at that figure and cried out softly, "Now it is clear why everyone on Antare knew of our marriage. Oh, Fredrick . . . not you, too."

His familiar voice reached her ears and it was then, feeling totally alone and betrayed much like the time when her parents had died, the first sharp stabbing pain pierced her head, made her stagger tediously on the bluff's edge. The entire incident stirred dark things in her mind that had been long buried. She did not wish to recall them, for then she would have to confront those awful feelings of loneliness and despair. The door was threatening to open and the horrible emotions escape.

"No . . . no," she gasped, terribly frightened. "I will not remember . . . I refuse to."

Reeling from the knowledge that Rayne had been using her to obtain knowledge of her family and to get the ring, Starlin fell back from the cliff and staggered back over the path that led to the cottage. She thought if she could lie down she could reason out what she must do next. She knew beyond any doubt that she had to escape and somehow warn Benton. His very life, and perhaps even hers, depended on it.

Starlin hurried through the darkened cottage straight to the bedchamber. She began gathering up some of the things that she would need and tossed them into a

380

carpetbag. After placing her shirt, trousers, and boots together where she could easily slip into them, she sat on the edge of the bed and habitually removed her clothes. She kept one ear trained on the front door, listening for Rayne's footsteps. After donning a satin nightshift, she blew out the candle and lay down upon the bed. Her heart was beating so terribly fast that she could hardly draw an even breath. Forcing herself to concentrate on the task at hand, she gradually became calm and was able to devise a plan of action—one that would see her safely off the island and to the Keys.

It was very late when Rayne came to bed, but Starlin was still wide awake. He slipped in quietly beside her, and as he did every night, drew her close to him.

Starlin did not protest, but she could not help the slight tensing of her body as he kissed the back of her neck and caressed the curve of her hip. She knew by the way his fingers hesitated for a moment before slipping beneath her gown that he had felt the motion. Yet even as she cried inwardly, her senses surrendered to his sweet touch, the tender urgency of his lips when they sought hers. She tried not to give him all of her, to hold back just a tiny part of her soul, but it was useless. Between Rayne and herself there would always be complete surrender in their lovemaking. She arched upward to meet his first thrust and was immediately lost to the magic of his possession. He made love to her as if somehow he knew it was their last time.

And when it was over, Starlin could not help burying her face in her pillow and crying softly.

Rayne heard her tears, felt her pain, and even though he did not know the true reason for them, began to seriously wonder for the first time whether any of it was truly worth so much. One part of him didn't want to hurt her. But his pride wouldn't let him spare her completely. He was going to abandon her, even knowing that he was losing the most precious thing in his life.

Just before Starlin fell into a restless sleep, she thought she heard him murmur quietly, "At first I wanted to hurt you . . . now all I want to do is make love to you." Then he swore softly, as if in disbelief, "Christ, can you figure that?"

When she awoke, Rayne's side of the bed was empty. It was still dark in the room. She rose bleary-eyed and lit a candle. He was gone. Lying on his pillow was a velvet pouch. It was painfully familiar. She knew it contained her stolen jewels.

A note lay beside it—simple, unsigned, and devoid of any sentiment. It read:

> One of these days I will explain, and you'll understand that my leaving was for the best.

The sun was just rising as the *Tempest's* sails were unfurled and she set sail for the Americas. On the shore there were shouts of farewell and groups of misty-eyed women. It was the usual scene, yet somehow, this time was different.

Starlin was nowhere to be seen.

Bettina and Jamie were at their usual place: the bluff overlooking the sea. They watched the ship sail away. Jamie was sad, but remained optimistic that Ely would come back to her soon. Bettina's heart was heavy, however. She did not know if Scorpio would ever return.

"You're very worried about something, aren't you?" Jamie asked her sister.

"Yes, I was disturbed by dreams last night. They were filled with violence and death."

Jamie grew frightened, for she knew Bettina had a strange ability to know of events before they had taken place. "Was Scorpio in your dreams?"

"Yes."

"And . . . Ely . . . was he?"

Bettina nodded. "But each in a different way. I saw them both clearly. Scorpio, bound in shackles, and Ely, sailing alone . . . master of the ship."

"Such a dream is too frightening to even imagine!" Jamie cried. She looked away. "I do not wish to hear any more."

"There is nothing more to say really. What shall come to pass will be—and nothing we do will alter the course." She glanced over at Jamie. "Have no fear, little one. Ely will return to you."

"And Scorpio . . . what of him?"

"I can't seem to foresee Scorpio's return" was the heavy reply.

Jamie's startled cry as she looked down at the cove below drew Bettina's attention to the schooner *Ice Princess,* moving out of the bay toward the open sea.

"Who is that at the helm?" Jamie asked her sister, astounded.

Bettina's answer was quick. "It is the English-woman."

Jamie whirled away from the bluff, with every intention, Bettina was certain, of somehow stopping Starlin. She grabbed the young girl by the arm.

"No! Let it be. You must not try and alter what must

transpire between them, Jamie."

"But . . . but she is all alone," Jamie protested. "And how will she survive the Triangle not knowing the way in and out?"

"Look closely," Bettina said. "You'll see how she is careful to follow far out of sight of his ship, yet along the same course. She must know of the route they're taking. She is confident of her abilities. And if you wish to see Scorpio live, then we must let her go. She is the only one who can save him."

On board the *Tempest* the mood was light despite the serious nature of the journey. The sails creaked aloft and a furrow of white foam curled around the hull as the vessel gained speed and sailed free of the island cove. As was the custom when leaving Antare, the *Tempest* fired a farewell salute.

The crew members worked swiftly at their tasks and those not so engaged promptly took up a game of dice in a quieter corner of the maindeck. Sailing safely away from the reefs surrounding Antare and through the Triangle took a skilled navigator. The crew had every faith in their captain, but if not involved in some task it helped to have one's mind occupied on this dangerous and eerie first leg of the journey.

The morning passed swiftly and uneventfully. Scorpio sailed the ship and crew safely through the sinister area and into the open sea. At noon, the intense sun raked the decks and the main sails were reefed as the wind increased. The men smiled, knowing it would be good sailing weather for the next several days. All hands not occupied went below for the midday meal.

Ely climbed up to the quarterdeck and approached the helm.

"Why don't you go below and get something to eat. I'll take over for you," he offered to his brother.

"I'm not hungry."

Ely saw that Rayne's eyes were riveted on a point of concentration far ahead in the distant sea. He was certain it was not the clear blue of the water, or the groups of cumulus clouds so low one felt they might reach out to them, that had captured his brother's attention. Quite likely, it was the memory of shining violet eyes and a cloud of ebony hair that kept him deep in brooding silence.

"What are you going to tell her when you get back?" Ely posed.

There was silence for several minutes, and then Rayne replied, "I don't know that I'll be going back. Fredrick is there to take her back home. He said it's safe for her now."

Ely frowned, then nudged Rayne. "Go on and get something to eat. You'll feel better for it." He took his place at the helm and heard Rayne walk away.

The sun was hot, and Starlin was terribly thirsty, but she did not want to lash the wheel. Later, maybe. But for now it gave her a measure of comfort to view the *Tempest*'s tall masts in the far distance. Starlin licked her dry lips, inwardly cursing her stupidity. She had thought of just about everything, but she had neglected to bring any water top deck. Dressed in shirt, trousers, and knee-high boots, she was protected from the sun's burning rays, but there was little wind to cool her.

Just a little while longer she told herself. Another hour or two and then I'll lash the wheel on a straightforward course. She tried to keep her mind off of her discomfort by recalling the many things that Rayne had taught her about the handling of a ship. She had always listened very carefully. She remembered his pointing out the various cloud formations, and explaining how she should learn to read the signals they gave forth.

"Study them carefully throughout the day. You'll know well in advance when a storm is likely brewing by their appearance and size."

She'd quickly learned everything there was to know about sailing the *Ice Princess,* but she'd never dreamed that she would one day be piloting it all alone.

Having overheard the men discussing the planned route to the Keys, Starlin had felt completely confident that she could plot the exact course. Utterly fearless, she'd boarded the ship just before daybreak and waited until she'd heard the farewell shot sound from the *Tempest.* Then she'd sent the little schooner skimming over the water following far behind the larger ship's wake.

Malcolm Wells sat in his private office on the second floor of the Cambridge warehouse near Mallory Square and leafed through the papers that his hired man had just turned over to him. The day was hot and sultry, typical of the climate in Key West. The windows were open wide to invite moist breezes into the room, the only sound that of the auctioneer's bell clanging loudly, proclaiming it nine o'clock and time for the

386

city's daily auction of the latest haul.

The man Malcolm had hired to do his dirty work for him had only just arrived from an arduous trek that saw him in London during and after the period that the attorney had been there. As soon as it became known that the Morgans had left London, he searched everywhere, at last discovering that Rayne Morgan had sailed for the Keys.

Malcolm was livid. "Foster, you sorely disappoint me. Why in the hell it took you this long to find out the man was on my very doorstep I don't know," he fumed. "And I never did receive that letter you claim you sent informing me of the girl's marriage." He flung down the papers, sending them flying about the room. "Damn! If Morgan brings Starlin to the estate and she discovers Benton's condition, she'll insist on poking her nose into the salvaging firm's business affairs."

"Perhaps she won't," Foster said with a sly smile.

He was a slick-looking bully of a man, with greasy hair and a well-oiled mustache. Malcolm detested him, but he needed someone with his smooth speech and various contacts to ensure his plans.

"You don't know that chit like I do. She was the talk of London, if you'll recall. Flitting about the earl's posh offices, issuing orders, overseeing business transactions."

Foster snorted. "I hardly think Morgan's the sort to allow his wife to make a spectacle of him."

"Did you say something earlier about Mayor Quincy having acquisitioned Morgan to chase down the pirates plaguing the wreckers and salvors in nearby waters?"

"Yes. The mayor knows Morgan well."

"Did you obtain this information from a reliable source?"

"Very dependable I would say," Foster chuckled. "The mayor himself."

Malcolm sat back in his chair, his eyes glinting with dangerous humor. "Quincy always did run off at the mouth too freely."

"My posing as a buyer from New York interested in bidding on those pharmaceuticals that Cambridge wrecker discovered rather helped our cause considerably, I'd say. Quincy was eager to talk about such a find." Foster laughed to himself.

Malcolm took his time in lighting a cigar before offering one to the other man. As Foster reached forward, Malcolm yanked the case back just a bit.

"Don't ever take too much for granted, sir. Least of all, Mayor Quincy's abilities. He's a shrewd hustler, even if he does talk too much at times. How do you think he got to be mayor of this money-grubbing town?"

Foster scowled darkly. "I can handle myself just fine, Wells. I don't need no instructions from you."

"You need to remember who is financing your charade, my good man," Malcolm stated authoritatively. "You're playing a role that is purely fictitious, remember that. There is no rich buyer from New York." He pointed a stubby finger directly at the silent man. "And don't forget it."

"Whatever you say, Mr. Wells," Foster was forced to relent quietly. "After all, you're the boss."

"Yes, I am. And it's time for us to round up the men and make ready for another strike immediately. And I don't have to tell you upon whom."

"You are worried about this Morgan fellow, aren't you?"

"He can be a deadly adversary. But then, so can I when someone has something that I want." Malcolm's eyes glittered. "And his lovely wife definitely has something that I want—and will get."

Twenty miles from the settlement of Key West, one of the crewman of the *Tempest* spotted a wrecker that had apparently laid claim to a bilged vessel. Rayne stood beside Ely on the quarterdeck, a spy glass trained at an angle across the vivid, turquoise water.

"It's one of Benton's wreckers all right. I can see that man of his, Cocoa, milling around on deck."

"Those red suspenders he wears are like waving a flag before a bull." Ely grinned. "He has no idea how often you watch for them."

"He's a dead giveaway for sure. But we won't be the ones to tell the old boy that, now will we?"

"How long they been there, you imagine?"

Rayne peered closely. "They're just now sending out their divers. And there appear to be no other ships around, so it's my guess our boy Cocoa is master of the wrecking operation. Otherwise you'd see ships all over these waters in hopes of staking their claim."

"Do you want to attack?" Ely asked the inevitable question.

The spy glass clicked briskly shut. "It's a Cambridge ship, isn't it?"

Dressed in the role of the brigand, with the gleaming hilt of the broadsword sheathed at his side, Rayne looked as fierce as any cutthroat to have sailed the seas of the Caribbean. He called to Riley, "Show them our colors! And issue the usual orders."

Riley nodded crisply before yelling to the crew, "There are to be no casualties if you can prevent it, men! But they must give quarter!"

The fearless crew began loading the smooth-bored long guns with cast-iron solid shot, the six pounders laid ready in case they were needed to cripple the ship. Even though the *Tempest* only had twelve guns, she boasted acurate gunners and a nimble cannon crew that could throw enough iron to easily capture any foe. The prospective boarding party quickly strapped on cutlasses and grabbed up pistols. If it necessitated a battle to take their prize they would stand ready. The black flag was hoisted up the mast. The crew looked sharp and chillingly dangerous.

The swift, twelve-gun brigantine hoisted additional canvas: square sails on the bowsprit rigging and studding sails to give her extra driving power. She bore down on the bulky wrecker before they had opportunity to fire off even one of their guns.

"Fire a shot across their starboard!" Rayne ordered.

The deafening roar of the cannon shook the brigantine, and the deck trembled in response. Thick black smoke lingered in the air, leaving a trail across the length of space between the two ships. The sound of men shouting frantically told Rayne that this crew would give up without a fight.

The *Tempest* glided smoothly next to the wrecker's hull. Cocoa was waving his arms back and forth, his expression fearful. He had heard of this rogue Scorpio and his fearsome crew. They had earned quite a reputation in these waters. He did not wish to become one of their victims.

"We give quarter! Don't shoot!"

"The grappling hooks, Mr. Riley!" Rayne called out with a wide grin. "And prepare the men to board."

Screaming like banshees and armed with weapons of every make and size, the crew of the *Tempest* swarmed over the fallen ship. Only Rayne stayed behind, and for good reason. It was important that his identity not be known.

Ely boarded the wrecker and faced the Bahamian captain.

"I mean you no harm," he told Cocoa. "I only want the wrecker. You and your men are free to leave."

"You are called Scorpio, aren't you?" Ely only smiled mysteriously.

"Why you do this thing to Mr. Cambridge?" Cocoa asked, shaking his head, puzzled. "He a good man."

"Let's just say it is for a debt owed. You can tell Benton Cambridge that it is retributive justice."

"Then my men and I are to be let go?"

"You and your crew are guilty of nothing," Ely said firmly. He saw Chevaz motioning for him to join him. "Now, if you will excuse me, Captain, one of my crew wishes to speak with me. I suggest you join your men at the longboats."

"What is it, Chevaz?" Ely inquired of the big man upon confronting him.

"Off the starboard, sir. A schooner is approaching fast."

Ely raced to the rail. The schooner was bearing down fast. He knew Rayne did not wish a confrontation which might result in unnecessary bloodshed.

"Damn," he swore softly, hitting the top of the rail with his closed fist. "How did she sneak up on us without our being aware?"

391

A pistol shot resounded from the deck of the *Tempest*. It was Rayne, firing off a warning. Whirling about, Ely raced back toward his men who stood with their guns trained upon the crew of the wrecker, awaiting further orders.

Rayne had stayed well out of view of the wrecker, confident that Ely could handle matters. And then he saw the tall masts in the distance making straight for them, and even though he knew his men could never make it back on board the *Tempest* before the other ship was upon them, had fired off a shot.

He trained the spy glass on the approaching vessel. A caustic smile abruptly curved his mouth.

"Ice Princess," he murmured. "I should have remembered never to underestimate you."

Chapter Twenty-two

It was difficult to say who was more surprised to see a women at the helm of the *Ice Princess* when the vessel swung into the wind next to the *Tempest*'s hull—the crew of the brigantine or the salvors. All eyes were fixed upon the fiery beauty at the wheel.

Rayne stood at the rail facing the schooner, his face set in harsh lines. Starlin took her time in securing the ship, knowing that by doing so she would force him to come to her. Her gaze swung across the water, caught his. Their emerald depths appeared sulfurous. But she knew him too well to be deceived by their fiery light. He was angry, but also uneasy. Good, she thought smugly. She wanted him distressed. She averted her gaze once again to stare out at the sea. She was not about to have come this far to let him browbeat her. If she wished to salvage her pride, she would have to show him that he could not order her about ever again. She caught a movement on the water. It was Riley rowing a longboat alongside the *Princess*. He boarded.

"Captain's ordered me to escort you back to the

Tempest," he said firmly.

"No! Emphatically no!" she said loud enough for the entire lot of them to hear, staring at her husband's narrow-eyed face across the expanse of water that separated the two ships. She crossed her arms over her bosom. "Mr. Riley, you can tell Milord Captain Pirate that I will not set foot on that marauding vessel—he is to come over here. And then perhaps we'll talk."

Riley coughed uneasily, not quite certain just what he should do now. He knew from experience that if Starlin had a mind not to do something, then she simply would not do it. He glanced over at Rayne and sheepishly shrugged his shoulders.

"Says she won't come, sir. Wants you to come over here."

Rayne scowled at the distraught man. "Bloody hell if I will!" he growled menacingly, spinning on his heel to address Ely who had joined him from the wrecker. Keeping his voice low, he said, "You could always talk with her easier than I, Brother. What say you try and reason with her? If we stay in these waters much longer we are asking for serious trouble."

"I'd say we already have just that," Ely returned with a glib smirk.

Rayne's eyes narrowed. "And whose side are you on here, might I ask. The Morgan's—or the Cambridges?"

"You forget she is a Morgan, too."

"And that, I might add, was one of the biggest mistakes of my life—to have married that hot-tempered little baggage."

"I disagree," Ely stated with bold assurance.

Rayne peered at Ely. "You would mutiny on me, I think, if she would ask it." He glanced around him at the passive faces of his crew—eyes scanning the stunned group of Cambridge men who were oblivious to anything but the vision of Starlin in those alluring, form-hugging breeches. "She has bewitched the lot of you—and I only have myself to blame."

He decided drastic measures were needed at once. He said slowly and quietly, "Issue the order to put the Cambridge lot adrift in boats, and prepare to fire the wrecker. His gaze swung across the deck to fix hotly upon Starlin, his eyes taking on a glint of steel as he strode determinedly to the rail, lips moving with mumbled words. He grasped the rope ladder.

"Look sharp, Mr. Riley! I await your escort!" and then scowling blackly at Starlin: "You have gone too far this time, madam! I will not tolerate this outrageous behavior from you!"

Starlin retreated below deck with no doubt in her mind that her open defiance before the men would bring his wrath down upon her. She feared she might have pushed him too far, but knew whatever she'd done he'd fully deserved it! If she had not arrived just in the nick of time, why he'd have overtaken the Cambridge wrecker and claimed the find for his own. She was knowledgeable enough of his dastardly ways to know that he would not have one qualm about stealing from her.

She recognized the sound of his lithe stride upon the teak deck, racing down the stairway. The cabin door that she'd left slightly ajar hit the wall with a resounding bang, and she tried not to flinch when his big frame filled the entryway.

"So you followed me, did you?" His eyes shot green fire.

"I followed you because I suspected you were up to no good. And I was right!"

"And you dared to gull me before my men—in front of my enemy's men!"

Starlin stiffened, her violet eyes appearing wide and luminous yet displaying no visible fear. He moved toward her. She took a step backward.

"They are my crew, too. You seem to have forgotten that half of the salvaging firm is mine. And don't come near me until you are ready to listen to reason," she said levelly.

"You have always made a spectacle of yourself, and now you seek to do the same to me—and the Morgan name."

Her wary eyes watched him draw ever closer until they were standing but a foot apart.

"That's all you really care about, isn't it—your precious family honor?" She bit her lip. "And stop looking at me like that. It's insulting."

His eyes glimmered with feral lights. "Tell the truth, Starlin. You really don't want me too close because you know that no matter how much we fight, you've found what you've been seeking in my arms."

"I am here to save Benton, and myself, from this insane quest of yours to destroy every last Cambridge. I heard you talking to your men before you left the island. I won't allow you to hurt anyone . . . I have to stop you."

"Do you really think that you can?" he said silkily as he reached for her. Cruelly his mouth came down on hers, punishing her lips, holding her in a crushing embrace until she whimpered in protest. Yet even though he physically dominated her, her proud spirit refused to bend. She remained rigid in his arms. Slowly, his lips ceased their harsh demands, became soft and persuasive, seeking to elicit her surrender in still another way.

Starlin clung to him, wanting never to let him go or face the dark stranger inside him again. Passion coiled in her stomach and heated her blood, but this time, she could not blot out the image of the harsh lover who held her. Lives were at stake. Even Rayne's, although he would never believe it. She deftly twisted free of him.

"It won't work this time, Rayne." She turned to leave.

"Where the hell do you think you are going?"

"I'm going on deck to release my men," she said, halting momentarily.

"Your men?" he snorted.

"I have half interest in the Cambridge firm—it makes that wrecker and her crew my concern." She took a tentative step forward.

Bedeviled by pride, Rayne could not let her simply walk out of his life. After viewing the contempt on her face he knew they were finished. Love—hate. Love— hate. It constantly swung like a pendulum between them.

"So be it then," he murmured, grabbing her hand. "It's time for the real strength of will, Starlin. I want you to come on deck with me."

"Why?"

"There is something that I want you to witness."

Starlin was pulled along after him through the hatch, immediately spying his crew standing on the deck of the *Tempest,* torches ready to heave onto the wrecker. And in the distance, the Cambridge crew at the rail, awaiting their turn to climb down into dinghies.

"What are you planning?" Her words were tinged with frightening suspicion.

He was already at the rail, calling back to her as he stared at the scene across from them.

"By your open defiance, and your admission, I'd say that you and I are on opposing sides." The fury in his eyes blazed once again. "I intend to see my enemy completely destroyed. Down to nothing but ashes drifting in the wind." He turned to regard her face. "You know the story, the reason. Can you blame me? And knowing that I intend to take everything away from Benton, from your inheritance, do you really think we stand a chance in hell of salvaging this marriage?"

Starlin swallowed painfully, watching the crew from the wrecker being herded into the dinghies that would carry them back to Key West. Her eyes darted to the Cambridge ship, her eyes stinging from the smoky torches and the tears that she could no longer hold back. She had come all of this way to prevent him from destroying everything; hoping that maybe he cared, too; and in the end, discovering that he really didn't give a damn about anyone.

"Damn you, why must you persist until you've destroyed everything! Why couldn't I have been enough for you?"

Starlin veered past him and stalked across the deck. Her intentions were obvious by the mutinous thrust of her chin.

"Starlin, I cannot let you leave." His voice held no

measure of warmth. It was cold and direct. Just as she passed Riley, Rayne gave a quick nod of his head.

Starlin felt her wrist grasped, and she was brought up short.

"Please, missus," Riley said quietly, "he means what he says. Come without a fight . . ."

She whirled around so swiftly that she took Riley by surprise. He held firm to her wrist, but his expression was bleak.

Her eyes shooting sparks at Rayne, she stated calmly, "You'll never be able to keep me, you know. I do not belong here any longer. While I understand what drives you, I cannot condone your methods of dealing with it. You can't go on blaming us for an unfortunate incident that involved two people. There is much that needs explaining—if you would only take the time to ask and listen."

He was glaring at her now, and Starlin knew he felt betrayed. No doubt he was thinking that she had gotten the information out of Ely in order to help her own cause. And, of course, he was certain that she would tell the authorities who had attacked the wrecker.

Yet all she really wanted to do was get away from him, salvage what she could of her pride. She wanted to go back to the Cambridge estate and look after Benton. Perhaps even investigate a few things on her own— talk to Benton and find out if he knew anything about Carl's involvement with April Morgan.

No one, it seemed, had ever heard the entire story from either Carl or April. Perhaps there had been more to his relationship with April Morgan than a sordid affair? April had proclaimed her innocence—yet not one soul had been willing to believe her. She and Carl had become victims of the tonnish gossip-mongers. Starlin knew how devastating that could be. She had been under their close scrutiny for many years.

Rayne ordered Riley to take Starlin to the *Tempest* and lock her in his cabin. The man looked stricken, but would not defy his captain.

"Come, little lady. We'd best do as he says."

Starlin's footsteps were weary as she followed beside Riley. She never once looked back at Rayne.

Riley saw Starlin to the captain's cabin with a heavy heart. He did not know why Scorpio was such a driven man, he only knew that he trusted his judgment, and if he said that the Cambridges had done his family a great injustice, then it was so. He only wished Lady Morgan did not have to suffer, too. It was these deep inner feelings that allowed his guard to slip just a bit, and Starlin to act.

He was just turning to leave the cabin when Starlin, forced to act out of desperation, slipped the jeweled dagger from her boot and crept up stealthily behind the man.

"Don't take another step." When Riley appeared as though he meant to turn on her, Starlin increased the pressure of the knife. "Please, Riley," she stated in a voice that trembled. "I don't wish to hurt you."

Riley froze, feeling the prick of the blade in his ribs. "You'll only bring his wrath down harder on you, girl. You can never make it off this ship."

"Move over to the bed," Starlin ordered. "And no more talking."

He reluctantly complied. After slipping the sash

from her waist, Starlin tied Riley's hands to the bedpost. With a quick apology, she gagged the man with his own neck scarf, then grabbed his gun and slipped it inside the waistband of her breeches.

"Someone will free you before very long. I'm sorry but your captain has left me no choice."

To Riley's begrudging admiration, she displayed even more clever cunning by slipping into a concealing slicker and overlarge seaman's cap, careful to stuff every last raven strand of her hair beneath the cap.

Unease thrummed through her, but she crept up through the aft hatch and peered around her. Most of the men were busy seeing the hostages into the boats. She did not see Rayne anywhere and her bravado slipped. Where was he? Was he watching her, just waiting to pounce at the right moment?

She saw that there was only one man guarding the forward stern of the *Tempest*. The last group of Cambridge men were preparing to climb over the rail to the rope ladder when Starlin made a quick dash into their midst. Glancing furtively about, she breathed a sigh of relief that she had not been detected. She put a finger to her lips when the men around her all turned to stare. They quickly gathered about Starlin to shield her from view. Surrounded by huge, bulky forms, Starlin stayed in their midst as they began to climb down the ladder.

Once inside the boat, she sat huddled among the crew, her hat pulled low over her face. Even though her heart was breaking, she could not help but feel a small measure of triumph for besting the arrogant Scorpio.

*　　*　　*

It was a shock to Starlin to find the Cambridge estate in such disrepair. The sun was about to descend into the Gulf when she arrived at the isolated house situated on a remote tip of the island. The two-story structure, which boasted verandas encircling each floor and a widow's walk, was badly in need of paint. Vines were tethered to the drops and perks of gingerbread and hanging from the huge banyan trees that were in front of the house.

Starlin walked toward the steps, pushing aside the limbs of kapok trees swamping the path. The tall windows were covered by louvered shutters and there appeared no movement behind them. The entire place looked deserted. She raised the knocker and let it fall. the massive door slowly creaked open and a small woman in a patched dress wearing a bandana around her head stared disbelievingly at Starlin.

"Lord a mercy," the woman gasped, "but I never thought I'd live to see you again, child!"

"Hello, Mammy Juno. How have you been?" Starlin said softly.

The spry old woman suddenly brightened and threw the door wide. "Why, quits your standing out there like you is some kind of a stranger. Come in, come in. This is your own home, after all."

Starlin smiled upon stepping into the hall and looking about at the familiar interior. Nothing had changed, except that everything was decidedly more worn. "It's good to be back . . . it has been far too long."

Mammy Juno ushered the young woman into the dimly lighted parlor. Candles were burning throughout the room and Starlin wrinkled her nose at the peculiar odor they emitted. She caught Mammy Juno's eyes.

"Still up to your old tricks?"

"Needs them, darlin', needs all the tricks Mammy Juno's got up her sleeve to keep the evil spirits from this house."

"You know that I never did believe in voodoo," Starlin said disdainfully.

The old woman smiled in understanding. "Same as most folks. Can't help it though. It's a century-old religion my ancestors brought with them from Cuba, and it bears great powers. Santeria, stresses the positive things in life, it is not like the evil black magic practiced by some that lives in these parts."

Starlin knew better than to argue. She had heard her mother have this same conversation with the woman countless times, and it had never changed a thing. Mammy Juno was too set in her own ways.

The woman motioned Starlin to a settee. "You sit a spell. It looks to me like you've had a rough journey." She sat down next to her with a sigh. "It is good that you have come, little one. I don't like what's been happening around here of late."

A loud groan made both women flinch. It was followed by a slur of garbled words.

"Who is that?" Starlin asked, her face visibly paler.

Mammy Juno glanced down at her hands that were twisting the ends of her apron. "It's Benton. He has been like that for days now."

"Like . . . what?" Starlin probed.

"Drunk—rambling out of his head about everything."

"How long has this been going on, Mammy Juno?"

"The last six months he's been getting worse. He don't appear to be drinking enough to get him so drunk—least not around me he don't. But he been keeping to his room more and more of late, and I've found bottles stashed about, and empty ones in the trash."

"You mean he doesn't go out, or see anyone?"

"No—only sees that attorney fella, Malcolm Wells."

Starlin was stunned at the disclosure. "Who is running the salvaging firm?"

"Mr. Wells comes here often with papers and such for Benton to sign. I suppose the attorney is overseeing much of the business."

Starlin shook her head. "Things are worse than I could have imagined. I don't understand why my solicitors in London never told me of this."

"Perhaps your grandfather did not wish you to know for fear you'd come home and see how much you're needed here," Mammy Juno said soberly.

Starlin leaned her head back on the settee and stared thoughtfully up at the ceiling. "You are probably correct. And I am needed here—more than I even realized."

"Benton will be glad to see you," the old woman stated somberly. "He may not let you see just how glad he is, but know this—I think you are the only one left that can help him."

A rueful smile curved Starlin's mouth. "You know better than that, Mammy Juno. We did nothing but fight when we were youngsters."

"People can change if they try hard enough,"

404

Mammy Juno stated defensively. "You'll see, even though he drinks a lot, he is a good man when he's sober."

"From the way it sounds, he isn't sober very often."

"I think you can change that," Mammy Juno said hopefully. "I have faith."

Rayne Morgan had been more than startled to enter his cabin expecting to see his wife, and, instead, finding Riley trussed-up, his face the same bright red color as his hair. Rayne had come to tell Starlin that he'd decided she would stay with him, and, together, they would seek a possible solution to their ongoing problems. But he forgot everything as soon as he saw Riley.

"Where is she?" he demanded tersely, untying the man.

Riley rubbed his wrists to stimulate the circulation. "Gone—put on your slicker and hat and took off with a wicked smile on her face that would put the devil's to shame."

"Why in blazes did you let her go?" Rayne roared.

"Let her!" Riley guffawed. "She tricked me with those witch eyes of hers, she did . . . looking so bereft. Then she jabbed a sticker in my ribs and told me exactly what she wanted me to do. I had no choice!"

Rayne was furious. He knew at once where she had gone. "Cambridge! She went with his crew."

"Aye, most likely did. And I say good riddance to her. Woman on a ship always was bad luck."

"Except that you're forgetting one thing, Riley. She's

even more bad luck off of this ship. For she knows who I really am. I can't take the chance that she'll keep her mouth shut . . . not after today."

Ely had just entered the cabin and was doing his best to bite back a smile. Starlin had managed to outfox his brother again! And he felt certain that she would not betray Rayne's identity. She had left because she was searching for answers. He could only hope that she would find them in time.

Rayne swore softly and ran his fingers through his hair. "The minx is enough to drive a man crazy."

"Give her some time to settle in at the estate, and then perhaps you might pay her a visit," Ely suggested.

Rayne looked harassed. "You saw what happened today. It's never going to change."

"Go to her after you both have a chance to cool your tempers."

"And she'll turn on me the same as she did Riley," Rayne snorted. "No thank you. I just might be tempted to apply a firm hand to her backside for what she did to the poor man."

"She is not one that you can browbeat, Rayne. If you try, she'll do her best to beat you every time."

"Well, the next move is mine. And when she least expects it, I think," Rayne said slyly.

"It would go easier if you would do the right thing."

"And just what is that?" Rayne shot back.

"Have her best interest at heart, for a change, instead of your own," Ely replied without hesitation.

"I think that you are the one who should have married Starlin, Brother. You certainly seem to know more about pleasing her than I."

"You're forgetting . . . she doesn't love me."

406

Rayne was silent for a moment, presumably considering Ely's words. A sly, tigerish smile suddenly curved his mouth. "Best interests, hmm? We'll just have to see if the lady agrees with you."

Morning saw Benton Cambridge passed out upon his bed. Mammy Juno arrived with a breakfast tray and set it on a table. She had not told him yet of Starlin's arrival. There would have been no sense in doing so. He would not have been in any condition to greet his sister. Perhaps today, she hoped. She shook him gently. There was no response, not even his usual groan of protest. The old woman bent over him. Even in the diffused light she could tell he had a sickly pallor, and his breathing appeared shallow. The room held an awful odor.

"Someone has got to convince him that he is killing himself," she murmured to herself, shaking her head sadly. She removed his house shoes and put a pillow beneath his head.

"Whatever it is that's been eating at you all of these years, I hope your sister can get it out of you," she said softly to his motionless form.

Starlin slept through most of the day. When she awoke the sun was casting long shadows across the carpet and the heat had settled in the bedchamber. She pushed back the mosquito netting surrounding the canopied bed and sat up. Her bedchamber was still the sunniest room in the house. She looked around. Not much had changed since that long-ago day when she had left to go live with her grandfather. Thinking of the earl, she longed to know how he was recovering.

The young woman decided she would speak with Benton today. There was little time to waste. She needed answers from Benton, and without delay.

He just had to remember something of the events that preceded their parents' tragedy, the clues that led them to the site. Even how Carl came to possess the ring?

It was the prayer-chanting that caught her attention first, then the movement of furniture that sounded as if it were coming from down the hallway. Starlin threw a wrapper about her nightrail and hurried toward Benton's bedchamber.

She paused at the door, heard Mammy Juno's voice clearly. Starlin knew immediately what to expect as she entered the room.

The rug had been rolled back and a circle of candles placed on the hardwood floor. Mammy Juno was on her knees in the center, her head bowed, chanting a prayer. She kept on, even though Starlin knew she had to be aware of her presence. Benton Cambridge was alseep on the bed, oblivious to anything.

"What is going on?" Starlin queried anxiously.

Mammy Juno paused to look up at the young woman. "He is under the powerful influence of evil. The whiskey is going to kill him if he doesn't stop his drinking."

"He does look terribly ill." Starlin murmured, moving to stand by his bedside. She felt deep remorse for the tormented man. He had always been weak, wanting so to have his father's admiration and respect, and never receiving it. The wound must have festered all these years until it became too much for him.

"Stay with him," she instructed Mammy Juno before

408

leaving the chamber, "and if he awakens, call me at once."

Hours passed, and there was no change in Benton's condition. Starlin became increasingly concerned. Something had to change, and soon, or so many people's lives stood to be ruined.

She left the house and stood out in the backyard staring at the playhouse that Carl had built for her, trying to recall all the happy hours she had spent here rather than the fact that this was the last place that she'd seen Carl Cambridge alive.

Starlin recalled fondly how Carl would read stories to her from the volumes of children's books that lined the shelves along one wall of the playhouse. Slowly, she walked toward the structure and stepped inside.

Everything was just as she had left it. The dolls, toys, and books were all there. It was like greeting old friends.

Chapter Twenty-three

Starlin spent the remainder of the day within the playhouse. The past was there, too, but somehow she was no longer afraid of the memories. Instead of being overwhelmed by haunting fears, she was willing to confront them, and look for answers. And in doing so, she was able to bury that part of the past which had always made her fearful of returning to Key West.

When she had left, she'd been a frightened, insecure child. Well, no longer. She had returned to seek answers for herself and the people she cared about. And she knew she was strong enough to accept whatever she might find.

She took one of the books from the shelf and sat down to thumb through the pages. It was covered with dust. She wiped a hand across the jacket. The dust scattered to partially reveal an intricate design swirling through the fine leather, and, glancing at the other volumes, she noticed that each book bore a different design. She had really never paid heed to that fact before, perhaps because she'd been so young and more enthralled with the contents.

She had enjoyed those times with Carl very much. He read to her a lot. And then other days, he'd encourage her to write her own tales.

Starlin grew thoughtful . . . remembering now one story that he'd helped her compose.

A particular tale about two lovers:

A poor lad and a rich girl, who, as fate would have it, were destined to live their lives apart. The lad told his love that he was off to seek his own fortune. The girl gave him a ring as a memento. He left, vowing to cherish the keepsake, and return. Later, he discovered his love had given him a most precious gift indeed. The ring held a secret to a fabulous treasure. Yet, there were clues missing. It took him years to finally decipher the clues. And by the time that he'd found the way, and discovered the treasure, his lady had been betrothed to a rich, powerful man.

Starlin did not realize that she was staring down at the intricate design on the volume she was perusing. Something clicked in her brain. The story—the ring—the design on each book. She had seen the design in the ring somewhere before? But . . . how long ago?

A deep voice broke through her contemplation and she snapped the book closed and swung about. A dark shape stood in the doorway. She blinked. It was a man, his keen eyes fixed upon her.

"I did not mean to startle you," he quickly offered.

"It's all right." Starlin fought to regain some semblance of composure. "I . . . I suppose I was lost in my musings. I didn't hear your approach."

412

"I did call out," he explained. "But I could see you were quite interested in your book." He smiled. "Might I come in? My name is Malcolm Wells, I am the attorney for Cambridge Salvaging."

"Oh, please come in, Mr. Wells." Starlin dusted off another chair for the man to sit down. "I am Starlin Cambridge Morgan. And I've been wondering when we might meet at last."

"This is quite a surprise." Malcolm sat down, careful not to muss his coattails. "I had no idea you were planning a visit here."

"It was rather unexpected." She tried to sound casual. "My husband has business here, and I thought . . . why not come along, too?"

The attorney paid careful attention to her facial expressions, the constant movement of her hands as she talked. Her mind appeared preoccupied. And what was she doing out here, in this child's playhouse, with those musty old books, so very deep in thought? What was here? "I'm sure Benton is overjoyed." He kept talking as he looked casually about. He wondered if she'd uncovered something that he should know about. "I had heard talk of your arrival. Something about the mayor offering your husband a commission to go after this band of pirates that are preying upon the ships in the area." He picked at an imaginary piece of lint on his coat sleeve. "A dangerous assignment unless one is experienced with these sort of men."

"I assure you, my husband is quite experienced."

For some reason the remark made Malcolm uneasy. He was anxious to ask Benton a few questions. "Is Benton up to having visitors this morning?"

"Benton is clearly not up to much of anything. And I

413

think that I shall start making some of the decisions regarding the firm." She did not relent at his scowl. "You've been too overworked. But from now on I'll approve the transactions. You've only to bring them to me."

Malcolm was clearly astounded. "What a preposterous suggestion! Surely, you cannot be serious."

"Oh, but I am," Starlin responded.

"You are a woman!"

"Yes . . . I am." She grinned.

"The clerks . . . the crew. Hmph! They'll not stand still for this!"

"Does that include you, Mr. Wells?" Starlin asked quietly.

Malcolm stared into Starlin's violet eyes and cleared his throat nervously. "No!" he replied quickly. "I am merely an adviser. I didn't mean any disrespect. I had come to inform Benton of another Cambridge ship being raided and destroyed yesterday. We have an explosive situation on our hands. The men are all threatening to quit. They're scared of this pirate, Scorpio. And rightly so."

Starlin faced him with forced calm and a fixed expression of authority.

"Then we must convince them not to quit; and can only hope that these pirate attacks will come to an end soon."

"Convince them—how?" Malcolm inquired.

"Tell the men nothing of Benton's illness. Tell them he is working from the estate, that his sister has come home for a visit and he wishes to spend time with her. I'll make the decisions in his place." Starlin's tone was firm. "And hire more men . . . able-bodied seamen to man our ships and protect our finds."

Malcolm frowned. Damn her! Just when he thought he had everything working in his favor, this little chit had to turn up—and with every intention of taking matters completely in hand.

"If you would allow a suggestion from someone who knows a bit more about the financial strain the firm is experiencing, I think you should really consider cutting your losses and getting out while you can. Benton is a drunk. He should be institutionalized. I think that you should take care of his needs, and allow me to worry about the firm. After all, that is what you pay me to do."

Her immediate response made him so angry he almost lost his calm composure.

"Absolutely not," she replied briskly. "Benton, and the firm, are both going to survive these rough times. I shall never put Benton in an asylum. And I won't be defeated by these pirates. I intend to personally see to both." She rose to her feet and stared down at the flustered attorney.

In no position at the moment to argue further, Malcolm simmered inwardly and gave an affirmative nod.

"Whatever you say, madam. And I meant no offense by my suggestion. It was merely that—and in your best interest, of course."

"Of course," Starlin agreed dryly.

Wells rose, and with a cool nod, left immediately. Starlin called after him, and smiled slightly at the stiffening of his shoulders.

"No one is to know of our discussion, or of my decision!"

The days passed swiftly for Starlin. One morning she looked in on Benton to find him sitting up in bed. He grinned snidely. She knew then, Benton sober, was worse than Benton drunk.

"Well, well. The lamb has returned to the fold. And in view of your recent marriage, what brings you to this barbaric country, my dear sister?"

It was not a good beginning, nor as the week ended, did it get any better. Benton refused to leave his room, remaining unshaven and unbathed. He was quarrelsome with Starlin and belligerent toward Mammy Juno. Starlin had hoped they might unite their common interests and work together to save the firm. He'd snickered at the suggestion, and after learning that the two women had broken the bottles of liquor they'd found in his room, flew into a rage that frightened them so badly they'd locked him in his bedchamber. He banged on the door until the women felt certain he'd knock it down.

Of course, Malcolm Wells picked the exact moment that Benton was swearing like a lunatic to arrive with papers for the proper signature. Starlin remained cool and collected, receiving Malcolm in the parlor, signing the necessary invoices, and, in general, ignoring his presence. He handed her a satchel of work for Benton, with the explanation that he thought it might do him some good to think he was still needed.

She accepted it and had one of Mammy Juno's sons take it to Benton. After several hours Benton had quieted, and Starlin opened the door. His window was thrown wide and he was nowhere to be seen. She thought the room smelled faintly of liquor, but didn't know how that could be possible. She gritted her teeth and sent Mammy Juno's eldest son, Arman, who was as strong as an ox, to fetch him back home again. Arman found him in one of the island's shanty bars. Benton gave him a good fight. But Arman's hulking size was indomitable.

Mammy Juno was the first to reach the door upon hearing the sound of a buggy in front of the house. Starlin was almost certain who it was. She went ahead to Benton's bedchamber to turn back the coverlet.

After sleeping the entire day, Benton awoke to find Starlin sitting in a chair beside his bed, dozing with her head lolling sideways on her shoulder. He tried to get up and noticed for the first time that his hands were firmly bound with strips of cloth and tied to the bedposts. Starlin, of course! Only she would dare something like this! He stared unbelieving for a moment, and then, instead of becoming furious with her, he smiled wryly. She had always been a stubborn minx, and it appeared she was still of the same mind. If she believed strongly in something—be it a cause or an individual—she never gave in. He wondered just what she had in mind for him? God, but it hurt his head even to think. He squinted his eyes.

"Do you intend to sleep the entire day away?" he said gruffly, watching her closely.

Starlin awoke instantly, her eyes regarding him warily. She sat up straight in the chair, groaning a bit at her stiff muscles.

"How long have you been awake?" she asked.

"I've had enough time to consider my position, if that is what you mean."

"You forced me to do this."

"Yeah, and I bet you hated every minute of it, too."

417

"I did not like it. And Mammy Juno feels terrible."

For the first time, Benton looked a tad remorseful. Starlin saw a ray of hope.

"She only stays on here because of you. She is worried what you'll do should she go and live with Arman. He wants her, too, you know."

Benton sighed heavily. "I can't say that I blame him. I know I'm an ornery cuss at times." He met Starlin's eyes. "It's just been too much to handle . . . the debts father left . . . those damned pirates." His expression was bleak. "You see I haven't changed very much. I'm still the same old Benton. Weak, ineffective, and—"

"Stop it!" Starlin said harshly.

Benton shrugged. "Very well. But you know it's true. Father always preferred you, Starlin, because he could face the truth. He always could."

"And the drinking—does it truly make you stronger?"

"No, but then I don't look for anything to accomplish that."

"You're killing yourself, can't you see that?" she inquired painfully.

"Yes—I know."

She stared at him, comprehension in her eyes. "You don't care at all, do you? But then, I felt the same way once. And you must fight it, Benton. Come to terms with the past."

"No!" he shouted. "It's more than that—more than anyone could even imagine!"

"Tell me! I'll understand anything . . . I want to help," she pleaded.

He studied her intense features, breathed deeply. "Do you now . . . ?"

"More than anything."

His eyes were brooding as he stared over her shoulder out of the window. "I've seen him, you know . . . out there . . . by the playhouse. He prowls about looking up at the house from time to time." Benton moaned. "Why is he doing this to me . . ." And then as if in answer to his own question: "Because I survived, that's why! And have managed to allow everything he worked so hard for to slip through my fingers."

Starlin felt a coldness grip her.

"Who are you referring to?" But deep in her heart she already knew the answer.

His bloodshot eyes met Starlin's.

"Why, Father. Who else?"

"That's not true and you know it," Mammy Juno told the young woman later as they sat peeling vegetables in the large, airy kitchen. "There is no truth in that. It's the evil liquor making him say them things."

"He was stone sober when he told me," Starlin said, tossing another potato in the pot.

Mammy Juno paused in peeling a carrot to consider Starlin's words.

"The ship was never found. No one survived, except Benton, and that was a miracle of sorts. Mr. Cambridge loved all of you very much. And I know if he could be around, he would not be sneaking about like some ghost. He is dead, or he'd have come back to help us in our time of need. Now I may be one to fear the spirits, but this one is not Mr. Cambridge. I know that."

"Well—something isn't right around here," Starlin

419

mumbled, jabbing the knife into a bad spot on a potato.

"What do you think it is?"

"Who—is more like it." Mammy Juno paused. "Maybe it's some other poor soul? Heaven knows them wicked coral reefs have left enough spirits around here."

Starlin knew she was referring to the countless number of ships that had gone down because of the deadly reefs which run parallel to the Keys and to the Dry Tortugas. Every person in Key West had his own tales of superstition and ghostly apparitions. Starlin had no idea why anyone would want to prowl the estate—and especially around the playhouse—at all hours of the night, but she thought perhaps she just might sit up a night or two and see if "this ghostly prowler" appeared.

Around seven o'clock she brought Benton his dinner, and, to her utter disbelief, saw that he was up and moving about his room. He watched her calmly as she entered the room.

"Dinner? Mmmm, it smells delicious." He sat at a nearby table and waited for her to place the tray before him.

She did so, and lifted the napkin off the pot roast and vegetables.

"Who untied you?"

He picked up a hot roll. "Mammy Juno." Biting into it, he favored her with a pleased smile. "These are really good. Did you make them?"

Starlin felt all of her patience slipping away. Was there no one she could trust. While she could understand Mammy Juno's reluctance, and even guilt at keeping Benton tied to his bed, she knew also that just as soon as he had the opportunity he'd be at the bottle once again. She shook the napkin out forcefully, her expression one of concern.

"Don't look so upset. Mammy Juno isn't to blame. I am. She's been taking care of me for so long now that she just can't say no to anything I ask her."

Starlin sighed. "Oh, Benton. I'm not mad at anyone. It's just that I want to help you so much. And now I know what you are going to do."

"Stop trying, Starlin. Just leave me be. I don't want your help—never did."

Starlin was saddened by his callous words. "We'd fare better in this house, if we could be friends at least."

He laughed harshly. "There isn't a chance in hell of that, darlin'. It's better if we just know where we stand with each other—point-blank. At one point, I'd thought it might be nice to see you again. But I've changed my mind. I don't like you here interfering in my life, and my business. And I'll be real happy when you leave." He took a bite of his food, chewed thoughtfully for a moment, then continued. "In the past, I blamed you because my father never loved me as much as he loved you, his stepchild. But I know it wasn't your fault now. I don't blame you. I just don't like you. You always were a strong, independent person—and everyone paid you notice. Instead of shunning you, perhaps I should have taken the time to study you, and learn something."

"You are a hard, bitter man," she said, feeling pity for him. "And I wish it were not so."

He sipped at his coffee and sat back to favor her assessingly. "It's too late for us to go back and mend fences, Starlin. Forget about me."

Starlin shook her head. "No . . . I can never forget you, Benton. And it's never too late to start over. I, for one, am not giving up."

His eyes followed her from the room.

Starlin told no one of her plans to watch the grounds at night. She waited until everyone had gone to bed, then went up to the widow's walk where she could observe the entire island, and sat and waited for the surreptitious ghost to appear. There was no sign of him on the first and second nights. On the third evening, she had to wait an especially long time for the house to quiet down, as Benton was having a particularly bad time of it this evening. He and Arman were passing the time playing cards in Benton's room. He was drinking again. Where he got the bottle she did not know, nor did she interfere.

Once again, there appeared nothing moving except the trees. Starlin was given to wonder if perhaps Benton had been imagining the figure he'd seen. She waited until past midnight and then she decided to turn in for the night. It was then she swore she saw a movement close to the house, darting behind a banyan tree. She waited, and watched, but there was nothing further. With a shrug, she went inside.

The house was quiet; everyone presumably had settled down for the remainder of the night. She went immediately to her bedroom and began to take off her clothes. It was hot and stuffy in her room. She threw open the doors leading out onto the veranda to allow air to circulate throughout. Padding barefoot back to her small dressing room, she shucked her chemise and underclothes and splashed water from the washbowl over her face and body. She reached for her nightrail, hanging on a hook on the wall, and slipped it over her head. With a tired yawn, she shuffled across the room, blew out the lamp, and slid into bed. She was asleep before her head even hit the pillow. And awake just as quickly when she felt someone sit on the bed right next to her. Her eyes flew open. A rough-calloused hand had already covered her mouth.

In the moonlight shadows, her eyes stared up at him, wide and not without fright. Rayne! her mind screamed. He answered as if he read her very thoughts.

"You didn't think I would allow you to get away from me that easily, did you, my beauty?"

"Mmmrrggr" came the enraged mumbling from beneath his palm, eyes shooting daggers at Rayne Morgan's grinning countenance.

"I want you to come back with me. You don't belong here anymore."

She shook her head negatively, trying to remain calm, but with his hand resting just beneath her breast, lightly pressing against her rib cage, she knew he could feel the frightened pounding of her heart.

"I have to talk to you, and I need answers. So I'm going to take my hand away from your mouth. But I swear to you—if you make so much as a peep to warn anyone, I'll make certain you don't sit for a week. Do you understand?"

Starlin glared reproachfully at him for a moment, and then nodded.

Slowly, never quite sure of her, Rayne removed his hand.

She shot up in bed, her face zeroing in so close to his that their noses were almost touching. "Ghosts! Benton said! Someone prowling about that looks like our father, he said!" She hissed in outrage. "I'd be willing to bet that 'the ghost' is sitting right here in my bed with me this very minute!"

"Dammit woman! What kind of nonsense are you talking about now?" Rayne grabbed her shoulders, his patience worn thin.

"Benton claims he's been seeing someone rather odd around the place at night. I'd say you fit the description."

Rayne glared. "Where exactly?"

"The playhouse mostly."

"You mean that miniature replica of this place is a playhouse?" he snorted.

"Yes," she gritted. "Carl had it built for me years ago. We spent many hours there together—happy times that I cherish."

Rayne released her and sat back to ponder her words. Starlin observed him closely.

"What are you thinking, Rayne?"

He looked at her.

"I was only there one time, Starlin—tonight."

She could not suppress a gasp.

"But I rather doubt it was a ghost the other times." And then his voice hardening. "I think it was someone who was very much alive prowling about—looking for something."

"Why is it that I have the distinct feeling that you are going to tell me that there is a deep, dark secret here. I know nothing about, but that you seem to?" Her eyes were wary.

She watched him remove the ring from his finger. He tossed it to her. She caught it and favored him with a puzzled frown.

"Look closely at the ring and tell me what you see."

The moonlight shone brightly on the stones. Starlin stared at it, glanced back up at him, then stared at it again. It was similar to the design on the books.

"A beautiful ring with a strange design . . ." Her eyes widened, ". . . swirling through the stone." A memory taunted her.

He grinned at her. "I see our minds are thinking alike for a change. I believe the ring is a clue to a journal that took Carl years to compile. He never gave up his quest for the treasure. It became his obsession."

"And of course *you* want it." Her voice rose. "You've been scheming the entire time to get your hands on it!"

"Believe whatever you like," he said unemotionally. "But I will have that journal."

"And what if I decide you won't?"

His laugh was infuriating to her.

"I doubt anyone can stop me. And if you don't help me find it your midnight prowler just might decide to enlist your help." He reached out to take her hand within his. She jerked it away from him as though his touch seared her.

"Such a smooth liar," she said acidly. "You've been after the journal the entire time, I think. You've done everything to destroy my business, my family—and me. But I swear to you, Rayne, if you keep burning my ships—"

"I didn't burn your ship the other day!" He cut her off.

"You didn't?" she exclaimed.

"Not that I didn't entertain the thought. But seeing you changed my mind, although someone is set on

425

destroying you. It's the same person who's been attacking many of the salvaging ships and burning warehouses in an effort to gain complete control of the industry. He's been using me as his shield. I admit, before I came to England and met you, I did intercept a few of your ships. But lately I seem to find myself merely confiscating your goods to keep them from this pirate. I'm not good at explaining things, but I want to help you. The last haul was pharmaceuticals. I already have a buyer for you who I think will pay handsomely."

"Stop it!" she cried, afraid to hope. "Why should I believe anything you say?"

He leaned forward to brush his lips across hers, as if he could not help himself any longer. "I've missed you—even your sharp little tongue—very much."

Starlin could only stare at him. "If you are lying to me again, I'll—"

"I'm not," he interceded, his eyes meeting hers and making her heart leap.

To cover her flustered nerves, she looked away from him and down at the ring. She studied it, and then she remembered. "The books in the playhouse have a similiar design. Carl bought them in Italy years ago."

"Your father, you mean?"

"My stepfather, actually."

Her statement nearly took his breath away. "Your . . . stepfather?"

Starlin nodded. "Yes. We loved each other as if we were true blood kin. My real father died when I was a baby. Carl adopted me and raised me as his own."

Rayne grew quiet. "What a bloody fool I have been," he muttered disgustedly. And then speaking slowly, as if humility were indeed hard for him to swallow, "I'm sick to death of all of it. The hatred, the bitterness."

Starlin took a deep breath. "Most of your bitterness was turned inward, upon yourself, Rayne. I think perhaps you are learning that now."

"What happens to us now, Starlin?" he asked quietly.

"I don't know," she said honestly. "You treated me very well in some respects, and you allowed me to express my opinions freely. Even if you didn't always agree with them. You were the only man who ever listened to me as if you truly were interested in my views—about some things, anyway. But you did your part to destroy something precious to me . . . and I can't easily forgive you for that."

"I'm not asking for your forgiveness. I just seek a truce, that's all." His voice was husky. "Help me, Starlin. And in return, I shall help you put an end to this treasure matter forever." He picked up her hand and kissed her fingertips. She was fighting hard for control.

"Lord, how I want to believe you."

"Then do."

Starlin decided to tell him everything. "I believe that Carl was in love with your mother at one time. I've considered many things of late. And I don't think he would have taken advantage of that love. Just as you say you cannot take advantage of mine. Don't you see . . . your mother and Carl knew they could not betray their love with a sordid affair. The ring was the only way that she could express her love to him. It was a symbol. She wanted somehow to make him happy."

She hesitated, recalling once again Carl's words the day that he'd given her the ring. "And he understood this. I think a part of the quest was for her also. He told me the ring had been given to him in love, and that love would guide me. It's time we put a bit of trust in the people that we love . . . and also in each other."

Chapter Twenty-four

Starlin followed Rayne into the dark playhouse. She could never remember having been here at night. In the shadows she sought out his hand.

"It doesn't look quite so cheery," she remarked.

Rayne released her hand. "Stay put until I light a candle."

"There's one sitting on the table beneath the window."

It was quiet, and then she heard him fumbling around.

"I found it."

Within minutes the candle flickered to life and the room glowed softly.

Starlin wasted no more time and approached the bookshelves to stare at the beautifully bound volumes.

"There are so many. This could take all night."

Rayne brought the candle over and stood beside her. "Look closely at the ring. The design on the book we're looking for should be identical to the one in the ring."

She saw that many of the books bore designs, some simple, others more intricate. "Yes, I think you're right." She was becoming more excited as her eyes skimmed each volume. There were shelves from the floor to the ceiling. She saw nothing that caught her attention. How strange, she mused, that she'd never seen the similarity between the design in the ring and that on the book covers. She paused and went back to examine one volume a bit closer. It was similar, but not exact. She was becoming frustrated.

"There isn't any that looks exactly like the ring."

"It has to be here," Rayne insisted, perusing another shelf.

Suddenly, with a startling flash of memory, Starlin recalled every detail of that last day she saw her parents alive. Carl had watched her closely while he told her to remember that love would guide her. Love! That was it. A book of romantic sonnets! She remembered Carl had composed a book of sonnets. He had never read any of it to her, yet had worked on it incessantly, sometimes even coming alone to the playhouse late at night to write. Her eyes searched for it on the bookshelves. It was nowhere to be seen.

And then she thought about where she would put it if she intended a small child to find it. How tall was she then? She dropped quickly to her knees and began removing books from the shelf. At last she found the book she was looking for.

Her heart beating a tattoo against her rib cage, she pried it loose. Holding the ring in the light of the candle, Starlin was able to discern that the design on the book's leather-bound cover was the same as on the ring.

She opened it slowly.

Carl's handwriting filled the pages. Tears formed in Starlin's eyes. "I think I've found it," she said, her tone a little breathless.

He had written down everything. His feelings, his hopes, and dreams. And as she sat down on the floor and continued reading, she became aware, that interwoven in the prose were cleverly phrased words, each interlinked with the word *Love*. And if she wrote it all down on paper, she was certain it would clearly point the way to the treasure.

Love will guide you, he had told her. At the time she'd been too young to understand. And after her parents' death she had never come into the playhouse again.

Rayne looked at her in anticipation. "Is that the journal?"

"Yes, it is." She met his eyes. "It's been here all along."

She saw a furtive movement behind Rayne. Someone had just stepped into the room. Starlin let out a relieved sigh. "Benton! What are you doing out here?"

His words were slurred. "I heard you two talking in your room. I was intrigued. I followed you."

She saw a flash of white teeth in the dim light.

"So, he had it hidden here the entire time. Waiting for you to grow up and find it, should he not return. It took a long time for you to come back. Father's been watching for you. I see him out here quite often now."

"Carl is dead, Benton," Starlin said firmly.

"Then why do I see him around the playhouse?" He appeared to consider his own question. "I think he's checking on me ... making certain I don't snoop around here and find it."

"You can't honestly believe that Carl—"

Rayne put a hand on Starlin's arm to quiet her.

"What is going on, Benton?" Rayne asked calmly.

Benton swayed on his feet, one eye focusing on Rayne. "You! . . . I heard everything you said to Starlin in her room. The man everyone thinks is a pirate-hunter . . . is a pirate himself." He laughed, bemused by it all. "And my dear Starlin is married to him!" He pointed a finger at her. "Even though Father wanted you to have it, Starlin, you will not. The treasure is rightfully mine, you know. I almost lost my life searching for it."

"I have a suspicion your brother knows more about that fateful day than he is admitting," Rayne said to Starlin.

"What really happened back then?" Starlin asked quietly. "I think now you are ready to tell it."

Benton sighed heavily. "Perhaps I am at that." He rubbed a hand across his eyes. "I have been running from it long enough, I think. From the start, the entire expedition was doomed. I never wanted to go to the Triangle. That place is cursed. Strange sights, ghostly fogs, and some sort of magnetic pull that draws boats off course, sometimes into reefs, others simply just disappearing. That force is the way to the treasure, don't you know? There is a specific area near the island of Antare where the magnetic pull is so powerful that you cannot steer out of it. Father sailed directly into it . . ."

"Dear God," Starlin gasped.

Benton came closer, leaning his shoulder against a wall, seemingly for support. "Father was certain he knew what he was doing. It was terribly strange there, in the eye of the Triangle, with those shifting mists upon the water and the storms that raged and whirled about. Father knew where he was headed—he was the only one who did. Gwen and I became frightened when we entered some sort of luminous, white water. We're here, Father said. Gwen and I just looked at each other. He dropped anchor and was eager to enter notations in the log. The galleon was directly below us, clearly visible on the reefs. I prepared to dive, even though I'd heard the stories of the area. I was afraid, but I didn't want him to know. So I dove—and I saw the ghostly wreck of the galleon looming before me. I had a line tied around me, and I swam toward the ship. Suddenly, the water changed. The temperature was frigid. I was freezing. I turned around to swim back, and it was then I came face to face with the largest barracuda I've ever seen. It was at least six feet long. And he did not wish me in his territory. I surfaced fast, and climbed on board the ship. I explained my reasoning. Father was adamant about staying in the area. We waited awhile, and then Father stated he was going to dive. Gwen and I tried to talk him out of it. He tied the line around himself, and grabbed a spear. Gwen held one end of the line. I was terrified and shivering with a chill I could not seem to disperse." He halted, his face crumbling. "It . . . was as if we weren't wanted there."

"I don't think you were," Rayne stated solemnly.

Benton swallowed, and continued. "I wanted to go back. Father surfaced several times for air and to tell us he had almost reached the galleon. The last dive, he was down so long. Too long. I told Gwen to pull him up, but she said Father would be furious if we did that. We waited . . . and waited . . . and finally I grabbed the line from her and pulled with all of my strength. The line felt light . . . and I knew even before I pulled it up that Father was no longer attached. Gwen became hysterical. She snatched the line out of my hand, and before I could stop her, she dove over the side. I was in shock, and it took me a few minutes to react." His voice fell to barely a whisper. "They died—both of them."

"And you just left them—without even trying to dive for them!" Starlin sobbed, her eyes wide from the horrible story he had just told.

Benton nodded miserably. "There was nothing left to do. I didn't wish to die, too!"

"And you were found in the ocean because the boat capsized," Rayne said.

"Yes. I don't know how I got out of there. It was a nightmare!" he sobbed. "Both of them . . . victims of that place. I can't really say what happened down there near the galleon. It might have been the barracuda. It was big enough to . . . to . . ." His shoulders were shaking and he bowed his head. "And I couldn't let anyone know what had happened . . . don't you see? How could I explain it. I knew they were dead—that the Devil's Sea had managed to claim them. I didn't want people to think I was such a coward. I just pretended I couldn't remember anything."

Starlin placed her hands over her face. Rayne wrapped a comforting arm about her.

"Tell me what you saw going on out here before tonight?" Rayne probed.

"A man has been out here, watching me . . . Father I'm certain." Benton glanced at Starlin. "You know that sailor's cap and jacket he always wore, Starlin. It

434

was him . . . or his ghost."

"I can't believe that," Starlin gasped, her hands falling to her sides.

"Nor I," Rayne agreed.

"Well, who else could it be?" Benton yelled. "Someone has been out here around this playhouse. And he looks just like my father . . . right down to the same clothes!"

"It's someone trying to scare you. He wants you to think it's Carl so that you stay away from here. I think he might suspect that something of great value is out here," Rayne explained.

"The journal." Benton laughed shrilly. "Let him have it. I'll never go back there again."

"Oh, Benton," Starlin breathed sadly. "All of these years you've carried this awful secret inside you."

"I have had a pretty good idea who is behind your problems," Rayne told them. "And I had even thought you were in league with him at one time, Benton."

"Who?" Benton and Starlin echoed in unison.

"I have to make certain that I have your word that you will keep quiet about my identity. I can't have my activities exposed until I've caught the culprit responsible for everything. The confiscation of your goods, the burning of your ships and warehouses."

"I was beginning to believe it was Father—or his ghost—come back to make certain that I never received anything. But, of course, in my sober moments I know how foolish that is." He held Rayne's gaze. "Very well, Morgan, I give you my word. Now, tell me this man's name?"

Rayne wasn't certain whether he could trust Benton. He considered it briefly, then said, "It's Wells . . . he's

435

your midnight prowler."

"My own attorney?" Benton was stunned.

"I am not surprised," Starlin said. "But how do you plan to expose him, Rayne?"

The nerves of everyone in the room were taut. Rayne was amazed to find himself actually contemplating saving the Cambridge salvaging operation. But then, his gaze shifted to Starlin. Her eyes were imploring him.

"There's talk that your attorney, Malcolm Wells, is behind a man by the name of Foster. He's buying out the salvors who reportedly have been financially ruined by Scorpio. Foster seems to know before anyone else when the salvors are close to bankruptcy and willing to sell out. Unfortunately, instead of manning the boats with the same crews, he mans his newly acquired ships with crewmen from other ports. Key West seamen are suffering double, while Wells is in the background, reaping a fortune on the side."

Suddenly, all of the pieces fell into place. The man responsible for their misfortunes was none other than the firm's own lawyer. Benton swore softly.

"What a fool I have been. Wells has been making certain that I'm kept supplied with liquor. And even when Starlin tried to dry me out, he'd send out satchels of papers for me to look over. Inside, he'd always place a bottle or two."

"I wondered about that, you know," Starlin said. "But Mammy Juno was always the one the satchel was delivered to. I never had a chance to get my hands on it before you did, Benton."

"Wells knows how easily I manipulate Mammy Juno," Benton explained. "He would make certain you were nowhere about before coming out here."

436

In the flickering darkness Starlin's eyes met Rayne's.

"And I'd be willing to bet that Malcolm Wells was the man behind the awful events in England," Starlin stated, her voice low.

"He was," Rayne replied. "Fredrick has a piece of cloth that Merlin tore from Wells's cloak at the scene of your grandfather's accident. Ely snuck into Wells's office at the warehouse one day. It was the exact color, and when he compared it to a mended section on the garment, it matched perfectly."

Starlin looked up at Rayne. "I have wondered about something. Fredrick. How is he involved in all of this?"

"He is my uncle—my mother's brother," Rayne explained. "But he is very loyal to you, Starlin. He has been your friend from the first time he met you. He wanted to make certain all was well with you, so he sailed from England to Antare to find out."

"Oh dear," Starlin said in dismay. "And I ran off again."

"I'm certain he'll understand," Rayne said wryly.

Benton appeared lost in his own thoughts. "Damn Wells. My own attorney seeking to destroy me?"

"You aren't the only one he sought to ruin," Rayne told him. "But you were making it easy for him. He thought he could have it all by simply encouraging you to stay drunk while he ran the business, charting the courses for your ships, his own men interceding and taking your finds to his warehouses. He knew there was a journal somewhere." He met Benton's bloodshot gaze. "I'd be willing to bet he's the one prowling about the estate. When he began to figure that Starlin might be the one with knowledge of the journal, he kept you both under constant surveillance. He's clever. But we can still beat him."

"How can we stop him, Rayne?" Starlin blurted angrily.

A cunning smile crossed Rayne's lips. "A friend of mine will help us out. She'll tell Wells that she has heard the Cambridges are going after a big find. After having met Starlin, he'll start to wonder if she's decided to search out the treasure."

"But won't that be risky?" Benton asked.

"We have no choice," Starlin said firmly.

"She's right, Benton. We either try and outsmart him, or he'll eventually get everything that he's after. He's giving a masquerade ball on Friday. It will be easy for us to slip in as guests, spread a few rumors, and then slip out without notice."

Benton looked dubious. "You can't tell me it's not going to be dangerous. His men are very good at what they do. They're true pirates in every sense of the word."

"It's going to take something like this to flush him out into the open," Rayne told them. "He has been blaming Scorpio for his evil deeds for so long now, that who will believe otherwise unless we catch him in the act. He's very much like that barracuda near the galleon. He waits, and watches, and guards his own safety well. But we'll have dangled the perfect bait before him. He'll come . . . and we'll be waiting."

"So you believe he'll follow us with every intention of forcing us to show him the way to the treasure?" Starlin asked tensely.

"There's no doubt in my mind," Rayne responded with a grim look.

Starlin shivered, and stared down at the journal. "I

438

know Carl never intended anything like this to happen. He only wished to leave us something special . . . something that was very meaningful to him."

"I won't allow anything to happen to you, love," Rayne assured her. "I'll watch you every minute." He favored her with a wolfish smile. "And I suppose that means that I'd better have my belongings moved from the ship over here."

Starlin was all too aware of those magnetic eyes as he watched her closely. She said nothing.

Rayne turned to Benton. "What say you, Cambridge? Can we depend on you to help us capture Wells and put an end to his piracy?"

"Well . . . I really have to think about it," Benton stammered, his hands shaking, his eyes cast downward.

Starlin was livid. "If you run from this, you may as well turn around and go back in the house and drink yourself into a stupor, for you'll never be able to hold your head up again. I think you owe it to both of our parents . . . don't you?"

Benton flinched, but he made no move to leave. With a huge sigh he said, "No, there will be no more running. You are right. I must take a stand if I am ever going to gain control of my life again."

"Then let's go inside and Starlin will make us some coffee. After you've sobered up a bit, we'll discuss the plan until everyone knows what they're expected to do," Rayne suggested.

Malcolm Wells took the last bite of his Key lime pie and sat back in his chair with a resplendent smile.

"That was divine," he told the woman sitting across

the table from him. "Extend my compliments to your cook."

Beaming, the big woman offered Malcolm a cigar from a pearl smoking case.

"Why thank you, Lucy, I don't mind if I do," Malcolm said. He watched in amusement as Lucy took a long, black cigar from the case and placed it between her own lips. A servant, who had been swishing a palm fan over them during the entire meal, hurried to light their cigars.

Lucy took a deep drag of her cigar and exhaled. Blue smoke floated upward about her face and drifted in wavering lines toward the ceiling.

"Vincente makes the best damn cigar on the island," she said, referring to the first man in Key West to open up a small cigar factory. "He's gonna be rich one of these days, I just can feel it in my bones," she added with a wide smile, her brown eyes all but disappearing in her fleshy face. "Cigars are gonna be a big business here. Don't take much to make a man rich in this town. Just a bit of forethought and the nerve to act."

"Yes, I think you are right about that on both counts," Malcolm agreed, looking around him at the occupants in the saloon. "Civilization is definitely creeping in on us. And all of them getting wealthier by every day by one means or another. Why, who ever would have thought that the wrecking industry would boom to such proportions in such a short period? Look around you, Lucy, all of your customers are associated with it in one way or the other. Auctioneers, salvors, even the wharf owners are making fortunes." He suddenly scowled. "I just happened to pick the wrong people to associate myself with, that's all."

Lucy Belle was a big, attractive Bahamian woman who had been one of the first to open a saloon with female entertainment and keep it running profitably. She tolerated no rowdies or toughs, and if a man wanted to buy himself some time with one of her "girls," he paid her a goodly sum for the honor. If there was any social class in the waterfront area, "Lucy's" was the place. The decor was flashy, with bright pink walls, tropical plants everywhere, and conch shells filled with fresh flowers. Lucy liked to give her customers the impression that her place was a homey establishment, where they could kick back and hang around a spell and relax. As long as they had the money to afford her high prices, of course.

"A hodgepodge of humanity," Lucy replied. "The wrecking business is turning this swamp into a boom town. Every one of them looking for the same thing as you and me—a way to turn a fast buck, and spend it just as quickly." She leaned closer to Benton, her ample bosom resting on the tabletop. "I heard tell from one of my girls that you just might be in for a substantial raise yourself, if everything goes as the Cambridge girl has it planned." Seeing his eyes widen slightly, she continued. "This is just hearsay, mind you. But it's something to do with the biggest find that anyone has ever come across. No word on the exact location, of course. But then, I expect you'll be hearing more about it from them any day now."

Malcolm was staring blankly at her as if he were taking it all in by slow degrees. "That chit knew all along. Damn, but I was right," he murmured softly.

"What's that sugar?" Lucy inquired.

Malcolm grunted. "A major find, huh?"

"That's what I heard. Everyone is right excited about it, too."

"Well, I certainly can see why. And I am, too. That's a real uplifting piece of news, sweet." Malcolm rose suddenly from his chair. "You don't mind if I make it a short visit tonight, do you, Lucy? I have a lot of extra work that needs my immediate attention."

Lucy shook her black ringlets. "You go right ahead, Malcolm, honey. Lucy knows where your heart would really rather be. You come back and visit me when you're less busy, and we'll have us a right good time."

Lucy Belle watched Wells depart and motioned to the servant. "Manuel," she said. "I want you to go the back way, through the alleys down to the pier. Don't give this message to anyone but Ely Morgan. He's waiting." She lowered her voice to a whisper. "Tell him the fish is swimming in the direction of the net, and all that he has to do is reach out and catch him."

Starlin took her time in dressing for the party at Malcolm Wells's home. She was thinking of the letter that she and Rayne had sent off to her grandfather, informing him of their safe arrival in the Keys and telling him that as soon as they concluded business matters they would return to England. Fredrick had told Rayne that the earl was recovering nicely and looking forward to their return to England. She was relieved.

And Starlin hoped they could go home soon. She placed her palms on her abdomen. There was no movement inside her yet, but soon . . . she mused with a gentle smile. She had been to see the doctor and he had confirmed her suspicions. She was going to have a baby in seven months. Wouldn't Rayne be thrilled—and Grandfather? A tingle raced down her spine. Just as soon as this nightmare was over, she would be able to tell them all her good news. But not yet. For she knew Rayne would never allow her to be a party to their clever scheme if he had the slightest suspicion that she was carrying their child.

Starlin closed her eyes for a minute, trying to envision just what their baby might look like. Boy or girl? She shrugged. That really did not matter. But she did hope the child would look a lot like Rayne. She imagined most women in love felt much the same way. And she did love her husband, more and more with every passing day. His deep voice behind her brought her eyes open immediately to stare at him through the cheval mirror.

"What were you dreaming about, my beauty?" he inquired, kissing the back of her neck, exposed by an upsweep of tumbling curls.

He was attired in only a burgundy robe. His hair was still damp from his bath and lay in unruly disorder about his forehead.

"Mmmmm . . . you smell wonderful," she said throatily.

"And you look wonderful. I'll have to watch you closely tonight, so those pirates don't steal you away." He pulled her against him, wrapping his arms about her waist and nuzzling her earlobe with his lips.

Starlin prayed it would always be this way between them. Yet there was still something so uncertain that kept him from becoming completely hers. Was she only imagining a coiled tenseness about him? And perhaps it was just because of the dangerous scheme they would set into motion on this night. Was he concerned for her? She hoped it was because he loved her too much to want to think of what his life would be like without her. She was not afraid—she trusted him. Trust. She tested the word in her thoughts. It was wonderful to have someone to share your hopes and dreams with. True, this venture tonight was not without risk, but she felt confident that they could accomplish it together.

He caressed her shining hair. "Damn! I hate having you involved in this. I'm almost tempted to send you back to Antare instead."

"I wouldn't go," Starlin said simply.

"And if I insisted."

"I still wouldn't go," she told him, an impish smile reflecting in the looking glass.

"And how did I know that you would say that?" Rayne teased, turning her in his arms and kissing the tip of her nose.

"Because you know me better than anyone."

"Yes," he murmured, "that I do."

She pressed her lips to the tip of his chin. "And I you."

"But I wonder if I shall ever know you completely, my darling. You are the most intriguing woman I have ever met."

Her arms encircled his neck and she peered up into his eyes. A slow flush of pleasure spread across his lean features. "As it should be. You will never grow bored with me then."

"That could never happen." Before she could protest, he had swept her up into his arms and carried her toward the bed.

"Rayne! We'll be terribly late for Wells's party."

"Merely an hour, madam," he offered with a light kiss and a rogue's smile. "We don't wish to be the first ones to arrive, now do we?"

Starlin favored him with a dubious look, even as his fingers moved swiftly over the fastenings of her gown.

"Heaven help me if I should ever seek to be a part of your clever planning again."

His lips moved across the perfumed softness of her throat. "Let me see if I might change your thinking."

"That's terribly unfair, applying such heavenly persuasion," she whispered near his ear, shivering in anticipation of his lovemaking.

"I never play fair."

"I discovered that long ago."

She pulled his head back down to hers.

Chapter Twenty-five

Malcolm Wells's home was situated in the middle of a swampy bayou, an island unto itself that suited the attorney's need for absolute privacy.

To reach his home, which Rayne found even more secure than his castle at Sontavon, one had to take a boat and wind through the swamps. The waterway was not the most appealing that Starlin had ever seen, but it was interesting, teeming with wildlife and unusual vegetation.

Starlin and Rayne arrived at Wells's dock shortly after sunset and were greeted by several men in pirate costumes. Benton was acting the part of their pilot, and would be remaining behind with the boat to ensure their safe departure.

Starlin met Rayne's eyes with a questioning look. The men all looked of disreputable character. What were they walking into?

Horse-drawn rigs transported them toward the house. The long road was especially dark. Starlin could hear all sorts of creatures scurrying about in the marshy forests. From behind her mask, she could barely make out the towering forms of huge willows lining the road on either side. After they had gone about a mile, she heard the sound of music and voices drifting over the swamp.

Lights were ablaze in every room in the house as they approached the looming structure. It was not a crude design, as she'd anticipated, but a two-story dwelling with double French doors leading out onto wide verandas. The doors were thrown wide on this exceedingly warm night, and Starlin could see that the house was filled to capacity with guests in costume dress.

Rayne said little to her on the drive for fear of being overheard, but once they'd departed from the buggy and the vehicle had rumbled off, he leaned over to whisper in her ear.

"Do not wander around on your own. Stay as close to me as possible—no matter what."

"Have no fear. I shall dog your every step," she replied. This was one time she planned to do exactly as he said, without protest.

The upper portion of her face was completely obscured behind a purple satin mask that enhanced her soft, alluring eyes. Her gown was of such a deep purple to almost appear black. It was soft and clinging, an enticing creation that Mammy Juno had slaved over for three nights in order to have it completed in time. She told Starlin that it was a copy of a high priestess's gown, and had even placed a delicate shell necklace about the young woman's throat, claiming it would ward off evil and protect her from harm.

Starlin favored Rayne with an admiring glance. He

448

was dressed to complement her costume: dark, clinging breeches and shirt open to the waist, and a voluminous black cloak thrown back over his broad shoulders. The severe color and the black half mask gave him the appearance of a fierce brigand. She knew that no one would dare harm her tonight if she stayed near to him. He took her hand and drew her along behind him toward the side of the house.

"We'll slip in through those doors over there," he told her, "and out the very same way. I'll let you know when it's time to leave. Bloody hell, but I hate taking you in there." He hesitated as if considering leaving her behind.

"You can't wander around without a lady on your arm," Starlin said quickly. "No one comes to a party like this alone. It would look suspicious."

He grinned. "All right, then, my adventurous vixen. Shall we make our entrance?"

Once inside the large parlor, they had little trouble losing themselves within the crowd of people. There were so many guests that it was difficult to keep track of Rayne.

At one point, she thought she heard Malcolm's familiar voice behind her, yet did not dare to turn around and look.

Rayne circulated freely, appearing to drink far too much, although in truth he was slipping the glasses of champagne to Starlin, who disposed of them wherever possible.

After awhile a couple standing next to her began talking excitedly about the Devil's treasure. The Cambridges, they said, had decided to seek it out once again and had enlisted a crew and planned a careful route. Within a short time the news had circulated throughout the entire room. Rayne's plan had succeeded.

Starlin had stepped out of the parlor to dispose of another glass of champagne when she saw Malcolm hurrying down the hall and into the study.

Starlin hurried down the hallway to pause before the door. What was he up to? She leaned over to try to peek through the narrow key hole only to sense someone standing directly behind her. She froze in motion.

"See something that captures your fancy?" said a gruff voice from over her shoulder.

Starlin weaved drunkenly and feigned a convincing hiccup.

"I think we'd better see what the boss has to say about you."

Before she could turn around, a hand went over her mouth and a huge arm wrapped about her tiny waist. Her angry struggles were useless. He squeezed her so tightly that she nearly swooned. Deciding that she might fare better if she did, she closed her eyes, let her body go slack in his arms. She felt her attacker nudge the door with the toe of his boot. It was quickly opened. She was dragged into the room and tossed roughly onto a leather couch. As she sprawled willy-nilly, she flung her arms across her face and slumped into a corner of the plush cushions. She forced herself to remain still when she heard Wells refer scathingly to Rayne.

"That drunken fool who's been rambling about the Devil's treasure since he got here has unknowingly given us all that we need to bring our association with the Cambridge family to an end at last. With the treasure in my possession, I'll be able to retire from this pirating business and live quite splendidly in Europe. And don't you dare fail me this time, Foster," she heard Wells say. "You have the crew ready to go first thing in the morning. They'll be heading into the Triangle and we'll follow."

Footsteps drew near her. She opened her eyes to mere slits to peek between her arms.

"What are you doing bringing some soused female in here like this?" Wells queried sharply.

Starlin didn't move a muscle.

"She appeared to be gettin' a bit too nosey, Boss. Found her trying to look through the keyhole."

"Hmph," Malcolm grunted. "There's one of them females at every party. Always wandering off in search of a little private party of their own."

"Wouldn't mind doing a bit of that myself with this one," Malcolms' thug snickered.

"Forget it, Foster. You've got to see that the ship and the men are ready, instead. Heard talk all over out there of Cambridge going after the treasure. The stupid fool doesn't know it yet, but I'm the only one who is going to get his hands on that find. I've earned it."

Starlin did her best to keep her face hidden while quietly listening. Malcolm Wells came closer.

"She looks a pretty little thing, doesn't she?" he said, his voice dropping to a husky whisper.

"I saw her first," Foster protested.

"Perhaps you might have her, after all—as incentive, shall we say." Malcolm laughed. "And when you tire of her, simply leave everything to me. She'll not say much and risk her reputation. Her kind knows when to keep her mouth shut."

Wells bent over her, and Starlin could feel his hot gaze roaming up and down her body. "She won't find the party dull where you'll be taking her, eh, Foster?"

Foster snickered.

"You'd best get out of here before anyone discovers that she's gone. Of course with all of that talk that drunken idiot is circulating in there about the treasure expedition, every fool and his friend will have his mind on the treasure . . . not his wife." He strode away from her. Starlin listened while he left the room.

The man, Foster, ran a caressing finger along her arm.

"You were looking for a private party with some fun, huh? Well, I'm sure gonna give you one, sweetie. And you'll be the belle of the ball."

One minute Rayne had seen Starlin standing nonchalantly in the hallway; the next, she had vanished. He wandered several times through the crowds of people but did not see her. Trying to appear calm, he walked out into the hallway and glanced about. Nothing.

A terrible feeling gripped him. Wells was behind her mysterious disappearance, he felt certain of it. Unholy fire blazed in his eyes.

As Rayne slipped unseen from the house and circled stealthily around the veranda, he thought he heard a shrill yell drift out through one of the windows. Before he had time to react, a man swearing profusely came bursting through a door onto the veranda, a thrashing, kicking virago imprisoned in his arms. He dragged her a foot, and she kicked him in the shin. Then he grabbed her again. He kept one hand across her mouth. She must have bitten his hand, for he released her and stood shaking the offended limb. The woman sprinted ahead of her attacker.

It was pitch-black, but Rayne knew immediately who she was. Starlin! There was no other female who found trouble so easily, or confronted it with such daring.

Forming a quick plan, Rayne swung himself up onto a low-lying branch hanging directly over their path. Unseen, and deadly quiet, he waited.

Starlin ran past on flying feet. The man gave quick pursuit. As he drew near, Rayne tensed to spring forward. Silently he pounced upon the stunned Foster and knocked him to the ground.

Rayne took pleasure in clipping the man soundly on the jaw. Foster gave a strangled cry and crumpled to the ground without having so much as seen what he had run into.

Spinning about, Rayne caught a fleeting glimpse of Starlin wasting no time in scurrying off in the direction of the boat dock. Rayne went after her.

Keeping well off the road, Starlin slowed her pace and took to the shadows, avoiding the departing guests who were returning to their boats.

She screamed when a man grasped her arm, but was silenced by his hand.

"Going somewhere without me?" Rayne drawled.

He dropped his hand.

"Oh, Rayne," Starlin said breathlessly, "I am glad to see you. Wells and his cohort are plotting just like you said they would. I was looking through a keyhole in one of the rooms because I thought I heard something going on . . . and you'll never guess what happened?" she said, wide-eyed.

"Let me try," he said, lifting one eyebrow.

Starlin ignored him, grabbing his hand and pulling him along behind her toward the dock.

"No, we don't have time. Let's just say that Wells bought our story about the treasure and he's gearing up for the confrontation."

Rayne gave a little smile behind her back before murmuring, "And a great time was had by all at the party."

When they reached the boat dock, Benton was waiting. He was playing dice with Malcolm's men. And they were all taking pulls from a big jug of rum. Benton was loaded, and doing a lot of talking. It made Rayne nervous. He would have liked to have drawn his gun, and shot the jug to pieces in Benton's hand. As it was, he could not afford to make a scene. He approached Benton and said loud enough for everyone to hear, "The lady isn't feeling well. She would like to go home."

Without drawing undue attention to themselves, they took their boat and headed back along the waterway, disappearing into the mists.

Starlin awoke at dawn the following morning. She glanced over at Rayne, who appeared to still be sleeping soundly. At the smell of frying bacon drifting upstairs from the kitchen, she wrinkled her nose and put a hand over her mouth. Her stomach lurched, and she swallowed several times. She tried lying perfectly still, not daring to move a muscle. Then with a smothered groan she dashed for the chamber pot. She was violently ill. When it was over she collapsed onto the floor with a sigh of relief.

Rayne was beside her, a damp cloth in his hand and concern for her in his expression. He hunkered down next to her and gently wiped her moist brow. He drew back to study her pale features, dawning awareness in his eyes. He smoothed back the tangled hair lying plastered to her forehead, and then his hand moved downward to lightly touch her abdomen. His eyes met hers.

"You are with child."

Starlin hesitated. "Yes," she sighed.

"How long were you going to keep your condition from me?" he inquired, his expression hardening.

"I—" Starlin began, but fell silent.

Rayne strode away to drag her trunk from the corner and began gathering up her clothes.

"What do you think you are doing?" she asked.

"You're leaving here—today. I want Benton to go with you."

"With me, where?"

"Back to Antare, at least until I've snared Wells." He snapped open a carpetbag and began tossing in her toiletries. "I can't trust Benton to stay away from the bottle and —"

"What you really mean is you have no use for anyone from the Cambridge family any longer. We've served our purpose," Starlin said in a tight voice.

"This is one time you'll do as your told, without argument."

She ran to the bed and grabbed Carl's book of carefully composed sonnets from under her pillow.

"This is what you were after all along, wasn't it? And now that you have it, you no longer need me. Your precious family treasure is still safe—no Cambridge will ever go near it again." She threw the journal at him in a rage.

Rayne knocked it aside and resumed packing. "You're going," he said.

Rayne stood on the crowded dock and watched the Cambridge ship glide away from the busy wharf. He could still feel Starlin in his arms, taste the salt of her tears on his lips as he'd kissed her good-bye. He saw her standing at the rail looking back at him, and cursed the fates over which he had no control. So much had transpired since that long-ago night when he'd boldly confronted his destiny on that isolated shoreline, that night his beloved enemy had come into his life. He stood there with Ely beside him, watching her go out of his life and feeling as if he'd just lost a part of himself.

"It won't be for long, Rayne," Ely said, trying his best to cheer his brother.

Rayne forced his gaze away from the *Ice Princess* disappearing on the horizon.

"Of course it won't," he agreed.

Ely placed a hand on Rayne's shoulder. "It was the right decision. Riley will take the ship through the Triangle by the route you indicated, far from our confrontation with Wells. And Benton may be a lot of things, but he won't let anything happen to her. He even seemed happy about the baby—more than . . ." Realizing what he had been about to say, Ely halted.

"More than I am? That's what you were about to say,

wasn't it?" Rayne finished for him.

"You aren't exactly overjoyed about it."

To his surprise, Rayne only swung around and strode briskly away from the wharf, leaving Ely to wonder if his mule-headed brother would ever find the peace he so desperately sought.

Malcolm Wells was not an easy man to defeat. A ruthless, cunning manipulator, he welcomed adversaries and concentrated all his efforts on beating them. In the pirate Scorpio, he had found a most worthy opponent. But every man has his weakness, he thought with a devious smile, sitting at his desk in the Cambridge warehouse. After repeatedly questioning some of his crew about several of their last sea raids—and discovering that Scorpio had intervened—he had come to the conclusion that it was more than chance that both Rayne Morgan and Scorpio had appeared in Key West at the same time.

It was true of course that no one but Wells and his men knew Scorpio had foiled their recent attacks on the Cambridge ships. His fingers thrummed upon the desk top.

"Why in the world would that pirate sail into these waters and suddenly start acting on behalf of the good people of Key West? When not long ago he sought to destroy Benton Cambridge as vengefully as I did." He leaned back in his chair. "And made it quite easy for me to blame him for everything. Could it be that he has formed some sort of pact with that devil, Rayne Morgan?" He rested his elbows on top of the desk and placed his hand beneath his chin. "Or . . . is there something else going on here that I haven't heeded—until now?"

Within seconds, his frustrations lessened, and he was almost amused.

"Damn! But it was right in front of my eyes this entire time. Morgan was clever . . . but every man has his weakness. And I would be willing to bet that Starlin Cambridge Morgan is a weakness that both Scorpio and Morgan share—quite intimately."

Wells suddenly sprang up from his chair and yanked open the door to call his secretary.

"Taylor! Get me the manifests of the Cambridge cargoes that have been lost most recently. And find out if the mayor is in his offices. I have something vitally important to discuss with him at once."

Chapter Twenty-six

The *Tempest* rode at anchor within an isolated section of water bordered on three sides by thick, green jungle foliage. It was a deep pool that she rested in, her top masts and lines shrouded in dark netting that made her appear to blend into the scenery.

Rayne Morgan paced back and forth upon the maindeck in agitation, a piece of paper clutched in his hand.

"What the hell is he up to?" he growled to his brother, who was equally distressed. "Wells claims to have Starlin held captive in a warehouse at the far end of Wharf Street. If I don't go there he says he'll kill her, without hesitation."

"I think this is nothng more than a ruse to delay our setting sail for the Triangle," Ely said. "How could he possibly have gotten to Starlin when he did not know she was leaving the Keys."

Rayne looked at Ely. "I agree. However, can I take a chance with her life?"

"How long ago did you receive this note?"

"About twenty minutes ago. One of our men was at Lucy Belle's. A man approached him and handed him the note, saying that he should make certain that his captian received it."

"It appears someone has been watching us closely to have known all of our haunts."

Rayne's lips curled slightly at Ely's words. "Or, doing a bit more talking than they should."

"Of course!" Ely growled, his expression bleak. "Benton."

"He can't resist the bottle, and Wells knows it. I should never have allowed him to know of my decision to send Starlin to Antare. There was the chance of his drinking too much . . . and talking more than he should."

Ely swore angrily. "Damn him! I knew his drinking was going to lead to trouble. Wells has undoubtedly been plying him with drink in order to get what he wants out of him—information."

Rayne nodded at Ely's words. "Yes, I think so. And you see why I cannot take risks. The warehouse is but an hour's ride from here. If I am not back by noon, sail on without me. The *Tempest* is a much faster ship than the *Princess*. The few hours delay in our departure won't hurt us. We should be able to catch her by nightfall."

"I don't like it," Ely retorted. "What if he doesn't have Starlin? You could be walking right into an ambush?"

"And what if, by a slim possibility, he does?"

Ely rammed his closed fist into his open palm. "Damnation!" He frowned, watching Rayne sheath his broadsword. "I'll go with you. The men can handle everything, including Wells's pirates."

"No! I don't want to have to worry about anyone else while I'm there. I can slip in and, if all goes well, get out. And remember—if I'm not back in time—go on."

Rayne scanned the swampy terrain behind the sandy shoreline. Nothing moved that appeared unnatural. He breathed a relieved sigh. That was good. It seemed that Wells had not discovered their hideaway . . . and perhaps was only bluffing about holding Starlin captive. Rayne knew he was in a precarious position. And he was certain it was Benton Cambridge who had put him there. Once again, he felt searing anger and a need to strike back at the name Cambridge.

Rayne glanced about him as he rode down the narrow street and turned his horse into an alleyway. Listening carefully to every movement, every creak and sigh of the wind, he halted his mount in back of the dark, silent building and tied off his horse. Only the shadows were waiting for him when he slipped inside the back door. He stepped quickly behind several stacked crates and waited for his eyes to adjust to the murky light. The interior of the warehouse was huge and deathly quiet, like being inside a mausoleum. There was no one about. Where, he thought, should I look first? He was just making his way toward a dark stairway that he assumed might lead to a basement when he heard someone walking up behind him. He whirled, and they stood there for a long, tense moment staring at each other.

"You're Wells' man?" he asked, jaw set rigidly.

"That's right."

461

"Where is she?"

"They're . . . waiting for you downstairs," he said. He had a pistol at Rayne's chest.

"Who?" Rayne had to force himself to keep his hands off the man.

Foster grinned. "You'll find out soon enough." He waved a hand toward the stairs. "We're wasting time. Get going, unless, of course, you don't give a damn whether that sweet little wife of yours stays so pretty anymore."

A coldness settled over Rayne. Foster's voice came from behind him.

"Don't turn around—just keep moving, Morgan."

He felt a gun at the back of his head. "Drop the sword . . . easy like."

Rayne swore softly, but knew he had to comply.

"You made it real easy for us," Foster said in a gloating voice. "I thought you would be tougher. I heard everyone talking about what a deadly foe you are. Well, you aren't so big and dangerous now, are you?" He grew braver and rammed the gun harder into Rayne's neck. "Well, just you wait and see what's in store for you, mister."

There was one lantern hanging overhead to light the dingy stairway. Rayne took his time, his brain racing, searching for a plan.

At the bottom of the stairs they made a sharp turn to the right and walked down a long tunnel carved into the ground. It was damp and dripping water, rats scurrying to escape booted feet.

As if he could hear his thoughts, Foster said, "You're wondering where I'm taking you, aren't you, Morgan?" and then proceeded to answer his own question. "To

462

the pit of hell, that's where!"

The back of Foster's hand came down on Rayne's neck. He stumbled forward, Foster's shrill laugh echoing in the tunnel.

"You're ruining my fun, Morgan, and I don't like it when I can't have a little fun on the job."

They reached a small cavernlike room. Rayne saw a woman with tangled black hair sitting in a chair with her back to him. There was only a single candle lending light to the chamber. The woman wasn't moving or talking. He assumed Wells had planned it just that way. His blood boiled. Several rats were scratching around her feet, and he could see her body shaking beneath the dark cloak. Damn them to hell! He'd kill Wells and Foster for this!

A hand clamped down on his shoulder. "That's close enough. Halt right where you are."

Rayne tried hard not to show his surprise upon seeing Malcolm Wells step out from the shadows. He really hadn't expected him to be here.

"I requested your presence here tonight, because I have decided it was time that we understood each other. I am the only one who shall call the shots, and you'd better listen well to what I have to say. I have a manifest here that I think might sound familiar to you," he stated with a leering smile. "After I read the list to you, I want your signature on it. Then, we'll see that your wife is released."

With slow deliberation Wells listed off cargoes that had been pirated from area ships in recent months. Wells smiled coolly. "The mayor has been informed of this list, though not yet where this merchandise can be found. I strongly suspect that we can convince you to confess having smuggled it out of Key West. You sign this manifest stating that you pirated the goods and come peaceful like to jail, and I'll see that your wife and your entire crew are left alone." His smile faded. "Oh— and one other detail. If you choose not to reveal yourself as Scorpio and sign this, then I will kill your wife before your very eyes."

"You knew just what to put on that list, didn't you?" Rayne shot back.

"Well . . . you might say that," Malcolm gloated.

"Aye, I thought as much," Rayne snorted. "Since you are the one who pirated all of it—not I."

The woman made a sudden movement, drawing his attention. In that split second, Rayne disregarded Foster and made a lunge for Malcolm, a snarl of fury reverberating throughout the room. Foster brought the butt of the gun down on his head. He doubled up and stumbled, but he refused to fall.

"You have nowhere to turn, Morgan," Malcolm crowed. "There is nothing left for you to do but sign, and rot in jail for smuggling. Benton's drunken ramblings have come in very handy. You really shouldn't have married into that family, you know." He shook his head slowly, mockingly. "A woman like Starlin is enough to tempt any man, but a brother-in-law like Benton no one should be stuck with. He's weak, the joker in your winning hand."

"He'll pay," Rayne growled, "just as you will."

Malcolm laughed and placed a quill in Rayne's hand. "Sign this . . . and then Foster and some of the boys will take you off my hands." He inclined his head toward the woman. "I'll untie her before I leave to rejoin the *Ice Princess* and Benton. I left him with some of my boys. They know just how to handle his sort so that he'll be more than ready to take me to the location of the Devil's Treasures." He shoved the paper beneath the quill Rayne was holding and wiped the back of his hand across his moist brow.

"Sweating a bit, Wells?" Rayne drawled, making no move to sign his name to the manifest. "What's got you so nervous?" His eyes were hard and unyielding as they held Malcolm's shifty gaze.

"Sign, you bastard!" Wells growled, suddenly becoming edgy and more than impatient. "You have no choice." He barely had the words out of his mouth when he knew it was a mistake to have uttered them. He was already cringing when he saw Morgan's fist snake out with lightning speed toward his face and his foot struck out back-kick Foster in the belly.

"I don't take to well to scum like you telling me what I've got to do," Rayne snarled. "And I don't like toughs manhandling my wife." The side of his hand chopped Foster in the throat. Foster fell like a stone and lay doubled up on the ground.

Wells was cringing against a wall, his hands protecting his bloodied face. "Stay away from me, Morgan!"

Rayne was before the huddled figure in the chair within moments. He grasped the woman's chin between his fingers and tilted her face forward.

Blue eyes, wide with fright, stared up at him.

"Who are you?" Rayne demanded with a sarcastic twisting of his lips, realizing what he had suspected all along. Starlin was not here. He could only hope that it meant Wells had not gotten to her after all.

"Please don't hurt me, mister!" the terrified young woman screamed, a jumble of words pouring forth. "Malcolm told me it would be easy . . . and he'd buy

465

me some ruby ear bobs if'n I did as he said. I thought it might be fun . . . I didn't know he would do this to me." She hung her head in shame.

Rayne unbound the girl and whirled about, only to find that Malcolm was gone. Only Foster still lay groaning upon the earthen floor.

He grasped Foster by the back of the shirt and hauled him to his feet, his fist doubled up threateningly before the man's frightened eyes.

"Tell me where he went, or I swear you'll be feeling a whole lot worse."

"To . . . to the wharf," Foster babbled freely. "He found out Benton is going with your wife to Antare. He was just waiting to make certain you were out of the way before he attacked their ship. He'll catch them in no time . . . he has the fastest ship in these waters."

Rayne flung Foster in the chair and tied him securely.

"You can't just leave me here like this!" Foster screamed. "I'll die . . . I'll starve to death!"

Green, merciless eyes viewed the terrified thug without compassion. "I imagine I can do just about anything I want . . . I don't see a soul around who's going to stop me."

Rayne strode away without one shred of conscience. He paid no heed to Foster's screams. He figured the girl would blurt the entire incident to Lucy just as soon as she got back, and someone would undoubtedly come to investigate. And if not? Well . . . he really didn't give a damn. He had only one thought right at the moment—to find Starlin.

* * *

Starlin heard the shout of "Sail ho!" from atop the mast, and her heart skipped a beat thinking that it might be Rayne. She hurried to the starboard and watched the vessel approaching. Benton joined her.

"Can you make out their colors?" he asked nervously.

Starlin placed a hand above her eyes to block the glare of the setting sun. She felt a prickle of fear at the unease she detected in Benton's voice. "No, it's too far away as yet." She glanced over at him. "Is there something wrong?"

"I hope not," he said, his expression bleak.

Starlin knew immediately that he was fearful of something . . . of that ship fast approaching them.

"Who do you think is out there, Benton?"

"No one. Why ask me?"

"Because you appear very nervous."

He shrugged quickly and attempted a reassuring smile. "I'm not. What do I have to be nervous about?" He spun on his heel and hurried off in the direction of his cabin.

Starlin wasted no time in heading for the quarter-deck. She climbed the stairs and saw Riley at the wheel. "Mr. Riley, how soon do you think that ship will be upon us?"

"I expect about an hour."

"Do you know who they are?"

He did not turn around. "We know it is not the captain, missus. Perhaps you might wish to wait in your cabin. I'll send the cabin boy to you just as soon as I have any news."

The cabin was warm. Starlin had only been sitting there for a few minutes, but it seemed like hours to her.

The ship was unusually hushed. Everyone was waiting. But for what? she wondered, twisting her hands in her lap.

Sometime later, an excited yell from above echoed across the water and through the open porthole.

"Pirates! They're looking to overtake the ship!"

Starlin jumped to her feet and ran to the porthole to peer out. She caught a fleeting glimpse of the approaching vessel, and saw that it flew the black flag. Her pulse raced rapidly. Should she stay here as Riley had told her, and possibly risk capture? Or should she put to use the skills that Rayne had taught her and fight to protect her life and that of her unborn child? There really was no choice, she knew that. She could not stay here waiting, she had to do something!

The cabin boy was pounding on the door, Benton's excited voice mingling with the lad's.

"Pirates are approaching. Hide Milady," Matthew blurted upon entering the cabin.

Benton hurried over to her, a cutlass in one hand. "Do as he says, Starlin. I'll . . . just help you find a safe place."

Starlin viewed him through narrowed eyes. "Why do I get the feeling that you are behind this somehow?" She noticed his shaking hands, his sickly pallor, and thought that at least he hadn't been drinking—as yet, anyway.

"I tried to warn you about me." He slid his arm around her waist and propelled her toward a large closet that was beneath the outside stairway. "I'm afraid I might have said a bit too much to the wrong people about our journey. I'm truly sorry . . . I was drunk."

Opening the closet door, they both jumped when a chilling boom reverberated throughout the cabin.

"Oh, Benton, how could you? Pirates yet! And they're opening fire on us." She tried to pull away from him. "I'm not about to hide in that closet—you can if you want to!"

A resounding blast came from the *Ice Princess*. The men would not allow the pirates to board without a good fight, but everyone knew that the smaller *Princess* could not withstand the full blast of a larger ship's guns and stay afloat.

"Don't argue, Milady, please!" Matthew shouted behind her. "Riley says he will protect you with his life, but at least help him by trying to stay out of those filthy beggars' sight."

'Give me that," Starlin hissed at Benton, grabbing the cutlass from his hand before he could stop her. "I doubt that you even know how to use it."

He lunged for her, but she stepped lithely aside and was out the aft hatch before he could stop her. Benton stared dumbly after her. He knew what a spitfire she was, but against these men? He didn't like to think what they might do to her.

The air was thick with smoke and reeked from the smell of gunpowder. Riley was trying his best to outrun the bigger ship, but Starlin could see that it was useless. Side by side now, the larger vessel sent a shooting, black missile into the *Princess*'s mainmast and wood splintered into the air. Chevaz, a knife between his teeth and long, gleaming rapier in his big hand, came hurtling toward her and grabbed her up under one arm to race out of the way of a fiery sail spiraling downward. Starlin watched it all through a haze of disbelief, the cutlass still within her grip.

There was no doubt in her mind that, if accosted, she would fight to the death anyone who threatened her.

"Go below!" Riley shouted to her after Chevaz deposited her safely beside the helm and raced back to the maindeck.

"No!" she screamed over the din of noise. "I'll not be trapped like a trembling mouse in a hole, Mr. Riley!"

Riley gnashed his teeth together, but a spark of admiration shone in his eyes. "The captain was right about you, you know. You never could do what you're told!"

Starlin lost some of her bravado seeing the first grappling hooks and iron sail through the air to ensnare the *Princess* and hold her prisoner. The ship shuddered from the force of the other craft's impact.

Clinging to a dangling ratline, Starlin did her best to remain on her feet. Riley was determined not to give up the wheel.

He was one of the first wounded in the ensuing foray of swords and gunfire. He slumped over the wheel, his knees buckling. Starlin hurried to stop the flow of blood streaming from his wounded shoulder. The sound of gunshots filled the air, but she would not flee. Laying the cutlass aside, she tore off a piece of her petticoat and applied it to Riley's wound. She was so intent on keeping pressure against his injury that she did not notice Malcolm Wells until it was too late.

With a shout of triumph, he yanked her roughly to him, his eyes gleaming wildly, a smoking pistol gripped in his hand. "Where's that drunken sot, Benton? He's the one I came to talk to. You I came to collect as a trophy."

"Leave me alone!" she railed. "Can't you see I must tend to this man or he will die from loss of blood!"

"What do I care if he dies or not?" Malcolm snapped, shoving her to the deck. "You'd better tell me where Benton is, my grand lady, or you just might join your friend here."

Starlin knew her hand lay inches from the cutlass she had previously laid on the deck, and her fingers stretched forward trying to touch the hilt. She kept talking in an effort to divert Malcolm's attention from her movements.

"Rayne will never let you get by with this. He'll find you no matter where you are . . . and you'll pay with your life."

"Not likely!" Malcolm sneered. "Where he is right now, I'd be willing to wager that he won't see blue sky for a long time."

Her stomach lurched. "What . . . are you saying?"

"I believe his good friend the mayor will probably have him arrested, and jailed by now. For smuggling, of course."

Just as her fingers curled around the hilt of the cutlass, Malcolm's heel ground down on the blade.

"No, you don't, sweet. I've no mind to give you the chance to skewer me. I know you would in a minute."

Blind anger chased away fear and Starlin came up from her knees to lunge for his eyes, sharp nails managing to rake a bloody gouge along the side of his cheek before he subdued her by grabbing her wrists in his hands. There was cold, killing fury in his eyes. Slowly, almost gleefully, he raised the pistol to place it between her breasts.

"Any last words for dear Benton?"

"Leave her alone, Wells!"

Starlin saw Benton climbing the stairs to the quarterdeck. He held the leg of a table as a club, his face set in determined lines.

"I can shoot her and you before you can reach me," Malcolm warned. "So, you'd better stop right there."

Benton froze. "If you shoot either of us, I won't take you to the treasure." Seeing the flicker of greed in Malcolm's eyes, he hurriedly added, "I am the only one who can, you know."

"A bargain then—is that what you wish to strike?"

"Yes, if you let her go."

"Benton . . . you can't trust him. He—" Starlin cried, and was cut off by a glancing blow from Wells.

"Stop it!" Benton roared. "Stop all of it . . . and I swear the treasure will be yours."

Pressing his advantage, Malcolm said, "Very well, you've a deal. But only if you dive for the treasure. I can't trust the others."

Benton paled, his shoulders slumping. "All right, anything that you say."

"No, Benton!" Starlin sobbed, standing all alone and feeling so helpless. She stared at Riley's inert form and then around her at the total devastation—a carnage of bodies and wounded men. They hadn't really stood a chance, but every one of Rayne's men had fought bravely. She saw no sign of Chevaz or Matthew, the cabin boy. A cold tremor ran down her spine. She knew Wells would kill them, too. She could see the bloodlust in his eyes.

Benton followed behind Malcolm who had given the word for his men to fall back. He was almost ecstatic when he faced Benton once again.

"Don't look so dejected, lad," he said. "Just think. You are going to be the one who finally brings the treasure to the surface. You'll be a celebrity—and all of Key West will respect you once again."

Starlin watched Malcolm intently, and knew very well that neither she or Benton, stood a chance of leaving the Triangle alive. As soon as he had his hands on that treasure, they would be killed. Oh, Rayne! she sobbed inwardly. Where are you?

Chapter Twenty-seven

Dusk was settling over the ocean. Rayne's nostrils flared slightly, sniffing the tangy salt air, cursing the sluggish breeze and wishing the miles away. He held the wheel steady, willing the sails to catch more wind, the *Tempest* to fly across the water if it were possible. Nothing appeared in his favor. There was little wind. And to make matters worse, he was short of good men. With a dozen of his best crewmen manning the *Ice Princess,* Rayne was working the skeleton crew hard. None complained, though, there was no time. Every minute, every second, was precious—everyone knew it.

When Rayne had first explained their mission, and that Malcolm Wells and his lecherous crew were in pursuit of Starlin's ship, the entire crew banded together to get the brigantine under way. It was difficult for him to keep his mind on the ship, for his every thought was on the woman he loved.

He cursed himself unmercifully for the countless hours he'd wasted, refusing so many times to say the words that could make her smile so beautifully.

"I love you, you violet-eyed temptress . . . I love you more than life itself," he whispered to the sighing wind.

With the dawn, they entered the Triangle. Starlin had never been more frightened in her life. It didn't look the same as the area she had sailed so boldly through when she had left Antare. She had not been afraid, even when she'd felt alone, trailing far behind Rayne's ship, determined that she would find a way for their love to survive. Would it? Would *she?* This morning, she felt totally helpless and without hope. She heard Malcolm yelling at Benton to make certain they were sailing in the right direction. They were both standing near the helm, Benton directing the ship deeper into the lost sea.

"This is where it gets dangerous. There's jagged reefs, and shoals lie very close to the surface. Take her in slow," he cautioned.

"I expect that will be easy. There isn't a drop of wind," the bosun's mate said.

Benton's only reaction was a sharp laugh, a sound that chilled Starlin's blood. "Here you don't need any."

Absolute silence prevailed. The crewmen in the masts scrambled down from their perches, their faces expressing grave concern.

Only Malcolm Wells looked satisfied. His dream was about to be realized.

"Just up ahead you'll pass the first line of reefs. Tell your man to keep going until he sees me raise my hand. We want to sail on past to the second reef . . . the galleon lies near there, her belly ripped open and the fortune she carried scattered for miles. There's several

476

shoals that you'll see before we reach the galleon." Benton kept talking, staring out over the water, his voice almost trancelike. "She must have been driven through here by a hell of a force of wind, bouncing off one reef, tearing her underside open . . . going on to hit the next and then . . ."

Starlin trembled, curiosity drawing her gaze over the side to peer down into the water. The ship appeared to gain momentum . . . the helmsman yelling that he had no control. They were being drawn helplessly along.

Starlin clutched Benton's arm.

The fierce-looking pirates appeared terrified enough to mutiny.

"I can only figure it's some sort of underwater currents," Benton explained so that only Starlin might hear. "But don't tell them. Stay calm. We're almost there."

"The water is so eerily motionless . . . how can it be currents?" Starlin turned to ask him.

Benton had not heard, for his attention was riveted on their location. "This is it, Wells," he stated abruptly, holding up his hand. "You can see part of the galleon if you look into the water on the starboard side." He pointed to a clear, translucent section of water.

Starlin remembered the white sea Benton had spoken of that night in the playhouse. It had been difficult to imagine the sea so clear it appeared almost pellucid. She saw the reef—and a wavering, dark shadow below. The galleon! It was lying in a kind of sand bowl next to the reef.

"Time for you to go over the side, Benton my boy," Wells said, almost with joy.

Benton was wearing a shirt and breeches. He was

barefoot, but wearing heavy gloves. The reef could cut a man to shreds. He knew to be careful. He removed a gold ring from his finger and held it out to Starlin. She took it, familiar with the seamen's stories of barracudas having attacked divers wearing anything that glinted golden beneath the sea.

Starlin thought of the creature Benton had talked about. She could only hope that it no longer inhabited the area. She glanced up at him, thinking that he appeared very calm for a man about to descend into water that, once before, had almost cost him his life. His eyes met hers, clear and alert. Under any other circumstances she would have smiled. Her eyes misted as she looked at him. His hair tousled and curling about his forehead made him appear even younger than his twenty-eight years. She could not help reaching out a hand to touch him.

"You don't have to do this."

He grinned. "Don't worry yourself so. This is not something that I'd do for anyone but myself, sister dear. You should know that."

"Don't get any notions in your head to defy me, Cambridge," Wells stated, grinning coldly. "I would have to turn our fair Starlin over to my men in retaliation. And I fear she would not appreciate their attentions."

Benton spun around and glared at Wells. "Like I said, no one could make me do this if I didn't have a score to even. But you can rest easy—I won't change my mind."

One of the men handed Benton a canvas bag and a line of rope. He tied one end of the line around his chest.

"I don't want anyone but you on the other end, Wells," Benton stated with a piercing glare. "So that means you'll have to come out in the dinghy with me. I'll be coming up and down with the bag. And I'm certain that you'll want to be the only one I hand it to."

"I'll be more than happy to accommodate you," Wells replied.

"Not having done this sort of thing for a while, give me some time to adjust to the sensation of being under water again."

"Just don't take too long," Wells warned. "I would not like to have to send one of the crew in to get you." That cold grin once more. "They're a greedy lot, you know. Couldn't trust them not to kill you down there just to get their hands on that treasure."

Benton was already climbing down to the rope ladder, preparing to jump into the small boat. Malcolm followed, a gleam of anticipated wealth in his eyes.

He rowed the dinghy directly over the sunken galleon. Without a glance in Starlin's direction, Benton stood and prepared to dive.

Starlin watched with undisguised fear in her eyes. Once in the water, Benton began testing the depths and his courage. Although the shoals were under no more than fifteen feet of water, Starlin knew he was finding it difficult to face his past. This is where it all had begun—and ended, in a sense. She prayed it would not be the same this time.

Wells grew impatient, and yelled out to Benton, "Dive, lad! I didn't come out here to admire your swimming!"

Starlin watched Benton disappear beneath the surface.

The first dive didn't last long. He came up for several minutes and went back down again. He didn't come up for several long minutes, and when he bobbed to the surface once again, Starlin observed him sling a gold chain of some sort to Malcolm. The attorney almost fell over the side of the dinghy in an effort to catch it. With a squeal of greedy delight, he snatched it out of the air and draped it about his neck.

It was then the first stirrings of mutiny must have entered the pirate crew's minds.

Over her shoulder Starlin heard the mate whispering something to another man, who did the same. She felt eyes staring at her back. Her flesh crawled. She wanted to cry out to Benton when she saw his head break the surface, but she knew what disaster would follow if she even hinted of the unrest sifting through the pirates.

The minutes crept slowly by beneath the water. Benton knew his fear of returning to this place had been for a good reason. It was one of the most beautiful underwater places he had ever seen. The quiet and the gentle embrace of the currents lulled one into a false sense of security. Benton knew the sea to be as treacherous as any foe. Let your guard down for a minute and she turned deadly. Kicking his feet, he dove deeper, his lungs already feeling as if they were going to burst. The galleon wavered just ahead. He thought he glimpsed a long, ominous flash dart back into her gaping hull. His heart began to pound in his rib cage.

All of the stories of the galleon being haunted by a shapely phantom who reportedly lured men into her embrace, and to death, flitted through his mind. As he swam back down to the shelflike lip of an underwater cave where jewels and golden objects lay scattered, a colorful school of fish glided curiously beside him. An inquisitive grouper darted past Benton's hand. The touch of the rough scales against his outstretched arm took Benton completely unawares. He jerked his arm to his body, then, seeing the fat grouper darting in the opposite direction, smiled with relief.

Benton glanced around him, back over at the galleon. Nothing moved except small schools of fish. So far, the ferocious form of the barracuda had not appeared. Swallowing to clear his ear pressure, he dove for a winking green stone that caught his eye. He snatched up a gold figure encrusted with emeralds and stuffed it in the bag. A few more gold coins were added to the loot, and then it was back topside once again. Breaking the surface, he was just about to toss the bag into the boat when Malcolm's hand snaked out to grab the bag from him.

"This is a great place, Cambridge," he chortled, scooping the treasure finds from the bag and examining each piece closely. "Why you were too yellow to come back here all of this time escapes me."

Benton hung on to the side of the boat, taking deep breaths.

"I saw something down there. I'm not certain what it was . . ." He was breathing deeply. "But I want a knife, just in case."

"A knife! Forget it!" Malcolm exclaimed with a hoot of laughter. "You'd be trying to stab me in the back just as soon as you could."

Favoring Wells with a dark scowl, Benton took a deep breath and dove back beneath the sea.

After several more dives, hauling up the bag filled with heavy gold objects encrusted with jewels, and coins of undetermined number, Benton was exhausted. Every muscle in his body burned fire, and the upper cavities of his nose were aching terribly. He knew from experience it was time to quit diving. He started to get into the boat. Malcolm's booted foot came down on his fingers and he yanked them away.

"Just what do you think you are doing?" Malcolm inquired, his jaw set rigidly.

"I've had enough for the day. I'm coming in!" Benton yelled.

"The hell, you say!"

"If I keep diving in this condition I might not make it back up the next time," Benton growled.

"You yellow scum Cambridge! I know what you're up to." He kicked at Benton's head and caught him a glancing blow.

Benton fell back in the water, stunned.

Starlin cried out, and it was then from behind her that a shot whizzed by the two men and zinged into the water. Malcolm's eyes darted toward the ship, his mouth falling agape upon seeing his men with their pistols aimed at him. He knew they had been standing there watching, just waiting to see if Benton would succeed in retrieving the riches from below. Now they were going to strike. Malcolm raised a clenched fist in the air.

"You'll never have it! It's mine, I tell you!"

Gunfire erupted all around the dinghy and Malcolm ducked down in the boat. Benton dove frantically beneath the water, and kicked downward.

Starlin whirled, thinking that the pirates behind her would surely open fire at Benton. She was amazed to see that their guns were trained upon Wells standing wide-eyed and helpless in the tiny boat. A shot whizzed past Malcolm's head, then another. He could not believe that anyone would have the nerve to defy him.

"Filthy wretches . . ." he choked, feeling a bullet tear into his shoulder.

Starlin slunk away from the crazed group of men. Pandemonium spread like wildfire. Men were diving over the side of the ship into the sea, greed for the riches it protected the only thing on their minds.

The loud roar of a cannon suddenly shook the length of the entire craft and sent the pirates remaining on the ship scrambling for cover. The missile tore through the mizzenmast, wood splintering into the air, smoke and orange-red flames billowing upward and spreading rapidly across the top sails. Men were screaming in panic and running for their lives, some diving overboard to escape the fiery debris raining down on the deck.

Starlin had found her way to the water barrels lining one side of the maindeck. She ducked down behind them, her only thought on survival. The onslaught had come so unexpectedly that no one had had time to identify their attacker. Starlin chanced to look over the top of a barrel toward the advancing brigantine, the figurehead of the scorpion a most welcome sight. She had to force herself not to leap up and cry out. She watched silently as the *Tempest,* guns roaring, advanced rapidly toward the crippled pirate ship.

Malcolm stood swaying on his feet in the dinghy and stared in stunned horror as all of his dreams of power and wealth began to disintegrate before his eyes. His ship was enveloped in flames, his men scattering like leaves in the wind. He could feel himself growing weak, felt blood trickling down his arm, and, with horror, looked down to see blood spurting from another wound in his chest. The pain wasn't overwhelming, but the sense of weakness in his limbs threatened to buckle his knees. He grasped the gold chain around his neck and clutched it to his breast. For a while, he thought, he had known what it was like to feel rich . . .

He saw Benton bobbing near the boat, grasping the side of the dinghy to haul himself inside. With supreme effort, Malcolm kicked outward. Benton deflected the impact with the back of his arm, upsetting the wounded man's balance. Malcolm teetered on the edge, his face a mask of terror. Below, through the transparent blue, he swore he saw a woman's shapely figure beckoning to him with open arms. Upward, she glided . . .

"Now, Wells, it's just you and me," Benton snarled, having managed at last to pull himself into the boat. He reached out to grasp hold of Malcolm and watched in stunned disbelief as the attorney lost his footing and toppled forward into the sea.

Benton dove after him. Malcolm was sinking rapidly, almost in peaceful surrender. The weight of the chain pulled him down like a stone. Benton had to give up at last. His lungs were near to bursting, and he knew he could not reach Wells.

Below him, he saw the heavy gold chain glinting brightly in the sun-dappled water, and then, with fear, he saw the enormous barracuda swimming far below on the sandy ocean floor fix a keen black eye on the flash of color above him. The sleek, dark blue body quivered, its lower jaw projecting beyond the snout falling open, teeth appearing like long, jagged spikes.

Malcolm thrashed and struggled against the heavy

weight of his prized treasure, desperate now to swim upward. He could not. He was rapidly sinking, water rushing in through his nose and lungs. The chain gleamed like a beacon, drawing the predator upward toward the flash of gold.

Intent on the chain around Malcolm's neck, the barracuda struck with the force of a battering ram, his jaw falling open, sharp teeth sinking into the soft flesh of Malcolm's throat. Blood flushed out the sides of the barracuda's mouth and wavered about the two forms beneath Benton. He looked down to see the barracuda swimming away with Malcolm dangling brokenly between his jaws. The gold chain gleamed brightly up at him, until at last he could see it no more.

Shudder after shudder encompassed Benton as he swam away from the scene of Malcolm's death struggle. He broke the surface, gulping deep breaths, sweet air rushing into his lungs. Grabbing the side of the boat he just barely had the strength to haul himself over the side.

On board the pirate ship, the flames were rapidly spreading. The swine who had not fled into the sea were locked in a battle to the death with the brigands from the *Tempest* who had overtaken the ship. The clash of steel and the screams of the wounded and dying echoed chillingly across the water.

Rayne Morgan had been the first to swing over onto the fiery deck after the two ships had been locked together by grappling hooks. His eyes were searching everywhere for Starlin even as he stood engaged in a fierce duel with two of Malcolm's men. Steel clashed against steel. Morgan's size and strength was in his favor, and he parried the thrusts from one man to the other with effortless ease. Neither man was as smooth with a blade as Morgan, but the fact that there were two against one gave them the definite advantage.

His back to the rail, Rayne let out a loud roar and lunged forward to cut down one man. Then he spun around and severed in two the sword hand of the other.

A shot whined past his ear, and the sound of a body falling behind him. Ely hurried to join him, a smoking pistol in one hand, a cutlass in the other.

"Thanks!" Rayne grinned. He glanced frantically about. "Have you seen her anywhere?"

"No, but Starlin's smart. She'll have picked a place to hide until we can find her."

"The fire is spreading quickly. Tell Chevaz to fall back with the men and prisoners. I'll look for Starlin."

Ely nodded and sprinted off.

It was then Rayne saw the top of an ebony head and a pair of wide violet eyes peeking over a barrel at him. Merlin had come to her rescue to snatch the ankle of a would-be attacker. With vicious snarls the wolfhound sent the blackguard running for the side of the ship. It was the only time Starlin had been truly glad to see the beast.

Relief surged through Rayne. There were flames and burning debris all around them, but he knew that nothing could keep him from reaching her.

"Stay there! I'll come to you. And do not defy me!" He saw her smile. For once he felt certain she would do as she was told.

Within minutes he was beside her, pulling her up into the curve of his arm and running toward a dangling grappling line. The ship was a blazing inferno, their only hope of escape was to flee the vessel at once before the gunpowder stored in her hold blew.

Ely was standing on the deck of the *Tempest* yelling encouragement.

Without another thought, Rayne grasped Starlin firmly against him and leaped up on the edge of the rail. Overhead a burning sail fluttered toward them.

"Rayne, the baby! I cannot do this!" Starlin screamed.

"We have no choice. I'll shield you as best I can. Hold on to me."

Trusting him completely, Starlin locked her arms around his strong neck and pressed herself close against his body.

She felt the searing heat all around them—even the soles of her feet felt on fire. Then, suddenly, cool blessed air whispered against her skin, in her hair, and when she opened her eyes they were safely on board the *Tempest*. She sobbed in relief, feeling Rayne's lips against her temple.

"I love you, Starlin," Rayne said softly just before his lips claimed hers and his soul surrendered completely to love.

The island Antare was in mourning this night. The *Tempest* and the crippled *Ice Princess* had returned earlier in the day. Many good men had lost their lives, others were recovering from wounds. Later, when the people had had sufficient time to grieve for their fallen comrades, they would celebrate the return of the survivors.

Chevaz and Riley had been wounded, but both men would recover. Ely had wasted little time in asking

Jamie to marry him. He'd told Rayne and Starlin that he'd wanted to ask her before, but he did not feel he could devote himself to a wife and family until he was certain that Rayne was able to take care of himself. They had all laughed heartily. It was a good feeling. Starlin and Rayne told him of their decision to sail for England for the birth of their child. Starlin was anxious to see her grandfather, and then they would be traveling on to Sontavon, to see April, and hopefully to help her to recover.

Exhausted, but feeling the luckiest of men, Rayne sat on the veranda with Starlin next to him and talked optimistically about the future. In his lap lay the journal that Starlin had once thrown at him. He had read it from beginning to end, seeking to put to rest lingering doubt. For two days, while Starlin had rested, he sat on the veranda and began to know and understand the man whom he had hated so intensely for so many years. He could hardly wait to go home to England, and Sontavon. He intended on reading the journal to his mother. She would find solace in Carl's words, and Rayne wanted so to tell her so many things. He had been a fool, and must ask her forgiveness.

"He must have loved her very much at one time, to have respected her decision to stay with my father and not try and persuade her to go away with him," Rayne said quietly.

"I'm sure he did," Starlin agreed. "Although, later, I think he learned to forget. For he was happy with my mother. We had a good life in Key West. I'll never forget either of them, but I know their souls must be truly at peace now. Benton and I are both ready to put the past behind us and accept the future."

Rayne smiled gently at her. "Your brother is in good hands. Romani and his wife will take very good care of him while he is a guest in their home."

"It was very kind of them to offer. I know he would not have been comfortable staying with us." She sighed. "I hope one day that he and I might at least be friends. Perhaps now that he has confronted his fears, as I did, we can both go forward with our lives."

"He told me that he will be going back to Key West to operate the salvaging firm, and that he will keep us informed of its progress."

Starlin looked surprised but pleased. "That sounds like there is hope, doesn't it?"

"For all of us, I think."

Starlin met his soft gaze.

"Will you miss it very much?" she asked.

"What?"

"The sea . . . the danger . . . your life here on the island?"

He shook his head slowly, a faraway look in his eyes. "No, not a bit. I was never really happy before. Nor was I free. Vengeance made me a slave."

"And now love, I hope," Starlin murmured with a catch in her voice.

His eyes locked on hers; jade depths shimmering with emotion. "You were my destiny from the beginning. I loved you even before we met that night on Torquay. You were the temptress of my dreams . . . and now of my life."

Epilogue

Sarah Beth Morgan was born with her father's tawny-gold hair and her mother's smoke-violet eyes. She was perfect and healthy, and squalled loudly in protest when the doctor whacked her lightly on the bottom.

Upon hearing the lusty cry echoing through the vast interior of Eaton Hall, Rayne had sprinted up the wide stairway and hurried into the bedchamber. At the sight of the doctor beaming proudly at the bundle in his arms, he stopped short. He glanced anxiously at the slender figure in the bed. Starlin looked pale, lines of exhaustion evident around her eyes, but she was smiling at him. It was a moment he would never forget.

"We have a beautiful girl, Rayne," she said softly.

He sat down on the bed next to her and took her hand within his.

"The baby is healthy and beautiful, and you are well. I am a grateful man." He bent down to kiss her tenderly on the lips.

"I'll leave you to rest," he said. "I must tell your grandfather and Fredrick the good news. They've been

pacing with me half the night. I don't know which of us was more nervous."

"Give them my love, will you, Rayne? And tell them that our families are truly united now—at last."

The wind blew a siren's song through the rigging as the *Ice Princess* skimmed over the rolling sea breakers toward Sontavon. Her billowing sails snapped in the breeze. The smell of freshly painted masts wafted in the air, and the brightness of her gleaming decks flashed in the moonlight. It was a cool night with a full moon shining brightly on teak decks and dancing across silver-crested waves. The pilot of the schooner stood alone at the helm, the wheel sliding expertly through agile fingers. The night was soothing, with the wind sighing and the endless sea stretching for miles in every direction. The pilot found it easy to reflect on life and its hardships, triumphs, the uncertain road ahead. But with confidence now, strong enough to accept whatever fate had yet to unveil. And on love. How wonderful it was to devote life and soul to one love, one person forever, and to share equally, receiving the same in return. Promise lingered in the stars and love's caress in night's shadow. There was so much to be thankful for.

The pilot smiled softly, and then on impulse lashed the wheel in place and left the helm.

A kiss, soft and tantalizing, roused him from the misty depths of sleep. Without even opening his eyes, he envisioned her, welcomed her. His hand reached out

caressed her soft cheek. He smiled and slowly opened his eyes.

"I thought you weren't sleepy?"

"I'm not . . . I'm wide awake as a matter of fact."

Their eyes met in that special way that was theirs alone; understanding without saying the words the message conveyed there.

"I was dreaming about you," he murmured huskily.

"Yes . . . I know," she whispered, one finger lovingly tracing his full, sensual lips.

He could see so much of his daughter in her beautiful face, in her bewitching smoke-violet eyes, her high, delicate cheekbones. And sometimes, in her temperament as well, and the stubborn outthrust of her chin. He glanced over in the corner where a tiny hammock swayed gently with the ship's rhythm, and Sarah, his other love, slept soundly, and secure. The tension between him and Starlin was gone now, and the burning need for vengeance with it.

The moonlight beamed through the open porthole, casting wavering silver shadows over their naked bodies.

He took her into his arms and slid his body over hers. "God, but I love you so very much," he murmured thickly, burying his lips in her rose-scented hair.

"Always and forever, I hope," Starlin replied in a whisper-soft voice.

"Yes, my love."

She closed her eyes and nestled against his solid chest, her limbs quivering from her need of him. He was her strength, as she was his. Nothing could ever come between them again. She breathed deeply his familiar scent and welcomed his gentle caress. Their

bodies came together in fiery abandonment, lips seeking hungrily to bring exquisite pleasure, sleek golden limbs trembling with passion. Desire, white-hot and overwhelming swept them into a spiraling vortex of passion. Deep within the spiritual passages of their souls the promise was conveyed and accepted.

Throughout the night they made love—giving, taking, sharing, becoming one in every way. And after the fires of passion cooled, he held her close and gave her a symbol of his love to carry with her always. He slipped the ring onto her finger, where it belonged.

The *Ice Princess* skimmed onward through the night across the silver-crested water toward the Castle Sontavon. The fierce brigand Scorpio had no more thirst for revenge. He was going home, his faith in love restored.

RAPTUROUS ROMANCE
by Phoebe Conn